Also by Denene Millner and Nick Chiles

Money, Power, Respect:
What Brothers Think, What Sistahs Know

What Brothers Think, What Sistahs Know About Sex:
The Real Deal on Passion, Loving, and Intimacy

What Brothers Think, What Sistahs Know:
The Real Deal on Love and Relationships

Also by Denene Millner

The Sistahs' Rules:
Secrets for Meeting, Getting, and Keeping a Good Black Man

Love Don't Live Here Anymore

DENENE MILLNER
and
NICK CHILES

NEW AMERICAN LIBRARY

New American Library
Published by New American Library, a division of
Penguin Putnam Inc., 375 Hudson Street, New York, New York 10014, U.S.A.
Penguin Books Ltd, 80 Strand, London WC2R 0RL, England
Penguin Books Australia Ltd, 250 Camberwell Road,
Camberwell, Victoria 3124, Australia
Penguin Books Canada Ltd, 10 Alcorn Avenue,
Toronto, Ontario, Canada M4V 3B2
Penguin Books (N.Z.) Ltd, 182–190 Wairau Road, Auckland 10, New Zealand

Penguin Books Ltd, Registered Offices: Harmondsworth, Middlesex, England

Published by New American Library, a division of Penguin Putnam Inc.
Previously published in a Dutton edition.

First New American Library Trade Paperback Printing, February 2003
1 3 5 7 9 10 8 6 4 2

 REGISTERED TRADEMARK—MARCA REGISTRADA

New American Library Trade Paperback ISBN: 0-451-20778-5

The Library of Congress has catalogued the hardcover edition of this title as follows:

Millner, Denene.
Love don't live here anymore / by Denene Millner and Nick Chiles.
p. cm.
ISBN 0-525-94641-1
1. Triangles (Interpersonal relations)—Fiction. 2. Brooklyn (New York, N.Y.)—
Fiction. 3. Separation (Psychology)—Fiction. 4. Americans—France—Fiction.
5. African Americans—Fiction. 6. Paris (France)—Fiction.
7. Married people—Fiction. I. Chiles, Nick. II. Title.

PS3613.I565 L6 2002
813'.54—dc21   2001040433

Printed in the United States of America
Set in Sabon
Designed by Leonard Telesca

Printed in the United States of America

BOOKS ARE AVAILABLE AT QUANTITY DISCOUNTS WHEN USED TO PROMOTE PRODUCTS OR SERVICES. FOR INFORMATION PLEASE WRITE TO PREMIUM MARKETING DIVISION, PENGUIN PUTNAM INC., 375 HUDSON STREET, NEW YORK, NEW YORK 10014.

To our union,
for it is truly blessed

ACKNOWLEDGMENTS

All honor, glory, and praise to our Savior, whose blessings come in abundance, even when we falter. Without Him, surely, we are nothing.

Our family gives us all the joy that we can stand. Thank you Bettye and James Millner; Troy Millner; Chikuyu and Migozo Chiles; James, Angelou, and Miles Ezeilo; Jameelah and Ndegwa Thornton; Zenzele Thornton; and Maia and Imani Cogen for your unequivocal love and support.

To our children, Mazi, Mari, and Lila, who bring us never-ending bliss and laughter—you receive every ounce of our love and devotion, now and forever.

Nick would like to thank friends old and new—Addette Williams and Mark Drossman—for providing a glimpse of the advertising world.

To all the people in cities and college campuses across the country who have shared some of their most intimate and painful experiences with us over the past three years, we appreciate your faith and kindness more than you know.

We are so pleased to have welcomed a new friend into our lives, Victoria Sanders, who also happens to be a wonderful agent.

And, we are honored to have been placed in the skilled and caring hands of senior editor Laurie Chittenden and her able sidekick, Stephanie Bowe.

He

As I walked from the conference room, I had to struggle with an over-powering urge to scream out. Of course the eyes of my new colleagues were following me closely, even if they were trying to pretend they weren't. They were looking for some sign that I had been surprised by those lovely words that floated through the small speaker and settled over the room as dramatically as a summer storm. But I was trying to cultivate an image as the cool, unfazed New Yorker—my ever-present cool brother pose—so I couldn't let these Paris folks witness my joy. I wanted them to think this kind of stuff happened to me all the time—no big deal.

"We want Randy to stay on in Paris to see this thing through." That was the first stunning announcement to the conference room. The sentence was rife with ambiguities that would take me hours to decode, but Peter Webber, the senior vice president of Trier-Stanton, wasn't through with me yet.

"When you come back, Randy, if everything goes according to plan, we're making you the director of creative. That comes with a title of vice president, as you know. But there'll certainly be more discussion on this."

I had glanced quickly around the room; my glance repelled the stares like a fan. Though most of the people in the large conference room were Parisians, and I couldn't be sure they'd have anything more than an envious curiosity about Webber's words, it was the eyes of my four fellow New Yorkers that held the most interest for me. What were they thinking, particularly the aloof and blond Eliza, who was the closest thing to an equal that I had in the room? That just as easily could have been her name falling from Webber's lips.

Catching no eyes with which to lock mine, I looked around the outer environs of the conference room, even managing to notice for about the twentieth time how remarkably bare this showcase meeting place looked to my untrained eye. I didn't have to ask to know that staggering sums of money had been spent on its decoration. Big money, with not much to show for it outside of a large, irregularly shaped conference table—I thought it looked just like the shape of the African continent, but maybe that was just me—and some extremely comfortable leather chairs. Not even any artwork, not even in Paris. It was that minimalist thing again. So understated. As with the entire city and its people, never had so much effort gone into looking like there had been no effort at all. I was from Brooklyn. By itself, that was a biography. I didn't at all think of myself as tacky or low-class, but if something was expensive as hell, I thought it should look expensive as hell. Otherwise, what was the point?

It wasn't until I was about to step—or *skip* might be more accurate—through the threshold of my little office that I even thought about Mikki. How weird was that? A dramatic promotion, and my wife doesn't even cross my mind? But it wasn't the promotion that triggered the somersaults in my stomach when the image of Mikki's round smooth face flashed through my mind. It was that first sentence Webber spoke: "We want Randy to stay on in Paris to see this thing through."

I had already been away from my wife for nearly two months. Exactly how much longer would it take to "see this thing through?" Did I even have the option of declining? Of course, I would never consider not accepting Webber's assignment, but I wasn't sure how I should feel about the effect it would have on my marriage. Though there had been very little passion and longing between me and Mikki in the months before I left for Paris, I had started to get some pretty sturdy erections of late when my mind wandered to thoughts of my wife. That was evidence of some feeling, wasn't it?

What I was being offered had the sound of a Faustian bargain of sorts: kiss your marriage good-bye and you'll get the job of a lifetime.

Mikki had been unhappy enough when I accepted the three-month transfer to Paris. The memory of those long, silent weeks in our Brooklyn brownstone leading up to the trip made me shudder. She was even reluctant to drive me to the airport, though she finally relented. I felt a small tug of pleasure when I saw alarm, or maybe surprise, cross her face when I pleaded for her to drive me.

"Come on, Mikki. I need to see the face of someone I love right before I step on an airplane and go halfway around the world." I laid it on with just the right touch of whine in my voice—about as much as my ego could stand. What I wanted to add, but held back because I found excessive melodrama more than a little distasteful, was that something terrible could happen to me and I'd never see her again.

Mikki knew those pleading words were about as theatrical as a love confession from me would ever get. She even smiled, something I hadn't seen probably in weeks. Do you understand how painful it is to live in a house with another person for weeks without a gesture as modest and easily conjured as a smile? I hated the silent treatment—at which Mikki excelled. I needed human interaction, conversation, contact. I wasn't exactly what some would call a "people person"—in fact, I despised that expression—but when Mikki wouldn't talk to me, I truly suffered.

"Mr. Murphy? Will you be needing me any longer?"

It was my secretary, Claudia, interrupting my meditation to ask in her heavily accented English whether she could go home. I smiled to myself. I still hadn't gotten used to her politeness. Back in New York, my secretary usually *announced* when she was leaving.

"No Claudia. Have a nice evening," I said.

"Thank you, sir. *Bonne nuit*."

"Yeah, bone newee to you, too."

I heard her hearty laugh through the open doorway. I knew she enjoyed my painful attempts at French enunciation. For a place with such an historic reputation for rudeness, Paris was about as ornery as a monastery compared to the New York I had just left. I had been braced for hostility but instead found gentility. But I suspected it might be a black thing: my white colleagues from New York had taken to complaining bitterly about their treatment, even as they absolutely cherished the idea that they were actually *living* in the world's most storied place. I spoke not a bit of French beyond the basic greetings, yet waiters and shopkeepers greeted my arrival with welcoming smiles and sincere courtesy. And the women. That was the biggest shock of all. There had been not a word from any friend or foe stateside to prepare me for the aggressive interest of these Parisian chicks. My God, it was enough to make me gaze into the mirror and wonder if I looked any different. White women openly staring at me on the street? I had no clue what to do with that. That just did not happen where I came from. They might steal glances when they believed no one was looking, but a bold-faced stare? And a welcoming smile? What was *that* all about?

I knew that quite a few black Americans over the years had reveled in the different treatment they found in Paris, from James Baldwin to virtually every bebopper of note. It was a popular destination for disaffected black folk, particularly males. The prevailing assumption was it was the warm cultural and artistic embrace that they sought among the French. But maybe I had stumbled upon some more carnal motivations that got less attention in the biographies and PBS specials.

When I glanced back down at my note pad and saw it was covered with doodles, I decided I was too juiced to get anything more done. I gathered up my things and hurriedly strode out of the office before my relatively early slide attracted too much attention from my New York colleagues. The Parisians didn't seem to appreciate the long hours that were put in by the New York team, but my colleagues and I had grown so accustomed to eating dinner at the office that we had a difficult time turning it off. Of course, nothing appalled the Parisians in the office more than the idea of eating dinner at the desk.

As had become my recent custom, I walked home to take in more of the city. Each night I tried to take a different series of streets, considering it part of my job to study the French, to observe the things that pleasured and angered them, to know what set their pulses racing. I was an ad man, a creative director at one of the world's largest, most far-flung advertising empires. Selling was what I did. It came as easily to me as breathing—or at least that's what I liked to think about myself in my most self-indulgent moments. Finding those clever, original, memorable phrases and ad campaigns that would move product. Or sell tickets, in this current assignment.

My last project had been hugely successful. I was the creative force behind the ad campaign that launched the Women's Professional Basketball League, which vastly outpaced projections in ticket sales and television viewership in its debut season. Impressed, the executives at Trier-Stanton gave me and my "team" an even more challenging assignment—sell the French on a women's professional soccer league. Or "football" league, as I had to learn to call it in Paris. Beneath their elegance and "joie de vivre"—ha, I already knew that one!—the French had rigid beliefs about who did what. Women could do many things, and did, but play football was not one of them. It was the same in many parts of the world, of course. How else could you explain the fact that the U.S., of all places, had the world's best women's soccer team? But a group of European billionaires had gambled very large sums on the hope that this mindset could be changed. Trier-Stanton had been hired to pull off the miracle.

The company had sent what was essentially two competing teams from the New York office to Paris—my team and Eliza's team. We were supposed to be working together, but everyone knew we wouldn't. Couldn't. It was an office joke in New York before we left—people snickering about which one of us would come back to Manhattan still breathing. We had too long a history of competition to make cooperation possible. Eliza's success had come a few years earlier when she convinced every child in America that they just *had* to own a silly little chirping bird that fit in a pocket or the palm of a small hand and flapped its mechanical, velvety wings whenever someone petted its head. Called "Flap-happies," the birds had caused near-riots in some toy stores when parents feared the dwindling supplies would leave their little Sam or Lisa in the cold.

By promoting me to vice president, Webber was acknowledging that my team had "won" in Paris. I couldn't help but stroll down Boulevard Saint-Germain toward my hotel and gleefully watch the Parisians on the streets and in the cafés put on a show of seeing whether they were being seen while pretending to be indifferent to it all. It was this studied indifference that I had skewered in the ad campaign for the women's soccer league. My commercials had shown beautiful, fashionably dressed Parisians sitting at café tables and whispering to each other, the camera zooming in to catch pretentious, superior looks on their faces, their unapproachable glamour. Then the narrator knowingly, conspiratorially, asked in French, "Haven't you always wanted to know what the hell they were talking about?" Long, pregnant pause . . . "Well, now you do." A soccer ball then was featured in close-up, flying directly at the screen, coming at the viewer, then the camera pulled back to show a lovely, sweaty woman in the blue, white, and red French colors, grinning as the crowd wildly cheered her goal. Eliza and the other New Yorkers had tried to warn me that the Parisians didn't like to be made fun of, but the Parisians loved the ads, as I knew they would. The people in this city were too damn smart not to get it. Surely they understood how ripe they are for gentle ridicule. And the point was proven: Tickets for Opening Day sold out in the first six hours, about a week faster than the Women's Professional Basketball League had. I knew it was these walks down Boulevard Saint-Germain, gazing into the cafés and watching the parade of beautiful women gliding down the streets, that had been my inspiration.

Swimming deep in my thoughts, I almost collided with a woman who was coming out of a clothing store. I was thoroughly embarrassed, and we both wound up apologizing simultaneously.

"Oh, wow, excuse me, ma'am," I said hurriedly.

"*Ça va, monsieur,*" the woman said abruptly, telling me in French that everything was okay. I looked into her face and was quite startled to find myself staring at a tall, stunning black woman. She had the narrow face and high cheekbones of a model. And she was scowling at me. This was the kind of look I was accustomed to receiving from beautiful women.

"Uh, well, have a good day," I mumbled, chastened by her expression. The woman nodded, her angry eyes flashing like emeralds. I hoped I wasn't the cause of her saltiness. Damn, it wasn't like I had knocked her over.

"I hope your day gets better," I added as an afterthought, flashing what I considered my most charming smile. Evidently it worked. The anguish melted off the woman's face like frost. She even managed to smile back.

"I'm sorry," she said in clear, slightly accented English. "I wasn't upset at you. It was the women in that damn store." She cut her eyes at the small boutique, whose French name I didn't recognize and couldn't pronounce. "They act like their clothes are on display in the Louvre or something."

I laughed, though it came out like a feminine little giggle that briefly embarrassed me. Where the hell did that come from, I wondered. This beautiful woman had moved from scary to engaging in seconds. Something about the way her eyes glinted when she talked, as if everything was a secret, reminded me of Mikki. Strangely, that comforted me—but it scared me stupid at the same time. That little voice that acted as my marital conscience told me I better get away from this fetching woman, whose fingers were noticeably free of wedding bands.

So why then, fifteen minutes later, was I seated at a table in one of those preening cafés I enjoyed ridiculing, smiling up into the face of this lovely woman whose name happened to be Marie? I guess my little voice needed to have the volume adjusted. In minutes, I had found out Marie was originally from Haiti and had lived in Paris for the past eight years, since she was twenty-one. And yes, she was a model. Or at least part of the time, when she found modeling work. The rest of the time she was a secretary at a music company. She was also hoping to get a record deal. The reason I already knew all this was because Marie liked to talk. I knew instantly that I could listen to her talk for hours and never get bored. That realization also frightened me; I told myself for about the thirtieth time in the past fifteen minutes that I needed to leave.

Marie was responding to me in obvious ways, smiling at my observations about Paris, looking down and blushing when my eyes caught hers for too long. I was thoroughly shaken by what was happening, but I was not locating the energy or the desire to stop and flee. Admittedly, I was enjoying myself too much.

"So, where did you say you were staying in Paris?" Marie asked, trying to make it sound casual. I wondered if it was casual, or if she was memorizing my vital facts.

"Oh, Hotel Saint-Germain. It's not far from here. It's near the Musée D'Orsay."

"Do you like it?" she asked. I wasn't sure if this was more small talk. What if I didn't like it? What then?

"Yeah, it's pretty nice. The room is kinda small, especially for the amount of time I'm supposed to be here, but it's all right."

She nodded. Our eyes locked again. This time she held it slightly longer, then she looked down again with an even fuller blush.

"Why do you keep blushing? A shy fashion model—is that what you are?" I asked, teasing just a little.

"Models can be shy, you know. Most of them are." She said this a little too seriously. I realized my comment might have offended her a bit. She hadn't yet succeeded as a model, so she wouldn't be taking kindly to any suggestion that she might be ill-equipped for the job.

"Anyway, you're married, and you're quite good looking. I probably shouldn't even be talking to you." She blushed again when she said it. I could almost feel my head expanding, filling with the drug of her compliment, which I fixated on so intensely that the second part of her statement barely registered. My ego was getting the gassing of its life. Sitting in an oh-so-fashionable café in Paris with a beautiful model telling me I was good looking? What more could a man ask for?

"You *did* say you were married, right?" Marie asked, staring at my wedding band for effect.

I quickly remembered the point she had been making. It wasn't about my looks, not really. She threw that part in to soften any blow I might feel from the I-stay-away-from-married-men brush-off. But even if the compliment was a throw-away, I was running with it anyway. Months into the future, I knew I'd still savor it whenever I happened to glance into a mirror.

"Yeah, I'm married," I said matter-of-factly, trying not to reveal how I felt about my union.

"Well, maybe we should be going our separate ways, then," Marie said. I noticed a small amount of hesitation in her voice, like she was hoping that I'd contradict her. But I knew she was right; I needed to get away from this woman. What every married man needed was a good pair of track shoes and the instinct to flee at the right time, like a long-surviving deer. Without those, his marriage was doomed. Unfortunately, the married man was first a man, and his DNA was likely to contain a strong predilection to run *toward* beautiful women, not away from them.

I struggled with my DNA at the café table. Marie even noticed.

"Why are you looking so pained?" she asked. Her English was precise, but it sounded heavily French-inflected, and quite lovely to boot.

"My wife is coming to visit in the next week. I'd love to see you again, but I know I shouldn't. I can't." I knew from my three years of marriage that honesty was best in these situations. It usually took the hard work of fleeing out of my hands because the woman would get the message and run away herself. Usually.

"Okay, Mr. Randolph Murphy. You be a good boy and go home to the Saint-Germain. I enjoyed your company very much."

I raised my wineglass. "I enjoyed your company too, Miss Marie Bautista. Here's to the best of luck in your career. Cheers."

She beamed back at me. "Thank you. *A votre santé.*"

I frowned. "What's that mean?" I asked.

"The same as what you said. Cheers."

As we were about to separate on the sidewalk out front, she threw me one more meaty, irresistible bone.

"By the way, Mr. Randolph Murphy, in case you wanted to know, my company is called Chaud. That means hot." I could have sworn there was a twinkle in her eye before she turned around with a little wave. She didn't even say good-bye, as if she knew we'd see each other again. I watched her round ass twisting under her short skirt. Her smooth, light-brown legs seemed to stretch all the way to her neck. Oh God, I thought, I better run like hell.

Once I touched down in my room, I would desperately search for activities to keep me busy so I wouldn't think about it, but I usually failed. Inevitably my wandering thoughts would bring me right back to Fort Greene, Brooklyn, and Mekhi Chance-Murphy, my wife of three years. When I thought about Mikki, the name by which she is widely known, I felt a peculiar mix of anger and confusion that combined to produce helplessness. I just did not understand what had happened to my marriage, to my unabashed loving. We'd met on a commercial shoot, me on the set to make sure it ran smoothly, Mikki as a stylist ensuring that the actors had the right "look". Our beginnings could have fit comfortably in a fairy tale: the wildness of the early courting, like having sex on a subway car—that wasn't empty; sleeping in Central Park for a night to see what creatures lurked in the dark; paying a horse-drawn carriage to gallop through Harlem; and my kicker—proposing to Mikki across the sheltering sky of New York City with a skywriting airplane painting the words for all to see, "Marry me, Mikki."

Mikki's initial response will never be forgotten: "Look, Randy, that airplane pilot is asking me to marry him!"

I wasn't sure if things had started to go bad before the Baby Wars. I suspected that they had. But maybe that was just my wish, to place the blame elsewhere, not on my own doorstep, because I knew I had pushed too hard with the baby thing. The conventional wisdom said that women were the only ones equipped with a biological clock, but I knew the truth—men could just as desperately crave the moment when the world's promises and possibilities multiplied exponentially because it now included your own human creation. Ever since I had entered adulthood—actually, even during my teen years—I had wanted a baby. It didn't even matter if it was a little boy or a little girl; I just wanted to cherish and nurture a tiny, helpless reflection of myself, showering it with as much love and protection as I could manage. I loved everything about them—their smell, their little whines, their grasping need, their velvety softness.

But Mikki wasn't having any of it, at least not now. She wasn't ready, she said over and over again. Wait! she virtually shouted to me. But I didn't want to wait, and I said some pretty awful things to her to make my point. Questioning her womanhood, her commitment to our marriage, her love for me. Things I wished I could take back. I had tried to apologize on many occasions, but the damage appeared to be done. Mikki had shut down on me, or so it seemed.

She would be in Paris in less than a week. That thought frightened me from my nearly clean-shaven head to my raggedy toenails. I had grown comfortable without the pressure, the stress, that had started to accompany us whenever we were together. It had started to become unbearable—which was a major reason I had jumped at the chance to come to Paris. Actually, considering how unpleasant our Brooklyn home had become, I was surprised that Mikki had reacted with such anger and bitterness at the announcement of my three-month stay in Paris. In fact, her reaction had been so extreme, so over-the-top, I wondered now for the first time if maybe she had been faking it. Maybe she was glad to see me go and she felt so guilty about it that she put on an Oscar-worthy performance for me, and even herself. Why had there been so little contact between us since my departure? The communication had dwindled to e-mails once or twice a week that were perfunctory in message and tone. It was almost like we no longer had anything to say to each other.

The more I thought about it, the more I dreaded Mikki's arrival. What would we talk about? I had an elaborate week planned, but would any of it matter? And now I had the extension of my stay to worry about. How would that go over? How should I break the news to her? Somehow, e-mail didn't seem sufficient. But it certainly was easier. Perhaps waiting until she arrived would be best, so I could tell her face-to-face. If I gave her forewarning, it might put a splash of cold water on our romantic Paris rendezvous before we could get around to "doing the do," as I used to jokingly say to her in our early days. She'd laugh and tell me that I was "soooo corny," but she'd add that "the do always needs doin'." Usually I'd chuckle happily at how lucky I was to have found such a sexy, sensuous woman.

I had invested in a modem for my laptop so that we could exchange e-mail whether I was at work or at "home" in the hotel, but I hadn't yet even connected the modem to see if it worked. Thus far I had done all my e-mailing from the office. As I threw off the last of my work clothes my eyes settled on the laptop across the room, and I felt a flash of inspiration pass through me like a zap of the same kind of energy I felt when I had just thought of a clever ad campaign or slogan. I was going to sit down and construct the sexiest, most romantic, toe-curling e-mail love letter for my wife. After reading it, she'd want to sprint to JFK Airport and hop on the first thing to Paris so she could hop on me.

Like most married men, my skill at writing love missives had grown rusty from disuse. I made my living as a writer of sorts—though I'd never make that claim around authors or journalists—but ad writers always went for the cute and clever, which was almost the opposite of the earnest, heartrending tones you needed in a good love letter. The more I thought about it, the more excited I got. Stripped down to my briefs for maximum comfort, I placed the computer on my lap and turned it on. As I listened to the familiar grunts and hums of the computer, I considered what message I wanted to get across. Was this going to be some sort of apology? If so, for what was I apologizing? If not, was I trying to wipe the slate clean and pretend none of the unpleasantness ever happened? Was it possible for us to start all over?

Yeah, starting over, I thought, nodding my head. That's the tone I would go for. I'd ask Mikki if we could jog back to the starting line and correct our mistakes. We could treat Paris like a week of those sexy, exciting nights we used to share racing around Manhattan from one hot spot to the next, hardly stopping to take a breath, sucking in the intoxicating scent of each other's company in the most scintillating place on earth. Well, now we were really going to be together in perhaps the most exciting place on earth. If Paris wasn't more exciting than New York, it certainly was more romantic. Romance had a tough time sustaining life in the cynical air of the five boroughs.

Twenty minutes later, I still hadn't gotten the modem to work properly. Wasn't that just so typical of my marriage—get in the mood for romance and things just can't seem to proceed according to plan. As I tried to get the computer to recognize the modem card for about the twelfth time, I considered stopping the whole production and pulling out some paper to write her an old-fashioned letter. Talk about a bygone era. When was the last time I had written anybody a letter? I couldn't even remember the feel of my hand sliding across the paper, trying to avoid the fresh ink. But if I had only six days until Mikki's arrival, what assurance would I have that she'd even receive the letter before she got on the plane? That would be a major drag—pen the most affecting letter ever written, only to have her arrive in the City of Lights without reading it and with that scowl still on her face. I knew a letter was too risky. I needed to hurry and get the damn computer working; I felt the romantic urgings slowly seeping from my body.

When I finally figured it out and opened up the message screen, a gigantic case of writer's block sat down on my lap, gazing back at me through the computer screen. I had no idea how to start. There had been such a long-standing impasse between us that I wasn't sure how much I needed to acknowledge it before trying to move things forward. I couldn't simply pretend that the past six months or so hadn't happened. The marathon arguments over babies, my late hours at the office, and Mikki's growing distance—would she allow me to jump over all that stuff with not a word of explanation or apology? I didn't think so, but how could I get through the unpleasantness without bogging down my love letter with negativity? A love message had to be inspirational, emotive, poetic. Not whiney and pathetic. How do you achieve the former when your entire being was suffused with the latter?

I took a deep breath and closed my eyes, letting my tired bones sink back into the bed. Maybe I should go to sleep first, take a nap before I tried to write. But just as I hit the pillows, my eyes flew open and I pushed my fingers across the keyboard. I couldn't afford sleep right now. I had a marriage to save.

Mikki: Damn. How do I start? How have I even gotten to this terrifying point where I'm not sure what I want to say or need to say to you? You are still the center of my universe—to which I'm sure you're responding, "Then why the hell are you in Paris instead of in Brooklyn with me?" That would be a legitimate question—one that you've asked before—but I'm not sure it's an entirely fair one. There are sacrifices we all must make for our careers, to advance our lives forward to get the things we want out of them. Working hard and staying in Paris is definitely one of those sacrifices. If I had declined this trip, it would have been difficult for me not to blame you for any stagnation I suffered throughout the rest of my career. Don't you think that would be an unfair burden for our marriage?

I want us to take this visit as an opportunity to start fresh, wipe the slate clean, if that's possible. We have flung enough angry statements at each other to last us the next thirty years; how about if we declare a truce and start all over again? Can we put the past unpleasantness behind us, for the sake of our lives and our love? I'm willing to purge it all from my mind. I hope you are, too.

As far as a baby is concerned, I am truly sorry for any pain I may have caused you with my insistent stubbornness. I just got the idea in my head and I had a hard time letting it go and seeing things from your perspective. You're absolutely right that you would be the one bearing the overwhelming burden of having a child and that it must be something you're totally ready for. If you had gone ahead and gotten pregnant just for me and not for you, you probably would have resented me for it—just as I would have resented you if I declined the job in Paris.

There are many times in a marriage when we must compromise and try to keep the other person's perspective foremost in our minds before we fly off the handle and start making crazy accusations. I was guilty of failing to do this over the last few months and I'm really sorry about that. We both need to become better at talking through problems before we let anger get the best of us and do things we'll regret. Maybe we could try going to a third party, like a marriage counselor, to help us resolve our problems. If you don't want to do that, we should at least make more of an effort to communicate instead of just shutting down. It doesn't get anything accomplished when you turn off and just stop talking to me, as if I no longer exist. It makes me wonder if you even enjoy being around me *anymore. Sometimes I still wonder that. When you come here, I'm going to pour it on pretty thick. You're going to get all the loving you can stand, and then some. I hope you're ready to be swept off your feet. I love you dearly and I can't wait to see you.*

    Love,

    Your husband.

    I read over the message several times, asking myself if I was accepting too much blame. I wasn't sure I really believed much of what I said in the note, but I felt it was necessary for me to show some contrition in order to get her attention and have any chance of her moving toward me. I still harbored some resentments about her not wanting to give me a baby right now. She had been saying "Now is not the time" for almost two years. I was starting to fear that she would never want a child, that there was something else going on that I didn't understand. This frightened me to my core. Maybe she had never planned on having a child, and she just refused to tell me. I knew those childless-by-choice women were out there, angrily refusing to accept the conventional wisdom that a woman wasn't really a woman unless she had produced offspring. But I knew that if my lack of trust grew, there was no way we could patch this thing up. I had to accept her decision to postpone the baby-making, and I had to believe that it would happen soon. I just didn't want her to wait too long. I had so thoroughly idealized my image of fatherhood—the sports I would teach my child to play, the marathon basketball games we would stage in the driveway of our future suburban home—that I had calculated how many years I could afford to wait before all my plans would be ruined because I'd be too old. At age thirty-two I was now about three years away from my age threshold, beyond which I'd be too old to be Athlete Dad. I didn't want to be in my fifties when the kid went through teenhood. I didn't want to be an aging, hobbled fifty-three, fifty-four, or fifty-five-year-old when my child turned sixteen. I wanted to be able to spank my sixteen-year-old in a game of one-on-one.

    When I pressed the send button, I felt a slight easing of the tension that had gripped me ever since I walked out of the café with Marie. I felt that I had taken a strong, proactive measure to rebuild my marriage. I had put out just enough apology and contrition for my headstrong wife to allow me back into her embrace without feeling she had compromised too much of her anger. Or at least that's what I thought. Mikki was so unpredictable that I could never really know how she was going to react. That's why the thought of her filled me with such tension of late. That unpredictability, that mercurial storminess had thrilled me in the beginning, but as with so much of a marriage, those early virtues had soured in my mind and become vices. Now instead of the thrill of discovery and the possibility of danger, what I felt in her presence was the fear of conflict. It sat in the pit of my stomach like an ulcer, gnawing away at my love for my wife. I found myself trying to postpone it, to stay away as long as possible to reduce the hours I'd have to sit amidst her vitriol. But of course it curved into a vicious cycle because the longer I stayed at work or the more I hit the bars and strip clubs with my buddies to stay away from her, the angrier and nastier she got.

I lunged for the television remote in search of a distraction. I couldn't understand anything except for the BBC's newscasts, so if I wasn't in the mood for world news, which I usually wasn't, distractions were hard to come by. Once in a while I'd stumble upon some peculiar Parisian show featuring scantily clad women with juicy, bouncy breasts, but I never seemed to find those shows when I was looking for them. I couldn't stand the French version of MTV. I didn't know what they were saying and I had no taste for the music they played—bizarre hip-hop–style phrasings over monotonous house music beats. You haven't been musically repulsed until you've heard a French rapper using a watered-down MC Hammer beat. After laughing for the first few days, I had taken to avoiding French MTV.

When I turned off the television, I heard the unmistakable sounds of rhythmic groans and grunts through the wall behind me. Unfortunately, the groaning had become a familiar visitor during my Paris stay. I was living in a Paris hotel in the heart of the fashionable Saint-Germain district, blocks away from the Louvre and Musée D'Orsay, and within shouting distance of some of the city's most important cafés. My hotel was bursting with newlyweds. Everywhere I turned, my eyes were met with lusty kisses, groping hands, and way too many smiles for my tastes. Mired in a marriage that was collapsing before my eyes, I found the omnipresent scent of romance suffocating. But it was even worse when I went to my room after the day darkened. At least a few times a week, my silent repose would be shattered by the rutting soundtrack of consummation. The first few times I heard it, I admit I was instantly aroused and once even slid my hand down to stroke my thickened penis to orgasm as the groans cheered me on in the background. But the arousal had eventually turned to annoyance, then depression, and now anger.

I slammed my head back down on the bed and covered my face with the pillow, but I could still hear the woman's high-pitched wails. I wondered if the wailer was the homely blonde I saw slipping from her room as I was coming home the night before. She was wearing a loose-fitting robe and as she swung around to head down the hall, the robe opened up enough for me to see her full breasts almost to the nipples. She stared me fully in the face as she walked by, making no attempt to cover herself. I had tried to read her expression, but as was so often the case while I had been in Europe, I could extract no information from the blankness of the stare. She brushed by me and I tried to stop myself from looking down, but at the last moment I succumbed to my erotic curiosity and dropped my eyes to catch what I would have sworn to friends and strangers was a tuft of blond pubic hair saluting me. Stunned, I watched the woman saunter down the hall, finally reaching down and tying her robe. Just before she turned into the alcove with the ice machine, she glanced back at me with an expression that I interpreted as bemusement—though, again, I could have been wrong.

As I heard the woman's wails reach an orgasmic pitch and then subside like a police siren fading into the night, I worked up a picture of the face I saw in the hall. The nose was much too large and hawkish and the eyes too close together, but perhaps she wasn't so ugly after all.

When the fucking sounds had been replaced by the faint irregular squawks of a distant television, I clicked off the light and slid under the covers. As was often the case, I chose sleep. Now I was horny—certainly even more reason for me to close my eyes and declare the day over. As a married man in Paris, I was afraid to choose entertainment or any distraction that involved stepping out of the hotel into the nighttime Paris streets and clubs. I was tired of reading. Television was hardly engaging. The sound of newlywed sex was torture. What else was there but sleep? I tried to slow down my breathing and paralyze my overactive mind in an effort to lure sleep into my bed. Before I dozed off, I was aware of a dull ache that still sat in my belly. It wasn't anxiety, I now realized. No, it was something harder to purge, something more deep-seated and affecting. It was loneliness.

She

Fool.

Look at her, twirlin' around in that dress like she don't have a lick of sense. Yeah, it looks nice on her and all, the way the white silk is slinking and clinging to her little bony hips and her little itty-bitty waist and those doctor-done-hooked-me-up breasts of hers. I do good work, I ain't gonna lie. But I wish I could walk over there and do her mouth like I used to do those sand faces I made at the beach when I was a kid—just take my hand and slide it across the mouth and the eyes and the nose. Erase every hint of a facial feature until there is no more nose, no more smiling eyes, no more lips spread wide. It'd be just a blank dirt circle.

She was irking me that much, singing that stupid-ass bridal march song.

"Oh, it's just beautiful, Mikki," she said to me, still twirling. "It looks just like the dress in your sketch and it fits me like a glove. You have such an amazing eye for detail. How do you do it, girl? You're an angel!"

Bitch.

"Oh, it's nothing, baby—just been making wedding dresses for a long time now," I said, putting on my best syrupy-sweet voice. "It does fit you beautifully. You're going to make a lovely bride."

"Oh, yes—thanks to you! Brian's mouth is going to drop to the floor when I walk down that aisle. We're getting married at the Akwaaba

Mansion in Bed-Stuy. It's going to be out in the garden with lots of flowers and harps and we're having a catered buffet . . ."

Damn. The last thing I want right now is to hear the details of her stupid wedding. I don't want to think about weddings, because weddings make me think about vows and vows make me think about relationships and relationships make me remember how my relationship with my husband, Randy, is unraveling like a ball of catnip-laced yarn at the claws of my nutty, mischievous cats. Thinking about other peoples' happiness—particularly their nuptials—bums me the hell out.

I don't need to be bummed.

Right now, what I need to do is think happy, happy, joy, joy because tomorrow morning I'm going to fly to Paris to meet him and I'd best have my face straightened out when I do it. I already called Angelou and told her I need her to help me pick out a new haircut, some kind of style or something, like one of those short, cute Halle Berry pixie cuts, or maybe even one of those supershort Jada Pinkett/bleach-it-blonde-slick-it-down dos, and some makeup. And a sexy getup from BCBG. Something. Anything. Because I know that if I don't have a new look to provide for that distraction when I rush into his arms at the Roissy Charles deGaulle Airport in France, my face is going to betray it all—the late-night dinners, the long lunch-hour phone talks, the Sunday-morning brunches—all of that stuff I've been doing with Marcus that I should have been saving for Randy.

Of course, if Randy's ass was home, I wouldn't have been on the stroll with Marcus.

Well, maybe that's not exactly true. Okay, okay, okay—it's a big, fat, round, bold-faced lie. I didn't want him to go to Paris at first—gave him hell when he told me he was going away for three months without me. I didn't particularly give a damn that it was for his job and that his commitment to this project would get him "mo' money, mo' money, mo' money." I wanted him home. I wanted him to slow down. I wanted us to work a few kinks out of our marriage. Okay, a whole lot of kinks. Three months in Paris wasn't going to accomplish any of the above.

At least that's what I thought when I dropped him off at Kennedy Airport.

But you know what? He's been there seven weeks, and I'm not mad at being without him anymore. I didn't realize how tired I was of the excuses, the headaches, the heartaches, the arguments, until his butt left. I got sick of him asking me to have a kid, sick of him telling me I should sell my shop and let him take care of me, sick of him making me sick. I didn't want to argue about it anymore—didn't even want to twirl it around in my thoughts for more than two seconds.

Oh, he tried to bring it up in our earlier phone conversations—"Babe, when I get back from Paris, I'll be set with the firm and I'll probably get a fly promotion. We'll be set financially, and if we're set financially then we can do this." I'd just find a way to cut him off: "Randy—let's not argue about this right now, baby. Let's talk about happy things."

"Oh, my bad—I thought having a baby with my wife was a happy thing."

Yeah. Right.

I mean, it's not like I don't like kids. My sister, Zaria, has two crumb-snatchers—James and Jasmine—and I guess I like them. I mean, they can be some bad asses. James came to my house a few months ago and decided he wanted to look out the window where I'd just hung my brand-new sheer off-white curtains while he was eating the cherry, lemon, and blue ice bomb pop I'd just sprung for from the ice cream truck. Blue and red sticky shit everywhere. I wanted to kill him, or at least inflict some pain on his little behind. I would have, too, if his sister hadn't busted her butt climbing up on my kitchen ladder and started screaming like a banshee. That's what she got for trying to grab for some cookies without asking. She was all right—and I guess I did a good job of comforting her and scolding him, but Lord I'm not ready to do that all day, everyday, especially if my husband isn't committed to being there to help. Zaria, their mom, knows I'm a good auntie, but she also knows that Auntie Mikki can't be left with the kids too long because she can't handle more than a two-hour dose of kids at any one time. Her kids are cute, so long as I can give them back when they really work my nerves. They work my nerves often. I am not around them too much.

I can only imagine that I'd feel the same way about a child born to a marriage that isn't all that stable, with one parent who can't keep his behind still long enough to have dinner, let alone raise a child, and another who much prefers sewing children's clothes to cleaning vomit off of them. Truth of the matter is that I'm scared to death of kids, both having them and rearing them. I saw my sister go through two pregnancies; her body was possessed. The birthing experience? It was an experience, all right. Probably the most violent experience I've ever witnessed in my life, next to that scene in *Scream 2*, where some guy with a death mask and a really big knife gives Jada Pinkett hers in twenty-eight places in a crowded movie theater. Everybody was watching Jada and cheering her on, without recognizing that homegirl was bleeding real blood, in serious pain, scared to death, and about to die. That would be the perfect description of Zaria and the hospital scenes when she was giving birth to both James and Jasmine.

I don't know nothing 'bout birthin' no babies. Ain't trying to anytime soon.

Besides, my shop, Mekhi's, is just getting off the ground; my client base is starting to build up and I think there's a buzz going on about my work. No, I'm not turning very much of a profit. In fact, I've lost money each of the three years that my shop's been operating. But I love being my own boss, and keeping my own time, and Randy makes enough money to get me through the first few years of my business's struggle for self-sufficiency. There's no need to bring a little person into this world while I'm trying to get my stuff together, no matter how desperate Randy is for a baby. Shoot, I need to spend this twenty-eight-year-old energy on Mekhi Chance-Murphy and my true baby—my shop. I got plenty of time to have a rugrat.

I'm not being foul; I'm just keepin' it real.

Now, Marcus, he understands all of that. He has a kid of his own —a five-year-old, Kofi—whom he loves, but didn't really want. His ex-wife, Marti, just straight up stopped taking her pills without telling him until, of course, it was too late. He wasn't ready, and he didn't think their marriage could stand it either. He was right.

They slept with each other maybe twice after the baby was born, and then she moved into the kid's room—talking about how she wanted to keep an eye on the baby. Before she knew it, he was turning into one long, bad husband cliché—working late during the week, staying out with the boys on the weekend, coming home with Calyx perfume on his collar. Marti didn't wear Calyx. Her husband's secretary did; she got a bottle of it from Marcus and Marti Peate for Christmas. Marti Peate picked it out.

I know these things because Marcus is Randy's best friend. They talk about everything under the sun—have done so since Marcus be- came Randy's mentor and ace boon coon back in college, at Yale—and Randy, being my husband, tells me everything (or at least he used to).

"Mikki? I'd like to try the headpiece on one more time, just to make sure that it's right for the dress. I saw another in a bridal magazine that looked like it might work better," Fool said.

If this little girl doesn't get out of my face quick, I'm going to hurt her. Bad.

"You know what? I think you should leave those magazines alone, be- cause you're always going to find something you think is more beautiful than what you have. I was the same way when I was getting married."

"Really? Wow! I thought I was the only one who became addicted to bridal magazines. Even though I've had most of my wedding planned for months, I can't help but to pick up the new ones when I get into one of those magazine stands. They're so expensive, though. Like, *Bride?* That one is just ridiculous . . ."

I really can't do this. She's going to make me go postal.

Anyway, back to Marcus. I also know all of his business because I am on the verge of having an affair with my man's boy.

Yes, I know that it is not right. Yes, I do feel bad about it—horrible, if you need to know the absolute truth. Yes, I know that this needs to come to an end, for the sake of my marriage, for the sake of my san- ity, and for the sake of the twelve-year friendship my husband and my kinda-boyfriend share.

But Marcus feels so good. His hands—Lord have mercy, his hands—they're just so soft, and gentle, and his breath, so sweet and sensual when he's tickling my ears with conversation about nothing in particular. I think—no, I know—I fell in love with him at the Meshell Ndegéocello concert at the Knitting Factory last weekend, just when Meshell started singing some love song she was dedicating to her new girlfriend.

"This song here, it's about love and commitment," she said into her microphone, her bass resting in the swell of her stomach and thighs. "I see y'all, looking at me like I'm crazy. Muthafuckas in New York are jaded; y'all don't believe in commitment. Y'all saying to yourselves right now, 'Commitment? Sheiit, alls I expect is that he'll have a job and he pay the rent on time.' "

Then she started strumming the most beautiful song I'd ever heard in my life, and the keyboardist just played this gorgeous melody and the crowd started swaying and I started to catch a buzz from the dude to my left who'd lit up a bud the second the host announced smoking wasn't allowed in the concert area and Marcus accidentally—or maybe it wasn't an accident—brushed the back of his hand across my ass and leaned into my neck and said, "Excuse me, baby, I didn't mean that," and then paused for exactly two beats and then leaned back into my neck and said, "That was nice."

"Sure was," I said, without realizing it was coming out of my mouth, and without hesitation.

And Meshell kept strumming and the crowd swayed some more and before I knew it I was burrowing my ass into Marcus's crotch and he was rubbing my thighs with those thick, strong hands of his and his face was this close to my neck and his lips brushed against my collarbone and I know he must have felt my pulse because it was racing and racing and racing and everybody in the crowd heard it, I know it, because it was keeping time with the drummer who'd begun pounding out this *boom-bap, de-boom-bap*, and I could hardly breathe. I was exhaling like a mug, in the middle of some smoky, trashy Manhattan club, with someone who was not my husband. I felt like a schoolgirl who'd graduated to her first PG-13 date.

And now, after thinking on it long and hard, (I think) I'm ready to make the R-rated version of this Marcus movie. No, really, I am. Marcus makes me feel sexy, and beautiful, and sweet—like a woman who deserves love and affection and all that syrupy shit you hear R&B singers whining about in all those stupid songs they play on the radio. He makes me feel like I'm the only woman in the world who deserves his attention. He's so smart and funny and he makes me feel like I'm smart and funny, too, you know? I love holding on to his big, muscular arm while we're walking down the street (of course, we only do this in the middle of the afternoon, in weird places where no one we know will ever see us, like Chinatown and Little Italy, and elementary school playgrounds in the Bronx). He makes me feel protected.

In fact, it was his protection I was seeking when we got ourselves into this predicament in the first place. In fact, it was Randy who suggested I call Marcus the night after I thought I heard somebody tramping through my pegonias out in the garden just outside our ground-floor window.

"But, Randy, I can't take it anymore, you all the way on the other side of the world. I need you here," I'd told him the next morning, exhausted from having had absolutely no sleep whatsoever. Too scared. "Some woman was coming home from work the other night—ten-thirty in the evening—and someone shot her in the head while she was getting out of her car. She was parking her car a block over on South Portland Street. The same guy that shot her could have been watching this apartment, figured out I'm here all alone, and decided he's going to rob us blind or rape me or both or—"

"Baby, calm down. You know that was probably one of your fool cats making noise," he joked, totally not taking me serious.

"Not outside—you know they don't go outside. And don't call Pootie and Mac fools. Aren't you the least bit concerned that I don't feel safe here all by myself? At all? I mean, damn." My voice was trembling and I was getting angrier with every word.

"I'm sorry, Mikki," Randy said, careful to remove the smirk from his voice this time. "Look, here's the deal. As soon as you hang up this phone, I want you to call Marcus and tell him to go over to the apartment and check all the locks on the doors and make sure the security system is hooked, okay? And tell him to do his ol' buddy a favor and stop by just before you turn in to make sure no one's waiting out in the bushes. Is that cool with you?"

"I don't want to call Marcus to do for me what my husband should be doing—can't you understand that? I need you here, Randolph Murphy. Not in fucking Europe, not in fucking Paris, not in fucking Manhattan, not in your fucking office, not anywhere else in this whole entire fucking world but H-E-R-E, Randolph. Here."

I'd worked myself into a tizzy, you see, and now Randy didn't know what the hell to do. He had no answers for me, no solutions that would amount to what I wanted right then and there. He had but one suggestion.

"Please, babe, calm down. Just call Marcus. He'll take good care of you until I get back, I promise you. I won't let anything happen to you, baby, please. Just—just call Marcus. I'll call him, whatever you want, okay?"

Silence.

"Okay?"

He was near begging mode. I mean, what the hell else was I supposed to say? He wasn't coming home, that was clear. He wasn't going to be here for another three months, that was clear. He didn't really care that I was scared shitless without him and I needed him to be with me, his wife—that was crystal.

"Fine. I'll call Marcus."

"Babe, everything is going to be fine, okay? I trust Marcus with my life, and I know I can trust him with yours, baby. Please. It's going to be all right. I'll be home before you know it. Call Marcus."

I called Marcus, all right.

And now, I don't particularly care if Randy stays in Paris for another three years. As far as I'm concerned he messed up when he left me here alone, and he messed up big time when he pushed—yes, pushed—me into the arms of his best friend. Had the nerve to send me a two-page-long e-mail, talking about "let's make a new start." I mean, he called himself apologizing and wanting to straighten shit out, but he asked me in a damn computer message. *A computer message.* You order T-shirts on the computer. You read newspapers on the computer. You send insignificant e-mail to the friends you kinda want to talk to, but not enough to run up your phone bill. You say, "the kids are fine," and "I went to see Wynton Marsalis in concert last week, he was great," and "Belize was the bomb." You do not use it to tell your wife that you want to put all the bad stuff behind so that there'll be no bad blood when she comes halfway across the earth to see you—which she wouldn't be doing if your ass was home where she wanted you to be in the first place.

My reply to him was simple and swift.

> *Randy: Did you forget the phone number here? Will I need to bring a computer with me so that we can "communicate"? I guess I'm not a big fan of marriage by e-mail.*
> *Mikki*

Perhaps it was too simple and swift, but I'm a blunt kinda girl, and Randy, being my husband for three years, should know this by now. Still, I felt instantly bad the moment I lifted my finger off the send button. Sometimes, though, I just get the feeling that he doesn't know me, and doesn't care to find out.

Don't get me wrong—I love my husband, see? He is a good man

and he takes care of his responsibilities, which is more than I can say for most of the trifling Negroes I've dated in my lifetime. But I can't give him cool points for that; he's *supposed* to be a good man and take care of responsibilities; that's what being a man is about. Being a husband? Now that's something altogether different. A good husband is supposed to be there for his wife—to love her unconditionally, to support her in all that she wants to do without pressure to do things his way or no way.

I'm not sure that Randy is capable of loving me unconditionally. He certainly isn't here for me, seeing as he's in France on yet another job assignment. Lord knows what he's doing over there, and with whom he's doing it. And homeboy wouldn't know the meaning of "no pressure" if it attached itself to the grill of a Mack truck and ran him down like a dog.

And I'm not so sure any of this would change if he was sitting right here next to me at this very moment.

Marcus? He's fine. He's intelligent. He treats me like the Queen of Sheba every moment we're together, which is beginning to be often.

My man is not here.

I'm beginning to think that he may be gone for good.

What's a girl to do?

"Mikki? Mikki? Girl, what you thinkin' about?"

"Hmm? Oh, um, I'm sorry—what were you saying?" This fool girl was still standing in front of me, well, the mirror—but she'd finally directed her attention to me, a minor miracle in and of itself.

"I said, should I come back for another fitting, or do you think this is it?"

I walked over toward her and put my hands on her shoulders, guiding her into a perfect-posture position. My eyes washed over her body, taking in every inch of the dress that I'd painstakingly sewn over the past three weeks to fit her shape to a T. There were flaws—the seams that traveled along the sides of her breasts and down to the hem of the gown weren't completely straight. The hem could have been about a quarter-inch shorter (she changed her shoes, again). And if she lost one more pound, the whole thing was just going to slink right off her body when she walks down the aisle, if she doesn't die from starvation first.

"No, you need to come back one more time so that I can make sure it's absolutely perfect. When is the date again?"

"October 23—one month, three days from now. God, I'm so excited."

Ugh. Bang, zoom, to the moon, Alice. This is one corny bitch.

"I'll come see you a week before then, okay? We'll take a final fitting and you'll be all set."

"Oh, thank you, Mikki—you're the best. I really love it."

"You're welcome," I said, practically pushing her back into the fitting room. "I'm going to make a phone call. Just hang the dress up after you get it off and leave it in the fitting room. I'll see you in three weeks."

"Okay," she said, muffled, through the fitting-room door.

I walked over to my desk and plopped into my chair, picking up my cordless on the way down. I'd been calling Angelou at this number for so long that I couldn't even remember it unless my fingers were flying over the keys.

"Hey, girl—whatchoo doin'?"

"I'm waiting for my very best friend to take me shopping," Angelou said sweetly into the receiver.

"Shopping?" I asked incredulously. "No, darling. I'm going shopping. You're coming with me. You are the designated helper—get it straight."

"Well, I'm figuring if you're going to drag me to the Village in this heat on my day off, the least you can do is hit a sistah off with a little BCBG goods, knowhatumsayin'?"

"Chile, please—you know damn well you don't have a job. Your day off. Bitch, please. You ready to go or what?"

"Now why I gotta be a bitch?"

"See you in, what, twenty minutes? Don't have me sitting there waiting all day long for you, Angie. You know how you do."

"Well, damn. A sistah just has no credibility whatsoever."

"None."

"Well, you don't have to pour more salt into the wound. You just be ready when I get there. Oh, and wait—don't hang up!"

"Yes, Angelou," I said, putting on the monotone of life.

"Joke of the day—you ready?"

"Oh, here you go."

"Okay. How are tornadoes and redneck divorces different?"

I didn't even bother thinking about it—didn't make sense to. "I give up. How are tornadoes and redneck divorces different, Angelou?"

"They aren't—either way, the trailer's gotta go." Then she started laughing hysterically. I swear this chile ain't got the good sense of a billy goat.

"Angelou?"

"What?" she asked, still giggling.

"You stoopid."

"Well, damn. Why I gotta be stupid?"

It was one of those sweet summer days—the kind where if you have an office job, you wished there were some outlets outside, or an extension cord long enough to allow you to move your computer and your phone and whatever other tools you need outside. If you're really smart, you don't dream about taking up residence on a park bench; you use up one of those sick days and you call in from a pay phone on the corner of West Broadway and Houston and tell your boss you have cramps and shit—you know, gross him out with some feminine stuff so that he won't ask questions and he'll rush off the phone—then you hang up and walk on over to the deli and pick you up one of those plastic cups of sweet watermelon and spit out the seeds onto the sidewalk while you're peeking into all the little boutiques and checking out all the fascinating dresses hanging in the windows and imagining all the crap you would buy if you had a little more money in your checking account or you hit the Lotto or something.

I don't have to call a boss—I *am* my boss. That means I get to enjoy these kinds of days regularly, because that's how the boss at Mekhi's rolls. Ha.

Angelou pretty much has the same luxury. She's auditioning right now—has been for the last three months since the chorus gig she had in a Disney Broadway musical closed. Between gigs she does interior decorating, freelancing for all these rich misses who're long on dough and time, but really short on creativity. She's bad, too. She bought this little raggedy brownstone over in Bed-Stuy out of foreclosure last year for virtually pennies, and, then, room by room, gutted the entire thing and created a virtual mansion with her own bare hands: there's Italian leather and afrocentric flourishes everywhere, walls in mauve and sandstone and amber and closets built into walls and walls that expand into French doors that kiss perfectly manicured sitting rooms. Simply lovely.

I let her hook up Mekhi's—but not because of what I saw her do to her own home. I knew girlfriend had a gift the moment I saw her dorm room back at Spelman, where we first met and became best friends. We'd gone to a sorority rush together for a young organization, Sigma Kappa Psi, and simultaneously fell in love with its promise of sister-hood, security, community leadership, and afrocentric values the group had promoted on its advertising flyers. Then the president of SKP, Chandon Patrik, opened her mouth. Complete and total ditz.

"Okay—joke, one-liner." Angelou didn't know me from a can of paint, but that didn't stop her from leaning into my right ear and whis-pering into it. She was altogether strange and familiar to me—like someone I'd met before, but, like, in a former life. I knew she didn't belong there, though, because she had these locks—long and pretty and shiny black, like baby doll hair rolled between the fingers of a child who'd gotten into her mama's Afro Sheen. They reached just past her ears; a decorative pin of cowrie shells gathered a bunch just past her forehead. I'd considered locking my hair a few months back, but my daddy told me he'd treat me like I stole something from him if I walked into his house with "those dirt worms crawling from your scalp." He's so dramatic. I settled on braids. Neither Angelou nor I looked like the light-skinned, long-haired baby dolls we were rushing. "If Barbie is so damn popular," Angelou asked, "why does everybody have to buy her friends?"

"No, you didn't," I said, my mouth wide open and full of giggles.

"I know you're not buying this bullshit. I do not want some girl making me wash her clothes in between classes and beating my ass after dinner for the next seven weeks so that I have the right to call her my sister. You can forget that," Angelou stage-whispered.

A few girls—they were wearing the organizational colors, lavender and beige—peered in our direction, making sure to swivel their necks just so, so that their hair could do that Pantene-commercial bounce when they turned. It was amazing. I rolled my eyes at one—some chick with long, sandy hair, a whole lotta makeup, and a white-girl nose—then leaned conspiratorially into the purveyor of bad jokes and said, "Come on—let's go get a cup of coffee or something."

Then we both stood up, careful to make as much noise as humanly possible as we excused and pardoned our way out of the room. We fell out of there and laughed all the way to the Student's Café across campus, through a cup of coffee and two scoops of ice cream, through the walk back to her dormitory, and way into the night. We were both the same age (19), both born the same month (her birthday is October 21, mine, October 8), both from northern New Jersey (she's from Englewood, I'm from South Orange) and both unsure of what we were going to major in at the almighty Spelman. We were both seeking a career in the arts. I liked to sew. She was the drama queen. We were instant best friends. We were inseparable.

We knew better than to become roommates in college; didn't want to ruin the friendship before it really got started. But a week after graduation, we moved into a squat two-bedroom walk-up in Manhattan Valley, 105th between Manhattan and Columbus Avenues. We were both searching for gigs, getting work anywhere we could find it. She hit up off-Broadway, singing in choruses, dancing in music videos, doing commercials and, in one theater production, playing an understudy and designing the sets of small but prominent plays; I hit the video and commercial circuit, becoming a stylist for the starving dancers and actors who made their living shaking ass for 100 dollars and a half-second of fame. There wasn't a single, solitary thing under the sun that Angelou and I didn't talk about—our crushes, our fears, our families, our period pains. I was there for her when that boy was beating her ass and she pressed charges against him and got a restraining order and he came after her anyway and we got him sent away to prison, and she was there for me when that other boy, the professional basketball player (who shall remain nameless because to this day I still can't admit I screwed his dumb behind) refused to kick that other woman out of his house so that he could make room for me, the one he claimed he loved.

"I'm telling you, Mikki," Angelou warned about my NBA escapade, "this shit is going to end. It's cool and all that he sends for you at the drop of a dime and flies you all around the earth and sends you nice gifts even when it's not your birthday. But he's not leaving her."

"But, he says—"

She never let me finish. "*He's not leaving her, Mikki.* The sooner you get that into your thick skull, the sooner you'll be able to handle your business."

"And what business, exactly, is that, Angelou," I said, disgusted, even though I'd heard the same argument at least 508 times since I'd started dating Mr. NBA five months earlier. I knew she was right, but

I wasn't used to not having a boyfriend, and I was feeling the itch. I wanted to be married, to get a husband who would support my dreams—and who could afford them, too—and eventually have a family. I thought Mr. NBA was the one. Angelou was trying to snap me out of it.

"Oh, your business is simple. Number one: Get as much shit as you can. Number two: Get tickets to the games. And number three?" She paused. I stared at her. She paused some more.

"Well, number three?" I asked, incredulous.

"Always, always, always," she said, adding another pause, "hook up yo' friends."

"Angelou?"

"I know, I know—I'm stoopid. But you know you gonna get kicked off the team the moment you tell him to get rid of that girl. I'm the one who'll be providing my shoulder—the one with my good shirt—for you to cry on. The least I can get is a hook-up. You know how I do."

"Lord have mercy—what am I going to do with you?" We tumbled into a five-minute giggling fit, then went to the movies. That's my girl, Angelou. She's certified. On some days, I don't know which she needs more, medication or Jesus. I do know something else, though: I don't know what I would do without her. I value her intellect, her silliness, and especially her opinion. In fact, it was her advice that I was heeding when I decided to hit on Randy when we first met him on the set of a commercial five years back. He was an assistant account executive, in charge of making sure the taping went well. I was on the set dressing the talent, which included Angelou. He walked in and introduced himself, checked out what Angelou was wearing, and asked to see her nails (it was a Domino's pizza commercial, and at some point, Angelou was supposed to drop grated cheese onto a pizza pie with sauce). Both of our mouths were watering, like, the entire ninety seconds he was in the room, and I'm almost sure the temperature rose a good twenty degrees, because I just got hot and flustered and began to sweat and stammer a little bit when he turned his attention to me, introduced himself, and flashed me this million-dollar smile. Boyfriend had barely gotten out of the door before both Angelou and I breathed again.

"Well, damn," Angelou said, loud as hell.

"Shhhh! He might hear you," I whispered. "Let me close the door first." We burst into giggles as soon as the door's latch clicked. "I'm saying, honey was fine! Did you see his eyes? And those lips? And his arm was as big as a tree."

"No—did you see how he was smiling at yo' ass?"

"Oh, stop it, Angelou. He wasn't paying me any mind—just being polite is all."

"Girl, please. If he grinned any harder, his mustache would have fallen off. Did you peep the mustache?"

"No—did you peep the beard?"

"No, what I peeped was him checking you out, girl. You better go talk to that man."

"Angie, what? Go talk to him? As far as he's concerned, I'm just the help—the little pee-on stylist. What on earth would he want with me?"

"First of all, you're not a pee-on. Second of all, he's not in charge, just the gopher for the guy in charge of making sure that everything is fine. There is a subtle difference, Mikki. You best recognize and go talk to that man."

I thought about it for a minute. "And what exactly am I supposed to say to him?"

"Oh, don't even try it, Mikki—acting like you don't know how to mack. Just go talk to the boy."

I looked at her as if she were crazy. Just as I was about to ask Ms. Go On and Talk To Him to help me out with something pithy to say, she was called in to the set to run lines. "You better talk to him, or I will," she warned before she squeezed into her corny red and blue Domino's jacket. She slammed the hat on her head. I fixed it so that it didn't completely muss up her shoulder-length bob. She winked at me and walked onto the set. I swear, you could be the cutest thing on this earth, but squeeze into one of those fast food restaurant uniforms, and you immediately become one of the goofiest muthafuckas on the planet.

I followed behind her.

"Go work that cheese, girl," I called after her. "And work that Domino's hat, too. Shoot, ain't nobody gonna tell you you ain't fly, girl. Work it!"

"Oh, hush," she said, laughing. Then she put on this weird face and jerked her head to the right. Mr. Assistant was standing there. Angelou made her eyes go like saucers, then she started making all these weird, funky faces—all of which were to tell me to get my ass over to Mr. Assistant so that I could kick a few words to him.

Randy never gave me a chance.

As soon as Angelou and her crazy behind got past him, he turned his attention to me. "So, can I get you a can of soda, some water, a cup of coffee—anything?"

I just looked at him. He had the most piercing dark-brown eyes I'd ever seen, framed perfectly by these shiny black eyebrows that kinda looked manicured, but without the abruptness we women get after the tweezers mold our brows into shape. He was the color of bare wood submerged in one coat of fresh mahogany stain—a weird kind of reddish brown, but pretty all the same. A nice height he was—about 6'1" or 6'2"—and I immediately started thinking about how far I'd have to crane my neck and arch my back to kiss his those big 'ol juicy lips of his, and whether it'd be worth it to get used to the pain getting into a serious lip lock would cause.

I surmised that any lower-back pain caused by his embrace would be well worth it.

"Um, I'll have a glass of wine, but since I never drink on the job, I guess you'll just have to take me out after we're finished."

"Well, you're certainly not shy."

"I decided a long time ago that shy isn't worth the bother. I'm a go-getter."

"Well, go-getters are just what I like. We're not going to be wrapping it up for another four hours or so, so if you'd like, I'll get you a ginger ale for now, and then I'll figure out a place where go-getters can get a nice meal and a glass of wine." His smile was infectious.

"Sounds like a plan," I said, trying hard not to show all thirty-two of my teeth. Just maybe, like, thirty. Angelou was practically climbing over the fake Domino's counter she was standing behind, craning her neck for a better look.

Now, the same woman who set us up, served as the maid-of-honor in our wedding, and set up the candles, hot bubble bath, flowers, champagne, and edible panties in our honeymoon suite is watching our marriage take a nose-dive, and she's being kinda wishy washy about which side she stands on. Angelou can't stand the fact that my husband is gone more than he's here, and she knows I'm hurting because it's her shoulders that I cry on when I feel like Randy just doesn't care about this marriage. Not to say that she's been coaxing me out of Randy's arms, but she hasn't exactly been encouraging me to stay away from Marcus, either. One thing about her encouragement, though, is that she's been trying to get me to be smart about all of it.

"Damn, girl. That e-mail was foul as hell," Angelou said. We were in Jean Jacques, a trendy hair salon in Soho—though the only thing trendy about the joint was that it was on a cobblestone street and the beauticians charged a good sixty dollars more for the haircut that I could have gotten uptown. But it was really pretty in this place, and they gave you coffee and pastries while you waited and all of their magazines were up-to-date and everybody in there dressed like they were about to step into a corporate board meeting at Goldman Sachs. Their hair? Always hooked. I like that. Can't stand letting a woman who can't comb her own hair messing in mine. "You didn't send it, did you?"

"Yeah, I did. I felt bad about it a few minutes after I did. I mean, he was trying to set it up so that we wouldn't spend an entire week in Paris angry at one another. But something as serious as this requires a conversation, not Randy's dictations, you know? I felt like he was just *telling* me how I was going to act when I got to Paris, and *telling* me I've been compromising our marriage and *telling* me how I'm supposed to respond to his wanting a child. Why couldn't he just pick up the phone and talk it out with me?" I quickly answered my own question. "Because he's not interested in how I feel about anything—it's all about him, all the time. He's going to set the tone for the way I should be acting, and I should just go on ahead with the set agenda because that's what Randy wants. What about what I want?"

"Okay—chill, Iyanla. You don't need to find the value in the valley for me. I understand."

"I'm glad you do, because this whole thing just confuses me. I mean, do I have a marriage or not? Should I just chill the fuck out and hope we can work everything out when he gets back? Should I even let him come back? And what about Marcus?"

"What about Marcus, Mikki?"

"I don't know, girl—I mean, we're definitely kickin' it. It clearly has the chance of turning into something else, at least I think it can."

"Mikki. That's your husband's best friend."

"You don't think I already know that?" Angelou was pretty much down with whatever decisions I'd made in my love department—always had been. She was also keen as hell when it came to insight on why things were happening the way they were, and she was pretty accurate most of the time, but I had to wonder how good she was at this love thing when she couldn't keep a man longer than a baseball season.

"You know what I think you don't know?" Angelou asked me. Her face was grave—serious. I knew to listen intently. "I think that you don't know that your heart needs a rest. It can't stand all this trauma, Mikki. I've known you for close to ten years, girl, and not once have you slowed your roll and just taken some time for yourself, you know what I mean? You go from boyfriend to boyfriend to boyfriend to husband, and I don't think you need to go to boyfriend in the middle of your marriage. But that's just me. If I were Mekhi Sidnei Chance-Murphy and I was considering removing that marriage hyphen from my name, I damn sure wouldn't jump into another relationship—particularly with my soon-to-be ex's best friend."

"Well, who said I was getting a divorce?"

"If Randy finds out you've been messing around with Marcus, you better hope all you get is a divorce."

"Yeah, okay."

"Act nonchalant all you want to—but you're going to need more than a haircut to make things all better with Randy, and a freakin' army if he ever finds out about Marcus. For real."

I was tired of her preaching. I'd run through the same thing over and over and over again in my mind after I sent Randy that e-mail, and frankly, I wasn't sure what I was going to do, even though I was leaving for Paris in less than twenty-four hours. But by the time Esperanza (she's my beautician) turned me around to the mirror to check out my new 'do, I'd decided that the Marcus thing was, indeed, ugly—we've kissed and hugged and touched, but no nookie has been had—and Randy shouldn't be privy to the 4-1-1 on that front. In fact, as I prepare myself to meet the man that I married three years ago, I feel downright guilty. There's no way in hell I'm going to bring it up. I'm going to call Marcus before I leave and let him know that this was all a big, big, B-I-G mistake, and end it right now.

And then Randy and I are going to have to take these next seven days to figure out what we're going to do about this marriage thing, because it's sinking—fast. I love that man—adore him to pieces. And I respect him and this marriage too much to let our union fail. Being in the most romantic city in the world might be the perfect elixir.

I pray it is, because all the short haircuts in the world aren't going to change the fact that I'm losing my man.

He

The words on the screen leered back at me, shocking me into near-hyperventilation. I tried to slow down my breathing, hoping to calm my stormy stomach. Was it possible that Mikki had written this terse, sarcastic, three-sentence message after she had read my heartfelt apology? This was her answer, this hard slap of the hand?

> *Randy: Did you forget the phone number here? Will I need to bring a computer with me so that we can "communicate"? I guess I'm not a big fan of marriage by e-mail.*
> *Mikki*

I read the message about two dozen times before I even dared to look away from the screen. I kept scrolling down to the bottom, looking for the "just kidding" addendum. Over and over I opened up the message box, looking for the follow-up message that would tell me this was Mikki's sometimes harsh sense of humor at play. But there was nothing at the bottom of the screen except blankness.

Finally, I slammed the laptop shut and pushed it away. Why was she having such a strong reaction to the e-mail? Had I made that grave a tactical error? Now what should I do? Calling her on the telephone was a possibility, but I'd have to climb a gigantic hurdle to do that: my pride. After all, I had just given her a peek inside of my heart—or, if not a true unveiling of the heart, at least I had been humble enough to make some statements that my ego found embarrassing. What did it matter where I had done it? Would she have had the same reaction to a letter? I suspected that if I called her on the telephone, she'd just use it as another opportunity to dis me. So I guess what I was really saying was that I was afraid to call her. That's a damning admission for a husband to make—though I'd guess that, if pushed, more than a few husbands out there regularly find themselves in similar situations.

Still reeling, I staggered over to the closet. This was always one of the more unpleasant parts of my day. My stomach was still in knots and my head felt so hot from rage that it might burst into flames, but I still had to get dressed and go to work in an office where there was no doubt that clothing made the man. In New York, I had been accustomed to being the best-dressed male around, but it was easy there. The white boys either grabbed a few suits off the rack at Brooks Brothers or they wore jeans and raggedy sweaters if they were trying to achieve the uncaring artsy look. They had nothing in between. My Donna Karans and Hugo Bosses stood out just as much as my chocolate face in a sea of vanilla.

The first day I walked into the Paris offices of Trier-Stanton with my New York colleagues, I nearly gasped when the young man at the reception desk stood up to welcome us in a three-button salmon-colored suit with the unmistakeable sheen of an Armani. I was convinced that it had to be a fluke, but I was jolted for the rest of the day by the creative and expensive combinations I saw on the Parisian men, stuff I thought men only wore on the pages of *GQ*, not in the real world. The account exec for the women's soccer league was even wearing a gold ascot that first day. I almost choked when I saw it. I had worn my most expensive suit, a midnight-blue double-breasted Hugo Boss, but it felt stale and boring next to the Parisians—even though Mr. Ascot had leaned over at one point and whispered to me that my suit was "bee-oot-y-full." I gave him a "Merci"—I had made sure I learned that one back in New York—but I felt insecure about my clothes ever since. After a few visits to men's clothing boutiques, where the prices had sent me staggering from the store, I didn't quite understand how anyone could afford these clothes. Maybe there was a secret Giorgio Armani bargain basement somewhere that only Parisians knew about.

After picking a gray, loose-fitting Donna Karan, one of my favorite suits—probably too favorite, to be honest—I hurried to the bathroom to check my face one more time before heading to work. I had learned the hard way how vital the face check was. After three years of marriage, I was used to having another pair of eyes in the house that appraised me every morning before I presented myself to the world. Those eyes wouldn't let me step out with excessive eye boogers or lint in the hair or sleep crust caked around the mouth. But Mikki wasn't here now. One morning during my first week, I happened to look up as I was washing my hands and glance in the bathroom mirror at the office. I nearly screamed when I saw the white flakes in my beard and the eye boogers on both sides. I had showered and was sure I had washed my face, but somehow I had missed it all. I had looked down at my watch and felt a distinct redness wash over my face when I realized that I had already spent nearly two hours—that included three meetings—in the office, smiling up in people's faces looking like a hygienically challenged Skid Row bum. I'll never make that mistake again.

Running a little late as usual, I rushed down to le metro for the short subway ride to Trier-Stanton. I thought the Paris subway system should be celebrated as a modern wonder of the world, more because of the people who rode it than the efficiency of the trains. I had been searching with a keen eye, but I had yet to find even a scrawl of graffiti anywhere. The city's obsessive cleanliness somehow extended even to the underground metro, a concept that this New Yorker had a hard time wrapping his cynical mind around. Where were the rowdy youths who had no respect for authority and the city's revered institutions? How could they leave an entire city sitting here in unblemished mockery of their rebellions? I had seen plenty of pissed-off-looking teenagers, with jacked-up hair and sullen scowls. Didn't they own any Magic Markers or spray paint?

When the train slid past the metro stop for the Louvre, I did my usual neck craning to eyeball the expensive statues and artwork lining the subway platform. As usual, I was the only rider at this early hour who even looked up from his newspaper or his deep thoughts—the tourists wouldn't be hitting the metro for a few hours. I shook my head for probably the twentieth time as I watched the art installation fly by. The first time I saw the subway art, after I recovered from my shock, I retained an admiration for this city's love of art. That these pieces from the most famous museum in the world could stay down there for years without as much as a fingerprint told me everything I needed to know about the difference between my city and this one. How long would works of art last at the subway stop for New York City's Metropolitan Museum of Art, I wondered? How long does it take to topple the Venus de Milo and draw a mustache on Mona Lisa? A couple of minutes, maybe five or ten if it's an artful mustache. That's how long artwork would last at the subway stop for the Met.

"Randy, I just wanted to congratulate you. You ran out so fast yesterday that I never got a chance."

Still looking down at the legal pad on which I was writing, I couldn't stop the small smile from overtaking the corners of my mouth. Eliza couldn't even get all the way through the doorway of my office and get the compliment fully out of her mouth before she was letting her spitefulness show. What she meant by me running out "so fast" yesterday was that I had left so early. This was her way of letting me know that she knew about my early slide and that she didn't approve—as if I cared.

I looked up, now grinning widely. It was a genuine grin of pleasure derived from her obvious displeasure. My relationship with Eliza was complex and often quite tiring. We had finally reached the point of grudging respect, but it had been a long bumpy road on the way there. I sensed that we both felt like we deserved more regard from each other, but that the reason we didn't get it was due to things totally out of our control. I believed she didn't give me my due because I was black and because Eliza just couldn't bring herself to believe a black man could be talented and capable; Eliza probably thought she didn't get hers because she was blonde and beautiful and that I figured any advancement or praise she got was because of how she looked. During our many disagreements, these accusations had been flung back and forth and we had both vehemently denied them—though I had to admit to myself that Eliza was pretty accurate in describing the disrespect I had for her accomplishments, which she said was based on my sexism and my inability to see past her looks. I didn't think my view was sexist, just uncompromisingly truthful. Because she had correctly nailed my thinking, I assumed I had nailed hers, particularly when she so vehemently objected to my charges of her racism. And during her defense, she had made that most common but costly of errors: she had claimed she didn't even see color.

"When I look at someone, I don't even think about color when I make judgments of their abilities," she had said. Naturally I had scoffed at that line, telling her it was not only improbable but it wasn't even preferable.

"I want you to see my color when you look at me," I had said. "I want you to see that it is a black man rising in this company, it is a black man creating these successful campaigns, it is a black man competing with you. So the next time you walk out of here and stumble across a different black man in a different place, you'll remember me and not be able to make any snap judgments about who he is and what he is capable of."

Of course, my speech was just as tired and run-of-the-mill as hers. How many times had I heard people in the black community use the same or similar words? But Eliza didn't know that. I could tell by the shade of crimson that spread across her face.

Now here she was in my office, not being able to resist showing me her anger over my advancement.

"Well, thanks for your congratulations," I said, still smiling. "I had to go 'home' "—I gestured with both hands to simulate the quotation marks—"to celebrate, you know? I would have invited you, but you looked busy."

She raised her eyebrow questioningly but allowed me to see her little grin. This was the other part of our relationship, the part that complicated things even more. We had become quite flirtatious over the years, in a challenging, overtly sexual kind of way. Eliza had started it early on by implying that she was so energetic and skilled in bed that I shouldn't even think about going there because I couldn't "handle" her anyway. I had asked her why she assumed I even wanted to—was it just because she was a blonde white girl and she assumed everyone wanted her? This had pissed her off to the highest of pisstivity and she couldn't even think of a pithy rejoinder. Since then, in between our angry competitive exchanges, we had engaged in a flirtatious wrestling match, each trying to use sexual references or sexual bravado to make the other uncomfortable. At times I had feared that the sexual double entendres and comments were going too far.

I couldn't tell anymore whether the tension, the heightened stimulation I felt whenever I was around her was sexual or just competitive in nature. I didn't think we'd ever find out—and yes, even though she was beautiful (although if ever I would go there with a white girl I always found brunettes more attractive), I wasn't sure I'd ever want to. The aftermath would be too uncomfortable and unworkable.

"Well, yes, I do get busy. I have all that research to do, after all," she said sarcastically. This was yet another challenge, her complaining that my team never researches our products and our market before firing off slogans that she contended were often serious misses. I knew she was partially right, but I had an abiding trust in my instincts—and those slogans we created by "feel" sometimes hit dead-on and we'd win the account while Eliza and her assistants were still slogging through demographic surveys.

"Well, as you know, I do my research with these," I said, pointing to my eyes. "They seem to have done their job this time, wouldn't you say?"

She scowled. "You always say that, as if you're the only one with fuckin' eyeballs. We *all* do research with our eyes, Randy." She shook her head in exasperation and pivoted on her high heels. I watched her switch from the office, though she didn't have much back there to pull off an effective switch. That was another reason I wouldn't have much interest in going there with Eliza—I needed some meat on the ass. Like Mikki, who had enough meat for herself and Eliza's entire family.

" 'Bye," I called out playfully.

" 'Bye," she said over her shoulder, sounding annoyed.

I grinned. I had clearly won that round. Not for the first time, I was tempted to start a tally board recording the results of our many face-offs. I suspected I'd be far ahead, but I knew she'd probably make the opposite contention. As I looked back down at my pad, I thought about Eliza's little ass—and I flashed on an image of Mikki. Her face brought that ache to my stomach once again. I knew the ache would probably become a permanent friend, at least until I had fixed the marriage. Some people were able to dive into their work and close off their personal problems into a little box where they stayed until the work was done, but that had never been me. Personal turmoil roiled my gut and sucked me into a depression, whether I was sitting in my office or in my living room. I had the weekend to get through, then my wife would be in my arms. I wasn't sure if that was something I should look forward to or dread.

The weekend crept by too slowly, with my anxiety increasing every time I allowed myself to think about my wife or her e-mail message. Though its harshness seemed quite clear, I held out some hope that perhaps I misinterpreted the message's tone. Maybe she was just being a smart-ass, as she is wont to do. When she delivered her cynical lines when we were together, I'd have a chance to witness the right eyebrow arching upward, telling me she was sending out sarcasm to be followed up with sincerity or kindness to reduce the sting. Mikki could pour on the kindness when she wanted to, when she wished to make someone feel special. In my mind there was nothing quite so ego-gratifying as being on the receiving end of Mikki's attentions—the wide eyes, the eager soothing voice, the flash of teeth, and the feel of her hands softly stroking my bare flesh, whether it was my arm, or hand, or face. The latter was my favorite, her hands cupping my face firmly while she leaned forward and applied the world's softest kiss with full perfect lips. I'd sometimes tell her she should have been a lipstick model— that's how precise they were. But I could see none of this through e-mail, could gather no clues from the tone of her voice and her body language. There were the words on the screen and that was it.

What those words told me was that I was getting the frost. I knew that just as effectively as she could pour on the attention, she could also shut it off like a faucet. I had watched it happen so many times that I didn't even need to close my eyes to picture the cloud moving over her face, telling me she wasn't happy. It was this cloud that I feared I'd see as soon as she stepped off the plane, and it wouldn't lift until—well, maybe it would never lift.

I couldn't bring myself to give thought to the possible breakup of my marriage. Whenever I felt my mind starting to drift to the possibility of life without Mikki, I'd forcefully move it somewhere else, to more pleasant thoughts. This didn't really work—I knew my mind was stubborn about how much pleasantness it would allow. If there were so many scary, heart-rending musings floating around in there, my brain wasn't going to let them drift by in search of joy—it was going to embrace them, wallow in their ability to bring misery. So as a result I spent a lot of time depressed, worried, upset—because there was always something to be miserable about. A troubled marriage was a biggie, an eight-hundred-pound gorilla that just never could be ignored because it was so all-consuming, following me to the office, to the dinner table where I usually ate alone, to my bed where I always slept alone. When you were by yourself in a strange place, how could you not obsess over the slow erosion of your relationship with your other half, the part that made you complete? I walked around Paris as a partial person, a diminished man. And I had no idea whether I would ever be able to find the rest of myself, to absorb the shocks to my system if I lost her and be able to move on to the next thing, the next person, the rest of my life. Of course I knew that men and women split every day, that something like half of all marriages ended in divorce, that there were millions of people whose beings were cleaved by bitter separation, and they all managed to survive, maybe even to flourish. But none of them did it without significant pain, or so I suspected. I didn't like pain. I had always done whatever I could to avoid pain. But though I could cancel dentist appointments, I couldn't avoid this looming encounter with my wife. If it wasn't happening Tuesday, it'd be some other time. But as I sleepwalked through my weekend, worrying about every detail of the week I had planned for us together—Mikki, the master of style and sophistication, was notoriously hard to please—my mind was consistently drawn back to one thing: What had gone wrong? Or, more specifically, what had I done wrong?

As Mikki walked toward me, a tentative smile resting on those perfect lips, I was acutely conscious of the joy that surrounded me as travelers were greeted by loved ones. Was she happy to see me? She got closer and I couldn't stop the frown from forming. Something looked different, radically different, about my wife. Her head was topped by a mop of yellow—her hair had been severely shorn, dyed blond, and swept to the side. She looked like that little white boy in *Home Alone*. What in the hell had she been thinking? I thought I had wiped away the frown as she got close enough to read my face, but she still saw it. As she stepped into my arms, neither one of us saying a word, I felt the hard, coiled tension of her arm and back muscles—I also felt the soft, cushiony press of her breasts against my chest—and it pained me to feel evidence of her fright. But she still felt wonderful nonetheless.

"How are you doing, baby?" I said softly in her ear. "I missed you so much."

As she drew back her head, her eyes moist and glistening, my focus was once again drawn to the hair, the artificial coloring, the new look which I thought was not at all flattering. A memory danced through my head of something I had once read about women getting drastic haircuts when they were going through inner turmoil. I wanted to squeeze her and ask, what's wrong, baby? But I saw her eyes locked into my gaze, which had been pointed at her hair.

"You don't like my haircut, do you?"

So those were the first words that fell from my wife's lips in Paris. They were an unfortunate omen of the mis-steps and stumbles we would make during the remainder of her stay. I didn't think it was possible for a trip that had been so meticulously planned and fervently anticipated to go so drastically wrong. But maybe that had been the problem—I had put too much pressure on the trip, expecting it to solve all our problems just because we were together in the world's most romantic city.

A week later, after Mikki had stepped back onto the plane to return to New York, I sat in the cab on the way back to my hotel and beat myself up, dissecting what had happened, what had we done wrong? Our marriage had become a bumbling waltz, performed by two dancers in their twilight, tripping over each other and stumbling across the floor with no apparent clue of the beat, no feel for the other's moves, no timing, no hope. It was as if someone changed the song in mid-dance and neither Mikki nor I had figured it out yet. I didn't know if it was possible for us to find our stride again.

The lavish meal that I had planned in the big fancy restaurant was supposed to impress my wife, to show her how wonderful and romantic our time together could be when I pulled out all the stops. But that was not the message that Mikki took away from the meal.

From the time the waiter brought us the menu, Mikki started complaining. Of course it was in French and of course she couldn't read any of it, I thought. We were in fuckin' France, for heaven's sake. I absorbed her bitching and held my tongue as long as I could. Finally, I had exploded: "Damn, Mekhi, could you just chill out? We'll see if the waiter can help us out, okay? What language did you expect the menu to be in, anyway?"

She had stared back at me, startled and obviously angry at my outburst. I was sorry right away—there were many better ways for me to have gotten the same message across. I had picked the worst possible one, implicitly insulting her intelligence and her lack of class.

"Well tell me, then, Mr. Fuckin' Parisian, what's the point of me holding this stupid menu in my hands if I can't read the damn thing?" She had leaned across the table and said this in a nasty hiss.

I knew that this was heading to a bad place in a hurry, so I scrambled to make it right. I took several deep breaths, desperately wanting to avoid an argument. Already I was worried that the evening might not include sex—I had been half expecting us to get busy when we hit my hotel room from the airport, but Mikki hadn't acted amorous in the least and I had gotten surprisingly shy and afraid about initiating. (Well, maybe it wasn't so surprising. The fact that the shyness didn't disappear was probably one of the biggest secrets I had discovered about marriage.) So I sat tensely on the edge of the bed while she went in the bathroom and changed, and we had gone back out to hit a few sights. All along, as I tried in my awful, tortured French pronunciations to get the cabdriver to slow down so we could actually see something, I was carrying the confident knowledge that we certainly would end this night in each other's arms. She had even leaned over and kissed me a few times, once quite tenderly. But a fight over dinner at nine p.m. was not a good thing at all.

The bad news compounded once our waiter introduced himself and we quickly discovered he spoke virtually no English. I had done quite well during my weeks in Paris in getting English-speaking waiters when I ate alone. In fact, I had found a few spots, one near my hotel, where virtually everyone spoke English. The food wasn't great in any of these places—in fact, I had had a very hard time finding any food I considered decent, much to my disappointment and shock—but I made the sacrifice to be able to converse with the person bringing me my food. Of all the nights to get a non-English-speaking waiter, this was the worst.

The waiter looked back and forth at us sorrowfully as we tried to ask him questions about the menu items. We discovered he did understand the word *chicken*—his eyes widened and he nodded vigorously as he repeated the word a few times—so we went down the menu, pointing to each item and him nodding yes or no, chicken or no chicken.

After a few minutes of this, Mikki was thoroughly confused and upset.

"So, after all that, what am I supposed to eat?" she said archly.

I thought the question was being directed at me, when actually she was saying it to herself, and I snarled back.

"Why can't you just pick something, Mikki?" I said nastily. I felt my stomach do a few flips as the words tumbled from my lips. Damn. Why did I say that?

She looked up, her eyes widening, and I saw the disgust on her face.

"I wasn't asking you, Randy. Obviously, *you* don't know what I should order."

This was not happening, I thought to myself. My big-deal dinner, for which I took at least a week of research in my office to select this restaurant, was quickly swirling down the drain.

I wondered what else could go wrong, and I found out as soon as our plates were placed in front of us. Mikki's food was covered with dark, oily chunks that looked like worms or snails. Homegirl was not pleased.

"Randy, what is this?" she said, looking down in horror.

But I was looking at my own plate, which was more like a bowl, filled with something mysterious and liquidy that resembled stew. Where was the chicken?

"Well, give it a try," I suggested, growing nervous as I watched her horror turn to disgust. "Maybe it tastes better than it looks."

It didn't. And neither did my meal. We tried to tell the waiter that our food was not agreeable, but he didn't understand—or he pretended not to understand. It pained me to shell out the wad of francs to cover a meal that neither one of us had eaten, but I had no other option. I threw the money down and hurried behind Mekhi, who was already out the front door, her round ass sashaying under the tight red dress she was wearing the hell out of. I had looked longingly at the ass as I slipped out of the restaurant and I'd wondered what were the chances of me palming it in my hands within the next two hours.

Mikki was silent on the way back to the hotel. I wanted to hear her say it was okay that the food sucked because at least we were together, but I got nothing. I was tempted to say it myself, but it wouldn't be the same coming from me, at least not in my eyes. I needed a sign from her that she was ecstatic about being here with me. What did it really

47

matter if the food was bad? We could chalk that one up to experience and warn everyone to stay away from that restaurant without a French-English dictionary clutched firmly in hand.

"I'm hungry," Mikki finally said as the taxi pulled up in front of the Hotel Saint-Germain.

I knew that was her way of letting me know that I hadn't gotten the job done. If we spent the next hour trying to find a café that was still serving on a Tuesday near midnight, my chances for intimacy would be slim to none, particularly after Mikki had been on a plane for much of the day. But she was my wife and she was hungry. This was not the time for me to be worrying about the care and feeding of my dick.

"All right," I said, keeping my sigh to myself.

After walking for a half hour, we found a small, nondescript cafe that was still serving sandwiches. Mikki looked down at the menu and pointed.

"Hey, look, Randy, I can understand what I'm getting here," she said, offering me a small smile. I gave her a real big one in return.

As we ate our sandwiches, Mikki started catching me up on how things were going back home, particularly with her best friend Angelou, whom I suspected was part of the reason that my wife had been acting so stank toward me. Angelou was one of those wild sistahs who never saw a situation or an experience that she wouldn't try at least once. No telling what that girl would have Mikki getting into without me around to act as a voice of sanity in my wife's ear. After a half hour of talk, I was curious that Mikki hadn't mentioned anything about my best friend, Marcus Peate, whom I had sort of put in charge of looking out for Mikki, or, more specifically, keeping an eye on Mikki. It wasn't that I didn't trust my wife; I didn't trust her best friend and I didn't trust Mikki's instincts when she was around her best friend. Mikki had made the mistake of telling me some pretty wild stories about her escapades with Angelou in college, many of them sexual in nature. If Marcus was doing his job, he should have been mentioned by now as a major player in Mikki's recounting of the news of the past two months.

"How's Marcus doing?" I asked.

She looked up quickly. "Why do you ask?" she said, her eyes slightly narrowing. I was slightly chastened—perhaps she had found out that I had told Marcus to keep an eye on her. In fact, I had even suggested that she call Marcus when she had told me over the telephone after my first week in Paris that she was afraid at night in the brownstone by herself.

"Well, I was just wondering if you had, uh, you know, called him after we talked that time. Or maybe he had called you."

Mikki looked over toward the waitress and gestured for the check. I felt a frown cross my face—she hadn't even asked me if I was ready to go. Obviously I *was* ready—shit, I was ready before we even got to the café—but I would have appreciated the request nonetheless.

"I guess *you're* ready to go," I said, unable to keep the sarcasm out of my voice. But she didn't even pick up on it. Maybe she was distracted, or maybe she was just tired. I decided to just let it go.

"So, I saw him once or twice. I guess he's fine," Mikki said as we walked the still-bustling blocks toward the hotel.

But my mind had been wandering back to the anticipation of our hotel room and I didn't remember about whom we had been talking.

"Who's fine?"

"You asked me about Marcus," she said, exasperated. "I'm answering your question."

"Oh! Marcus. Yeah, I'm sorry. I forgot I asked you about him."

I was trying hard now to keep things moving at a peaceful, even keel before we re-entered the room. I was trying to figure out how I was going to initiate the sex if she didn't bring it up. I had bought some scented candles specifically for this occasion. And that morning I had placed the *Best of Sade* CD on the bedside table, ready to pop into the CD player when she was ready to pop out of her clothes.

When we had returned to the room, I put the card outside the door announcing our desire to be left alone.

"Randy, come here, baby," Mikki had called out to me from across the room. I could never mistake that silky, come-hither tone. That was the invitation to bone, I had no doubt. I practically skipped across the room and stepped into a deep embrace with my wife. Our lips locked together, I felt her tongue push its way into my mouth. Mikki liked wet, sloppy, juicy kisses, but it slightly grossed me out. I'd never told her this, however, so I'd always have to suffer through the early moments of foreplay when she liked to slobber. As far as suffering went, I knew there were much worse forms of torture.

I reached around and clutched Mikki's firm round ass through the red dress. God, I had missed that booty. Mikki abruptly pulled her mouth away.

"Excuse me, I have to snee—aawwwchooo!" She let go a noisy, wet sneeze that left a visible line of snot trailing down her nose.

"Excuse me, baby," she said apologetically. Then she smiled and moved her face toward me. "Now where were we?" I saw the snot-line heading my way, leering at me like a big glistening cootie. She didn't know it was there. As her mouth opened again and the snot grew closer, I was momentarily frozen. I didn't want to damage the mood, but my stomach wouldn't let me kiss her with the knowledge that the snot would wind up smeared all over my face. That was about a hundred times worse than a slobbering kiss. Just before she made contact, I wrenched my face away from hers.

"Wait! I'm so sorry, baby. But you need to wipe your nose," I said, pointing to the snot-line.

I saw the horror cross over her face. She started to reach up and touch it, but she thought better of it.

"Ewwww! Damn, that's so gross, I'm sorry," she'd said as she sprinted toward the bathroom. I shook off the tremors of nausea that were trying to down me, and I decided to make a move for my instruments of seduction, the candles and the music. No doubt they'd work nicely to jumpstart the sexual tension when she returned.

"Okay, we are here, sir," the cabbie said, interrupting my reflections of that first night. I had planned on going into the office for the afternoon, but my heart was not in it. I was so shaken from the week with Mikki that I wondered if I'd be able to get any work done anytime soon.

When I got upstairs, I sprawled out on the bed and felt thoroughly sorry for myself. What had happened to the intense sexual fires that used to keep us in a constant state of inflammation? I thought absence made the heart grow fonder and the loins hungrier, but somehow we had forgotten how to do it. For Mikki at least, it must have been more of "out of sight, out of mind." Out of mind, indeed—that's where I felt like I was heading, out of my mind. I knew these sorts of problems plagued long-married couples trying to figure out how to fabricate some passion after two or three decades of marriage, but we had been husband and wife for three years. Weren't we still supposed to be humping like rabbits? I looked across the room at the beige cloth chair sitting in front of the small writing desk. I painfully recalled how we had tried to use that chair the previous night, her last in Paris, but every time I thought I was hard enough for Mikki to lower herself on top of me and slide it in, she'd reach down to find that I had gone soft again. That had been so predictable—that the pressure of the entire week and the painfully cold sexual encounters would produce such a heightened state of tension and worry in me that I'd be unable to perform—but that didn't lessen the severe humiliation that I'd felt then and I continued to feel now. It had been best on that first night, and even then there was something strangely discordant and off-key about the sex.

When she had walked back into the room after ridding her face of the snot-line, I had been instantly aroused by the sight of her smooth chocolatey body in a black thong with a black lace bra. She had removed the dress—perhaps purposely trying to make me forget the snot-line. It had worked. She smiled when she saw my candles. She rhythmically moved her head to Sade's sexy, hypnotic beat.

"Mmmm, Sade. You know how to get a sistah's juices *flowing*, baby."

I smiled back. "Uh, can you turn around so I can get the, uh, back view?" I had said, gesturing for her to pivot. She obliged and my smile nearly cracked my face in half. Damn. Now *that* was an ass, I had thought, remembering the sight of Eliza trying to switch her bony little thing as she left my office the week before. Mikki had more than enough meat—in fact, she had generations of meat back there, no doubt the finest stock of booty had sent that meat coursing on down through the years, through the decades of proud and bountiful Chance women, to produce the sight that Mikki jiggled before me. I had reached out and pulled Mikki's butt closer to me. I slowly rubbed my face and lips across its round smoothness, delighting in the silky touch, the perfection of each booty sphere.

"Damn, I missed this ass," I mumbled into her cheeks, eliciting a laugh from Mikki. "Paris has never seen an ass like this."

She quickly pivoted, snatching the booty away. "How do *you* know what kind of asses Paris has seen, Mr. Murphy? What have you been doing, field research?"

My mouth hanging open, my breathing heavy from the close ass contact, I was stunned. Was she serious or kidding? I tried to catch the expression on her face, but the candles didn't provide enough light to tell.

"Damn, Mikki. What are you *talking* about? Bring that booty back over here."

I reached out for it again, but there was no return of the butt.

"You *can't* be serious, Mikki. Are you?"

"Why wouldn't I be serious, Randy? That was a strange comment to make, like maybe you were subconsciously trying to tell me something."

I had flopped back down on the bed in exasperation. This was not happening, I had thought once again. But before I could work myself up into real frustration, Mikki had hopped onto the bed and crawled on top of me, pressing her lips against my chest and flicking out her tongue to tease my nipples. Okay, so she was kidding after all. Everything quickly flew from my mind so I could concentrate on the exquisite sensation of her lips and tongue exploring my most sensitive areas. She hadn't forgotten what they were, I had thought, smiling to myself.

When we were both naked and thoroughly aroused, I had looked over at the nightstand for the condom I remembered placing there. But there was nothing on the small table except for the hotel-issue clock radio. Where was the damn condom? I lunged across the bed and felt around on the other nightstand. Nothing. I felt a panic start tightening my chest. I caught myself and took a deep breath. No reason to panic yet.

"What's wrong, baby?" Mikki said, pushing herself up onto her elbows.

"Uh, nothing. Nothing's wrong." I wasn't ready yet to shut down the moment and shift our focus to finding the condom. I slid off the side of the bed to look on the floor. Nothing. How could the condom have walked away, like it didn't want to be used?

"You can't find the condom, right?" she said. She paused, then added, "Don't worry, babe."

I tensed. What did she mean by that? Was that another baby comment? Was she telling me she was now down with the baby-making? I pushed myself into action again, thrusting my hand underneath the nightstand. As I groped around, I ran her last comment back a few times. Maybe I was reading too much into it. Mikki wasn't so cold as to bring up the baby thing at a sensitive, tender moment such as this. Right? I felt my finger nudge a piece of plastic. I grasped the condom and clutched it in my hand, exhaling at that familiar strange feel of the slimy lubricant inside the plastic.

"I found it," I said, thrusting it triumphantly in her face. Mikki smiled. "All right, don't just sit there grinning, put the damn thing to use, homey," she said.

Thankfully, Mikki reached out and helped me get hard again before I tried to slip the condom on. I'd always found that one of intercourse's most peculiar times, when me or my partner had to use rapid hand movements, performed so clinically and purposefully, for the deed to be able to be done. But finally everything was in its proper state, all equipment applied and checked. We got busy.

I remembered thinking at some point during the midst of the act that something was missing, some key ingredient had been left out. I was assuming the position of a chef standing over the stew, frowning at the familiar yet not totally satisfying taste. I was enjoying myself but wondering why it wasn't blowing my mind. Was I too distracted? Why was I even thinking about the sex in the middle of it? I didn't remember doing that before, except maybe the rare occasions when I allowed my mind to drift—it was inevitable in a marriage for the mind to drift sometimes during sex—and think about the work I had to get done. Once my mind had drifted to Eliza during sex with my wife, keeping me awake for several hours that night as I convinced myself that it hadn't meant anything.

I considered Mikki, looking down at her face, which was twisted into a mask of ecstasy. She usually made a lot more noise—in fact, I had been hoping one of those honeymooning couples was next door when she visited so I could return the favor and let the whole building hear that I wasn't as lame and pathetic as I had looked. But all I was hearing were little squeals and yelps of pleasure, nothing like the yells and full screams I usually got. Did that mean anything? Was she not enjoying this?

Suddenly, I felt myself being shoved into the air. As my body fell to the side of the bed, the latex-sheathed penis bobbing like a rear-window car toy, I looked over in alarm just in time to see Mikki turn and unleash another giant sneeze.

"Awwchhoooo!"

She jumped from the bed and once again scurried to the bathroom.

"I'm so sorry, babe," she called out over her shoulder. "I must be catching a cold or something."

She closed the bathroom door for some reason and stayed inside for at least three or four minutes, leaving me sitting on my knees in the same position, stunned and confused and more than a little angry. This was supposed to be the orgasmic reunion I had been dreaming about for weeks; instead it was turning into a Three Stooges routine.

At one point during our coupling, the entire production switched into something I hadn't felt in a long time—a mechanical thrusting, back and forth, in and out, for the specific purpose of achieving orgasm rather than fully enjoying the moment. I had looked down and watched myself disappearing inside, I had collected my jumbled thoughts into an awe at the beauty of the perfectly mated sexual organs, my view had swept upward and taken in Mikki's jiggling breasts, their bouncing a coordinated syncopation with the thrust of my hips. I hadn't broken the act of intercourse down into so many distinct parts since my single days, when I'd slip into bed with a new woman just to relish the newness, the jarring yet familiar feel of her lips and breasts and butt and taste. The act of sex itself would be fulfilling and even fun, but I wouldn't know what real lovemaking was until I had felt the overwhelming emotion and longing along with the thrusting and moaning. That hadn't come until I had met Mikki. Once I had even thought I was in love with a light-skinned, light-eyed sistah named Felicia, but after a month's time the emotion drained away and I was back to thrusting. That had been infatuation. Well, maybe not even that. More like lust. There was no mistaking the difference between making love and making lust until you had experienced the former and realized what you had been doing before was like an anthill next to Everest, a Stockton layup next to a Jordan slam. No comparison, not even really the same act.

When I had come back to the present, deep inside my wife, and had realized what had been dancing through my dreamstate, I was thoroughly shaken, even frightened. What did that mean? Was I no longer in love with my wife? For you couldn't fool the basset-hound-like sensitivities of the loins. They knew right away if it was the real thing or just a thing. I had tried closing my eyes and willing back passion, forcefully trying to reintroduce emotion and dripping intensity into my marriage bed, but all I got in return was a worried stare from Mikki, or so I thought. I frowned and thrust my face closer to hers to make sure, but it was gone, whatever had crossed her face. She smiled at me softly, as if nothing had happened, nothing was wrong. But there had been something there, something akin to the worry that was roiling my gut. Mikki, too, had been scared; I was sure of it. Well, I wasn't exactly sure, but I knew I had seen something. When we were done, I had flipped around after staring off into the darkness and I caught Mikki just as she slammed her eyes shut. She had also been staring into the shadows of the room. I was sure of it. Well, not exactly sure. But even if my eyes were deceiving me, my heart surely wasn't. Something was wrong. Why couldn't I just reach out and grab her and pull things back to where they were supposed to be?

Finally, before I drifted off, I had broken the silence with a question. I thought it was the question that was hovering above us both, but the way Mikki reacted told me I thought wrong. Tragically wrong.

"Is something wrong, Mikki?"

I thought I heard a gurgling sound from her, like she had choked on the question.

"What?!" she spit out, almost in disgust. "Why would you ask me that?"

"I, I just thought that that didn't, uh, go as well as maybe it usually does?"

"Well, you think that was my fault?" she demanded.

Her question sat there for a long moment. I didn't want to touch it. I felt weak, inadequate, stupid for even bringing it up. Was I blaming her? I wasn't sure if I was blaming anyone. It was what it was—uninspired, somewhat affectionless sex. Boring. Since when had our sex been boring? Maybe it *was* my fault.

"Never mind," I said delicately. In response, Mikki flipped over, giving me her back. I looked at it, the sharp slope downward from her shoulders to her narrow waist, the drastic slope back up and around her hips, the entrancing peek of booty crack. I wanted to slide over and "spoon" her, as she used to playfully demand after sex. That's what I had wanted to do, but I didn't do it. I just closed my eyes and hoped sleep would come and find me.

She

Now, I thought my little haircut was cute. You remember that Revlon ad Halle Berry's in—the BrazenBerry one, where her hair, with its subtle shades of cherry blond and raspberry-iced-tea red, is cropped into this really cool side-sweep, with the back tapered to the nape? On me, it's equally beautiful. I admit it takes a few minutes to get used to the idea of Mekhi Chance-Murphy with a short, blond-red haircut; I've had, for as long as most people who know me can remember, shoulder-length, jet black hair, trimmed neatly into a bob that's wrapped into its straight shape. I'd always hesitated at cutting it because of my father's stupid southern traditions—"Ladies don't cut their hair, Mikki; it's not ladylike and it's bad luck." Daddy used to deliver me to the beauty parlor every two weeks with a warning to the hairdresser that if she trimmed so much as an eighth of an inch off my ends, somebody was going to get hurt. "That's not a threat, darling—I promise," he'd say with the most syrupy-sweet voice.

I'd braided my hair once, and kept it that way for most of my time at Spelman. It was just easier to manage and I was into this Afrocentric thing and too afraid to get dreds and . . . anyway. I admit that the one thing on me that never changed was my hair. But I figured, why not make a new start, Mekhi? Why not blow your husband away with a romantic new look for your romantic vacation in the most romantic city in the world? He'll love it and fall to his knees, but only after he sweeps you into his embrace and rushes you back to the hotel, rips your clothes off, and makes love to you over and over and over again, saying "I'm so sorry darling" between his tender kisses, and "I'm coming home to you."

In my fucking dreams.

Do you know what this Negro did? He sees me—his wife of three years, whom he hasn't laid eyes on for almost two months now—and frowns. *Frowns*, y'all. A big ole ridiculous, "what the fuck?" frown—like something stinking had just wafted to his nose or his eyes had laid upon a sight so incredibly foul that he couldn't take his eyes off of it, for its disgust was so ingrained in his pupils that they ceased all function.

You'd think I was bald-headed.

I didn't notice it at first; when I stepped off the plane, I was too busy trying to get the hell out of that airport. Everybody—and I mean everybody—was smoking like a damn chimney. Mothers, daughters, grandfathers, sons, hell, I thought I saw a kid who didn't look old enough to have pubic hairs lighting up. I can't stand cigarette smoke—stinks up your clothes, gets in your hair, makes your eyes water. This was a brand-new BCBG dress, a slinky one with a really sexy slit up my left thigh. Angelou said it would make Randy drool. Damn if it doesn't smell like a pack of Winstons.

I forgot about the smoke when I saw him standing there, this big humongous smile on his face, waiting for me, his wife. The tears that formed from the smoke gave way to hot tears of joy—the kind that come when your head warms and the heat rushes from your temples down to your nose and into the pit of your stomach. That was my husband standing over there. I was happy to see him, which kind of shocked me, because weeks ago, I'd gotten over the initial shock of not having him in our bed, in our home—felt just a dull flutter in the part of my stomach that burned like fire the first few days after he'd left me. I'd roll over in our queen-sized bed, suddenly awakened by the slightest creak and barely aware of my surroundings, and reach for him. The palm of my hand would simply stroke the fluffy mint-colored sheets, the cold searing my hands and shocking me back into the hard reality: I was the only person in that bed (not counting Pootie and Mac, who took advantage of the fact that Randy wasn't home and lounged their hairy little booties in his space). Today, my heart was fluttering at the thought of falling into his arms. I wanted him to snatch me up off my feet, I wanted him to press his thick, wet lips all over my face, I wanted him. I could barely see, the tears were so thick; the blur was blinding.

But the closer I got to him, the more apparent was the horror in his eyes. I didn't realize it at first 'cause, you know, I was all teared up. But when I fell into his arms, I saw the lines formed around the corners of his eyes, the wrinkle of his brow, the weird, awkward, Kool-Aid smile on his face, the kind that people spread across their lips to lull themselves into thinking they're putting on a credible front but that everyone else can tell is fake as a mug. My mother used to smile like that when my sister would fall out in the middle of the store, screaming over her decision to deny her some snack she'd decided she wanted, like, now. You saw that smile and you knew that she was embarrassed as shit, and that as soon as the coast was clear, my sister was going to get slapped. Hard.

"How are you doing, baby? I missed you so much."

He was whispering in my ear and pressing my head into his chest, and, at the same time, running his fingers through my 'do. I lifted my head and looked him in his eyes, or at least attempted to—but he was too busy staring at my head.

"You don't like my haircut, do you?" It was the only thing I could think to say. Not "Hi, baby—I missed you, too," not, "Take me back to the hotel and let's get busy," "Not, okay, I'll have your baby." I had to ask him about my damn haircut. I immediately felt horrible. What the hell was I thinking, chopping my hair off and dying it blond? I mean, what the fuck. This was all wrong—all wrong.

He mumbled something, and then said, more confidently, "Let's go get your bags."

It just got worse from there.

"Wait—okay, so let me get this straight. You went halfway across the earth to see your husband whom, might I add, you hadn't seen in two months, stayed there for seven whole days, and you two had sex only twice?"

Angelou is undone. Now I think she really wants this thing to work—more than maybe even me and Randy. For some reason, which I've yet to quite figure out, homegirl was under the impression that shit was going to work itself out in the Murphy household once its principles met up in Paris. To tell the truth, so was I, which makes me just as dumb as Angelou.

"Twice?" she asked me, her eyes wide as saucers. The pointer and middle fingers of her left hand formed a peace sign and made tracks in the air, landing about an eighth of an inch from my right eye.

"No, homey—try once. The second time, ol' boy couldn't even get it up. My own husband wasn't even turned on by his wife's booty. He's probably fucking one of those blonde Parisian bitches—that's all the brothers want over there, anyway. A nation full of jungle fever. It was just the worst week in my entire pitiful life."

And it was, y'all, but not just because Randy and I didn't do it. Shoot, that was the least of our problems. We just fought the entire seven days—non-stop. Over stupid shit. Where to eat. When to sleep. What to wear. Where to go. Who to visit. The white girls that kept giving my man the eye every time we walked past one. Randy's implying that I was emotionally distant.

Actually, that's what set it off—that emotionally distant talk. I wasn't upset with the accusation, I was mad because he'd called it. I was happy as hell to see him, don't get me wrong. He's my husband, and I vowed to him in front of my mama, my daddy, my friends, and the good Lord that come hell, high water, rain, sleet or snow, I'd stand by his ass. But Marcus stirred up a stone cold South Pole blizzard while I was making my way to the airport, and he turned my whole plan for reuniting into a confused mess. "There's something we need to discuss," I'd told him.

"Mekhi"—he always called me by my full name, said Mikki sounded "entirely too childlike for such a complete woman"—"baby, don't be sad. It'll only be a week that you're gone, and it'll zoom by before you know it."

"No—Marcus, that's not it." I was starting to sweat, which only happened when I was extremely nervous, like then. I took a deep breath and let it go. "I can't, um, we can't do this anymore. I love Randy so very much and I love you too, but not the way I love my husband. I'm afraid that if we don't cut this off right here, right now, none of us will ever recover. Let's just pretend this didn't happen."

"Mekhi? What happened—what's wrong?"

"Nothing's wrong, Marcus. I'm on my way to Paris to visit Randy, and I'm planning on us fixing whatever needs to be fixed in our marriage. That just can't happen if I'm messing around with his best friend. I can't do that to him, I just can't. And I can't do it to you."

"But Mekhi—"

"No—baby, don't. I can't do this, okay, Marcus?" I was starting to get a little worked up. My head was getting hot—the kind of hot that meant some tears were on the verge.

"But Mekhi—" The phone was starting to break up, the battery was dying, but I could still tell that his voice was starting to get shaky, too. I could only hear bits and pieces of his sentences, like, "you . . . special woman . . . never . . . one like you." I cut him off, because I needed him to be clear.

"Marcus, please. Just understand that this stops today."

"I love you."

That part came in clear as a Kathleen Battle riff. The car pulled into the right lane—the one that leads to the "departures" exit. The phone went dead. My heart was pounding; my head was throbbing. Had there been any flies in the vicinity, they'd have flown straight into my mouth, which, by now, had dropped down to exactly two millimeters of an inch from my lap. That boy said he loved me. His words echoed in my head for the entire six hours I was on the flight. Randy's face had been replaced by Marcus's.

I think I'm in love with him, too—and not the kind of love you reserve for a friend.

Now how was I supposed to keep my mind off of that? In front of my husband? Who'd practically abandoned me two months ago and was now acting all crazy and deranged toward me?

That's right, crazy and deranged. From that first moment in the airport, Randy was trippin'. I had told the boy I was hungry. He knows how I get when I'm hungry. I hadn't had time to eat before I left for the airport, I hadn't had time to eat once I got to the airport (after that Marcus phone call, my appetite was shot, anyway) and I didn't want to eat on the airplane (maybe it's just me, but I figure if you pay all that money to get to the other side of the world, the least they can do is give you something edible to eat. I mean, come on—drippy eggs, French bread, and fake orange juice? Pah-leeze.) So I was famished. And after we both got over the airport/hair incident, Randy promised that he was going to take me to a really nice restaurant. "The best in town," he promised.

Now, you figure that "best in town" is supposed to mean something because, like, the best cooks in the world are supposed to be French, right? I mean, I beg to differ, particularly since I grew up greasin' on my mama's fried fish, grits, and cornbread every Friday night, and her roast beef and signature macaroni-and-five-cheeses on every other Sunday. But you know what? I was ready to eat a fucking cow—raw—by the time I'd unpacked my suitcase, brushed my teeth, and freshened up my makeup, so "best in town" could have meant a dirty McDonald's in Mexico for all I cared. Then we walked into this restaurant, and the maître d' acted like he didn't want to seat somebody. So I immediately caught a bigger attitude—I'd gotten a pretty sizable one as we made our way over to the restaurant because this white girl stared my husband down, right in my face!—and made a point of showing it when the man finally seated us and sent over the waiter.

"Is everyone in France just a big ass?" I asked to no one in particular. Randy shifted in his seat. The waiter dropped the menus on the table and started speaking French. I looked at Randy. He looked at me, then the waiter.

"I'm sorry—I don't understand," Randy said feebly.

The waiter kept rambling. I opened the menu. Nothing but French. I started bitching some more. Then Randy flipped on me.

"Damn, Mekhi, could you just chill out? We'll see if the waiter can help us out, okay? What language did you expect the menu to be in, anyway?"

Now, see—he didn't need to take it there. First the maître d' was acting like we weren't good enough to be in the restaurant, then the waiter—and now my own husband was yelling at me like a damn child and acting like I was somehow less than those Parisians because I couldn't speak their language. English is the world's language; how come they weren't up on it?

I leaned across the table and hissed the words. "Well tell me, then, Mr. Fuckin' Parisian, what's the point of me holding this stupid menu in my hands if I can't read the damn thing?"

If he were white, he would have turned at least eight shades of red. Instead, Randy rubbed his brow. His eyes were tired and the lids were heavy, like those of a person who'd been sitting in the sun all day long, reading and gazing at the sky and the sea and the pretty women walking on the beach. Except that person would have a look of contentment. Randy? He just looked like he wanted to be somewhere else—anywhere, like in a bar. In Brooklyn. On a Saturday. With his boys. Several pitchers later. Pre-marriage, of course.

But he wasn't. He was here, with me, embarrassed that I was acting a stone cold ass. I obviously didn't care, he could see it in my face. So he avoided looking at it, instead training his tired eyes on the menu. He tried his best to get the waiter to point out something with chicken in it. It wasn't working. He might as well have told the waiter we wanted to eat a horse, live. He wouldn't have known to say it wasn't on the menu anyway. Frustrated, Randy simply shrugged, then slunk further into his chair.

"So, after all that, what am I supposed to eat?"

The look in Randy's eyes changed. Quickly. He looked at me as if I'd had a booger in my nose—just disgusted. Twisted his mouth all up and spit out, "Why can't you just pick something, Mikki?"

Oh, it was on. "I wasn't asking you, Randy. Obviously, *you* don't know what I should order."

Randy rolled his eyes at me and then trained them back on the waiter. "Chicken? You know, chicken—*pollo?*"

"That's Spanish, Randy," I snarled. "*Pollo* is Spanish."

He ignored me—made this sound with his tongue. Probably to avoid telling me to shut the hell up. "Chicken," he said, looking at me. The waiter called over a co-worker and said something in French to him, then looked at Randy, who said "chicken" again, then nodded furiously back to our waiter. "*Poulet.*" Pronounced "pool-ay." A huge smile crossed everyone's face. We all nodded furiously, saying "*Poulet!* Yes, *poulet*—chicken, yes, *poulet!*" over and over again. Both waiters trotted off, smiling. Randy was smiling, too. I'd at least taken the frown off my face.

Then the waiter stepped back over to the table with this, this—stuff—that, if you just thought about it slightly, looked just like worms swimming in, like, vomit. He sat that in front of me. Randy's dish wasn't any better—sort of like dirt soup, with pieces of red chicken tossed in it. Randy looked perplexed; he peered at me with these helpless, "I'm so sorry" eyes, but I wasn't even checkin' for it. Mama was hungry, okay? And now she was just stank, to boot, which, when tossed all together, meant that this evening, the one that was supposed to put our marriage back on track, was turning out to be a complete and total disaster. I did not want this. I don't think he wanted this either, at least I hoped not. I wanted to go to sleep and wake up and start all over again—like that movie *Groundhog Day*, where Bill Murray wakes up every morning to live the same day over and over again until he figures out how to be human enough to fall in love with this chick who started out thinking he was an ignorant ogre. If a genie had popped out in front of us right then and granted three wishes, mine would have been to rewind the whole day back to, like, before I talked to Marcus, and begin anew. Marcus wouldn't have said what he said on the cell phone, I wouldn't have said what I said from the moment my feet touched French soil, and Randy, the man with whom I'm in love but can't get it together, would be happy with this whole setup. In fact, I'd rewind all the way back to when Randy left my behind in Brooklyn. Wish number one would be Randy telling me that he wasn't leaving. Wish number two would be our marriage made perfect. Wish number three would be that Marcus did not exist.

But there was no genie there. Randy was still in Paris (and not leaving anytime soon) and Marcus was still heavy on my mind. I knew I couldn't change the former, but I had figured I'd at least forget the latter for the week I was in France. While we were together, I could tell by the look on Randy's face and the rush in his step that I had better stop poking my bottom lip out and give the boy some play—or the whole reconciliation was going to go straight to hell, do not pass go, do not collect two hundred dollars.

"I'm hungry," I told him, as we strolled the Champs Élysée. He looked at me with those big, round, brown eyes, and I swear I could see the gleam come back into them. He grabbed my hand and started walking a little faster. "Well, let's find my baby something to eat, then." We walked around for a good twenty or thirty minutes looking for something that was still open. It was closing in on midnight, and most of the cafés in the Saint-Germain district were closed. But when we crossed back over into the area near the hotel we found a cute little sandwich shop with normal food, like ham and cheese and salami and white bread. I hooked me up one of those tuna salads on a croissant, and I was straight. We sat and talked and ate and drank coffee and talked some more—about Angelou and her auditioning for a new Broadway play, my mother and father and my crazy sister and her bad-ass kids. I made a point of not bringing up Marcus—just knowing that I wouldn't be able to sustain a rational conversation about him without Randy seeing in my eyes exactly what was going on back home. But that was his best friend and it was just a matter of time before he did it. When he finally said, "How's Marcus doing?" I almost choked on my espresso.

"Why do you ask?" I tried to say calmly. I'm not so sure it came out that way.

"Well, I was just wondering if you had, uh, you know, called him after we talked that time. Or maybe he had called you."

I couldn't say a thing. I wanted this subject to change. Fast. The waitress was walking by, thank God. I signaled to her to bring the check. It was the easiest way for me to avoid looking into Randy's eyes.

"I guess you're ready to go," Randy said, bass in his voice. I ignored it, because I didn't want to get into it with him. But I knew I'd better answer his question, or he was going to suspect something.

"So, I saw him once or twice. I guess he's fine," I said.

"Who's fine?" Damn, he'd forgotten about Marcus, and I brought it back up. Dummy. Okay, play it cool, I said to myself.

"You asked me about Marcus," I said to him. "I'm answering your question."

"Oh! Marcus. Yeah, I'm sorry. I forgot I asked you about him."

I was trying hard to keep it cool, to figure out a way to keep him from hearing my heart pound and seeing the beads of sweat forming just above my brow. I smiled, grabbed onto his hand, and started acting downright giddy. I practically skipped back to the hotel.

Now, I was going to make it right. I was going to give Randy some.

"Randy, come here, baby," I said, just as I heard the click of the lock on the hotel room door. He turned toward me, then skipped across the room—and dove right into my arms. We kissed—one of those big, sloppy, juicy kisses. God, it turned me on to feel his tongue and his thick lips pressed against mine. Always liked a man with some big, juicy lips. The kind you fall into. He caressed my ass through my red dress, and it felt so damn good. I imagined that it was Marcus, not on purpose, my mind just roamed there. It happened so fast, I didn't even realize what I was doing. I let Marcus's hands roam over every inch of my body, invited his fingers to entangle themselves into the straps of my thong. He was tugging and caressing and tugging some more, exploring with his hands, his tongue. Just as his fingers made it to my spot, I felt a sneeze coming on. I tried to fight it.

"Excuse me, I have to snee—aawwwchooo!" I opened my eyes, and Randy was standing in front of me. I was temporarily dazed, partly from the powerful sneeze, partly from the fact that Randy had morphed into Marcus into Randy again, right before my eyes. I tried to shake it off as gracefully as possible. "Excuse me, baby," I said, smiling. "Now where were we?" Then I leaned into him, and he jerked his head away. God, he knows, I thought in terror.

"Wait! I'm so sorry, baby. But you need to wipe your nose," he said, pointing to my face. I almost lost it. I didn't know what the hell to do, except to apologize and make a mad dash for the bathroom. I silently thanked Jesus that he hadn't given Randy the gift of mind-reading. "Ewwww! Damn, that's so gross," I said, my hand instantly flying to my nose. "I'm sorry." I got into the bathroom, and, after I finished washing my face with this really hard toilet paper, I just stared at myself in the mirror. How the hell was I going to do this?

I recovered nicely by stripping off my dress and strolling back into the room with nothing on but my lace bra and panties. Randy loves my ass—he's a butt man. I knew whatever it was that'd grossed him out and got him worried would instantly be forgotten. Obviously, he'd been thinking the same thing, because when I walked back into the room Randy had lit some vanilla-scented candles. Sade was whispering "No Ordinary Love" through the speakers of a tiny box Randy had on the windowsill.

"Mmmm, Sade. You know how to get a sistah's juices *flowing*, baby."

He smiled back. "Uh, can you turn around so I can get the, uh, back view?"

I obliged, and I swear that if his lips weren't attached to the rest of his face, they'd have just fallen off his body—that's how hard he was smiling. "Damn, I missed this ass," he mumbled into my left cheek. I laughed. "Paris has never seen an ass like this."

What? What the hell did he mean, Paris'd never seen an ass like mine? Whose asses had he been comparing to his wife's? Probably some white bitch's. Probably fucked her, too. Right here in the bed he was about to lay me down in. Oh, hell no. I turned and faced him, quick. "How do *you* know what kind of asses Paris has seen, Mr. Murphy? What have you been doing, field research?"

He was temporarily stunned—just looked at me for a minute.

"Damn, Mikki. What are you *talking* about? Bring that booty back over here." He reached for my ass again, but I snatched myself away from him. "You *can't* be serious, Mikki. Are you?" He was getting disgusted. I didn't give a damn.

"Why wouldn't I be serious, Randy? That was a strange comment to make, like maybe you were subconsciously trying to tell me something."

Randy sat down on the bed and sighed, hard—with his dramatic behind. I looked at him and thought about what I'd just said. I had a lot of nerve, didn't I? I mean, a minute ago, I was pretending it was his friend's hands that were palming my behind, right? I figured I'd better stop trippin' before it got ugly and I said something I'd regret—like, "Marcus and I are fooling around."

I jumped onto the bed and straddled him, smothering his face and nipples and bellybutton with kisses. I let him peel my bra and panties off, then I returned the favor. I wanted him, desperately—hadn't felt his touch in two months. In just this small piece of time, I remembered why I married this man, and it wasn't my libido talking, this was real. I didn't want to divorce him, I wanted to work this out. I didn't want to be mad at him, I wanted us to have some of that happily-ever-after stuff. Maybe even have some kids. I mean, I'm not getting any younger—and he wants some anyway. It's going to happen eventually. Damn, wouldn't it be fly if I got pregnant here in Paris? God, Randy could come back home to the surprise of his natural born life. Maybe I should tell him to forget about the condom. Of course, that's what he was searching for at the very moment I was thinking this. It was taking up more time than just a little bit. What the hell was he doing?

"What's wrong, baby?" I asked, pushing myself up onto my elbows.

"Uh, nothing. Nothing's wrong."

"You can't find the condom, right? Don't worry, babe."

Randy looked at me like I'd grown a second head. Then he went back to thrusting his hand over the side of the bed. I'd probably just thrown him for a total loop. "I found it," he said, thrusting it in my face. I smiled, then hesitated a little. I started to tell him to put it back where he found it, then I chickened out. I smiled some more. "All right," I said. "Don't just sit there grinning, put the damn thing to use, homey."

I reached out and touched him gently, feeling him grow hard in my palms. He slipped the condom on, and then lowered himself atop me. I lost myself in him—moved my hips to his rhythm, felt his fingers probing every crevice of my thighs and my ass and my back and my shoulders—everywhere. He was holding me and caressing me and whispering in my ear and Sade was wailing about sweet taboos. Umm, ummm, ummm. I needed to open my eyes—to see his face.

"I love you, Mekhi," he said in my ear. I opened my eyes and smiled. Marcus was on top of me.

I stared in horror, but my body kept moving. Instinctively, I pushed him off me. When my hands left his chest, it was Randy again. His brows were creased, his mouth was wide open, he looked dazed and confused. I faked a sneeze so that I wouldn't have to explain why I pushed my husband off of me in the middle of our lovemaking session, then excused myself. "I'm so sorry, babe," I called out over my shoulder. "I must be catching a cold or something." I rushed into the bathroom and shut the door. I sat down on the toilet and ran my hands through my hair. What the fuck was I doing? This, this is just so un-explainable, inexplicable—whatever the fuck. My husband was lying out there, waiting for me, waiting to make love to me, and all I could think of was Marcus. Unreal. Truly. I couldn't go back out there; he's my husband, and I just knew he was going to know something was up. That would invite questions, and I just couldn't face any of that right now. I was so confused—so out of it. I felt like someone had punched me straight in the stomach—knocked the wind out of me like this big butch girl named Stacey did once in high school, during a basketball game in which the guarding got a little out of hand. I couldn't get my ass up off that gym floor, didn't want to get up, because that would in-vite more of the same pain. That's how I was feeling then—didn't want to get up off that cold toilet seat.

But I had to.

I raised myself up and looked in the mirror again. I feigned a sneeze to make it seem like there was a reason why I was in the bathroom for so long. Then I ran some water over my hands and my breasts and walked back out into the bedroom—tried to start over again. But every time I opened my eyes, every time Randy touched my thigh, every time he whispered, "I love you," I saw Marcus in the Knitting Factory, palming my ass, and heard his voice telling me he loved me, too.

I tried to play it off, and I guess it worked because Randy came. I didn't. The air was awkward, tense, thick.

"Is there something wrong, Mikki?"

I almost choked. Oh shit, he knows. "What?! Why would you ask me that?"

"I, I just thought that that didn't, uh, go as well as maybe it usually does."

He got that right. There was no explaining the Marcus factor, so I had to go on the defensive. Maybe he'd just leave all of this alone. "Well, you think that was my fault?" I asked, with a whole lotta bass in my voice.

There was a long, pregnant pause. Then, Randy said quietly, "Never mind."

And that was the last time we touched each other, really, for the rest of the trip. We'd stop talking to each other one day—I hated that he wasted an entire day dragging me around Versailles, this disgusting monstrosity of a city (no wonder they chopped off Marie Antoinette's head—wasting all the peoples' money on that gold and red and garden mess). And then we'd make up the next (the antique shop—particularly the vanilla bean–colored French window seat Randy bought for me—was awesome). We'd cuddle the day after that—but I didn't feel like having sex then—then piss each other off again. Before we knew it, my time there was up, and it seemed only right that we try to, you know, have sex before I went back to Brooklyn, before I left my husband and didn't see him for another month. I initiated it, figured I'd lay it on him before I went back to America. There was this chair in the hotel room—had my eye on it from the moment I dropped my suitcase on the floor. I knew I wanted to straddle him on it, like we did once on the lawn chair back in the garden in Brooklyn. I saw the Taylors' teenage daughter watching from her window, but she never said anything because she knew she was supposed to be in bed and I never said anything because I didn't need anyone else to know about our little garden rendezvous. Besides, the idea of someone watching kinda turned me on—disgusting, but true. Didn't have to worry about anyone watching us this time, though. We were going to get on that chair.

At least I thought we were.

Every time I thought that I'd gotten him excited, I'd reach down to help him enter me and I'd find him limp—barely there. He was acting like he wanted to, but penises don't lie. He didn't want me. I sat on his lap and looked him in his eyes. My fingers and his dick and our thighs had been wrestling for a good half hour now, and it was clear nothing was going to happen. I rested my palms on each of his cheeks and kissed each one of his eyelids, and then, tenderly, his lips. None of this was right, and we both knew that by now. What we didn't know was if any of it would ever be right again.

We barely spoke on the way to the airport the next morning. Just really sanitized, irrelevant drivel that was designed more to warm the chill that clung in the air, like, "So I called the airport service in New York and it says that the flight should be clear and on time," and "So, that cornflake batter on the French toast this morning was really good—have to try that at home." It was obvious that we were uncomfortable with each other, just sort of trying to pass time until I stepped onto that plane. There was more of that while we checked my bags and secured my boarding pass. Usually, when Randy is dropping me somewhere, I kiss him good-bye, hug him really tight, wave to him as I take my first steps, then turn around and wave good-bye again, perhaps blow a kiss.

This time, we simply hugged—one of those long and lingering but still quite tentative hugs. We did not kiss. And when I walked away, I waved once, but I didn't look back.

We knew. Randy and I both knew. It was obvious that our marriage was on the brink. All that was left was for one of us to just come on out and say it.

He

Being at the office became a form of torture to me, knowing that I'd be expected to put my private life aside and concentrate. I know men are supposed to be masters at this particular mental exercise, but I was a mess. My lack of focus got so bad that Eliza, my arch rival, the bane of my office existence, felt compelled to mention it to me. At first I thought she was using it as an opportunity to gloat, but when our eyes locked momentarily, I could have sworn I saw real concern.

"I just wondered if you needed to talk to anybody, that's all," she said gently. "I know it can get lonely over here. Sometimes I feel so alone it hurts."

This was an actual revelation, not the fake stuff in which colleagues usually engage in the office. I was moved by her honesty. I almost wanted to reach out and hug her.

"Yeah, I definitely know that feeling," I said. "That feeling of being alone. I thought it would, uh, you know, get better, feel lessened, when Mikki came, but I think it's gotten worse. It hasn't even been a week since she left, but I just feel so . . ."

I turned my face away from her and stared at the bare mauve wall near the doorway. Suddenly I was afraid I'd start crying if I continued. I wasn't ready to show Eliza that kind of weakness. Hell, I wasn't ready to show *anybody* that kind of weakness. What I needed was my friend Marcus, the only person I'd ever been able to really open up to besides my wife. Ever since our days together at Yale, when I was a scared, clueless freshman and Marcus was the wise, calm junior, I had reached out to him when I needed to talk through women (or, later, woman) troubles or work troubles or life troubles. But now Marcus was thousands of miles away—how many thousands? I didn't even know—inaccessible except for the rare short phone conversation. Besides Marcus, I didn't have anybody.

"Hey, you want to go get a bite together after work?" Eliza said, trying to appear chipper. I was still somewhat suspicious, but it couldn't hurt, right?

"All right, that sounds like a plan," I said, nodding.

"Great!" Eliza beamed, popping up from her chair. What was she doing, exactly? She must realize that if I was depressed and distracted, it would be a boon to her career, right? I didn't quite understand, but I was frantic for company. She spun around before she exited, probably catching me fixated on her ass but pretending not to notice. She'd caught me once before and made a big deal about it, teasing me for weeks. But now she was willing to let it go.

"I'll be ready about six-thirty or so. That sound good for you?"

I nodded and gave her a small wave. Before her perfume had even drifted from my senses, I was already second-guessing myself. How smart was it to reveal some of my most private thoughts to the woman who represented the most danger to my career? Sure, I had outshone her so far in Paris, but the war between us was far from over. When we got to New York, I expected her to be shooting for me and my new job at every opportunity. Maybe we could consider these days in Paris as a truce, like a détente, and any information shared could not be used during subsequent skirmishes. Yeah, right.

Three hours later and near the bottom of our second bottle of red wine, I was spilling out all my business to my co-worker, including even some vague references to our intimacy problems during Mikki's stay.

"Wait! Let me get this straight," Eliza said, holding out her palm like a black girl. I briefly wondered where she had learned that move. She was laughing now with her mouth wide open and I was trying to deny the thickening I was starting to feel in my crotch area. No, I was *not* getting turned on by this bony, bitchy blonde, I said to myself several times. She reached her hand across the table and ran it softly over the top of my right hand. It appeared to be a subconscious gesture while she laughed—if it was one of her seduction moves, I was impressed by its nonchalance.

"Your wife was here for a whole week? Your wife! And you only fucked once?!!"

Eliza doubled over from laughter, pushing her chair back from the table and attracting the attention of several Parisians at surrounding tables.

"Come on, Eliza. That's not funny." I was more than a little embarrassed. I hadn't intended the revelation to be received like a routine at the Improv. It wasn't *that* funny; in fact, it was kinda sad.

"I know, I know, I know," Eliza said, pressing her right hand to her chest as if it would help her suppress her laughter. "I'm sorry. It's sad, actually. I'd be going out of my mind if that had happened to me. Excuse me for saying this, but the whole institution of marriage just sounds fucked up and confusing as hell."

I couldn't argue with that observation. I had said the same thing myself of late.

"Yeah, I can't argue with that," I said. "It's kinda like trying to sail a boat on the high seas with no sailing lessons and no navigational equipment. You're just kind of adrift."

"Hey, that's pretty good," Eliza said, still smiling. "That metaphor works for me. Or how about this one—marriage is like flying a plane with no landing gear."

I frowned. "I don't know about that one, Eliza. No landing gear? The idea is that you're not sure where you're going and even if you did know, you're not sure how to get there. How does landing gear fit into that?"

Eliza shrugged. "Hey, man, I'm drunk, okay?" she said, laughing. "Excuse me if I'm not able to compete with Mr. Metaphor."

I laughed, but I wondered at the same time what was happening here. We were both lonely, a little drunk, and obviously enjoying each other's company. Sex seemed like a natural destination. But did I really want to go there? There were negative implications popping out all over the place. I was married; she was a colleague and a rival; she was white. I hadn't slept with a white girl since college. I might have had a few opportunities over the years if I had pushed, but the last thing I had wanted was to fall in love with a white girl. I couldn't even picture the expression that would cross my mother's face if I stepped into their house in West Orange with a white girl on my arm. She'd no doubt have imploded, right there where she was standing. My pops would have calmed her down eventually, but she'd have figured a childhood of enlightening me about my heritage and the importance of community and unity had been lost. If I let this thing with Eliza play itself out, I had no doubt that I'd regret it, probably sooner rather than later.

"I've noticed that there are a lot of interracial couples here in Paris—haven't you?" Eliza asked, trying to sound casual.

I'm sure my eyes widened, if only just slightly. She wanted to talk about race?

"Uh, yeah, I have kinda noticed that," I said, wanting to sound casual myself.

"Why do you think that is?" she said, leaning toward me across the table.

Wow. How much truth did I want to give her? I could blow off the question with something pithy and vague, or I could really bore in to the core of the issue: racism and white America. Is that what she wanted to hear, or did she really have no clue? Surely she must have some ideas on the topic.

"Well, I think maybe the French have a different attitude toward blacks than white Americans do," I said, hoping to leave it there.

Eliza nodded. "Yeah, I was sorta thinking that myself. I remember you telling us that the people here have been really nice to you. We think they're mean. Mike and I talked about it once at the office. He thought it was just you, but I said it was probably a race thing. You think black guys over here are more interested in white women?"

Damn. Where to go with that question? Was she completely unaware of how huge an issue this was in the black community at home? Was it my job to tell her these things?

"I don't really know, Eliza. I can't speak on how interested brothers over here are in white women. I can only speak for the ones back home. Back home, some brothers are very interested, but most aren't. They'd think it wasn't worth it for the hell they'd have to pay in the community and within their family."

There was a long pause as Eliza absorbed this information. I knew what was coming next.

"Well, how do *you* feel about white women?" she asked, somewhat haltingly, no longer even trying to fake nonchalance.

Well, there it was. That was clearly the point of this exercise. I knew my answer would have all kinds of implications. It would likely play a huge part in determining how this night ended. It would therefore impact many nights to come. It could change my work relationship with Eliza, thus impacting on either or both of our careers at Trier-Stanton. Lastly, it could devastate my marriage. I had never cheated on Mikki. There were moments when temptation had nearly brought tears to my eyes—sistahs could be pretty damn aggressive about making their feelings and desires known—but I'd always been able to flee before any damage was done. I wondered what my wife would think if she knew how close I was to going there with a white girl. I flashed on the memory of that sistah-girl coffee table scene in Spike Lee's *Jungle Fever*, when Spike allowed the sistahs to fling their vitriol all over the room when Wesley Snipes's character had strayed with a white woman. I knew that same scene would be repeated in Fort Greene, Brooklyn, with Mikki and her girl Angelou leading the line of marchers as my picture-framed face burned in effigy.

"What's wrong, Randy? Is that the wrong question to ask?" Eliza was leaning in toward me, her eyes wide, her lips slightly parted, waiting.

"I'm not sure how I feel, Eliza," I said. That was mostly a lie, but it was the best I could do on such short notice. "But it's something I don't really have to worry about because I'm not married to one, you know?"

Eliza sat back in her chair and nodded. She clearly got the picture. That was my way of letting out the air, releasing the tension, giving her an answer without making it unpleasant or painful. I thought I saw her shoulders droop slightly, but maybe that was just my ego seeing things that weren't really there.

"Hey," Eliza said, brightening, "so what was it like in Versailles? You didn't tell me how the trip went."

I sighed deeply, both because I was glad to change the subject and because the Versailles trip with Mikki had been such a disaster that just the mention of the place multiplied my melancholy.

"Another disaster," I said, shaking my head. "I'm just a simple guy from Brooklyn, so maybe I don't understand all this fancy stuff, but—"

"I thought you were from New Jersey, from Orange or something?" Eliza interrupted.

"West Orange. My parents moved there when I was a teenager, but

I mostly grew up in Brooklyn, where I was born. Can I continue?" I asked playfully.

Eliza nodded, grinning.

"Now, the whole idea was to bring Mikki on a short day trip some- where outside of Paris. I had heard a lot about Versailles, so I thought, 'Why not?' But let me tell you, Eliza, this place was wild. It was hideous. It was like it had been built by Donald Trump on crack. It was so outlandish, so overdone, that it was disturbing. It showed how fucked up the whole concept of monarchy is, that one person could have that much power and be that self-indulgent to think that such a place was necessary. It took fifty years to finish it and they poured I don't know how much of the people's tax money into the thing. It could hold twenty thousand guests at one time. Pretty damn practical, huh? Mikki called it an immense, gaudy housing project. Louis XIV was a trip.

"Anyway, Mikki is getting more and more upset. She keeps asking me, 'Why did you bring me here? Am I supposed to be impressed?' I was like, 'What kind of question is that?' It was a damn day trip out- side of Paris to a famous site. That was the purpose. I didn't really know what we were going to find there. I was as disturbed as she was. But it was like she was blaming me for the fact that this palace upset her so much. That really pissed me off. It was, like, symbolic of her whole trip."

Eliza was shaking her head. The earlier sexual tension had been sig- nificantly reduced; now she was just a friend commiserating with me over my troubles. Our eyes locked a few more times, but one or both of us would look away or attempt an innocent smile. I was amazed, frankly, at how quickly my relationship with Eliza had turned. For years I had viewed her as the rival, the cold Ice Queen, but now that our loneliness had pretty much forced us together she had softened considerably. She was actually sweet and funny. Or she could be when she wanted. I was curious whether she'd start showing me sweet and funny in the workplace—or if she'd throw me the booty even more in- tently now that we had shared this intimacy.

She

If Angelou's mouth stays open any wider and any longer, something is going to fly right into it, go straight down her throat, into her stomach. She'll discover she's pregnant with some exotic fruit fly in about two weeks.

"Hello—are you there?" I asked her, knocking on her head with my fist.

"Oh, hell yeah, I'm here," she said. "And I heard you loud and clear. You're getting a divorce, aren't you? And you're going to try to get with Marcus. Have you lost your natural born mind, Mekhi?"

"The one thing I haven't lost is my mind, Angelou. I know now that it's not going to get any better, and I know that he's not willing to fix any of it. I wasn't so sure before I went to Paris, but now, I am."

"Oh sure—now you are, huh? You went there fully expecting that shit wasn't going to work out, Mekhi, come on, admit it. You didn't have to pick all those fights with the boy."

"No, I didn't Angelou, you've got it all wrong. I wanted it to work, but it didn't and it won't. And I don't know what I'm going to do about Marcus." I was thinking about it, though—but I wasn't about to tell Angelou. She was in her self-righteous mode, the one where she defends Randy and blames everything on me. "Look, boo—mama's tired, she needs a little somethin' to eat and she needs to unpack these dirty clothes, because if she don't do it now, it ain't ever gonna get done. Unless you're gonna cook, unpack, and tuck my ass into bed, I suggest you get to steppin'. Don't you have an audition to go to or something?"

"Oh—oh. Now you trying to get rid of me because you don't like my truth, huh?"

"Your truth?"

"Yes, my truth," she said, bracing both hands on the arms of the chair to hoist herself up. "My version of the truth is that you best talk to yo' husband before you haul off and start thinking about drawing up papers on his ass. Randy is a good man, Mikki, and you're not taking any of that into account. I wish you would." She was standing and heading for the door. "Now, I'm going to kindly remove myself from your apartment because the energy in here is just funky. I fed Pootie and Mac, but I didn't pet the little hairy bastards—know I can't stand those little animals. Shoulda left the front door open—put us all out of our misery," she said, waving her hands in the air. She was wrinkling her nose like something stank. "But I'm your best friend, so I know you appreciate my truth. I love you, darling."

"Yeah, yeah, yeah—I love you too, though my cats don't. Take your energy up on outta my house." I gave her a smile, a crooked, weak one. She laughed and left.

I surveyed the room and breathed a really heavy sigh. Our place is so empty—almost cavernous. It's a classic New York brownstone with all the flourishes. The steps can make you tired, and when alone, it's kinda scary. But it's a blessing when there are two people in the house and you feel like you need to get away. When Randy was around and I didn't feel like being bothered with him, I usually slipped down to our entertainment center on the second floor with one of my favorite tapes—*love jones* or *Soul Food* or *Devil in a Blue Dress* or *Jerry Maguire*—and wrapped myself into a big 'ole blanket, curled up on the floor, and forgot that he was there.

Now, I simply felt like I was alone. Pootie and Mac were hiding somewhere, no doubt completely oblivious to the fact that Angelou was gone and it was their mommy floating around the house. They'd show their faces soon.

I walked up the stairs and past the office, into the bedroom, and dropped myself stomach first across the bed. In the same swift motion, I smashed my finger against the play button on the answering machine.

Amazingly, only four dummies left messages on the machine, even after hearing my nasty message:

"Hey—neither Mikki nor Randy are here to talk to you and we won't be returning your phone call until mid-September. You'd be smart to wait until then to call back, because we don't like coming home to a full answering machine. You decide."

The first message was from some mortgage company, offering low-interest loans for . . . it was a recording, which always pissed me off. I didn't bother to finish listening to it, just went straight for the delete button. The second was from some woman asking me to call her "the moment you set foot in Brooklyn because I heard that you are the best wedding dress maker on this earth and I really, really, really want you to make my dress for me. My name is Joan Silver and you can reach me at . . ." I pushed the skip button. Wasn't in the mood yet for clients. How'd she get the home number, anyway? The third was Marcus. His voice was soft and inviting. "Hey, Mekhi. Just wanted to make sure you called me when you got back so that I could resume my body-guard duties." He knew not to say anything risqué—Randy could check the messages from anywhere if he wanted to, although he hadn't the whole time he was away in Paris. Marcus kept it simple. But he hesitated before he spoke again. "Hope you had a, um, a nice trip. Call me, okay?"

I pushed repeat a couple of times and listened for the words be-tween his words, searching for any sign that he'd been thinking, "I love you, Mekhi." I heard it—heard it in the pause, just after the "um," just before "a nice trip." I picked up the cordless and started dialing. The phone was in the middle of the first ring when I heard my sister's voice.

"Mikki, call me when you get this message okay? It's important." There was a pause and I thought she was hanging up the phone. Then she spoke again. "It's about Mommy and Daddy."

I pushed reset on the cordless immediately and dialed my parents' house. I was scared beyond my wits—afraid that something happened to my mom or dad. The older I got, the more I started thinking about their mortality, and what I would do if and when they left this earth. It was a frightening feeling, and I hated to think about it, but it'd been creeping into my thoughts since the moment I turned twenty-one and moved out on my own for good. I worried about them like you wouldn't believe, and really got freaked out sometime later that year when my mom called me at my new apartment over in Boerum Hill to tell me that Daddy was getting baptized. Now, my father wasn't a religious man by any stretch of the imagination. While my mom trotted off to church every Sunday, me and Zaria in tow, Daddy would sleep the entire morning away, completely oblivious to the fact that we were on our way out the door—except on the mornings when Mommy made us hit him up for church money. He'd told me a few times that he loved the Lord, but he thought church was a crock—"All those holy rollers acting like saints on Sunday and sinners every other day of the week." Church just wasn't his bag. But he'd always said that he wanted to get baptized before he died, so that he could see his mother again. "Woman was a saint," he'd always said about my grandmother. I hated when he talked like that—all that death stuff. Mommy too, with her morbid behind. Last year, she put some money down on two plots, one for herself and one for Daddy, so that, as she put it, "You kids won't have to worry about scraping up money to bury us." But I got freaked out even more the day my mom called and told me that Dad was getting baptized. That night, I almost lost it. He swore he was just ready to give his life to the Lord. But to me, his rush to get baptized was symbolic of his preparation to die. I didn't want to think about my father in a casket—gone from this earth, gone from me. I was just sick over it for days, even though Mommy told me I was being silly. But death was on my mind whenever I left them for long periods of time. When I visited them at their house in New Jersey—and I know this is going to sound jacked up—I'd treasure it each time like it was my last. Every time I pulled away in my beat-up Nissan Sentra, I'd wave to them, a tear working in my eye, and honk the horn and wave furiously. I couldn't imagine life without them.

And now my sister was telling me there was something wrong with them? Oh, hell no—I needed to talk to someone, *now*. Maybe I should go out there.

"Hello?" It was my mother.

"Mommy?"

"Hey, baby girl—what's up? You're back from Paris—welcome home! How was your trip, baby?"

"Nothing's up, it was fine. How are you? Zaria left me a message saying there was something wrong."

"She did, huh?"

"Is Daddy okay?"

"Daddy's fine, dear. What did Zaria say? Something was wrong?"

"She just left this message—something like call me now, something's wrong with Mommy and Daddy."

"She said something was wrong, huh?"

"Mommy—where's Daddy?"

"He's not here." She said it calm, like, "I'm from South Carolina, my mother's name is Lila Mae and yo' daddy ain't here. What?"

"What do you mean he's not there, Mommy? Where is he?"

"Look, me and your daddy had a little problem and he left for a couple of days so that we can sort this out. Don't worry, okay, sweetie? Everything's going to be fine. You haven't told me about your trip. Tell me about your trip."

"Mommy, what is it that you two are trying to sort out?"

"Look, Mekhi." Her voice had taken on a dark tone, like, "Look, I'm the mother and you're the child and I said this conversation is over so it's over. Period." "I don't want to talk about this. So, unless you're going to tell me how that beautiful husband of yours is, or how your trip to Paris was, you might as well hang up this phone and get you some rest. We can talk about your daddy and me some other time."

"But Mommy, what's going on? Why can't we talk—"

"Mikki? I said that's all there is to say right now. Why don't you get some rest. We'll talk this weekend."

"But Mom—"

"Good-bye, Mekhi. I'll talk to you this weekend."

And she hung up. Nothing but dial tone. Just like that. Oh, my God. My fingers flew over the buttons on the cordless so fast that I dialed Zaria's phone number wrong three times before I got it right.

"Hello. You've reached 718-555-2344. Zaria, James Jr., and Jasmine aren't in right now, but if you leave your name, number, and a brief message, we'll get back to you as soon as possible. Say bye-bye guys!" Her monsters, with their faces no doubt two millimeters from the speaker of the answering machine, yelled into the phone, "Bye-bye!"

It beeped.

"Hey Zaria—it's me. I'm back. What's up with Daddy? I tried to get Mom to tell me what's going on, but she—"

Zaria picked up the reciever. "Hold on, okay? I just got to make sure JJ isn't beating Jasmine down." She put her hand over the receiver, but I could still hear her screams although they were muffled. "JJ? If I come out there and you're anywhere within a ten-foot radius of your sister, that's your ass, do you hear me?!"

"Zaria, damn, why you cursing at them kids with they bad asses?"

"What did you say?" Zaria said. "I didn't hear what you said. These some badass kids."

"Yeah, well—forget about them for a minute and tell me what's going on with Mommy and Daddy."

"Ooooh, Mekhi—girl, it's a mess over there."

"Well, is Daddy okay?"

"Oh, Daddy's fine."

"Where is he?"

"He's over at Uncle Leo's house," she said, just before turning her attention back to her kids and telling Jasmine to get off of JJ. "Don't make me have to come in there—or you'll both be sorry. Do you hear me?"

"Zaria."

"Yeah?" she asked, annoyed.

"Look—cut the bullshit and tell me what the hell is going on already, damn."

"Okay, okay. Hold on, let me get the cordless and get into the bedroom. I can barely hear you."

For the next ten minutes, Zaria told me a story I could hardly fathom. Yesterday, as I was spending what probably would be the last day I'd spend with Randy as his wife, my mother, who'd been married to my daddy for, what, almost thirty-nine years now, was kicking my father out of their house. Told him to bounce. Hit the road. Get to steppin'. Over something that happened thirty-two years ago. By accident. At least Daddy said it was an accident. And that accident's been calling my mama's house almost every other day for the last two months, trying to get "acquainted" with my dad—his dad.

I have—and I'm having a problem even letting these words touch my tongue—a brother. A brother, man. A half-one, at least. His name is Jason (Zaria didn't pick up anything on the last name, except that it's not my dad's) and he lives in Laurelton, the town in Queens, N.Y., where my mother and father met and fell in love and got married and lived the first five years of their marriage, before they got pregnant with Zaria. He is thirty-two. Which means that his mother got pregnant right around the time that my parents were celebrating their third year of marriage. Just as my mom was about to get pregnant with Zaria. My dad cheated on my mom.

"Mikki?" Zaria paused. She was trying to give me time, but she couldn't stand the silence much. "Mikki?! You all right?"

"Am I all right? What in the hell do you mean, all right? What exactly is all right supposed to mean in this context? You just told me that my father not only cheated on my mother, but that he made a baby with some woman who is not my mother. Am I all right?"

"Look, I know this isn't easy to digest right now; it nearly knocked the wind out of me when Mommy called me crying about it yesterday."

"Oh, no—Mom was crying?" I felt like crying. I was going to cry. My forehead was getting hot, and my nose was starting to hurt. Tears, definitely.

"Yeah, well, could you blame her? Some little boy is calling her house, trying to call her husband 'Dad.' I'm surprised all she did was cry."

"Well, obviously that's not all she did. Where did you say Mason was?" I wasn't so sure I wanted to call him Dad now, even though I was sad for him.

"Mason? Oh, he's not Daddy anymore?" Zaria was being venemous. She was always jealous of the relationship Daddy and I have (damn, had), and mad that she wasn't a part of the special bond that Daddy and I share (shoot, shared.) While she was out running in the streets, getting into trouble with this boy and that boy, getting put on punishment for weeks at a time, getting bad grades, being a plain bad ass, Daddy and I were busy being the best of friends. He'd take me on his errands, buy me pizza at our favorite shop, Ray's, down on Maplewood Avenue, spoil me with ice cream sundaes at the mall, where we'd sit on the benches in front of Friendly's and lick our spoons and talk about the people walking by and just crack each other up. We'd watch the games together and put bogus bets on the boxing matches. I always put my money on Sugar Ray Leonard, and later Felix Trinidad. Those boys have punches like the grill of a speeding mack truck. Daddy loved the old school, Sugar Ray, Julio Cesar Chavez, all them. Zaria hated sports, unless it involved checking out the guys who played them. Daddy always hated that about her. I always hated that she made fun of me and Daddy's relationship. Just like she was doing now.

"I need to know more."

"What else is there to know?" Zaria asked, with a sigh. "He cheated on Mommy, he has a son that none of us knew about, and now he's not with our mother anymore. Not much more to it than that."

"Where's Daddy?" I asked again, trying hard to block out what she was saying.

"He's over to Uncle Leo's house. How many times are you going to ask me?"

I ignored that. "You talked to him?"

"I ain't got nothin' to say to him. I need some time before I can even hear his voice, I'm so mad. You know that boy's been calling over to the house, trying to talk to Mommy, knowing that Daddy's not there? I mean, what's the point—she's got nothing to do with this. Daddy messed up and she has to live with it for the rest of her life, but she doesn't have to face it every time she hears the phone ring. She was crying so hard the last week her eyes are going to pop out of her head. She can't hardly see straight, she's so upset. Naw, I ain't got nothing to say to Mason."

"I'm going to call him."

"I knew you would."

"Yeah, okay, Zaria. Go get your kids, before they tear your house down. I gotta go."

"Wait—how was Paris?"

"I, um," I started. I didn't really feel like talking about this right now, particularly in light of the fact that it turned out that my parents' marriage appeared to be going in the same exact direction as mine. So I lied. "It was really nice," I said, quietly.

"Good. I'm glad you had a good time. I know you brought me something back," she said, trying to joke. I wasn't in the mood.

"I got you a little something, but don't get all excited and shit. It ain't all that special."

"Yeah, okay. One of these days, you're going to be sorry you weren't nice to me. You know this, Mikki?"

"Yeah, okay."

"And how's that fine ass husband of yours?"

"Stop worrying about my fine ass husband and get one of your own, why don't you?"

"Oh, see—that wasn't necessary." Zaria refused to marry Ricky, even though she gave her kids his last name, Fish. I don't blame her; he's way too trifling to get his measly little pea brain around the concept of marriage. But then, I thought my dad was the model husband, and he turned out to be every bit as trifling as Fish. Damn, Daddy screwed around on Mom. "Don't worry about my marriage situation."

"Zaria?"

"What?"

"Can you hang up now?"

All I heard was dial tone. Zaria's stupid like that.

I tried dialing my Uncle Leo's number, like, four times—but I just couldn't get my fingers to work. It was like this dream that I kept having a few weeks ago, after Randy started calling me and leaving me messages, asking me if there was something wrong with my fingers because I hadn't called him in a while. After the third message, I dreamed that I was trying to dial Paris, but I kept misdialing the numbers. I'd push one instead of two, five instead of eight—it was awful. I woke up laughing, because I was suffering in my dream what Randy said I'd been suffering in real life: Something was wrong with my fingers. Get it? Anyway, I just couldn't dial my Uncle Leo's number, so I gave up. It was probably some subliminal stuff, like, I really didn't want to talk to my dad. So I gave up. It was late, anyway, and Daddy was probably asleep. He turned in early if there wasn't a game on—as did Uncle Leo—so my calling there close to midnight probably wasn't a good idea anyway.

I didn't feel like calling Angelou. She would just start preaching or something—again—and I definitely wasn't in the mood for that. You know how sometimes you just want a person to listen to you bitch and be there to wipe your tears but not say anything? Like, don't say a word, just hear what you've got to say? Angelou couldn't do that if the person looking to release a load off their chest offered her a cool million dollars. She's a Libra; she's gotta hear all sides of the story, ponder it, talk about it, ponder it some more, talk about it some more, then mete out a fair and sizable decision on how you should go about tackling the problem. It never quite occurs to her that she should just shut the hell up and be there.

God, maybe I should call Randy. He's a good listener, a great one, actually. He's the only man I know who can listen to the problem and refrain from making like he's Dr. Ruth with all the pat solutions and answers. Guys usually aren't good at that; just want you to state your problem in ten words or less and then be very, very quiet while they give you the game plan for dealing with it. Randy wasn't like that. He'd listen, and hold you in his arms if you really, really looked like you needed it, then kiss you on the forehead and hold you some more until your heart just wasn't as heavy anymore. It was a refreshing salve for the soul to have someone like that around.

I could call Randy. It's about six p.m. in Paris, and he would understand the gravity of my parents' breakup and do what he could to make me feel better, even if it was just a little bit better. I need one of his big, teddy bear hugs. I need to hear him tell me that everything was going to be all right. I need him.

Randy isn't here.

I called Marcus instead. But instead of his sexy baritone, I heard really soft, sexy music blow into my receiver—Adriana Edwards' "Say You Won't." Really sweet song—like a 90s version of Aretha's "Daydreaming," but with a way softer edge. Marcus's voice was hypnotizing. "Hi— I'm not here right now, but you know what to do. Do it after the beep."

Shit. I didn't know what to say. What was I supposed to say? Oh shit. Um. "Hey, Marcus, it's Mikki. I got your message. Um, call me when you get in."

And where the hell was he, just two minutes before midnight? God, where is everybody?

I'm going to sleep.

He

I knew it was time. There was only one week remaining of my supposed three-month stay and I still hadn't told my wife that I wasn't coming home. Because of my cowardice, I had now waited much too long. I had allowed my return to become imminent, expected in Mikki's mind, no doubt. Now how much more disappointing was it going to be to her, how much more upsetting, hearing the news just days before she was to pick me up?

I looked up at the clock on my office wall. Four-thirty. That meant it was ten-thirty a.m. in Brooklyn. Mikki should be settled in her boutique, Mekhi's, by now. It would be bad if she were working on a customer, but that was less likely to be the case in the morning. I was proud of the progress Mikki had made in her boutique, in a few short years becoming one of the city's premier African-American wedding dress designers. She had other stuff in the store besides wedding dresses too; it had even become a popular shopping stop for white women.

I picked up the phone, paused, then put it down again. I was embarrassed that I had forgotten the phone number for Mekhi's—a number I used to call about three times a day. Damn, how quickly things had changed. Well, I hoped they hadn't changed too much. I dug into my briefcase for my electronic organizer.

"Mekhi's," she said, pronouncing the store name in a sing-song. I heard her voice and tried to assess her mental state from the one word. I guessed tired but not unhappy.

"Hi, Mikki."

There was a pause. "Hey, baby." She didn't sound too thrilled, more like subdued. I felt my gut starting to twist.

"You busy?" I asked.

"Nah, not yet. I have an appointment for a fitting in about twenty minutes, though. So, how's it going over there on the other side of the world? How's gay Par-ee? You ready to come back?"

I nodded, though she couldn't see me. "I'm definitely ready to come back. But that's actually what I wanted to talk to you about."

I didn't continue. I should have, but I waited.

"Yeah, okay. Go 'head. Talk." Her voice sounded guarded but not too troubled. Yet.

"Well, there's actually good news and bad news. I'll give you the good news first. When I come back, I'm going to be a vice president, in charge of the whole creative department."

"Really? Wow. That sounds impressive."

I caught her use of the word "sounds," as if she were telling me she wasn't impressed. But I thought I knew what she was thinking: Vice president in charge of creative sounds like even longer hours. And she'd be right.

"I'd get a pretty huge raise. From $90,000 to about $150 or so. We still have to work out the details."

"That's great, Randy. I know this is something you wanted. Well, actually I'm not sure I really know what you want anymore. But I guess you should be complimented."

Her tone was just all wrong. She was almost spitting her responses at me. I heard no joy coming from Fort Greene, Brooklyn. So if that was the good news, how was she going to receive the bad?

"So, what's the bad news?" she said, her voice almost sounding resigned.

I took a deep breath. "Well, they want me to stay here for a while longer."

I heard an audible sigh. "How much longer is 'a while'?" she asked. I heard no outrage. I thought it still sounded like resignation.

"I don't know, honestly. Probably another three or four months. Maybe a little longer; maybe a little less."

This time the pause, the silence, stretched on interminably, unbearably. I wanted her to be the one to break it.

"Well, all right. You know what? If that's what you want to do, Randy, go for it."

I frowned. I wasn't sure exactly what that meant. "Go for it"? Like an exhortation from a lame high school football coach. That didn't sound like Mikki at all. That certainly wasn't what I was expecting. I was braced for anger, some tears, some painful expressions of grief. Not this. Not "go for it."

"Uh, I'll try to make it back to New York once a month during the rest of my time here." Silence. "Okay?"

"Sure, Randy. That sounds great. Once a month. I'm excited."

Damn, she was giving me the harshest response imaginable—resigned indifference. She was acting like she didn't care when I came back, or how often I went back to visit. What was happening here?

"Mikki?"

"Yes, Randy."

"Uh, what's wrong, babe? I expected you to be more, uh, I don't know . . ."

"Angry?" she offered.

"Yeah, I guess angry."

"You want to know the truth? I guess I've started to get used to my life here without you. So a few more months probably won't make much of a difference."

Now it was my turn to pause. My head was spinning. I put the phone receiver down on the desk and leaned back in my chair. I realized virtually every muscle in my body had been balled into knots for the past five minutes. I tried to relax, thinking that would slow the room down, make it stop orbiting on its axis. This was not the conversation I expected to have with my wife. She had just told me she didn't care whether I returned. How was that possible? Was she bluffing? If not, it didn't sound like I even had a marriage anymore.

"Damn, Mekhi." I swallowed. "That's kinda harsh, isn't it?"

"Harsh? I guess it is kinda harsh. But you know I've never been one to hold my tongue, Randy. I'm just being honest with you. You know, 'keeping it real.'" She said that last in the gruff, put-on voice of a young hip-hopper. So she was so calm, unperturbed right now that she was even joking around with me? I felt a cold line of sweat run down from my left underarm all the way to the waistband of my boxers. Gross. This was not happening. I wanted to try to shake her, to get some more emotion from her, but what I really wanted was to get off the phone.

"All right, Mikki," I said shakily. "Uh, I'll call you, uh, soon. Okay? I, um, gotta go now."

"All right," she said, unaffected, uncaring. "Talk to you soon."

I hung up the phone and stared at the clock. But I didn't really see it. I let out a deep, sad gust of air and slumped back in my chair. I looked down and saw that my hands were trembling. I got that sharp ache in my throat that told me I was about to cry.

I waited for what I thought was a suitably respectful time period before I slid back the covers and headed for my hotel bathroom.

"Excuse me," I said back over my shoulder as I staggered toward the bathroom light.

"Of course," she said back to me. Without even looking back, I knew she was smiling warmly, too warmly, as she so often did in my presence. Paula was a fairly low-level employee in the graphics department at Trier-Stanton's Paris office and she had been sending out take-me signals almost since day one. I was sometimes slightly embarrassed in her presence but several days after my painful conversation with Mikki, Paula and I had shared two bottles of wine at an intimate café, raced back to my hotel room and, with head-spinning alacrity, I became an adulterer.

I stared in the bathroom mirror, checking to see if I looked any different, if perhaps I now had a big, festering Hester Prynn–like scarlet letter plastered on my chest. But all the mirror showed me was a slightly bloodshot, slightly groggy-looking black man whose eyes carried a tinge of sadness.

"Ran-dee," Paula called out to me, putting the harder accent on the second syllable as the French were wont to pronounce my name. "Is everything okay?"

I couldn't lie—the sex had been good. No, more than good. With her energetic bedroom acrobatics and bodily contortions, Paula could probably get an audition with Ringling Brothers.

But—there was always a "but," wasn't there?—her skills weren't even close to enough to ease the thunderous guilt I felt. Of all the people with whom to desecrate the sanctity of my marriage vows, I had picked her? A woman I not only didn't really know, but whose last name

I had never been able to pronounce correctly? It was spelled Bourgogne-Ramatuelle, but my tongue had difficulty wrapping around all that, so I just avoided using her last name. The encounter had been exciting, I couldn't deny that, but far from fulfilling. I thought back to Marie, the tall, stunning model/record company receptionist I had run into a few weeks back. If I was going to slide, shouldn't it have been with someone like her? But then again, maybe someone like her was too dangerous, too enthralling. What about Eliza? I shook my head quickly. Oh, hell no, not Eliza. That'd be as wise as setting myself on fire to stop an itch.

"Ran-dee?" Paula repeated. I heard her muffled footsteps heading toward the bathroom.

"Everything is just wonderful," I said, smiling to her as she stepped into the light. She was so comfortable with her body and her sexuality that she hadn't even bothered to cover herself up, even though I had never *really* seen her naked. That was extremely attractive—and maybe just a little scary. I didn't think I had ever met another woman like her. I'd certainly never slept with one.

I couldn't keep my gaze from sweeping down her body as she leaned jauntily against the door frame. She wasn't very tall, but she still had long legs and a torso that managed to make her look willowy. Her hips and ass, I had been pleased to see, were surprisingly round and full. None of those jutting bones I associated with white girls. In fact, it was a body of which I could easily grow quite fond. I certainly didn't want that to happen.

Paula stepped into the bathroom and invited herself into my arms. I embraced her and let my hands slide down to cup her behind. She sweetly nuzzled my neck and let her left hand drift to my chest, where she softly stroked my nipple. Instantly, I started to harden. I knew she could feel it. She pulled her head back and smiled up at me.

"I am very happy with you, Randy Murphy," she said. The gleaming in her eyes startled me a little. I hoped I wouldn't have any difficulty getting rid of this woman when I was through. But as she reached down and squeezed my thickening member, bringing it to full erection in seconds, I told myself I would leap that hurdle in due time. If I let her go now, all I'd be left with were my depression and bitter loneliness. At least now I could have some momentary feelings of soaring lust to go along with this guilt. She smiled up at me again, her tousled dark hair and full lips exacerbating her natural sensuality. I smiled back at her. She wasn't beautiful, but she had an open, welcoming face. She started kissing my chest and heading southward. No, I wasn't quite through yet. And I sensed that guilt was one of the more malleable of the emotions. With a little mental work, I could probably shape it into something else, something like anger. That wouldn't be too hard, I told myself as I let out an involuntary moan. God, this woman was talented. Maybe all the things I'd ever heard about French women were true. I smiled to myself. Yeah, sure. Just like the black male myth was true, right?

I walked through the next week in a daze. I desperately wanted to call my wife, but I was afraid of the emotional havoc such a conversation might create. I still hadn't managed to work through the guilt I was harboring over my evening of sexual gymnastics with Paula. Part of the guilt lingered because I still got so terribly aroused when I thought of Paula. I knew it was important for me to avoid being alone with her because it wouldn't take much for her to talk me into an encore performance. Talk wouldn't even be necessary. Feeling like I needed to avoid this woman was weak and pathetic to me; feeling weak and pathetic saddened me too, leaving a lethal combination of pitiful emotions.

On Friday afternoon, I heard a soft knock on my office door and looked up to find Eliza peeking in at me.

"Can I come in?" she asked, somewhat hesitantly.

I nodded and waved her in. I had also been avoiding Eliza since we had shared those intimate moments over dinner, so I wasn't eager to hear what she had to say.

"Mind if I sit down?" she asked. She didn't usually ask.

I nodded again and waved toward the chair facing me. My dread was rapidly increasing, though I was trying to appear nonchalant.

"Why have you been keeping your door closed?" she asked. "You never used to close your door before."

I shrugged. I had hoped it wouldn't be that noticeable; leave it to Eliza to call me out on it.

"I don't know. I've just felt like I wanted a little privacy, that's all."

Eliza was watching my face closely. I found it somewhat unnerving. I was tempted to turn away from her, but that would only make it worse. What was she looking for?

"I just felt like I needed to tell you, Randy, that people are starting to get a little concerned about you."

People? Who exactly was "people"? Did she mean herself?

"People?" I repeated.

Eliza shrugged. "Yeah, you know, your colleagues? Some of us have worked around you practically every day for the past seven or eight years. We know when something is wrong with you. Look, I know about what's been happening with your wife and all—"

My head snapped up in worry and suspicion; I studied her closely. Was she spreading all my business around the office?

"—but I certainly haven't told anybody about it," she quickly added, sensing the meaning of my look. "The main thing is, some people have noticed that your work is starting to, uh, like, suffer a little bit. We were just worried, so I thought I'd talk to you about it."

Right away I was leery. This was exactly one of the scenarios I feared after that night with Eliza, after the wine and the intimate talk: that she'd somehow use the information against me. Which Eliza was I sitting across from now, the intimate friend or the cutthroat competitor? How could I know? Maybe I should ask her to wear horns when she meant to do me harm.

"Did anyone happen to mention to you in what ways my work is suffering?" I said, perhaps a bit too testily. I didn't want to chase her away just yet.

"No, not really," she said, shrugging, trying unsuccessfully to remain nonchalant herself. "That's just something I heard, um, a few of the people that work with you talking about. They were saying that you seemed a little distracted of late. I felt like I knew why, but I didn't say anything to them about it. I didn't . . ."

She appeared slightly uncomfortable with what she was saying. She paused and then found renewed conviction.

"Look, Randy. Things got quite, uh, interesting, that night in the restaurant. I'm not going to deny that I was, was, uh, attracted to you. I guess I still am. I don't know." She threw her hair back in a nervous gesture I had seen before. "But we have this really weird competitive thing at the same time that I think will always prevent us from totally trusting each other. That's too bad."

If there was one thing that I appreciated about Eliza, it was her frankness. The lady did not pull many punches. But I wasn't sure how much frankness I could spare at the moment.

"Yeah, we definitely do have our history of competition," I said.

I wasn't sure whether I wanted to acknowledge the attraction thing. That was a slippery slope that I already appeared to be heading down. I didn't need to push anything with Eliza that would accelerate my descent.

I smiled. "I've decided that I'm going to trust you, Eliza. If you say that you haven't told anybody else about my business, then I believe that you haven't. If you say that others believe my work is suffering, then I'll make sure it doesn't happen anymore. And I'll leave it at that."

I knew she had probably told half my co-workers already, but I also knew that if I set it up this way, she'd be so chastened by her indiscretion that I'd have an upper hand in our future dealings. Our eyes met. There was an intensity to her look that I couldn't quite read. Did she want more, like an admission that I also found her attractive? If that's what she wanted, she wasn't going to get it. That would be begging the next step, wouldn't it? After both of us acknowledge our mutual attraction, human nature dictates that we act on it, doesn't it?

Finally, Eliza spoke. "Okay." She said it quickly, telling me I had effectively made my point, that she understood and was ready to move on. She popped up from the chair and headed for the door. I put my head down and strained to keep it there to avoid watching her ass. I knew she had on a short, tight skirt, and I didn't doubt that she'd be expecting me to look. I waited until her footsteps were out of the room, then I snapped my head up to get a last-second glance. To my horror, she was staring directly at me, apparently waiting for me to get my look. She caught the startled expression on my face and she laughed. I felt the blood rush to my face and I was glad that she was too far away to notice. Eliza gave me a little wave, a little knowing smile, and made a saucy pivot on her pumps. If I had been keeping a running tally, I knew she would have considered herself the victor of that round.

I tried to slow my breathing as I dialed the numbers to my Brooklyn home. I was relieved that I still remembered what the number was. A part of me was hoping that Mikki had gone to church so that I could converse with the answering machine rather than my wife. But that would only be delaying the inevitable; it was better to get this over with.

I still had her incredibly memorable statement rattling around in my head, damaging every tender emotion that appeared in its path up there: "I guess I've started to get used to my life here without you. So a few more months probably won't make much of a difference."

I shook my head to try to purge that thought. I heard the phone ring six times, then my own voice came on the line to say no one was home. I sighed and started running through the message I would leave, telling myself that the tone had to be just right. I got the beep, took a deep breath and started talking.

"Hello, Mikki. You know who this is. I haven't talked to you in about two weeks. When was the last time we went—"

"Hello! Hello! Randy?!" Mikki's voice filled my ears. She sounded out of breath.

"Hey, babe," I said. "You didn't go to church, huh?"

"Uh, no, I haven't made it there in a few weeks," she said, still breathing heavy. "Gosh, I'm a little out of breath. Guess I'm out of shape."

I chuckled loud enough for her to hear. "Nah, I bet your shape looks wonderful."

There was a pause. "Well, thank you, Randy," she finally said. I couldn't really read her tone, but I almost felt like I heard annoyance. Now she was annoyed at my compliments? This was crazy.

"So, how're things going there? How's the shop?" I asked, hoping that maybe small talk would loosen her up.

"Everything's fine, Randy."

I could feel the chill all the way across the Atlantic. Mikki had never much appreciated small talk—neither did I, actually—but when she threw my name in there, she was conveying more than annoyance at the small talk. She was telling me that she really didn't want to talk to me at all, that my call was disturbing her. I tried to swallow the giant lump in my throat and push onward.

"Uh, so, how's the weather?" I winced as soon as it left my lips. The weather? How incredibly lame was that? As if Mikki would engage me in a lengthy conversation about the weather.

I heard a heavy sigh. "The weather? Come on, Randy. Do you really care what the weather's like here? Let's cut to the chase, shall we? You called because you need my approval for you to stay over there for another six months, or whatever it is, right? You want me to tell you that this is wonderful for your career and that I'm behind you, whatever you do, right? Okay, if that's what you need to hear, then I'll say it. Randy, this is wonderful for your career and I'm behind you, whatever you do."

I could hear her heavy breathing. I wondered if she could hear mine. I was so stunned that I didn't know what to say. She seemed so far away from me, so unreachable. I didn't know how to bring her back, or where I needed to go to even find her. Her bristling anger was evident, but even that I didn't completely understand. I didn't feel like I had done enough to her to warrant all this—well, I *had* cheated on her, but she couldn't know about that, right? I know common lore said wives had that intuition, that sixth sense, but that could not possibly be what was going on here. Her hostility was glistening up in my face long before I brought Paula into my bed.

"Randy, you there?" Mikki asked. There still was no softness in her voice, none of the welcoming warmth I was accustomed to getting from her. I had no idea what to say to her.

"Yeah, uh, I'm here." I paused. "Damn, Mikki. I wasn't calling you for all that. I was just calling you because you're my wife and I love you and I haven't spoken to you for two weeks, which is probably the longest time we've ever gone without speaking since we met five years ago. So I don't understand why you're jumping down my throat like that."

"You don't understand? Is that what you said? You don't know why I'm acting this way. You have no idea, huh?"

I took another deep breath. I knew she was about to go into her abandonment speech. I had bumblingly pushed her into it.

"Well, let me tell you what this all looks like in my world, Mr. Randy Murphy. Yeah, I know you love and miss me and all that, but you are not here with me. I am here alone, in this scary city, in this big 'ole house, all by my damn self. Talking on the telephone just doesn't cut it, you know? 'Cause when we hang up, there's just gonna be me and these four walls. What was your solution to all that? You said I should call your best friend. Somehow Marcus was supposed to comfort me or something in your place, right? But Randy, you know what? I'm not married to Marcus. I'm married to you. And you are nowhere to be found for me right now."

Each of her words was burning through my gut, rustling up a firestorm in my stomach and sending a sharp ache to my head. She had laid it all out there, all her feelings, all her frustration, and how lame I had sounded in sending someone else to her to do my job. What exactly did I expect Marcus to be able to do, anyway? Was he going to slide into her bed late at night and hold her when the windows started to creak and the sirens went screaming by outside? Or even just to look into her eyes and tell her she's beautiful? No, that was my job. And I was not there to do my job. For perhaps the first time, I started to find the empathy to see this from Mikki's perspective, if only just a little. But it was enough to make me feel awful about what I was putting her through. And I felt particularly awful about cheating on her. That was so predictable, so clichéd, so common. Move to Paris for a few months and hop into bed with some hot Parisian chick. Not much originality in that. I hated feeling common and clichéd.

"Mikki, I'm so sorry, babe. I'm going to call the New York office tomorrow and see if I can't find a way to come home very soon. Okay?" I said this last word so tentatively, so weakly, that I wasn't even sure if she heard it. I almost didn't want her to hear me sounding so weak and pathetic, but I also knew she needed to hear the deep sorrow in my voice.

Mikki sighed again. "Randy, I don't want you to come rushing home if you don't feel like you're ready to come. This is a decision that you need to make yourself, not one that you make because I said something to you over the telephone. If it didn't occur to you before this conversation that you should make that call to New York, then maybe you shouldn't make it."

Now I was confused. Did she want me to come home or not? I was getting a throbbing headache to go along with my roiling stomach.

"But I *do* want to come home, Mikki." I knew I sounded like a small child pleading with his mother.

"Randy, come on now. Be truthful. Were you thinking about calling the New York office before you picked up the phone and called me this morning?"

I felt the beads of sweat pop out from my nose and forehead, just that fast. Damn, it had gotten hot in the room. I looked around the space and felt like it was closing in on me, getting smaller, more constricting. I needed some air. She had just asked me a question that I didn't want to answer.

"Well, I had been thinking before, that there was a problem here, like you were there alone and very upset. Then when you came I knew something was wrong. So I figured I probably—no, definitely—needed to, uh, do something about it. Like come home . . . or something."

"Come home or something?" Of course, Mikki had picked up right away on my indecision, my lameness. This was turning into the conversation from hell. Maybe I shouldn't have called her after all.

"Randy, it doesn't sound like you answered my question. But that's all right, because that's just as good as an answer. I guess the bottom line is this: don't come home if you think you're doing me any favors, okay? You really need to check yourself, you know what I'm saying? You've become so self-centered that it's not even possible to look at your actions from somebody else's perspective and see the impact it has on them. What did SWV say in that song? 'It's all about you.' But I really don't want to drag out this conversation any longer. I'll talk to you soon, I guess. Bye, Randy."

I heard the click. But I didn't move for at least thirty seconds. I dangled my legs over the side of the bed, threw the covers into a jumbled heap; my heart was pounding, my head throbbing, and my palms gripped the phone as tightly as the jaws of a well-trained pit bull. Slowly I placed the phone back on the base. I slid back into the bed, unconsciously curling myself into a ball. I pulled the covers up to my eyes because now I was shivering uncontrollably. I closed my eyes and felt sleep take over. Just before I drifted off, I wondered if maybe I was starting to go crazy. Maybe I had imagined everything that had just happened. Maybe it was a dream.

No, make that a nightmare.

She

"Oooooooh! Scandalous!"

I swear, sometimes I wonder why I tell Angelou anything. I don't need to hear, "oooooh, scandalous." Damn. I need some good, solid advice. And a prescription. And an altar call. Because right now, the only three things that are going to keep me from going straight to hell is a good talking to, some Prozac, and some serious prayer. Getting the drugs won't be a problem; I can just set up an appointment with a shrink with a liberal prescription pad. And I plan on being in the front pew at the Varick Memorial Church on Sunday so that when altar call does come, I can be the first one on my knees asking God to forgive me.

But right now? I am not feeling Angie's communication skills because girlfriend is not helping me figure out how to climb out of this mess right here. See, I slept with Marcus. No—let me rephrase. I fucked Marcus. And I enjoyed it. And then, with his scent still on my inner thighs, I told Randy to stay his ass in Paris, for all I care. See what I mean? Talk. Drugs. Jesus.

"Wait—so, let me get this straight," Angelou begged. "You invited Marcus to go with you to church and ol' boy showed up at your doorstep to pick you up and instead of going to Varick you two hit it?" Her eyes were as wide as saucers, her left hand draped her mouth. Angelou was gape-jawed and, finally, speechless—a rarity for her.

"We didn't just hit it, girl. We hit it," I said. Then I did the strangest thing; I laughed. A strong, hardy guffaw. I can't tell you where it came from, really, maybe from nervous energy, perhaps from the sheer excitement of it all. I mean, I'm scared witless of the fact that I cheated on my husband—with his best friend, no less—but I'm all butterflies and roses because I'm in love. I think. Well, at least this is what I remember it feeling like when I was falling in love—stomach tied up in knots, giggling at a whim, constantly thinking about him, constantly wanting to be with him, wondering where he is when he's not around, never wanting him to leave when he is. I just want to be with him, touch him, feel him, smell him, laugh with him, stare at him, rub him, hug him. Love him.

"Excuse me, honey, but this does not appear to be a time for giggles," Angelou said, looking at me incredulously. "You fucked Marcus."

"I know."

"Mikki," Angelou said, leaning in so close to my face I could smell the scent of the peppermint Tic-Tac she'd just popped into her mouth. "You fucked Marcus."

"I know."

"You know, huh? What about Randy?"

"What about Randy?"

"What do you mean, 'What about Randy?' He's your husband! Are you getting a divorce?"

"Well, damn," I said, snapping to attention. "How the hell did we get to divorce?"

"How did I get to divorce, Mikki? You fucked Marcus. If Randy finds out—"

"Randy is not going to find out," I said quickly, curtly. "Not until I'm ready for him to find out."

Which was not going to be anytime soon. Shoot, I'm still trying to figure out what I just did. Ain't no way I'd be able to tell Randy what I just did with his best friend—much less explain why it happened. I mean, I can't even tell you why I had sex with Marcus. I don't know if I did it because I wanted to, or because the passion made me lose my fucking mind, or if I was screwing him to get back at Randy, or a combination of all three.

All I know is he showed up to my door in his church clothes—had on this bad ass Donna Karan suit, single-breasted, four-button, light gray, with faint off-white pinstripes. And closed-toe sandals—black. And sunglasses—the cool kind, with the wraparound pitch-black shades. Everything fit . . . just . . . right. I was so busy watching his arm muscle rub against the material that I almost forgot to say "Hello" when I opened the door, and he leaned in, gave me a kiss on my cheek, and brushed past me and into the apartment foyer. It was the first time I'd seen him since arriving back from my disastrous trip to Paris. He was busy, you know—work and baby-mama-drama. And I was trying to deal with the whole Daddy-Mommy situation and trying to figure things out for myself. We played phone tag for a few days, and then finally we caught up with each other late Thursday night. I told him about how much I thought about him while I lay in my husband's arms, how much I missed hearing his voice. How confused I was by the whole thing—sure that I was falling out of love with Randy but unsure about my fling with his best friend. How much I hated my father right now for breaking my mother's heart. That I had a brother—some boy that was busting up my long-happy home. Marcus was a great listener, an apt counselor. By conversation's end, we'd both decided that going to church would help lift the loads we were carrying around— he with his ex-wife, me with my husband and parents, us with each other. And then we promised each other we'd sit down over a nice lunch and figure out what we were going to do about us.

"Umm. Hello back at ya," I said breathlessly, trying quite unsuccessfully to contain my smile as I took in how beautiful he looked standing in my door. "You going to church or to a fashion shoot?"

Marcus looked down at his body as if he'd just realized how good he looked, then turned his attention to me, looking me up and down. His tongue flicked at his bottom lip, then he bit it as his eyes finally met mine. "Well, you know, I was trying to make sure I could keep up with you, with your fine self."

Um, I did look good, y'all. I was wearing this beautiful rosy pink strapless number—fitted, but not too tight, long, but not too far past the knee, with a back split that showed just enough of my calf to tease, but not over-expose. Found it in a little boutique in Soho, my second home. I had already put on one high-heeled black sandal by the time I let Marcus in; so enthralled was I by the way he looked that I had forgotten I was holding the other in my hand until I almost fell trying to walk after him into the living room.

"Whoa, you okay there, cutie?" Marcus said, catching me as I stumbled toward the hardwood floor. He looked down at my hand, then at my feet. "Come here—sit down on the couch and let me help you with your sandal."

I gladly obliged. Twirled my little ass (well, it's hardly little, but you understand what I mean) onto the couch and offered up my pedicured right foot. God, his hands were so soft against my skin. He took my foot into his hand and promptly started to massage the padded skin just under my toes. It tickled and felt like heaven all at the same time. I didn't know whether to laugh or moan, so I laid back in the sofa and did both.

"You have beautiful feet," Marcus said. And then he set it off. He kissed my toes, one, by one, by one, by one. And then licked the last. I squirmed into my couch. My smile was uncontrollable.

"Marcus," I said, nearly whispering. "What are you doing?"

"I'm kissing your beautiful feet."

"Marcus?" I said, whispering again.

"Yes?" he said back, between sucking and kissing and licking and rubbing.

"You probably shouldn't be doing that, seeing as we're going to church and all," I whispered, a strained smile fighting against my laughter. It tickled, but it felt good as hell, too. I didn't want him to stop. But I knew he needed to stop.

He didn't. Wouldn't.

And I couldn't.

We were sweaty, sex-funky, twisted in a heap on the living room carpet when the phone rang. Probably wasn't nobody but that damn Angelou, calling to harrass me about Randy and Marcus, or my sister to tell me some more jacked-up news about my folks. I didn't want to talk to either one of them—didn't want them bringing down my high. I was feeling simply glorious and I didn't want to leave Marcus's embrace, or stop feeling his fingers running up and down my thigh, or his super-soft feet rubbing against mine. I wanted to drink him—every ounce—and talking to Angelou or Zaria would seriously mess up my thirst. So I decided to just let the answering machine pick it up.

Well, what did I do that for?

It was Randy.

I think Marcus heard his voice first; his body went limp, his hands stiff. I knew something was wrong, but it didn't click until I heard "I haven't talked to you in the last two weeks." I swear I flew up from that floor and over to the phone in the foyer so fast Michael Johnson would have been envious. I broke a record, y'all. I had no idea what I was going to say to my husband. I'd just had sex with Randy's best friend, and now, just minutes later, I was accepting a phone call from him. The guilt was written in big bold scarlet letters across both our faces; Randy's words made crystal clear to us that we'd just fucked and fucked up. I didn't know what I was going to say to Randy, but I knew I needed to get away from Marcus and save him, too—from the humiliation of having to hear Randy leave a sappy, corny love message to me as we lay. And I had to save myself, from the funky pall gathering at the pit of my stomach, the dull, achy pain settling at the base of my skull. I'd cheated on my husband—had committed the ultimate sin against our relationship. I was unfaithful to him. And there was no turning back. No matter if Randy and I worked things out, and this was looking extremely remote, I'd given my most precious gift to my husband—myself—to another man. What had I done to Randy? To me? To Marcus?

I had to stop him before he left a message, talk to him. I was dizzy from running, from screwing, from nervousness.

Until Randy got to talking—about my shop, my body, the weather. Huh? What the hell did he know about my shape? The last time we'd made love—oh, sorry, I mean *attempted* to make love—he couldn't even get excited enough about me to keep his erection. Which means that he had no right to comment on my figure. It obviously didn't excite him. Now, I know it didn't go down all that well in Paris, but we'd never, ever let anger stop us from communicating—not for no damn two weeks. Two hours, maybe. Two days once, when he hauled off and called Angelou a bitch to her face for telling him he didn't know what he was talking about. Long story. But two weeks? Scandalous. Particularly when he started it out by commenting on my figure, which, might I remind, he hadn't seen in two weeks because he was clean across the other side of the world.

Just hearing Randy's voice was pissing me off.

I didn't want him talking about my figure. I didn't want him asking me how my business was going. I didn't want him to waste his long-distance phone card minutes trying to engage me in small talk. And before I even realized how mad I was, I was laying him out—my anger further fueled by his trying to fake the funk like he couldn't understand why a sistah was pissed.

The truth of it was that with each word that dripped from Randy's lips, I longed that much more for Marcus. He was here, in my arms, on my skin, in my mouth, my bed (well, floor), my body. His whispers were in my ear, his thoughts on my mind, his feelings on my heart, fluttering about my chest. Marcus . . . is . . . mine. Gloriously.

I made up my mind right then and there that I wanted Randy to stay in Paris until I could figure out just how to work all this out. I knew Randy wanted to be there, and so did he. It would just take a little prodding and a few angry words on my behalf to convince him that he really didn't want to come back to Brooklyn.

"I guess the bottom line is this: don't come home if you think you're doing me any favors, okay?"

And I hung up.

Just like that.

But my legs were stiff, my hand stuck to the phone receiver. Although my heart was telling me to run back into Marcus's arms, my mind was asking me if I'd gone completely mad. In a matter of seconds, I was running through a mental series of really hard questions. Had I just lurched myself further in the direction of divorce? Was it over between me and Randy? Did I hate him? Or was I just mad at him? Or was I falling in love with someone else? Did I even love Marcus? Did I really need another man in my bed? Would Randy lose his natural born mind if he ever found out another man slept with his wife? You know how guys are; they can tramp with other women until the cows jump over the moon, and then turn around and convince us that it didn't mean anything, it was just a physical thang. But dammit, don't let us get ours. We'd be deemed hoes immediately—scandalous tricks who defiled the sanctity of the relationship to take up with some unworthy nigger with a big dick. And you know that's what it always comes down to, don't you? The big dick. Oh, yeah—a woman couldn't possibly cheat on her mate with another man because he is a better person, or a better listener or a better whatever. A sistah who takes up with another man on her mate's watch is simply mining for a bigger dick, or so that's what men think. Sex as sport, which man has the bigger, better, bestest penis. Brothers can't handle the idea that some other brother might be laying the pipe better than he is.

Oh, God. Randy would lose his mind. I slept with his best friend. And his best friend knew that I'd cheated on my husband, which was practically just as bad—if not in some cases, worse—than if Randy found out about the rendezvous some other way. I mean, come on—Randy has his self-respect, you know. Wouldn't he feel like a punk if his best friend knew his wife was gaming him? Wouldn't his best friend think I was a trick, too? Did I want to face Marcus right now, this minute?

Not really. All at once, I was embarrassed and ashamed to be standing in the middle of my foyer, naked, in front of the man my husband calls his boy. Marcus stood beside us at our wedding, held our rings, our vows. I couldn't lift my eyes to look in his direction. My feet were glued to the floor. I was cold. I wanted out of there.

I folded my hands across my breasts and made the decision to walk quickly through the living room and to the bathroom to grab a towel and find a way to politely tell Marcus I needed to be alone. But he'd beat me to it. Marcus had already climbed into his underwear, pants and shirt, and was collecting his suit jacket and sandals from the floor. He was headed for the bathroom.

"I'm going to, uh, get dressed and go," he said quietly. "I have a few errands to run, and then I need to get back home to do some work for a case I'm in court for tomorrow. I'll, um, call you later, okay?"

He closed the bathroom door before I had a chance to answer.

I walked up the stairs, my legs stiff and heavy like cinderblocks. Into my bed I climbed—buried myself under my comforter and sheets and cats.

There was nothing more to say.

I heard Marcus quietly close the front door behind him.

"Girl," Angelou whispered. "I don't know what you gonna do to get outta this one."

Frankly, neither did I.

He

If I had been on a witness stand a year later, being grilled by an attorney who wanted to know why I picked up the telephone the next day and called the stunning Marie Bautista, I would have been red-faced and speechless. I had no explanation, no rationale—I just did it. She had been rooting around in my subconscious since the day I met her, but I had been strong enough to resist the urges to reach out to her. But after the conversation with my wife, I was sapped. I knew not whether I was coming or going, as the saying goes.

Immediately I recalled the name of Marie's company: "Chaud. That means hot." I couldn't forget that if I tried.

"Hello?" I heard her voice and caught a flashing image of her breathtaking face. What in the world was I doing?

"Hello? Marie? I don't know if you remember me. My name is—"

"Randolph Murphy," she said, finishing my sentence for me. For that split second, just that tiny sliver of time it took her to say my first name and last, I was more flattered than I had ever been in my life. "Of course I remember you, darling. How could I forget such a lovely man? You are still here in Paris?"

I felt the blush blooming on my cheeks. I was glad I was in my office, with the door closed.

"Yes, I'm still here in Paris." That statement made me think of my wife again. I fought hard to push any thoughts of Mikki far away. At times like this, I wondered if the minister had implanted a chip in my brain while we were repeating our wedding vows, forcing images of my wife to flood my thoughts whenever I was tempted to stray.

"I presume you are still married?" Marie said. I blushed again. She certainly got right to the point, didn't she?

I took a deep breath. What did I want to happen here, anyway? Scratch that—I knew damn well what I wanted to happen. It was almost too thrilling for even the raciest regions of my imagination to wonder what her skin, her form, would look like unclothed.

"Yeah, I'm still married. But I was thinking about you a lot and I wanted to give you a ring."

"How long have you been away from your wife?"

Damn, what was she getting at? Was she trying to ask me whether this was a booty call?

"Uh, well, I've been in Paris for a few months. My wife came to visit a few weeks ago." I wanted to ask her why she wanted to know, but I also wanted to move the conversation off my wife as soon as possible.

"So maybe you're not calling me just because you are terribly lonely and—how shall I put it?—horny?"

Wow. She just came right out with it. Yeah, of course I was calling her for those very reasons.

"No, of course not," I said. "That would be terribly crass, wouldn't it? If I was merely looking for company or for sex, there are plenty of places to find those things in this city. But no, that's certainly not the reason I'm calling you, Marie. I'm almost hurt that you would ask me that."

The feigned sensitivity and vulnerability usually worked well with American women, so I thought I'd try it across the Atlantic.

"Oh, my, the American's feelings have been hurt by the mean French lady, huh? Well, Mr. Murphy, I'm sure you'll get over your pain," she said, chuckling. I winced. Damn, she blocked that shot into the stands.

"I was just, uh, wondering"—come on and spit it out—"if, like, we could maybe meet again and talk. That's what I really need in this city, someone I can talk to."

I had just thought of that one, but it sounded pretty good. At least it did to me. It might even have been a little true, though that was hardly necessary in the situation.

"Oh, is that all you need? Talk?" Marie said playfully. Was she teasing me? Was she flirting with me? Her frankness had put me slightly off guard, knocked me off my stride a little. Should I go for honesty right now, too, or continue the little dance with her?

"Well, a beautiful face to look at never hurt either," I said, opting to reach for a little of both.

"Yes, I also believe that's a good—what is it?—motto. Some talk and some beauty. What else is there, right, Mr. Murphy?"

Oh, so she was baiting me to continue the dance, right? I was only happy to oblige.

"Well, I can think of a few other things that would serve as a wonderful complement to those two," I said.

There was a pause. We were both waiting.

"Okay. Like what?" Marie said. She was clearly playing along now, nudging me on to see where I would take it.

I took a deep breath. This response was crucial. I didn't want to push the flirtation too hard, but she obviously was expecting something saucy yet clever.

"Well, in addition to engaging our brains with talk and our eyes with beauty, there are some other senses that can't be left ignored," I said, hoping that she didn't pick up on the fact that engaging the brain with talk wasn't exactly one of the senses.

But Marie was having too much fun now to nitpick. "You're right," she said giddily. "I'm a firm believer that we should engage as many senses as possible as much as possible. That keeps them all sharp."

I felt like I could hear her smiling. Oh, Lordy, I remembered the glint in her eyes as she sat across the table at the café. I now desperately wanted to see that glint again, even if it did remind me of my wife a wee bit. But I was so intoxicated by the lavish attentions of this funny, gorgeous woman that I had nowhere near the discipline needed to pull back at that moment. Onward I plunged.

"I think you are a genius, Miss Bautista. Like right now, for instance, I'm sitting here gently stroking the arm of my leather desk chair. I guess that means my sense of touch has been underused lately. And I'm sniffing around the room, catching the faint scent of the Cool Water cologne I put on this morning. But that cologne isn't doing nearly enough for me. I want to smell even more lovely scents. And I can't leave out the all-important taste. I'm hungry as hell right now and I'm not tasting anything. What I think I need more than anything is to eat."

I heard my breathing when I stopped. It was too audible, but I didn't know how to bring it down a few notches without fainting.

"Mmm-mmm-mmm. You are too much," Marie said, giggling. "All right, all right. You've convinced me. You don't need to, uh, twist my leg anymore."

Now it was my turn to giggle. "I think you mean 'twist my arm,' " I said.

"Oh, of course, it is the *arm* that gets twisted. Not the leg. I always get that wrong."

"Maybe I can give you a crash course in stupid American clichés," I said. "There are a million of them. Maybe we can start tomorrow night. We need to get on top, uh, I mean, we need to get on it, as soon as possible."

I winced again at that last line. I didn't want to sound so transparent as to be silly—though it would be difficult to be more transparent than I'd already been. I had just told the woman I needed more than anything to eat. Marie knew I wasn't talking about a hamburger.

She agreed to meet me the next evening at a café on the boulevard where we first collided. The setting could not have been made more romantic.

That night, my emotional state veered wildly from deliriously excited about my hot date to enormously depressed and conflicted about my crumbling marriage. I didn't need a marriage counselor to tell me that the best way to finish off a troubled relationship was to form an intimate attachment to someone else—particularly if that someone else happened to be so much more beautiful and exotic and clever than the original partner. As that thought reached my consciousness, I realized with alarm that it was the first time I had been willing to admit to myself that another woman was more beautiful than Mikki.

I had come to discover over the years that men can perform some impressively elaborate mental gymnastics to convince ourselves of the surpassing beauty of our mates. It was something we needed to believe about our women and thus ourselves—that we were worthy and important and handsome and talented enough to attract the cream of the female crop. A few things were necessary to keep the thought alive: one, we would find it worthwhile to make as few direct comparisons as possible between our mates and other women. This was especially true with celebrity or famously beautiful women. The male would admire every inch of the celebrity's face and body, but he'd sprint like an Olympic champion to avoid putting his wife up next to her. Two, we'd need to keep handy a fresh image of our wife at her most attractive—even if that was fifteen years and thirty-five pounds ago—if ever anything close to a comparison was going to be made. It was like those newspaper columnists who continued for decades to put an ancient picture of themselves at their spry young best above their columns.

So now that I had made the comparison and Mikki had come up short—not far short, I might add—what did it all mean? If I was no longer willing to fly through the gymnastics anymore to protect my wife's pulchritudinous honor, did that mean I no longer loved her? In fact, it was the first time since I hit Paris that I had been willing to engage the question of whether my feelings toward Mikki had indeed changed in that fundamental way. How does one discern the difference between dissipated love and growing animosity? I was becoming more upset and frustrated at the changes my wife was putting me through and I approached conversations with her now with a sense of dread, but did that all mean I no longer loved the woman? How would I know? Who would come along and provide me with the answers? And, more important, did I need to have some answers before I sat down at a café and smiled goofily up in Marie Bautista's lovely face?

As I watched Marie approach my table, I offhandedly wondered why I was now grappling with a sudden case of jangled nerves. I could feel the moist clamminess start to spread across my palms and I could nearly hear the throbbing of my heart, but it wasn't necessarily the approaching presence of this beautiful woman that was the culprit—i.e., those old adolescent fears about saying and doing the right thing. What I was frightened about was what would happen if the evening ended like I suspected it might—with me handing my heart to this woman to do with as she pleased. And after that would come another date, and another, and then the possibility that I might not ever want to ask for my heart back. That could not be allowed to happen. After all, I was on my way back to New York City soon, right?

"You look wonderful," Marie said breezily as she sat down next to me. I had expected her to sit opposite me, but she didn't even pause before she sat down in the chair to my right, and her left leg immediately snuggled up against my right leg. Before Marie had even ordered a drink, before I had even finished drinking in the fresh sweetness of her perfume, I was feeling a thickening in my crotch. Oh, this evening was going to be deadly.

"You look pretty damn wonderful yourself," I said, giving her the big goofy grin I knew I couldn't hold back.

It was all so perfect, the seduction so clearly visible before me. Maybe I'd teach her the cliché about taking candy from a baby—that's how easy this was going to be.

So three hours later, as I rode back to my hotel in a taxi, I could not comprehend how grandly I must have screwed up to warrant the kind of dismissal I got from Marie. She had done it so effortlessly, so matter-of-factly, like shooing away a lingering fly, that I almost believed I had been set up. Like Marie was some sort of spy hired by Mikki to see how far her poor, clueless, horny husband would go to slip into the bed of a beautiful stranger. And I had failed—oh, how miserably I had failed—the spy test. I was practically a drooling puppy when we finally hit the front door of her apartment, which was in a seedy neighborhood in the far northern reaches of the city, much farther north than the Moulin Rouge cabaret and the bohemian craziness of Montmartre that I had visited with my office colleagues during our first weekend in Paris. I didn't even know the arrondissements—Paris's numbering system for its neighborhoods—went as high as eighteen. I thought that the slow, intimate mating dance had proceeded spectacularly, that this ripe, young, sweet-smelling essence of woman was poised, trembling, ready to offer her tendermost secrets to me for the plucking. But the dance had ended not with throbbing expressions of passion but with me being tripped and rudely slammed to the ground.

"Okay, now that I am here safely, you must leave," she had said less than a minute after we had crossed her apartment threshold. I had practically choked from the shock.

"Leave?" I repeated, not believing I had heard her correctly. And she had been so willing to play along with my wildly flirtatious sex talk.

"Yes, Mr. Randolph Murphy, you must leave now. You didn't think that I would make love to you, did you?"

I focused most immediately on the phrasing of the question, rather than the question itself. She'd said it in a way that made her the active doer, not the passive receiver. In other words, her conception of love-making was that it was something she did to somebody else. I felt a shiver pass through me at the deliciousness of that thought. But wait—it was not being offered to me. In fact, I wasn't even being allowed to drink in any more of her presence. She was tossing me out.

"Make love?" I repeated that phrase, too. "What do you mean, Marie?"

Of course I knew damn well what she meant, but I thought playing dumb might buy me a few more minutes—as if she just needed more time to return to her senses. But playing dumb only seemed to increase her sudden annoyance.

"So now you don't know what make love means, is that what you're telling me?" she said, laughing at me. "Oh, you are very funny. You are a—wait, what is it?—a character? Yes, a character. Or what's the other one? A card? Is that it? But that doesn't sound correct. A card. Anyway, I think you know exactly what I mean. Don't you?"

"But, Marie. Does—do—why does it have to be so, uh, fast? Can't we just talk some more, or something?" I sounded whiney and desperate now. I knew that most women would not find this appealing. When they heard the whine, they most *certainly* were not opening up the legs.

I thought I saw anger flash across her eyes. I hoped I was wrong.

"Okay, Randy, I'm getting sleepy now. I have to get up in the morning for church."

Church? I hadn't heard her mention anything about church. I sensed that she was lying to me. She was pulling two of the tricks out of the bag at the same time—fatigue and church. She must have suddenly considered me an extreme case, in need of a thorough and ignoble dismissal. I thought about challenging her on the church thing, but I knew it wouldn't yield me anything, even if I turned out to be right. It would only make things worse.

"Damn, Marie. I don't understand." I had consciously pulled the whine out of my voice. Now I was shooting for confused. If she allowed me to continue, I hoped soon to get to outraged—as if she had guaranteed me some pussy and was now reneging on the contract. But she shot down confused with a quick bow shot directly to the crotch.

"What is there to not understand?" she said. "I don't want to sleep with you. That's obviously what you want, right? That's what you thought would happen here, right? You probably wouldn't have even wanted to come all the way up here with me in the taxi if you didn't think we'd wind up in my bed. So I'm saying, 'No!' That's all. You can go back to your room in the Saint-Germain and think about your wife."

With that, she gave me a backhanded wave of the hand, the way she'd probably chase away a misbehaving cat. The wave was in the direction of her front door. I instantly felt the humiliation of a thousand rejections, all crashing down on my head. I knew she'd get to the wife eventually, and I'd been right. She'd saved it for the final flourish, the victorious closing statement. She'd used Mikki like an exclamation point. My eyes immediately dropped to the floor. I couldn't look at her anymore; it hurt. More than anything in the world, at that moment I wanted to be gone, away from her, from her tiny, dank, little apartment in this dark, gloomy neighborhood. Maybe it was even time to be gone from the entire amusement park ride of a city. Maybe it was time to go back to Brooklyn. After all, no scene with Mikki could ever be as bad as the one I had just lived through. Mikki didn't lunge for my self-respect and harshly pry it away from me. Or at least she hadn't yet.

She

I really didn't want to see him. I mean, he'd cheated on my mom; made a baby with some other woman and allowed the little bastard to call her phone and harass her—reminding her that her husband tipped out on her and dipped his dick where it didn't belong. Now, I love Dad, that'll never change. But right about now, I can't like him. At all. He made Mommy cry, and me, too. And all the things that I thought made him a good father—his love, his dedication, his ability to step up and be a responsible man for his family—have been thrown into question by the fact that he left his home-wrecking whore knocked up with a manchild that he never, ever even acknowledged existed, much less took responsiblity for. He couldn't possibly live up to the image I'd created for him. Our family couldn't either, for that matter. For the first time in my life, I realized that he ain't Ozzie, Mommy's not Harriet, and I damn sure ain't the Beaver.

This is what Daddy wanted to make clear over brunch, which I finally agreed to have with him after making him beg me over the answering machine for the last two weeks to just hear him out. Shit, to tell you the truth, he'd still be begging if I wasn't so confused about Marcus and too afraid to sit with myself for longer than half an hour at a time. No, I had no intentions of telling Daddy what I'd done. I am, after all, still his daughter and though we share a lot—well, used to anyway—I've never talked to him about sex, you know? I'm well into my 20s and I still blush when love scenes come on the TV screen while

Dad is in my presence. There's just some things to which daddies aren't privy, and their daughters' sexual proclivities and cheating ways are at the top of that list. But I needed the company. And to deal with somebody else's problems, instead of thinking about my own. And Daddy promised to tell me the whole story behind the whore and her bastard, and I really wanted to hear this shit, even if I couldn't stand my father's ass.

"She was so beautiful, so sweet and kind." Daddy didn't waste any time cutting to the chase. We were at some dive of a diner in Harlem. He didn't even seem nervous or ashamed. Ordered a big ol' plate of porgies and grits and got to grubbing as he told me about the nurse who'd worked at the bakery and took care of him when he suffered an asthma attack on the cake line. "We didn't start out looking for a relationship," Daddy continued. "It just, well, it just happened."

I was using my straw to spin the ice cubes in my orange juice. I wasn't hungry. I was indifferent. Daddy was rambling.

"I didn't find out about Jason until he called your mama. She quit the bakery and I assumed it was because I told her that under no circumstances did I intend to leave my wife for her. I ended it, baby, and she left. And that was the end of it, as far as I was concerned. I never did see her around—not until years later, at the hospital, when your mother had her first back operation. I'd gone to get your mama some ice chips, you know, her throat was dry. And who did I run into in the hallway but Delphine. She was holding this little boy's hand—had to be 'bout six or seven at the time. We ain't said nothing to one another, just ' 'Scuse me.' And she walked on down the hallway and I walked down the hallway and we didn't see each other no more."

Daddy was quiet for a minute. I was shifting in my seat. My head hurt, and I was starting to get cramps—and just for a minute I was saying a silent "Thank you" to God because you know Marcus and I didn't use any protection that day and I was scared shitless that this whole affair thing that we started was going to blow up in our faces in the form of a crumb-snatcher. And then what was I going to do? Have an abortion? Have the kid? Oh yeah, that would have been a good one—giving birth to a child that was conceived with my husband's best friend while my husband was off working in Paris. Who would take care of it, me and Marcus? Huh—I hadn't even talked to Marcus since it happened, which was exactly five days, three hours and ten minutes ago, if my watch is working right today. Been talking to each other's answering machines. And if I didn't know any better, I'd think he was calling mine when he knew I wouldn't be home, which is exactly what I was doing to his ass. I'm not ready to deal with this just yet. But yay for the cramps . . . my bad. I digressed. Where was I? Oh, right, right —not giving a water drop's chance in hell about why my father cheated.

"You know, your mama and I were doing okay at the time, I guess," he said, taking a sip of water from his glass. He swallowed hard, like he'd just taken a shot of Cuervo. "Things had gotten a little thick, you know, when we moved from Long Island to New Jersey and all. I was commuting back and forth to Bayshore. I was staying there for three nights and commuting for two more, then coming back on the weekends. Those were some hard times, baby girl. We didn't have a whole lot of money and your mama, well, even though I didn't want her to, she had to go to work to make ends meet because I couldn't find work out on the Island and the plastics factory in Jersey wasn't paying no money. By the time I finished spending all that cash on travel expenses and hotel rooms, wasn't much left over for her or that great big ol' house we'd just bought. Then I quit and your mama was bringing in the bread while I looked. That's when it got really rough. Your mama and I, we were going through it over that. No money coming in, I'm sitting at home, not really sure about what to do, and feeling like I'd failed my wife."

"Oh, and tipping out on her was going to make her feel better about all this?" I snapped. Daddy just sighed. He knew instinctively that this wasn't going to be easy, and he'd just sailed into rough seas.

"No, baby," he said quitely. "Tipping out, or whatever you want to call it, had nothing to do with me trying to hurt your mother. I was doing it for myself. See, Delphine listened to my problems, baby. She understood how thick it'd gotten in our house between your mama and me, and how even though I'd gotten the gig at the bakery, things needed fixing. Your mother and I were to the point where we weren't even talking to each other. And I was all sick, you know, all that flour and sugar and heat clogging up my airways and blocking my breathing. I hadn't been on that job more than two months and I had three asthma attacks. Here I was thinking I was going to die, and your mother? She was barely talking to me. Delphine listened. She wasn't judgmental of me or your mama. Never said an unkind word toward her, as a matter of fact."

"Well, who needs words to hurt? She just fucked my mother's husband instead," I said. I was livid now, and Daddy could see he needed, desperately, to reel this one in, wrap it up, and hope I'd think about it later when I'd calmed down.

"Look, honey—I'm not trying to convince you that what I did was okay. It wasn't," he said gently. "But there's more to it than me messing around on your mama. And in the end, I knew that it was her that I wanted, not Delphine. Try to understand that, okay? Can you do that—for me?" There were tears in his eyes, gathered up in the corner, fighting one another for space on his cheeks. His face was red, whether from the heat of embarrassment, or shame, or guilt, I don't know. He lifted his hand, his thumb and pointer finger rubbing slowly across his eyebrows. He wouldn't look at me, didn't want his daughter to see her hero crying. To tell you the truth, I didn't want to see him crying, either, because his tears and his guilt and his admittance was making me get teary, too. I mean, here I am trying to judge my own daddy not even a week after I tussled with Marcus on my living room floor, on top of my church clothes, no less. Some nerve, huh? Now my guilt was kicking me in the ass like a mug. My tears were tracking down my face, too—and I'm not so sure if it was because of Daddy's crying or because I knew I'd fucked up my marriage. We were quiet, still, for what seemed an eternity.

"Daddy?" I said, sniffling. "Do you ever wonder what would have happened if you'd left Mommy for Delphine?"

So quiet was he for so long that I wondered if he'd even heard me. Or if he just didn't want to answer, for fear that I really didn't want to hear the truth. He took a sip of water, and then another, and instinctively wiped his brow some more.

"Delphine was a beautiful, special woman," he said, finally. "She was—God—she was perfect in every way—attentive, tender, kind. Just a lovely person." I didn't think I wanted to hear any more. "But I am married to the love of my life, Mikki, and no temporary lapse in judgment is going to change that. What I did three decades ago was wrong, baby, but I don't want it to ruin the heaven I've found in your mama—in our family. God intended for us to be together, and that's the way I want it.

"Now, I don't know how I'm going to do this, but I need to get her back. I want her back, Mikki." He was sounding like a desperate man. And then he got quiet again. "But you know I have to do what's right, don't you, baby? I have to make it up to Jason—to be the daddy that he didn't have. I didn't know he was out there before, but I do now, and I'll be damned if I let another week go by without stepping up and doing what's right. I am his father."

Damn. Now there's two kind of men in this world—baby daddies and fathers. Baby daddies don't do anything for their kids but make them hate men in general, fatherhood in particular, and women en masse. They give the ultimate disrespect to what God intended the seed of Adam to be—a provider, a teacher, a leader, a responsible man who does right by his children and his woman. *Jerry Springer, Ricki Lake, Sally Jessy Raphael*—full of baby daddies. So are the street corners and basketball courts—a gang of black men bouncing balls and drinking beer and smoking weed and spending what little bit they got on the latest Nikes instead of Huggies, baby wipes, Gerber oatmeal, and Similac.

Now, the father—he's the one who looks at the baby daddies wasting time on the courts and corners as he makes his way to work. He works anywhere, does anything to support his wife and children—to love them, help them live.

Daddy? He's a father, always has been. I've always loved that about him, admired that though he was a blue-collar worker, he took care of his family like we were royalty living in a castle. All it took was hard work—that and a little bit of imagination. We didn't have the best, but we had what we needed and what we wanted, too. Daddy made sure of that. Was thirty-eight years of happiness to just go down the drain because shit got rough and Mommy was being unbearably mean and Daddy temporarily sought solace in the arms of another woman when things got a little rocky? Should this be some kind of sign that I need to stop this mess with Marcus and work this thing out with Randy, the love of my life? Could it be that Marcus is the love of my life?

My head felt like it was going to burst.

"Daddy?" I sniffed. I traced a drop of water on my glass with my finger. "How do you know after all these years that it's Mommy you want? I mean, if Delphine walked into your life right now, this very minute, would you remember what you could have had with her and leave Mommy, or would you pass Delphine by again and stay?"

Daddy didn't hesitate.

"I love your mother, Mekhi. That's all there is to it."

He didn't answer the question, either.

So, Mom has a date with some old geezer named Joe she met at some book club she joined last week to ease her mind over the whole Daddy/Delphine/Jason thing. Zaria, with her bitter, nosy, meddlesome ass, told Mommy to get out of the house and do something interesting to take her mind off of it, so she walked on down the block to the Mahogany Space African Art and Books Gallery, stumbled in on the book club gathering, and flirted with this Joe person enough to get his home phone number and then later ask him out on a date. He's taking her out to some fancy restaurant in Manhattan, the one place no one could ever get Mommy to go because she'd convinced herself over two decades ago that she would die at the hands of some crazy, deranged, toothless, stinky, homeless guy the moment the front tires of her Lincoln crossed over to the New York side of the Holland Tunnel.

Does Mommy think she's going to die tonight? Noooo—because Joe's taking her out.

"He's a nice guy, really," Zaria told me as she marched across her back lawn and over into the neighbors'. I'd gone over to Zaria's to tell her about my conversation with Daddy, and before I could get in a word edgewise, she was telling me all about Mommy's new man and how they met and how cute they were together and how she promised our mother she would see them off on their date. Of course, I was all like, "What the fuck are you talking about?"

"He's a retired professor, lives in Maplewood, divorced father of three," Zaria continued. "And from what Mommy told me, he's fine, too."

"Fine? Mommy told you he was fine?" I was incredulous. What the hell did my mother know about fine? For the twenty-eight years I'd been on this earth, she'd never once mentioned what she liked in a man's looks, what she found attractive, what kind of personality attributes turned her on. I guess I just assumed that my father was her end all to be all, and that she never even once considered that any other man on this earth would be capable of giving her the pleasure and satisfaction she got from my dad. Shit—to tell you the truth, I never really thought of my dad giving her pleasure and satisfaction. Not something you really want to consider when it comes to the 'rents.

"Yeah, Mommy said he was fine," Zaria said, her patience growing thin—though I couldn't tell if it was because I was playing stupid, or because the next-door neighbor wasn't answering the door. Zaria was trying to track down her bad ass kids, who were supposed to be over there playing with the neighbor's three bad ass kids. The five of them probably had her behind tied up in the basement somewhere. "Mommy's got eyes, Mikki. She can tell if a man is good looking or not. Jesus, grow up. And where the fuck is Karen?" she said, simultaneously laying into the buzzer and banging on the glass doors.

"What do you mean grow up?"

"Just what I said—grow up. This shit between Mom and Dad is major, Mikki. Mom's not Mother Love—she ain't trying to forgive and forget. She's trying to leave. And I can't say that I blame her."

"Huh? You want them to break up?" I said. My eyebrows were furrowed so hard that my forehead was starting to hurt. And my voice? It was beginning to crack. "Don't you care anything about their marriage? That's your mother and father, Zaria. Damn."

"Oh please, Mikki. Of course I care about their marriage," Zaria said, backing off just a little bit. She could see I was getting mad as hell, and I don't think she was in the mood for one of our knock-down, drag-outs. Besides, my purpose in her life today was to drive her and the kids from Teaneck to South Orange so that she could cheer Mommy on, and she knew that wasn't going to happen if she got me too mad. But she's still my big sister, so she was only going to bend but so much.

"I also care about my mother's mental health and her happiness, and right now, this is what she thinks she needs to get past this mess. I'm not going to stand in her way, and you know what? You shouldn't either."

Now, there's something you need to understand about my sister. She's—well, how can I put this?—damn near anti-male. She walks around, proudly proclaiming herself "happily single," whatever that's supposed to mean, and telling anyone who will listen that she has everything she's ever wanted and doesn't need a man to "complete her," whatever that's supposed to mean. I mean, I guess it comes from her being bitter about her babies' daddy, whom she dated through high school, had two babies with, and still couldn't get the ring.

But because he was a fool and didn't marry her after sixteen years or take care of their children like he was supposed to, she got to thinking that all men are fucked up and unworthy of her good goddamn time. So she lives alone. And raises her kids alone, too. Goes out to eat alone, or with her girls. Goes on vacation alone or with the kids or the girls. And when she does choose to let a man take her out or occupy some of her precious time, guaranteed within a month she'll find something that in her eyes is earth-shatteringly wrong with him and bounce the man out of her life. Zaria is the queen bee of the she-girl man hater's club, and now she's trying to make my mother a member.

Not if I can help it. I wanted to go over to my mother's house so that I could straighten out this mess, and keep her from becoming a Zaria-ite.

"Whatever, Zaria," I huffed. "Why don't you let the kids stay so we can talk to Mommy without interruption? And hurry up. I'll meet you at the car."

"Yeah, whatever, Mekhi," Zaria called back, just as Karen, all disheveled and red-faced, opened her doors. Within seconds, Zaria came jogging over to the Beemer. "Karen's going to watch Jas and James until we get back. You are bringing me back, right?"

I just rolled my eyes at her. We were silent during the half-hour ride to South Orange; the radio was the only noise to cut through the thickness of our quietude.

I'd barely gotten my key into the lock before a man I assumed was Joe swung open the door. I was all like, what the hell? How is a man I don't know going to be opening my front door? I didn't say a word to him. Zaria pushed me out of the way.

"You must be Joe," she said, extending her hand. She took off her sunglasses to get a better look at him. He was handsome—had this salt-and-pepper thing happening, and these bushy eyebrows and really pretty doe eyes. Had a beard too, very distinguished looking, but in a sexy way. Like Ed Bradley, but without the earring and not quite as fine. I would have been impressed if he wasn't trying to date my mother. Zaria, on the other hand, was practically drooling. "Boy, my mother sure wasn't lying when she said you were a looker."

I rolled my eyes, and just as I sucked my teeth and let out a little huff, my mother appeared behind him. I swear, if that woman could have thrown daggers from her eyeballs, I'd be one dead bitch. She never took her eyes off me. "Joe, I see you've met my girls. This is Zaria and this is Mekhi," she said, as each of us walked through the door. "Joe, I'm almost ready to go; I just have to take care of a few more girl things. Help yourself to a glass of wine; I'll be down shortly."

Wine? My father has an occasional beer when he can find a Miller High Life somewhere—which is hardly ever—but the closest my mom's ever gotten to spirits is communion on first Sundays. Where in the hell did the liquor come from, and why was ol' boy getting lifted before he took my mom out this house?

"Come on upstairs, girls—help me finish getting dressed," Mommy said. But she directed it to me, and it was clear we were going to be doing more than freshening up. We filed into my parents' room, and Mommy quietly shut the door behind us. Zaria kicked off the discussion, talking about how cute Joe is, but Mommy wasn't trying to hear it. No—she was going to goad me, first.

"Joe's taking me to the Soul Café," she said to me as she pushed her diamonds into her ears. "Is that a nice place, dear?"

"I guess."

"You guess? You've been there before, haven't you? Either it's nice or it's not."

"It's all right."

Mommy looked into the mirror and added a dash of peachy-orange lipstick to her lips. She blotted them on a small piece of tissue, leaned into the mirror for a final check on her flawlessly made-up face, then turned around to face me.

"What's the problem, Mekhi," she said. She only called me Mekhi when I was in trouble—and it was clear from the tension ringing the "khi" that I was about to get laid the fuck out.

"You're going out," I said slowly, "with a man who is not my father."

"Oh—like your father never went out with a woman who wasn't his wife," she said, obviously disgusted.

That's it—I'd set it off and it was on. Honestly, I really didn't come over here to get cursed out, just to tell her what my father said and be the voice of reason in this whole Joe thing. But my mother, never one to pass up a good tongue-lashing, was going to let me have it for remotely suggesting that she was somehow wrong in this wholly complicated mess that my father had dragged his family into.

"Sit down there for a minute," my mother said, pointing at her bed. I slowly eased myself onto the neat, gray comforter hugging the king-size mattress. Zaria and I had spent a lot of time on this bed—cuddled up between my mother and father, bogarding their sleep and their space in our quest to warm up our icy toes and fingers and get a little extra TLC in the process. Perched on that mattress, my sister and I watched *Sesame Street*, and later, *Zoom*, and then more grown-up shows like *General Hospital* and *Oprah*, and *The Cosby Show*. We watched Mommy put on her makeup from that bed, and Daddy tie his ties there, too. It was the makeshift couch in our makeshift family room, the only place in the house besides the dining room table where we gathered on the regular to keep each other company and laugh and giggle and discuss and debate and just, you know, be a family. I loved waking up there—my mother yanking my toes from my father's ear or cheeks or nose, where they'd inevitably end up after a wild night of tossing and turning in my sleep. Daddy would just smile; Mommy would shake her head and laugh. Zaria would make fun and we'd all hug—big hearty, drunken embraces.

That was for the birds now.

"Let me tell you something, sweetheart," she said. Her words were biting, her breath searing. "Your father fucked up." Damn. Mommy was using the "F" word. She didn't say "fuck" unless she was pissed off to the highest of pistivity—and when she reached that point, um, you really didn't want to be on the other end of it. I'd walked right on into it, then invited it into the house. "Don't you try to give me your high-and-mighty, Daddy-is-always-right attitude, hear? Because some little boy is calling my goddamn house and reminding me on a constant basis that your father fucked around on me. And I will not sit here and let you act like I'm the one who's wrong here, because I am not. I did nothing but love your father unconditionally—through two children, unemployment, mortgages, and high interest rates and very little money, honey. Everything I did was in support of your father—even when I didn't agree with his decisions. That's what wives do—they stick it out.

"But dammit, there's some things I'm not going to tolerate and let that begin with little bastards calling my house and reminding me that my husband got another woman pregnant while his wife was carrying his child. I know that's your daddy and he's the love of your life, but open your eyes, Mikki. He's not perfect and I'm human and some things just don't fly with me. Cheating husbands is one of them. Illegitimate kids? Oh, yeah, you bet that's on my list, too."

She was breathing hard by the time she finished. My mouth was simply open. I really didn't know what to say. I mean, my mother had never really cursed me out, or anyone else, for that matter. Oh, she talked a good game—had everyone believing that because she could put two words together and mix it with a little attitude that she was much more an independent new millennium woman who did what she pleased and kept my father in check while she did it. Reality was this: Mommy is straight-up old school. She married young, bore and raised babies, cooked and cleaned and laundered and stroked. She did her fair share of complaining, too—but she always made sure that Daddy was taken care of. Always. So it was just weird to hear her talking all this here shit, you know? Because I expected her to, you know, toe the line, give Daddy a little grief, then get over it. And here she was going out on a date.

"I think it's great she's going out and having a good time," Zaria said. I swear, sometimes I just want to put her head under my sewing machine and permanently thread her lips shut.

"You would, Zaria."

"And just what the hell is that supposed to mean?" she asked, incredulously.

"It means that you seem to thrive off of being alone, as if the only way you can be happy is to *not* have a man. And now you're sucking Mommy straight down the same path, and I don't like it."

Mommy's turn.

"What the hell are you talking about, Mekhi? Are you suggesting that you can't be happy unless you're married?"

"I'm saying that she knocks marriage like it's some kind of disease."

"Oh—and it's not?" Mommy charged back.

"No. You and Daddy were happy for a long time," I said firmly. "And Randy and I are happy, too." Okay, so the second part came out weak as hell. I'd walked smack dab in the middle of some bull and was getting ready to get smoked.

"Oh, really," Mommy hissed. "You and Randy are happy, huh? Well, where's your husband, Mrs. Chance-Murphy? When's the last time you seen him? As I recall, you didn't exactly come back from Paris singing his praises, either. What's going on in your house that your husband is living clean in another country on the other side of the world? Let me tell you something, Mekhi. You better pull your head out of your behind and recognize that it's not peaches and cream in your household, either, honey. If you knew what was best for you, you'd do what makes you happy, rather than what makes him happy—because his happy Paris-hopping self obviously ain't thinking about yours.

"Now, I'm through with this conversation. I'm going to the Soul Café, with Joe, in Manhattan. And I plan on having me the time of my life. I ain't thinking about your daddy."

And with that, Mommy twirled around on her heel, kissed Zaria good-bye, and waltzed down the stairs, straight into Joe's arms. From my mother's window, I could see them walking down the front walkway. They were locked arm-in-arm. He opened the passenger-side door for her, and helped her into the car. She smiled back at him as he walked around to his side, and climbed in. They said something to each other—I don't know what—but Mommy put her hand over her mouth and laughed.

She looked beautiful. Happy. Content.

I felt awful.

She was right. Here I was, screaming about the virtues of wifedom and marriage, and my own house was a stark-raving mess. My husband had been in Paris for three months and was planning to stay another six—despite what I said. And who knows what he was doing over there and with whom. Randy is an extremely sexual person and I know that it will be just a matter of time before he hooks up with some big-booty Parisian bitch to get some ass. That's if he hasn't already.

And truth of the matter is that when I'm with Marcus, I feel the way Mommy looked in that car with Joe. Maybe I was deluding myself about Randy and marriage and commitment. Maybe I did just need to have a good time with Marcus, and enjoy the ride of singledom.

"Let's go, Zaria," I said to my sister. I said a silent "thank you" to God for not letting her light into my ass about my mother's cursing me out. I already felt like ten pounds of shit in a three-pound bag. She didn't need to add anything to it. "You should get home before your kids think you ran away."

*   *   *

The first message on my machine was from Fool. She wanted to make sure, I guess, that the shop didn't burn down and I wasn't dead and still able to meet with her to go over the dress one more time before she got hitched this Saturday. The second was a loan company begging for me to refinance our home for "spectacularly lower rates than your current lender." Yeah.

The third was this: "Hey, you. What you up to? I wanted to come over to, um, make sure everything was cool—you know, no prowlers in the bushes. Give me a call when you get in."

It was Marcus.

And he wanted to come over.

And I wanted him to come over.

He did.

He

If I was calling Mom, it meant I had reached the nadir, the dregs. My calls to Mom had grown less frequent since I had married, much to her annoyance, but when I wasn't sure what to do next I still found solace in her voice, her soothing assurance that whatever I decided was the right thing to do. But she would always manage during the conversation to steer me in the direction that she thought I should go in.

I knew my mother liked Mikki, which would make this call easier and more difficult at the same time. It would be easier because I'd be more trusting of her advice than I'd be if she disliked my wife. But she'd also have less patience for our recent difficulties, and she'd probably be annoyed at me for going to Paris in the first place if it was going to endanger my marriage.

But, as frequently happened when I tried to anticipate my mother's reactions, I turned out to be completely wrong.

"Can't you just go on back there and visit a few times, like once a month or something? It's not like she doesn't know where you are and what you're doing, right?" Mrs. Earline Murphy asked me. I heard the lack of intolerance in her voice. I could sense Mikki was not going to fare well in this conversation.

I had stayed at work later than usual so I could call my mother from the office. I swiveled in my chair and stared out at the faint twinkle of office lights I could see from my tenth floor window. Paris didn't have the jungle of skyscrapers that I was used to, so when night fell there really wasn't much I could see from my chair. If I stood up and craned my neck, I could see the spectacular nighttime illumination of the 130-year-old Opera, which boasted the world's largest stage and which supposedly was the setting for the *Phantom of the Opera*. I had yet to hit those more high-falutin' tourist spots.

"Of course I could go back and visit, Ma, but she thinks that I'm, like, I don't know, putting the job before our marriage," I said.

"Well"—she paused for dramatic effect—"is that what you're doing?"

I was a little surprised by the question. I thought my mother knew how much I loved Mikki.

"No, of course not, Ma. This is a great opportunity for me, and I thought she would be able to see that. I'll go home as a vice president, you know? In charge of the whole department. How could I turn that down?"

"I know that's what you've been working toward all these years that you've been at Trier-Stanton. And I guess Mikki knows that, too. I think sometimes you young people have some unrealistic ideas of what a marriage . . . of what's supposed to happen in a marriage."

I knew that she was thinking of her own marriage. When she first married my now-deceased father, she had to stay home alone for weeks at a time while he was on the road selling air-conditioning systems to businesses across the country. Surely that couldn't have been easy for her, but she never complained—at least I don't think she complained.

"Was it hard for you when Dad went out on the road for long periods of time?"

"Hard? Shoot, of course it was hard. Especially after we had you and your sister. But you learn how to deal with it."

I suddenly latched on to something I hadn't recalled in a long time. When my father would return from a long trip, my mother would dance around the house with me and my sister, singing a song she had made up: "It's so nice to have a daddy around the house. . . . It's so nice to have a daddy around the house."

That was the song's only line, and we'd all sing it together while my father looked at us and grinned. The memory, as strong and vivid as if it had occurred yesterday, caused me to get a little misty-eyed, something that hadn't happened to me since the months right after he died four years earlier.

"Dealing with it" was practically an Earline Murphy specialty. Not for the first time, I wondered why the women and wives of my generation seemed so less able to deal with it—the "it" always on the verge of breaking them down. Were the men of my generation to blame? Had we failed our women in some fundamental way that I couldn't see or understand?

"Well, how do I get that idea across to my wife?" I asked my mother. "The last time we talked, she acted almost like she didn't care anymore, Ma."

"Oh, I'm sure she still cares, Randy. She probably wants you to think she doesn't care anymore. Maybe she thinks that'll hurt you, and apparently it did. Maybe she feels like you're hurting her and she's just trying to get back at you."

Up to that point, I hadn't really focused on the possibility that I was "hurting" my wife. She said she felt lonely and scared back in Brooklyn, but a part of me always immediately dismissed that claim because she had lived by herself in Brooklyn just four years ago, before we moved in together the year before we got married. But *had* she succeeded in hurting me? I guessed that she had, otherwise I wouldn't be torturing myself over it and even calling my mommy. In fact, it was the hurt that had sent me into the arms of another woman. Well, maybe it wasn't the hurt alone—perhaps my straining and lonely erections had had something to do with that, too.

I suddenly felt overwhelmed by the confusion of all this guessing and game-playing. Mikki had sent me into this funk and I didn't know how to get out of it.

"This is all so stupid, Ma! I mean, she knows what I'm doing here and why I'm here. Why can't she just hold on and wait till I get home? Why put me through all this mess?"

I heard my mother's sigh. "I don't know, Randy. Maybe there's more going on than you even know about."

I thought about that one. "What do you mean? More going on like what?"

"I don't know." I imagined her shrugging her shoulders. "I'm just saying that maybe she hasn't told you everything she's feeling. So that's why it's so confusing to you."

"So you think I should ask her why she's doing this?"

"Well, it sounds like you've already done that." She paused

again. "I don't know, son, sometimes you really can't know or hear everything over the telephone. And certainly not over the computer, that e-mail stuff. Sometimes you have to be there, talking it over in person."

"So you think I should go back home?" I was anxious now; I thought I was getting some hard advice, a clue about what to do.

"I'm not telling you what to do, Randy. I'm not necessarily saying you should go back home. But I *am* saying that you can't possibly know everything that's going on with your wife when you're thousands—how far away is Paris, anyway?—thousands of miles away from each other."

I thought about that one for a long while. I was still thinking about it that night when I lay in my bed at the Saint-Germain, waiting for sleep to come. Just before I drifted off, I decided that I would call my boss, Peter Webber, and talk my way to cutting short my stay in Paris. I'd tell Webber that Eliza could handle everything on this side of the Atlantic in my absence. I even smiled to myself just before I drifted off because I had more peace of mind than I had had in weeks. I had made a decision.

The conversation with Webber turned out to be a lot easier than I had anticipated. In fact, its ease worried me. Webber had been a little too willing to put the soccer account in Eliza's hands.

"Of course, I'll continue to monitor the soccer league from New York," I had added, a bit nervously.

"Okay, that's fine, Randy. I'm sure you're leaving things in good shape over there. If you feel like you need to come back, by all means come on back. Your personal life and your marriage are of the utmost concern here."

I was alarmed at the way Webber had inserted "your marriage" in there. I hadn't told him enough to make the boss conclude that my *marriage* was in any kind of danger. I had said I needed to go back to my wife, like she was the problem, not the entire marriage itself. I was tempted to correct my boss—the last thing I wanted was for him to go around the office telling everyone that my marriage was in some kind of trouble—but I decided to let it go. It wasn't worth getting into that kind of nitpicking with Webber. Besides, he would sense my alarm and determine that things were even worse than he had imagined. What I really hoped was that my boss was too busy to be walking around the office talking about my personal life anyway.

It took no more than forty-five minutes for the news to hit Eliza and for her to sprint to my office for details. I knew to expect her, but I didn't think it'd be so fast. Webber must have called her right away.

"I just heard the news," she said, peeking through my door, which was slightly ajar. "Can I come in?"

I was bothered that Webber had called her so quickly, that the boss had been so eager to give Blondie the wonderful news. I waved her in. I was curious to see which approach Eliza was going to take, how much she would try to hide her pleasure.

"So, is everything okay?" she said with a slight hesitation. So I got my answer right away: she was going to play the concerned colleague. I looked in her eyes and thought I saw genuine concern. It occurred to me that maybe I was being too hard on her. Maybe she actually did care why I was leaving.

I shrugged. I didn't want to tell her too much; I knew *Eliza* wasn't too busy to be walking around the office talking about my personal life.

"I'm not sure how things are, Eliza. That's why I'm going back to New York."

She nodded, as if she understood everything. I wanted to tell her to stop nodding, to shout at her that she didn't know a damn thing. The nodding bothered me; lots of things about her bothered me. (Lots of things in general bothered me lately.) I shuddered with the memory of how close I had been to having sex with this woman. Damn, that would have been disastrous.

I knew she wanted to ask about the job, to say something about the fact that Webber had put her in charge of the account. I wanted to see her face when I told her that I had been the one to suggest it to Webber.

"I don't think there's anything to worry about with the women's soccer league," she said. "Pretty much the whole campaign is done, most of the print and television has already been purchased. We just have to do radio and stick around to clean up whatever messes come up. There are always messes."

I nodded in agreement. Of course I already knew all that. Eliza was just showing me that *she* also knew. I wondered if this was a good time to tell her.

"I'm sure you'll do fine," I said. "That's why I told Webber to leave it all in your capable hands."

I watched her face carefully, but to my disappointment I saw no surprise.

"Yeah, Webber told me that you recommended me. That means a lot to me, Randy. Thank you."

She reached across the desk and patted me on the hand. She let her hand linger there. Once again, I wondered what was going through Eliza's head.

"When are you leaving? You have time to go out and get drunk again?" she asked, taking her hand away.

Surely she remembered what happened the last time we got drunk—was she telling me she wanted to go through all that again, maybe push it further this time?

As if reading my racing thoughts, Eliza added, "Maybe we can invite a few people from the office. I'm sure some of the Parisians will want to come. You were quite a popular guy here."

She said that last teasingly, making me wonder if there was a subtext that I was missing. Why did I so often wonder if there was another conversation going on beneath the surface when I talked to Eliza? That's why conversations with her could be exciting and infuriating at the same time. I suspected that I *was* in fact popular here in the office. I had gone out of my way to be as warm and open with my Parisian colleagues as possible. I could tell that they were impressed with my wit and my obvious talent for the job. I wondered if maybe Eliza could see all that too and she was jealous. Or perhaps she was merely alluding to the race thing—that Parisians liked African Americans more than they liked white Americans. As if I should feel bad or guilty about that.

"Okay, sure," I said, relieved that the invitation to get drunk wasn't a come-on. "I was planning on leaving this weekend, though I haven't bought my ticket yet. Maybe we could do it tomorrow night, or even Friday night—though if I'm going to leave on Saturday I'd prefer being able to get some rest on Friday night."

"Okay, tomorrow night it is, then. I'll pass the word around."

She popped up from the chair and darted from the office. I didn't have much difficulty keeping my eyes off her behind this time. I was already anxiously looking forward to the call to Brooklyn that I was about to make.

"Mikki, guess what, I'm coming home." I said it as soon as she had picked up the phone at the house. Contained in my words, of course, was an abundance of pride that I had finally made the decision, in my mind, to put the interests of my wife and marriage above all else. I expected to hear an equal amount of gratitude and excitement from her. But that's not what I got, not really. I wasn't sure what I got.

"You're coming to visit or you're coming to stay?" she asked. Was that alarm in her voice, or excitement?

"I'm coming to stay, honey. I decided that Brooklyn is where I should be, where my wife is, where my life is."

There was a pause. "Hmmm. What finally brought you to this decision?" she asked.

I caught the "finally" right away. So she was going to punish me for the past, for all the lost time, rather than taking it from here and being happy that I was returning. Why did women have to focus on the negative to the exclusion of everything else, like happiness, I wondered. Couldn't she just get over it?

"Well, like I said, Mikki, I thought it was time for me to come home. It's that simple."

Another pause. I thought I heard a sigh. "Well, I'm glad you're coming home, Randy. That's wonderful news."

But her voice almost had a certain resignation to it, like she was saying this because she knew that's what she was supposed to say. Was she not excited about my return? Why was I hearing so much—what was it?—almost indifference in her voice? Had things gotten that bad? I felt my stomach begin its slow roil that usually accompanied conversations with my wife these days. How was I going to get things back to the way they were? Would I know what to do, what to say? The questions frightened me, shook me. I took a deep breath.

"Is anything wrong, Mikki?"

I heard another sigh. "Are we back to that, Randy? Am I not showing the right response here, is that it? I don't sound excited enough?"

"Well, as a matter of fact, you don't really sound as excited as I expected you to." I tensed up even more because I knew she wouldn't accept that statement in the spirit of peace.

"You know, I'm not sure what you want from me sometimes, Randy. Pardon me if my reactions can't always live up to your expectations. Perhaps you can give me some warning first, let me know how I'm supposed to react to all your little announcements. Then I'll be better able to live up to your expectations."

I was growing angrier by the second, but I wasn't really sure if my anger was justified. She had me so flustered that I couldn't even really gauge what the appropriate responses and emotions were during our encounters. Was she doing this on purpose? Was she trying to keep me off balance? Was that part of what my mother said, her efforts to hurt me back?

"Okay, can we move on?" I said. "I don't know anymore what I expect of you. I don't really understand what's happening here. But maybe part of the problem is that these conversations by telephone just aren't cutting it. Maybe things will be better when we're actually face-to-face."

Another pause. What was with these pauses?

"Well, I hope so," she said. I was trying to locate the right word to describe the tone of her voice. Indifferent wasn't quite it. The voice was lacking a certain energy that I had grown used to hearing from Mikki. Maybe lackadaisical? Nonchalant? Listless? Detached? Maybe detached was it. Like she was just going through the motions, responding but not really feeling.

"When are you going to be here?" Mikki asked.

"I don't know exactly when. I'm going to try to get on the Saturday morning flight. Delta has a flight that leaves Paris at about ten-thirty and arrives at JFK at about one o'clock in the afternoon. I'll call and see if I can get on that flight. Can you pick me up at one p.m. on Saturday?"

"Sure I can pick you up. I think I have a fitting at noon, but I'll just reschedule it."

I waited to see if she wanted to say anything else. But all I got was dead air. Damn, talk about a major letdown. This conversation contained none of the excitement, the heartfelt expressions of love and longing, that had I expected it would.

"All rightie then, Mikki. I guess I'll see you in a few days. After I make the flight reservation, I'll call you back and let you know the definites. All right?"

"All right, Randy. 'Bye."

" 'Bye," I said.

She

This is all taking me just a little too fast, y'all. See, when Randy called with his happy behind to tell me he was on his way home, I liked to died—not because my heart was racing with joy, but because it was pounding with fear. Marcus was there. Half naked. Sprinkling rose petals all over my house. And lighting candles and hurricane lamps and shit. Singing along with D'Angelo's "Brown Sugar," the song he said reminded him so much of me that he made a special trip to the Hustler store in Hollywood while he was in L.A. on business last week to buy me a little teeny weeny brown tank top with the words "Brown Sugar" emblazoned in orange sparkled neon across the chest. I was slinking around my kitchen in that shirt and a chocolate brown see-through thong, struggling with an ear of corn and my *Joy of Cooking* book, when the phone rang.

To be honest with you, I didn't know what to say—how to respond to Randy. I was all at once scared and confused, more scared than anything. I thought for sure Randy could hear Marcus singing, along with D'Angelo, talking 'bout getting high off her love. Just when Marcus joined D'Angelo on the chorus—all off-key, at the top of his lungs, he was hollering with conviction, about wanting summa my brown suga—Randy stopped talking. And just when he grew silent, my heart damn near rushed out of that orange sparkled neon and straight into my frying pan full of corn, which was on its way to burning. I was struggling to wipe up the popping grease and heavy cream that had spilled all over the counter, floor, and my cookbook when I accidently dropped the corn husk into my mixing bowl—a ridiculously clumsy set of events that could have awakened the dead. Which scared me even more because the last thing I wanted Randy to ask me was what I was doing, because then I would have had to explain to him that I was cooking, which he knew I only did on special occasions for special people, which would have meant that someone was in our house. He didn't need to know anyone else was in the house.

What Randy did need to do was get off the phone. The easiest way to make him do that was to get loud and rude with him. So I did.

Just as I hung up the phone, Marcus walked into the kitchen—sans shirt, a single long-stem red rose in his left hand. "How's it going, beautiful?" he boomed. "A rose for my brown sugar." I rushed past him and into the living room. I leaned down to turn the stereo down, then tried to muster the strength to stand back up. Marcus, obviously flustered, stood in the doorway, looking at me with a "What the fuck?" look on his face. "Mikki? Everything okay?" I didn't answer him. He walked slowly toward me, and put his hand on my near-naked ass. His touch shocked me out of my trance. I stood up and pushed his hand off my flesh like he was some stranger making an unauthorized grab in a smoky hip hop club.

"Mikki?"

"He's coming home," I said slowly.

"Who?" Marcus said, the look on his face shuffling from startled to concerned.

"Randy. Randy's leaving Paris and coming home," I said. I felt weird, dizzy. I needed to sit down. That's what I did—right on the checkered tablecloth Marcus had spread across the living room floor for our romantic indoor picnic. My back was facing Marcus; I was too embarrassed to look at him. Here I was, a half-naked married woman twisting my ass all up in front of a man who wasn't my husband—with the man who is my husband on the phone professing his love for me and telling me he's on his way home.

There was silence. Neither of us said a word for what seemed like forever. Finally, I said it. "What are we going to do?" I said, burying my head in my hands. They were sticky from the corn milk that had dripped clean up to my elbow. I turned my head slowly toward him, and then my entire body.

"What," I said, more deliberately this time, "are we going to do?"

Marcus was looking dead at me—our eyes locked. He took in a deep breath, then let it loose. He said nothing. Then finally, "We're not going to do anything, Mikki."

"I don't understand. What do you mean, we're not going to do anything?" I was getting more confused, and even more flustered. "Randy is on his way home and we're together. You. And me. Together. How are we going to do that if he's here, Marcus?"

More silence.

Neither of us could bring ourselves, really, to look at each other. I wanted to get up and go into the bathroom or back into the kitchen or to Botswana—anywhere—but I couldn't move.

Marcus got up and walked to the window, then turned around and looked me dead in my eyes, which, by now, were tearing. The crying started slowly, quietly, then turned into a hot rush down my face. Before I knew it, I was sobbing.

"Mikki, baby," Marcus said as he rushed over to me. "Don't cry, honey. Don't cry. We're going to work this out—just you and me."

"How?" I said, sniffling. "I mean, are we going to tell him? We can't possibly keep this up with him in town. I can't take all the sneaking around and hiding and ducking into schoolyards already, and it's only going to get worse when he comes home."

"No."

Marcus said it so loud that it startled me. Then he started talking more quietly. "No. Mikki, listen to me. We can't tell Randy anything until we figure out just what to do, baby, do you understand? I know him, Mikki. I know him too well. We've been boys for a long time now and I know what he would do if he found out you were having an affair. And I know what he would do if he found out you were having an affair with me. We can't tell him anything yet."

"Then what? What are we going to do, Marcus?" My voice was tinged with desperation, and I couldn't stop sobbing. I felt like an idiot. He walked over and took a spot on the tablecloth. I felt his hand touch my shoulder. His fingers, warm and smooth and soft, began caressing my shoulder.

"How about we just enjoy each other tonight," he said, leaning down to kiss the spot he'd just rubbed. "We're going to eat that beautiful meal you've prepared and we're going to make love and lay in each other's arms and pretend tonight that nothing else matters." And just as I was about to say, "Negro, have you lost your damn mind," he said it, the words that would lead me straight down the path of destruction, just a minute away from sheer hell. "I love you, Mikki," he said, using his fingers to turn my chin toward him. He kissed my lips so softly, I almost didn't feel it. And then he said it again.

"I love you, Mikki, and I don't want this to end." He kissed me again. And then again. And then again. "We'll tell Randy about us in our own time. But right now, we have to be smart about it if we're going to be together, understand? I want to be with you, Mikki, but we have to do this right."

Truthfully? I didn't really hear the rest of what he said after the "I love you" part. Here was this beautiful man, right here in my arms, not only saying how he felt, but showing it—something Randy hadn't done in months. I was excited. Elated. Ecstatic. Horny. I wanted him, desperately, madly. And with my corn chowder burning my pot to a crisp on my stove, with the candles flickering all around us, and D'Angelo's falsetto slowly, deliberately crooning his "Shit, Damn, Muthafucka" ditty—the tale of a man who, after discovering his best friend and wife in bed together, suffers the consequences of shooting the two of them dead in the ass—Marcus and I made slow, passionate, sweet love, the kind reserved for people who truly loved one another.

He set it off when his tongue licked the pressure point on my neck. I was sure he could feel my heartbeat racing, dancing with his tastebuds, surely lit up by the extra spritz of Issey Miyake I'd sprayed there just about an hour before. He used his tongue to explore every inch of my body: the tips of my ears, the bottom of my chin, the ticklish patch of skin just beneath my armpit, the sides of my hips, the backs of my knees, the pads of my toes. I was dripping wet, hips writhing like a crack fiend waiting for her next fix, anxious to see where his tongue was going to take me next. He moved slowly up my leg, kissing every centimeter on his way up to my vagina. He teased me. He made me throb. And within seconds of his tongue-kissing the cat, I came—squeezed my ass and hoisted my hips into the air and felt the burst climb from the tips of my toes, up my ankles, past my knees, through my thighs, straight to my clit. I was bucking like a damn Clydesdale, and Marcus was my jockey, riding and steering me and goading me to leap over boundaries I'd never before jumped. I was amazed at what my body did that night.

I was equally amazed when Marcus—sweaty, panting from exertion, and obviously satisfied—raised up off my picnic sheet and began to pull his underwear, then pants, then shirt and socks and shoes, back onto his beautifully shaped frame. He was quiet, didn't really make eye contact with me. Not even after I began to question why he was in such a hurry to leave.

"Baby, calm down, okay?" he said to me, as he took a quick look at his watch. Um, I was calm. I just wanted to know where he was going, and why he couldn't spend the night with a sistah, perhaps work on a round two or something. That he seemed annoyed with what I thought was a pretty simple, straightforward question bothered me, even if it were just a little bit.

"I have to be in court early tomorrow morning, you know—gotta do work," he said, a little less bass in his voice. "You don't want your man to lose the case because he rolled into superior court on C.P. time, do you?"

"I'm not stressing you or anything," I said, trying not to sound disappointed. Or desperate. I got up and stood before him, helped him button his shirt. And then I ran my fingers across his chest, and kissed his nipples, first the right, then the left. He didn't really respond. In fact, it seemed a little like he was trying to put some distance between us, trying a little too hard, if you ask me. He turned his back toward me, took a step forward, and ran his fingers through his hair. "I was just thinking it would be nice if you spent the night tonight—if we could wake up in each other's arms."

"Maybe some other time, baby, okay?" Marcus said coolly, quickly. He turned around and pecked my forehead. Then, noticing my disappointment, he eased up just a little bit and smiled. "There is nothing that I would love to do more than to wake up to your beautiful face, but, unfortunately, I have to be staring in Judge Lance Owens' mug at nine a.m. or else my case will be ruined and my client will sue me for malpractice."

He walked toward the front door, and I followed, pulling my shirt over my torso as I moved. He kissed me, ever so gently, then placed his hands on my shoulders and slowly took me in with his eyes, from my hair down to my toes. "Uh, uh, uh. My sweet brown sugar. I'll call you tomorrow when I get out of court, okay?"

And without another word shared between us, he walked out into the cool Brooklyn night.

*   *   *

"See, if I were you, I'd be thanking God he hasn't ever tried to move the party to the marital bed or spent the night because now you don't have to fumigate his scent from your mattress before Randy comes home."

Lord, Angelou can be crass. I've always known she could be a bit too plain-spoken, but dammit, you'd think she was Randy's personal cheerleader or something, which is why I never told her the full story. I invited her to Jenny's Nail Salon for two reasons: first, to give her a congratulatory pedicure for officially getting a boyfriend. He's some guy she met out on an audition (Lord, another actor, but hey, he's a man and she seems happy so, whatever) and they've been kicking it for a few weeks and she's been over to his house and he over to hers and, by all indications, they've fallen madly, ridiculously, head over heels in love. I guess he's a nice guy—good looking, well mannered and, by all indications when she introduced me to boyfriend at our jazz dance/aerobics class last week, cuckoo over some Angelou.

And secondly, because I need her to help me figure out if Marcus is trying to distance himself from me now that Randy's coming home or if my adulterous behavior has made me more paranoid than usual. But noooo, mama's not going to work with me on this. She's going to sit there in that chair, all on her high horse, and call me out for my transgressions while she gets her toes done. On my dime, dammit.

"Come on, Ang, I'm serious," I said, a hint of desperation tinging my voice.

"I know you're serious," she snapped back. "That's what's bothering the shit out of me. Mikki, say it with me: Randy's coming home. Your husband. The man whose ring you're wearing on that perfectly manicured finger. Doesn't that mean anything to you?"

"What do you mean, 'doesn't it mean anything'? Of course it does." I was getting impatient with her. We were both starting to fidget in our chairs, and a few of the other ladies of leisure in the salon were starting to direct their attention to our conversation, which I certainly didn't want to happen because the last thing I needed was for people I didn't even know to get all up in the middle of this business. I lowered my voice, and I shot Angelou a look that surely signaled she should do the same.

"Randy is coming back from Paris, but after all these months I'm not so sure I really want him back. Why is that so hard for you to understand?"

"Because the reason why you don't know if you want your husband to come home is because that home-wrecker of a boyfriend has your panties all in a twist." The woman painting Angelou's toes looked up at me, then said something in Korean to the lady doing my toes. When she stopped talking, they both started laughing. I swear I need to learn how to say "I know you're making fun of us and I'm going to jack you up if you say another word" in Korean, just to shock the mess out of them. Instead, I shushed Angelou.

"Not so loud, damn," I said, whispering. "You want all of Brooklyn *and* Seoul, Korea, to know my business?"

"Well somebody else in Brooklyn might be able to talk some good sense into your ass, because what I have to say obviously doesn't count for much."

"Okay—now you can cut the self-righteousness, Angelou. You think just because you're getting a little dick now means you know how to get and keep a committed relationship? Little girl, I'm a married woman with serious, grown-up problems. This isn't some little two-week romance with a two-minute brother I hardly know. Personally, I don't think you're all that qualified to sit here and be my judge and jury."

I said it all in one breath and, in the next instance, I wished I could take it all back equally fast. Angelou's mouth was wide open. She was speechless, and, after all the venom I'd just spewed in her direction, so was I.

"God—Angelou, I'm sorry. I'm sorry."

Angelou was staring at her feet. Her pedicurist was applying the top coat to her last two toes. She didn't say anything at first, and it was clear she didn't intend to. I'd gone too far. My apology wasn't going to mean a thing to her.

"You know," she finally said quietly. "I may not have a ring on my finger, but I'd rather be single and sure of my choices than married, fucking my husband's best friend, and on my way to a divorce because I can't get a clue." Then she reached into her purse, pulled out a twenty-dollar bill, tossed it at the Korean lady, and hopped down from her chair.

"Good luck with Randy," she snarled, as she snatched on her shoes.

"Or Marcus, or whoever the hell it is you choose to be with next week."

And with that, she turned on her heel and headed for the door. "Oh, and thanks for the pedicure. I had a lovely time. Tell your mother I might see her at the dinner on Friday. Then again, I might not."

I called after her, said something stupid, you know, like, "Let's talk this out," or "Don't go." But she kept on walking. My man is gone. My other man is going. And now I think I've lost my best friend, too.

He

I wouldn't have called it spying exactly, but I was trying to utilize all the information available to me when I picked up the phone early the next morning and called my best friend, Marcus Peate. Marcus had always been a great listener, one of those rare souls able to sit quietly and hear another person lay out an entire story or dilemma. Marcus was able to put his own stuff to the side and really focus in on someone else. Most people can't do that; most people can't even sit through thirty seconds of someone else's troubles without quickly reverting the conversation right back to themselves. I knew I was guilty of that personality flaw myself. Because of watching Marcus operate over the past decade, I had become conscious of it and was trying to get better.

I had to dig into my electronic organizer to find Marcus's number at his big Wall Street law firm. Marcus was on that workaholic partner track, trying to put in the requisite hours to make partner before thirty-five. That meant he practically lived at the firm—a fact that did not sit well with his wife. That was one of the reasons—in addition to an affair with his secretary—why Marcus and Marti had separated about six months earlier. If anybody could understand how confusing this work-marriage stuff could get, it was Marcus.

Marcus had barely gotten out his "Hello" before I launched into the story about the problems I had been having with Mikki.

"I don't know what's happening, Marcus," I concluded, hoping I didn't sound too whiny.

"Whew. That's some heavy shit, Randy. I kind of got a few clues that things weren't all that great, but I didn't know it was that bad."

"Clues? You did?! What did she say?" I held my breath. This was exactly the kind of stuff I was looking for from Marcus—insight from a neutral third party.

"Well, the few times that I went over there, she mentioned that you two weren't really speaking as much as you should have been. That was kind of upsetting to her. But she didn't know what to do about it. She wasn't sure if she should call you more herself, or if she should just wait for you to call. Then when—"

"Damn, that sounds like high school!" I said, interrupting my friend's report. "You believe that shit, Marcus?"

"It does sound a little crazy, Randy. But, you know, we can get into some pretty silly stuff in our relationships."

"You got that right! I can't believe we're still tripping over who's calling who."

"I was about to say that she mentioned something about an e-mail. She didn't seem to appreciate y'all communicating by the computer. She thought it was impersonal."

Wow, she had even told Marcus about the e-mail? Suddenly, I was a little embarrassed. I didn't expect my friend to know this much detail. Apparently Mikki had really confided in him. Didn't she realize how dangerous that was, considering that Marcus was my best friend in the whole world? She had to know it would get right back to me, right? Or maybe that was her intent, part of her plan. Maybe this was one of her ways of communicating with her husband. But it seemed so indirect, so uncertain.

"Yeah, well, I realized the e-mail thing hadn't gone over too well. But at the time it seemed like a great idea, you know, taking advantage of the available technology. I was at home, I mean at the hotel, and there was the laptop. It was a much cheaper way of communicating, I thought. Well, I'll never do that shit again."

"So, what day are you coming back?" Marcus asked.

When did I tell Marcus I was returning to Brooklyn? I didn't remember mentioning it earlier in the conversation.

"How did you know I was about to go back home?" I asked, my brow furrowing.

"What? Waddaya mean? I *didn't* know. That's why I asked, what date are you coming back?"

"Oh, I thought you said what *day*."

"Nah, I said *date*."

I unfurrowed my brow. I was just *too* suspicious these days. What did I think, that Webber had called Marcus, too? I chuckled to myself at the absurdity of my suspicion.

"I'll be there on Saturday afternoon. I just made the reservations."

"This Saturday?! Damn, you don't waste no time, huh? Well, brother, we must definitely get together soon. Maybe next week. Like, uh . . ."

I knew Marcus was looking down at his calendar, checking which night he'd be able to get away from the office before ten p.m.

"How 'bout next Wednesday?" Marcus said.

"All right. Wednesday it is."

"And you're gonna have to tell me all about those French women. I hear they can't get enough of the brothers, especially American brothers."

I chuckled. "Yeah, well, I got plenty to tell you. Plenty."

"Oh, really?" Marcus said. "Plenty, huh?"

I knew he was guessing that I had sampled some of the French fare. Should I lie right away and tell him that wasn't the case? Marcus and I had always been painfully honest with each other, but I wasn't sure if I was comfortable giving my friend that kind of information.

"Let's just wait until Wednesday," I said finally.

By the time dinner was served, it was clear to me that most of my colleagues were looking at my going away as an excuse to get drunk. In some cases, very drunk. I had noticed Eliza guzzling down several glasses of white wine on an empty stomach, so it didn't take long for her to hit cloud nine. I was alarmed to see that Paula wasn't far behind her. I wasn't sure what I was in store for, with both of them already laced, but I could sense it wouldn't be pretty.

Paula had already let me know that she wasn't happy about the way I had avoided her after our night together. She had done this one memorable afternoon by marching into my office, slamming the door behind her, and assaulting me with "Why the fuck are you avoiding me?"

I had been not only stunned but also a little frightened. I had seen enough Hollywood stalker flicks to know that stranger things had happened in these situations than Paula pulling out a butcher knife and plunging it into my wildly pounding heart. Or Paula yanking a little silver .22 out of her bag and feeding me a bullet through my forehead. How would that one be explained in *Le Monde*? I could picture the headline back home in the *Daily News*: "New Yorker shot in head by Paris lover after adulterous sex romp."

After a bit of hemming and stuttering, I had babbled something about feeling so much for her that I was afraid of spending too much time with her because I wouldn't want to go back home to my wife. I had stared up at her, wide-eyed, waiting for her reaction.

"Really?!" she had said, her chest still heaving from the energy and adrenaline it must have taken her to walk in my office like an assassin. To my amazement, she was buying it! I had expected her to laugh in my face over the lameness of that line. That's what a New York girl would have done. But apparently Paula hadn't had much game run on her by the Parisian playas, so she couldn't smell a playa line even when it smacked her upside the head.

On this night, Paula wasn't shy about staring over at me as she downed wine and chatted with her co-workers. I had to do a little last-minute musical-chairs maneuvering to avoid sitting next to her. It mainly consisted of starting a deep conversation with Eliza about the soccer league account and forcing Paula to make her seating choice without knowing where I was going to sit. If I wasn't so nervous about it, I might consider her excessive attention to be flattering—after all, Paula was an attractive woman with a great body. But now she was scaring the hell out of me. How easy it would be for her to let slip a mention of our encounter, then for the gossip mill to kick in and spread the news like a California forest fire, then for it to leap across the Atlantic and follow me back to the New York office, then for one of those evil little horny and hostile spinsters that filled the New York office to find a way to get the news to Mikki. I felt the line of sweat race down my torso from just the thought. Paula gave me a big seductive grin and I turned my head away as quickly as I could without making her feel like I was disrespecting her. Oh, God, I thought, it was time to run home to my wife—not that that was the most appetizing thought in the world either.

Eliza leaned over to whisper in my ear.

"That guy sitting over there next to Paula—I think his name is John-Pierre or something real French like that—he's hot as hell. He's mine."

I looked down to see whom she was talking about. Of course, Paula thought I was looking at her and threw me another big smile. The guy next to her had dark hair and a narrow face. I had seen him before in the graphics department, where Paula works. He looked a little bit like Tom Cruise, so I could easily see white girls throwing booty at him from all directions.

"Not if I get to him first," I said, leaning toward her. Eliza laughed much too loudly.

"That was pretty funny, Randy. Maybe I'll call you Mr. One-Liner from now on."

She leaned closer this time, even more conspiratorially. "I think I want to sit next to him. I'm going to ask Paula to switch seats with me."

Before I had a chance to object or to rush to the bathroom and slit my wrists, Eliza was up and switching her narrow behind to the other end of the table. I saw her lean over and say something to Paula, whose face instantly brightened. I sighed. Okay, if I really had only one more night to spend around these people—of the fifteen or so people seated around the table in the small restaurant, only about four, including myself and Eliza, were from New York—I could find the grace within me to be kind to this woman for the next couple of hours. But under no circumstances, I promised myself as she slinked her way toward me, would I allow my tongue to be inserted down her throat.

"Hello, Ran-dee," she said chirpily. In her mouth, my name sounded like the word's other meaning, the freaky nasty one.

"Hello, Paula," I said, giving her a bright smile. This was a delicate operation here, to give her enough encouragement to feel loved and desired, but not enough for us to wind up back in my bed.

"I'm going to miss you," she said sadly. She turned down the corners of her mouth and poked out her lips at the same time to demonstrate her sadness. To me, she looked like one of those fish staring up open-mouthed from the blanket of ice at the meat counter. I almost felt like sharing that with her, but I didn't think she'd see the same humor in it.

"Yeah, I know, Paula. I'm going to miss you, too. I was starting to really get used to this city. It's a unique place, so different from New York."

Paula perked up at the mention of New York.

"I've always wanted to go to New York," she said. "Maybe I can visit you there."

If I had had any wine in my mouth, I probably would have sprayed it all over Paula. If I tried for a hundred years, I likely couldn't have come up with a worse idea than that one.

"Hmmm. Well, uh, you want to visit, huh? Well—" I just had no idea what to say. I looked away and tried to come up with something. But Paula mercifully rescued me.

"I know you're married, Ran-dee," she said, leaning in close. If she were any closer, I'd be able to tell the year of the wine that lingered on her breath and assaulted my nose.

"Don't worry," she said. "This is our secret."

I breathed audibly. I didn't mean for the sigh to be that obvious. I looked up at her quickly, ready to apologize if she was offended. But she wasn't even noticing. To my horror, she was busy sliding her left hand up my thigh until it was about two or three inches from my crotch. I looked around to see if anyone was watching us, but the party was in full swing now and all I saw were a lot of dental crowns and bicuspids as the table roared with laughter.

"It won't be a secret for much longer if you keep going with your hand," I said, leaning over to her ear and trying to close the distance between us so her hand in my crotch couldn't be detected.

Paula thought that was a joke. "Ha, you're funny, Ran-dee Murphy."

But she did remove her hand. However, over the next forty-five minutes, I felt like a teenage girl fighting with her boyfriend in a darkened movie theater as I tried to keep her hands off me without cursing at the woman. Even after her food came, she still managed to put down her knife every few minutes to stroke my right thigh. Did she think she was turning me on? Well, actually the stroking *was* giving me an erection that I didn't want. But a wanton erection was not enough to make me succumb. Not on this night.

"Excuse me," I said to Paula and the others around us, as I realized I could escape for a while in the men's room. Most of the people at the table were speaking in French, which limited the number of conversations I could join in—and which effectively lashed me to Paula.

I rushed downstairs to the toilet, wondering how long I could get away with staying down there. I even considered running from the restaurant and back to the hotel, but I couldn't bail from my own going-away party. I'd never live it down. I stepped into the stinky bathroom and knew right away that I'd only be able to survive for about three minutes in there without passing out. That was about as long as I could hold my breath. At no point during my stay in France had I been very impressed with the hygiene habits of the French. Sure, they had the world's most developed and refined aesthetic sensibilities, but they were also slobs.

When I opened the bathroom door to leave, I got a thunderbolt of shock. Right outside the door, about three feet away from my eyes, was Eliza, pinned against the wall by Tom Cruise of the graphics department, tongue wrestling and sending their hands on frantic search missions across each other's bodies. Mr. Graphics had his right hand, the one I could see more clearly, underneath Eliza's skirt and appeared to be fingering her crotch area. I could have sworn Eliza's right hand was down the man's pants.

I stepped back into the bathroom but kept the door open enough for me to look out and get a clear view of the porn movie that was developing in front of me. On the few occasions when I had had a chance to watch a couple amorously involved, I had been enormously turned on. This time was no exception. The fact that it was Eliza, who admittedly had been the star of many of my sexual fantasies, only heightened my arousal. Mr. Graphics pulled up Eliza's skirt now high enough for me to see the black lace of her panties. Damn, she wore black lace panties to work? That would certainly change the way I looked at my colleague. I could hear both of them moaning. I wondered if they were afraid of getting caught, but perhaps that was part of the excitement for them. I could see Eliza's right hand thrashing about and I realized she was pulling old boy's dick out of his pants. It looked like they were actually going to have sex, right here in the basement of the restaurant! I could not believe how freaky and daring Eliza was.

I opened the door a little wider to get a better look. What happened next truly stunned me: Eliza plainly looked right at me, stared for several seconds, then winked at me. She knew I was there all along. Wow. I was staggered. In effect, she was performing for me. Maybe she had even seen me go to the bathroom and had led Mr. Graphics downstairs on purpose. Or, maybe I was being incredibly self-centered and egotistical to even imagine such a scenario. At any rate, she saw me and she wasn't slowing down a bit.

Eliza lifted up her right leg, the one on the other side from me, and wrapped it around Frenchman's waist. He dropped his left arm down to hold her leg up. Eliza reached down and grasped his dick with her left hand now. I could see it snaking out of the man's pants. It looked quite large from where I stood. Eliza was guiding it into the blonde thatch that I could clearly see peeking out from under the lace panties. It appeared that they had some difficulty gaining entry.

"Hold up a minute," Eliza said. I could hear her so clearly, it almost seemed like she was talking to me. She pushed Mr. Graphics back slightly, then in a graceful, impressively quick motion, she bent down and slipped off her panties. She pulled the man back to her and in the same motion she tossed the pair of panties right at my face. I gasped as they hit the frame of the doorway and dropped at my feet. I was almost afraid to bend over and pick them up—if I held them in my hands, I'd almost certainly ejaculate right into my Jockeys.

I heard Eliza moan as Mr. Graphics slid inside of her. I bent my knees slowly and gathered the panties into my left hand. I was so excited that I didn't even notice the bathroom's odor anymore. I just prayed that no one would come downstairs and interrupt.

The couple made a rhythmic pounding noise as he thrust her ass back up against the wall, again and again. There was no way I could have stopped myself from bringing the panties up to my nose. I sniffed deeply and smelled Eliza's pungent scent of moist arousal. I looked up at them and saw her watching me. She grinned when she saw me take a sniff. All these years, when this woman had been bragging to me and teasing me about her advanced sexuality, she hadn't been exaggerating. This was one of the most erotic moments of my life and I wasn't even the one having sex.

All three of us heard the footsteps at the same time. But, to my astonishment, I seemed to be the only one who was bothered by it. These two rutting beasts didn't even pause their thrusting. Whoever it was must have bore brief witness to the scene and raced back upstairs. I wondered about birth control; did Eliza take the pill or something? What about safe sex? Wasn't she worried about that? Apparently not. And neither was Mr. Graphics, whose groaning had elevated a few decibels, announcing that he was about to come.

"Wait, hold on," Eliza said. She abruptly moved back so he would slide out. Then she did something that almost caused me to burst. She turned around and bent over, offering herself from the rear. As Mr.

Graphics squatted down slightly to get the best angle, Eliza turned her head and gave him another order: "Hurry up, baby."

Mr. Graphics grunted in assent and thrust inside her again. After only about five thrusts, Eliza began squealing like a trapped puppy, though I could tell she was trying to keep the noise contained. She had both hands up against the wall and at that moment I was sure she was the freakiest woman I had ever encountered, even including Paula. Mr. Graphics joined her seconds later; he pulled out and let it spray onto her backside. As her moans slowed to whimpers, Eliza reached back and spread his cream over her ass, like she was applying Nivea.

I staggered back into the bathroom, sweating and almost on the verge of orgasm myself. I hurriedly unzipped my pants, yanked out my piece and finished the job off, tugging on it so frantically as I leaned over the toilet bowl that it was almost painful. When the fluid finally drained out of me, much of it missing the toilet and spotting the floor, I leaned back against the wall and tried to catch my breath.

Five minutes later, when I approached the table, Eliza and Mr. Graphics weren't to be found. Maybe they had gone home for round two. They must have had the energy of bunny rabbits, because I myself was already spent. I sat back down next to Paula and I felt emboldened enough to give her a broad smile. I had already had my orgasm for the evening. There was no way I was in any danger of going anywhere with this woman now. She smiled back at me, pleased to be on the receiving end of my attentions. I could smile all night. Smiles didn't cost anything.

No matter how long I stayed away, even if for just a weekend, I considered it one of life's glorious gifts to the New Yorker that I got to circle over Manhattan as the plane headed to the Queens airports. The Manhattan skyline, viewed above from an airplane, sent tingles coursing up and down my spine—all those lofty, glorious buildings, tightly packed together for miles and miles, winding down to the V of lower Manhattan. In unison, every passenger on the plane usually craned to get a glimpse, silently saying a prayer if they happened to be on the side with the breathtaking view.

I was grateful for the respite the view provided, because I had been a bundle of over-stressed nerves for the last hour of the flight. I was not sure what to expect when I saw Mikki; I was afraid that the thing would start off as badly as it did when she visited me in Paris and never get any better. Under this circumstance, that meant separation and anger and tears and divorce. I really, really didn't want that. I loved my wife and wanted to squeeze her into my arms and never let go.

As I stepped from the walkway and into the terminal, I looked around anxiously but I didn't see any sign of her. Okay, not many people did the boarding gate anymore. Surely she was at baggage claim. I told myself about every thirty seconds that no matter what she looked like, no matter what crazy and drastic thing she might have done to her hair or any other part of her, I had to appear utterly ecstatic to see her. Like a starving man sitting down to a four-course meal. I would not allow a repeat of the Paris fiasco, when I had been so dazed by the blond hair that I had distractedly let my displeasure show. I hadn't even gotten up the nerve since she returned to New York to ask her if the blond dye was still in her hair and if she was letting it grow out again. I thought her face was lovely enough to pull off the short hairstyle—I wasn't one of those black men who spit at the idea of speaking to a woman with short hair—but in combination with the blondness it had been enough to do me in.

"Randy!"

I heard her voice from behind and my heart skipped several beats. I could also hear the excitement in her voice and that made me want to smile. I pivoted around and saw my wife running toward me, her arms open wide and a big grin creasing her face. She was smiling! Damn, that made me real happy.

"Welcome home, baby," Mikki said as she walked into my arms and held me tightly. I heard a few sniffles and was surprised to discover they had come from me. I didn't want to break out into sobs here in the middle of the Delta terminal, but I knew I couldn't hold back the moisture from my eyes.

Mikki pushed back and looked at my face, her gaze sweeping over my eyes—I saw her notice the moisture—taking in my nose and my lips. She ran a soft hand over my face and slowly moved her mouth toward mine. Her hair was a dark brown, almost back to black, and it was now past her ears, surely heading toward the way it was when I first left for Paris. We met in a long, soft, passionate kiss, the kind of kiss that I had been expecting to get in Paris. I breathed a long, meaningful sigh.

"It feels so good to be holding you again," I said. "I missed you so much, Mikki. I'm sorry I left you for so long, baby."

Now I could hear Mikki's sniffles.

"It's okay. You're back now. You're home. We're together now."

On the ride back to Brooklyn, I quickly realized it had been a long while since I had been behind the wheel. My driving skills were rusty, especially with the distraction of me and Mikki staring at each other almost as if each had forgotten what the other looked like. Hitting New York City traffic wasn't the ideal way to re-acquaint yourself with the steering wheel. I loved to feel the power of the BMW beneath me. We had fought over the purchase of the car—Mikki thought it was too expensive for our blood; I just couldn't resist when I had the misfortune of test-driving one, after which I couldn't get the smooth intoxicating ride and race car–like acceleration out of my system. After a few weeks, though, Mikki was just as much in love with the car as I was.

There was a growing silence in the car between us that was strange and uncomfortable. I wasn't sure what to say to her. It dawned on me that we were suffering through the same kind of awkwardness that two people might find on a first date—not wanting to say the wrong thing, wanting to make the best possible impression, nervousness about where it might all lead. How could that be the case with my wife?

"So, did you reschedule your appointment?" I asked. It was lame, but it was the only thing I could come up with.

"My appointment?" Mikki repeated. She clearly was expecting me to talk about us, but I didn't know how to start. Thus the lameness.

"Yeah, you said you needed to reschedule an appointment to be able to pick me up this afternoon."

"Oh, that." Mikki dismissed it with a wave of her hand. "Yeah, of course. It wasn't a problem."

More silence. Wow, I didn't expect this. I was starting to panic. We could no longer talk to each other? Is that what was going on; there had been so many bad feelings between us that every step toward an actual conversation seemed too fraught with mines to even give it a try?

I waited a few minutes more, to see if perhaps all this was just a fig-ment of my overactive imagination. But nothing happened. We weren't even stealing glances at each other anymore. All we saw now was the road.

When we got back to Fort Greene, Brooklyn, I thought of some-thing.

"You want me to come to the store with you to keep you company for the rest of the afternoon?" As soon as I said it, I knew it was a bril-liant idea. She'd be grateful and we'd get to spend the rest of the day together.

"Nah, that's okay," she said. "We're really busy. I wouldn't be able to give you any time. I'll just see you when I get home later."

That was that. She hadn't even given it a consideration. When she first opened up the store, I used to spend entire Saturday afternoons with her, sitting to the side and watching her lovingly as she stuck pins in her customers and heard them complain—every single one, from the obese to the hanger-thin—about being too fat. But I supposed three years ago was a long time in relationship years, though it hadn't seemed that long to me.

"All right," I said. I tried not to let my disappointment show, but she caught it anyway. She studied me closely.

"I didn't mean for it to sound like I didn't want to be around you, Randy. I'm really glad to have you home. But you might not like sit-ting there in the store and having me pay no attention to you. That's all I'm saying. We got fittings all the way up to seven o'clock tonight. But that's only, what"—she looked down at her watch—"about five more hours. In the meantime, you can go home and get a little rest." She paused. "And get ready for me."

I cut a quick glance at her to see if she meant it as amorously as it sounded. The way she was smiling at me told me that she did. Okay, that sounded much better. She was sending out those strong signals, in-forming me that there was definitely some booty in my near future. I wouldn't have to spend the rest of the day wondering, like I had in Paris. I was grateful for the heads-up.

"Okay, that sounds like a plan. A great plan, as a matter of fact," I said, grinning. Maybe the silence had only been a manifestation of our nerves, which were assuredly somewhat frayed after the last few months. We had gotten accustomed to not seeing each other, even when we talked on the phone, so it made sense that we'd be a little unsettled in each other's actual presence. Right?

Mikki grinned back at me. Apparently she, too, was a little more at ease now. My gaze lingered an extra minute; I so thoroughly enjoyed watching her when she didn't know I was watching. Her big brown eyes and smooth skin and exceptional lips sent a chill through me. Oooh, my woman was fine!

I eased the car through the somewhat narrow streets of our Brooklyn neighborhood. It felt nice to be back, the surroundings so familiar, so comforting. The brownstones were as proud and elaborate as ever, the brothers and sistahs walking the streets still oh-so-hip and stylish.

I pulled the car up in front of her store. I looked appraisingly at the front window and the awning. Something was different.

"Something looks different," I said. Was it the colors of the awning, or the style of the "Mekhi's" painted on the plate glass?

"Really? You can tell?"

"Yeah. I can tell something's different."

"It's not much. We found this young brother, a painter, who re-did the sign on the glass. It's much fancier now. Actually, Marcus knows him."

"Marcus?" I said, raising my eyebrows. I couldn't imagine Marcus being down with any hip young Fort Greene artist types. "My friend, Marcus?"

"Yes, your friend Marcus," Mikki said, looking at me questioningly. "Why do you say it like that?"

"I don't know. I just didn't know Marcus hung around with any painter types."

Mikki shrugged. "I don't know that he 'hangs out' with the brother. But he recommended him to us, and we were happy with the work. Doesn't it look nice?"

I nodded. It looked all right. I didn't think it was the most professional look in the world, but I knew it'd set Mikki off if I told her that. I wanted to ask her how much she paid this young painter, but I held my tongue. No use getting into something over a stupid painter.

"All right, so I'll see you in a few hours then? You want me to pick you up?"

Mikki shook her head. "Nah, that's not necessary. I can walk. It's nice out today."

Our brownstone was only about six blocks from the store, but I didn't feel real comfortable about Mikki walking. But she insisted on doing it anyway. I shrugged. I had pressed this walking thing before, but there was no use getting into it again. Let her walk.

"All right, I'll see you in—" I looked down at my watch and did some quick calculating. I had already changed the time back on the plane. "In four hours, twenty-six minutes and, uh, thirty-six seconds." I gave her another grin, but she was already out of the car and didn't see it.

" 'Bye," she said, waving and pivoting. I loved watching her walk away, the way her full, firm buttocks marched together in unison, lifting up and down, back and forth, like a well-practiced drill team in a rhythmic syncopation. But she wore a long stylish black overcoat, very loose and flowing, and I could see no ass. She turned and waved again as she pushed open the front door. I saw an unfamiliar woman watching me through the plate glass. Did she get a new assistant in the store without telling me? Apparently she had. I drove off, thinking back longingly to the days when she consulted with me before she even purchased a new lightbulb for the store—after all, the store theoretically belonged to both of us. Now she was making hires without even telling me there was an opening. I shook my head. Things had changed.

She

"So, you think he's going to notice the scarlet letter when he reaches for the panties tonight?"

I knew that asking Zaria to come meet me at the store was a dumb idea the moment I walked through the door and saw her twirling her stupid ass around on my cashier's chair. She didn't even have sense enough to come alone—brought her next door neighbor with her because she wanted to make her trip to the city a help-Mikki/shopping-in-the-big-city day. I thought for sure when that block-headed girl opened the door that Randy had seen her, and I started an immediate panic, thinking he would stop the car and come into the shop and see Zaria there, which would invite all kinds of questions as to why she was there in the first place.

I could just hear the conversation: "Zaria! Good to see you! What you doing here?" And stupid ass would say, "Oh—you know, gonna help Mikki figure out how she's going to continue screwing your best friend until she can figure out what to do with you, then me and block-head here are going shopping."

Zaria made me sorry I'd given her the key to the shop. But I couldn't call Angelou. Judging from the lack of phone calls from her, I'm assuming she's not feeling me either. And there was no way in hell I was going to talk to Marcus again, seeing as he'd already made me cry this morning. Called the house about a half hour before I left to pick Randy up at the airport, he said to give me a pep talk, you know, help me through this. But his voice—and his advice, or lack thereof—just set me off, mainly because he got all smart ass and surprisingly jealous on me.

"So, listen," he began. "Just act like you're happy to see him when he gets off the plane. You know, hug him, smile. I guess you'll have to kiss him, but don't go enjoying that shit."

Now, I let that go. But then he turned around and told me in practically the same breath that I should treat Randy like nothing's wrong and "avoid fucking him, because I don't want sloppy seconds."

"What," I asked incredulously, "is that supposed to mean?" He then got quiet.

"Nothing, baby—just go get your man."

"Why are you doing this?" I said, tears welling up in my eyes. "You're acting like I wanted this to happen."

Then, just like that, he got to cleaning up his mistake. Even softened his tone, got rid of the smart-alecky attitude. "Babe, I know this is a shock to your system. All I'm saying is you have to act as normal as possible when he gets off that plane and for the next couple of days, at least until we get things under control." See why I couldn't call Marcus to calm me?

And seeing as I didn't have any friends, Zaria and blockhead were going to have to be it.

"Are you going to listen to me, or are you going to just sit here and make jokes? Because I can just turn my Chris Rock tape on and laugh at someone who's much funnier than you," I told Zaria, annoyed by her scarlet letter remark.

"Okay, okay," she said. "So tell me what happened when Mr. Gay Pa-ree got off the plane."

Well, I kinda missed Randy's grand entrance. While he was strolling up toward the boarding gate, I was in the bathroom searching my eyes, my face, my cheeks, my lips, my fingertips for evidence—evidence that could have implicated me in a tragic adulterous mess that would surely end my marriage before the Beemer even made it onto the Van Wyck Expressway. And by the time he'd actually made it into the airport, the cleaning woman was handing me tissue and asking me in Spanglish if I needed help. It took me a minute to get the smeared Maybelline from under my eyelashes and freshen up my lip gloss in preparation for my grand entrance. And then I said a short prayer, something like, "Dear

God, I swear, if you just get me through the next five minutes, I promise I'll cut one of them off and dedicate myself to the other." Yeah, like God was into helping an adulterer. I wasn't even dealing in absolutes, for Christ's sake. Learned in Sunday School that the one thing He hates more than an adulterer is a wishy-washy adulterer who says she'll stop but doesn't really intend to. Lord. I gave a final smile to Mrs. Clean and made my way into the waiting area, where Randy had, apparently, been waiting.

He had his back to me at first, but he turned around in time enough to see me coming up slowly behind him. And when I saw his face, I got dizzy. Because it was the first time in all those months he'd been away that I realized I'd really, truly missed my husband. Really—I had. After all the mess. And from the tears, I could tell that he'd missed me, too. We cried together—held each other hard, hugged each other strong—right there in the middle of the international terminal, like no one else was there. Spanglish walked by with her mop and pail in hand, smiling like she'd seen the perfect ending to a romantic movie. "*Buenos dias*, Miss," she said as she moved past us. I gave her a curt wave, took Randy by the arm, and walked off into the sunset.

And then reality hit when we got to the car. I didn't know what to say. I didn't have anything to say. I didn't want to say anything. I was too afraid to talk—afraid that whatever I said would be a dead giveaway. So I kept it simple, asked how the plane ride was, if he'd eaten, whether he'd gotten any rest on the ride over, if the in-flight movie was interesting. And after I'd run through the list of wack "how was the flight" questions, I decided to shut my mouth. And in an instant, it was weird between us again. The ride to Brooklyn couldn't have possibly gotten any longer.

"Come on, Zaria, tell me what to do," I said, dropping my face into my hands.

"Oh, my bad," she said right back. "I didn't think I was qualified to give relationship advice, seeing as I've never really had one."

What the hell did I invite this girl over here for? It was clear she had no intention of helping me out, that she was here simply to be all up in my Kool-Aid. I got the feeling pretty quickly that she only wanted to make me feel worse than I already did, like she was trying to take said Kool-Aid and drop it all over my good, clean, new silk suit. My sister.

"You know what? Never mind, Zaria," I said angrily. "Why don't you just go shopping. Make yourself useful and go buy some shoes or something."

"Okay, okay," she said, easing up. "It was a joke, damn. You ain't got no kind of a sense of humor, Mikki. First, what you need to do is lighten the hell up."

"Lighten up? You want me to lighten up?"

"Yes, lighten up," she said. "If you keep stomping around here acting like someone knocked your mother upside the head and left her for dead, Randy's going to know something's up. It's that simple." She was right. "Now, did you do what I told you to do with the lipstick?"

I have to admit, the lipstick thing was a good idea. After my midnight condom search last night, I'd gone over to Zaria's to drop off the shop key and there she was, half-sleep, talking about "tell him you missed him with lipstick."

"Huh?" I said. "Lipstick? What are you talking about?"

She rolled her eyes, then yawned. "I said, take your lipstick—preferably a nice red one—and draw an 'I Miss You' message on the mirror. That way, when he walks into your bedroom, he'll know you were thinking good things about him, even if you act crazy at the airport."

Turns out it was a brilliant idea. The lipstick booty I'd left on the mirror would surely divert his attention from my acting a complete fool in the car and telling him he couldn't hang out with me at the shop. He'd see it and think, immediately, about the implications: an explicit "I Miss You" note would translate easily into a "You're Going to Get Some When I Get Home" message. I'd been involved with Randy long enough to know that the easiest way to divert his attention from anything under the sun—high credit card bills, missed utility payments, unauthorized clothing expenditures, terroristic bomb threats—was to throw some ass in his face. The question was, what would happen after the lovemaking session was over?

Of course, I didn't have time to consider any of this last night; I was on a serious mission. Do you know how hard it is to find an economy pack of Sheik ultra sensitive lambskin condoms in a black urban neighborhood in the middle of the damn night? Let me break it down for you, so that it will forever be broke: you can barely find milk, fresh eggs, unmolded bread, and fly-free mystery meat in Brooklyn in the daytime, much less a box of contraceptives just before midnight. Fort Greene is no exception. Don't let the press fool you; the *New York Times* has convinced white folks that because this neighborhood has some well-to-do, overly hip buppies and yuppies with great jobs, some nice ethnic restaurants, and a few cool summer concerts in Fort Greene Park that it is the place to be if you're an African American with money or you're one of those white folks with a strange allegiance to blacks. One could very well find herself buying into it, too, what with all the stars who live there mingling with the dredlocked, poetry-spewing twenty-somethings walking the streets, draped in their Afrocentric designs and cowrie shells, quoting Erykah Badu, talking about Negro revolution.

But you know what? I'm from New Jersey, the 'burbs. Where they pick up the garbage at least twice a week. All of it. And you can walk from one corner to the next after nightfall without fear that you just might not make it back. And know that when you wake up, all the air bags in your car will be where you left them the night before. Where you can safely assume that your next door neighbor's neighbor ain't running a crack den in his attic. And somebody—don't know who, exactly, but somebody—goes into the park and cuts the grass so that the vermin won't come and bite your kid while he makes his way to the swing. And dammit, you can find a Pathmark or a ShopRight or a Grand Union somewhere that's open late at night and stocks fresh meat, milk, fruit, eggs, and several kinds of jumbo boxes of condoms.

But I wasn't in South Orange the night before Randy came home. I was in Brooklyn. Running around our brownstone like a mad woman, trying my best to erase every semblance of Marcus from my living room and my closets and my bathroom and, especially, my bedroom. I smelled him in the sheets. Saw him in the mirrors. Noticed him on the rim of the toilet, where he'd peed late in the night and missed the target. Found him in my sink, where my dishes were piled up in twos—two plates from dinner the other night, two cups from coffee the other morning, two spoons from the ice cream we snacked on after we'd last made love. It was all evidence—evidence I was sure Randy would use to discover what I didn't want him to know: that I'd been screwing around. So, in the middle of the night, I stripped off my clothes, climbed into my exercise gear, ducked down under my kitchen sink, pulled out my bucket of cleaning solvents and rags, and turned myself into a damn cleaning fool. I scrubbed. I rubbed. I shined. I mopped. I vacuumed. I changed sheets. I washed dishes. I swept up the little, teeny weeny hairs on the side of the bathtub that I thought for sure were left there the time Marcus, fresh from the barber's chair, stopped by my house to wash the cut hair from his neck and get a little sumthin', sumthin' afterward.

I'd actually stopped crying by the time I made it to the bedroom with the Pledge in one hand, the Carpet Fresh in the other. It was the last room I had to scrub down—the easiest by far, because there wasn't much furniture there. I've always been the type who preferred space over things—never liked more than a bed and a TV hutch in my room. Randy and I fought bitterly over what kind of furniture would occupy our personal living quarters; I wanted a king-sized sleigh bed and a wall-length armoire/tv hutch. He wanted that, two dressers, two nightstands, and several standing lamps. We finally settled on a beautiful mahogany bed and matching nightstands, and I had my armoire custom made to include drawer space for clothes. It was stunning and simplistic in design, really classy, regal. And easy to clean. All I had to do was put clean sheets on the bed, wipe down the nightstands and vacuum, then I could take my behind to bed. Or so I thought, when I went to empty the garbage can and found a condom wrapper. I swear, I thought I was hit by lightning—like God had finally had enough of me and decided to take me out. That's how my body felt when I twirled around, leapt at Randy's nightstand, and grabbed at the condom box. There were five left. Out of a box of thirty-six. And I couldn't remember for the life of me how many I'd used with Randy and how many I'd used with Marcus. Now, I don't know if guys do this, but I know damn well women do: whether she trusts him or not, she makes a point of counting the condoms so that whenever she comes back from wherever she went, she can get a close-to-accurate accounting of whether her man's been slipping with some other girl.

Not that he couldn't just go out and buy another condom for the other woman, but you know how sloppy men can be about dipping their things where they don't belong. They don't think through the details. It's how they always get caught. And by the looks of it, I was about to get busted, too—because I know damn well there were more than five condoms left in that box before Randy left for Paris. I looked up at the clock. It was 1:03 a.m. Where in the hell was I going to find a box of condoms that time in the morning? In Brooklyn? Where there was a store on every corner, but each of them stocked with more substandard, over-priced products than the last? I was jacked. And I wasn't even rational, because I never considered finding them in the morning.

I pulled on my sneakers, grabbed my keys from the sofa console, and rushed out into the cool night air. I drove the Beemer to the corner bodega. Nothing but condom singles. Then to another a few blocks into Clinton Hill. More singles. Cut across a few blocks into Bed-Stuy, then drove about ten minutes back downtown to Boerum Hill and Park Slope, then to a few stores and an all-night supermarket in Brooklyn Heights. Nothing. Before I knew it, my fingers were flying over the number pads of my cell phone. Zaria would have to get over my calling her so late. She answered after two rings.

"Zaria! Wake up," I yelled into the phone.

"What? What's wrong?" she said back, a hint of worry mixing with the sleep in her voice. "Mikki?"

"How late does that CVS around the corner from your house stay open?"

"What?" Zaria was awake now. "Mikki? What time is it?"

"It's after two," I answered in a rush. "Listen, I need to find a box of condoms—a specific kind—and I need to go to a drugstore to get them. Is that CVS still open?"

"Okay—I can't believe you are calling me two o'clock in the morning to ask me about some damn condoms, Mikki. What the fuck?"

"Just tell me if the damn store is open, Zaria. You can curse me out some other time, okay?"

"It's a twenty-four-hour store, Mikki. That means it's open twenty-four hours a day. That means unless the shit burned down or the cashier dropped dead and they're in the middle of an investigation into how he died, it's open."

"Thanks, Zaria," I said in a hurry. "I'm on my way over there."

"On your way—" she said, then changed her thought mid-sentence. "Mikki. What are you doing? What's gotten into you? Are you losing your mind?"

"No—I'm going to lose my husband if he opens up his nightstand and finds someone else used up all his condoms with his wife." Zaria was silent for a moment. And then she simply said, "Oh."

"Oh," I said back nastily. "Yeah, oh. Now you understand, huh? Randy's coming back home tomorrow and I need to make sure those condoms are in his nightstand . . ." Now I was the one who couldn't finish the sentence. The tears welled in my eyes, blurring my vision and making it hard for me to drive. Thank God I had to stop for the yellow then red light, or I would have surely crashed my ride.

"Mikki?" Zaria, recognizing I was in the middle of a nervous breakdown, had removed the bass from her voice. "Why don't you come over here after you stop by CVS. We can talk and you can rest here until the morning."

"I'll stop by and drop off the shop key so that we can talk tomorrow, because right now, I don't really feel like talking, Zaria," I said back to her, collecting myself. "I just want to get those condoms and finish straightening up the house. Randy's coming home." And with that, I hung up the phone.

He

I wandered aimlessly around my house for at least an hour after I hit the front door. I really liked where I lived, the way the inside of my house made me feel. When I was younger and I imagined life for well-to-do black people in New York City, this is the kind of house I imagined living in, with dark polished wood everywhere, fireplaces, marble mantels, elaborate mahogany banisters, old artful window frames that had the dramatic lines of sculpture, sparkling expensive-looking light hardwood floors that reflected the sunlight with just the right intensity. And with Mikki's decorative flair—and expensive tastes—we had created the kind of home that made our friends and guests gush. It had taken us a year and a half to get it just right, in fact, we had only considered ourselves done just before I left for Paris, and the last thing I wanted to think about was the possibility of leaving my magnificent abode.

In the bedroom, Mikki had a surprise waiting for me: on the large mirror above her vanity table, in bright red lipstick, she had written the words "Welcome Back" alongside a big red heart. I chuckled because Mikki had drawn the "W" in "Welcome" to look like the torso and big round perfect ass of a woman. With an ass like that, certainly a black woman. In fact, it could have been a self-portrait. Mikki did know where my tastes ran. As I stared at the "W," I thought back to Paula and flashed on a disconcerting image of her offering her ass to me, wiggling it as she perched on the edge of the hotel bed on her hands and knees, looking back at me with a lascivious grin. I felt the thickening start in my pants, against my will. I shook my head, trying to clear away the picture. I did not want this happening, these unwelcome memories of the freaky Frenchwoman piercing the sanctity of my home. I just prayed that the images would stay away when me and Mikki were in the midst of lovemaking.

I started to remove my clothes. What I wanted more than anything at that moment was to slip in a steaming hot bath and stay there for hours. And that's exactly what I did. I even drifted off to sleep, with the faint smell of Mikki's perfume hanging over the room, soothing and exciting me at the same time. I wondered how much longer I had to wait.

"Randy! You fell asleep in the bathtub? How long have you been in there?"

My eyes flew open to find Mikki standing over me, a bemused expression on her face. How long *had* I been in there? I had no idea.

"What time is it?" I said, fighting the cobwebs in my head and the cottony dryness in my mouth.

"It's six o'clock. What time did you get in the bathtub?"

I didn't really know what time I had gotten into the bathtub. It couldn't have been much later than four.

"I don't know, probably about two hours ago," I said. When I moved, I felt the icy coldness of the water. "Damn, this water is cold as hell," I said.

"I hope you haven't shriveled up into a prune," Mikki said, grinning. I wondered if she was talking about what I thought she might be.

"If that most important part is shriveled, I'm sure you'll figure out some way to make it grow again." I grinned back at her and heard her girlish giggle. Yep, that's exactly what she was talking about. I raised my hands and looked in wonderment at the crinkly, deformed-looking skin on my fingers. I pushed myself out of the tub and stood in front of my wife in all my naked glory.

She looked me in the face, then let her gaze sweep down over my body. I hadn't done a lot of exercise in Paris, but my metabolism luckily seemed to assiduously deny any fat from forming on my lanky but solid frame. The word to describe my body was sinewy. That was Mikki's word. She said she had always liked sinewy. Now she smiled.

"I've always loved your body," she said. Just her gaze and her words made me start to stir in the crotch. The water hadn't messed with that. Finally, having shown off enough, I reached for the towel and started drying.

"I think maybe I need to join you in your nakedness," Mikki said. She reached around and unzipped her skirt, letting it drop to the floor. In one motion, she pulled her blouse over her head. She wasn't wearing a bra; her full breasts bounced and jiggled as she brought her arms back to her sides. I stared at them and felt my penis start to rise up. Her panties were white and sheer, so I could see the dark patch of her pubic hair.

I stepped out of the tub and pulled her into my arms. We kissed hungrily, as if we could devour each other. I didn't even care that Mikki's open mouth was feeding me healthy portions of her slobber; I was willing to go along with her sloppy, wet kisses because I knew they excited her that much more. After breaking off the kiss, we looked into each other's eyes and rushed toward the bed. Without even pulling back the cover, Mikki leapt on top of the comforter—which she normally would never do—and spread her legs before me. I realized this must be a special occasion for her if she was willing to sacrifice a comforter for expediency's sake. I dived on top of her. I knew I didn't have a condom, but I didn't want to stop. But Mikki wasn't quite *that* excited.

"You're forgetting something, aren't you?" she asked, pointing to the nightstand that held the condoms.

It could have bothered me, the implications of her sending me to the condom drawer, but I let it go by. I reached into the drawer and pulled out the box. It was unopened. Things must have been pretty bad before I went away for us to have a brand-new, unopened box in the drawer. Because I wouldn't have bought a new box before I left if I wasn't expecting to get some. I thought about mentioning the new box to Mikki, but I let that go by, too. No need to get her upset.

Once the condom was on and I was inside of her, I tried to block out all thoughts except for the thrill shooting from my groin. I was almost successful, but then I looked down and realized that Mikki wasn't really moving that much. In fact, she never really moved that much. She was much more content to spread her legs far apart and then let me do most of the back-and-forth work. That had never been a problem for me at all until the evening with Paula. Paula moved so

much that she had even thrown me off one time, like a bronco bucking off a rodeo cowboy. But my wife was far from a bucking bronco.

Once again, I grew angry at myself for allowing these European
memories to mess things up. So what, Paula had moved more? What
did it matter? I was still enjoying myself right now, making love to my
darling wife, right? How acrobatic, how enthusiastic, how athletic, did
sex have to be to be considered good sex, anyway? Mikki wasn't a
gymnast and would never be one. So what?

A few minutes later, after she had flipped around and I was looking
down at the big round sphere of her ass pointed up at me, I smiled.
Paula had nothing on her in the ass department, that was for sure. A
big round booty was certainly enough to keep a black man happy,
wasn't it? I slapped it a few times to watch it jiggle. Forget acrobatics—this was the good stuff, right here.

She

Sleeping with my husband four months after he'd left our bed for Paris was—God, how do I describe it?—wonderful. And awful.

Sleeping with Marcus two days later was just plain gross. Not because Marcus is nasty—not at all. I love him to death and I enjoy making love with him, the way he moves, the way he feels, the way he makes me feel. I don't think that's ever going to change. But his sexual prowess and tenderness—well, he wasn't really tender that time, but I'll get to that—didn't mean anything to me that Monday afternoon because all I could think of was what a slut I'd become. I was at my dregs, a bottom crawler. I was sleeping with two men, mixing body fluids with the two of them like some prostitute on HBO's *Pimps Up, Hoes Down*.

I hadn't done something like that since college. But at Spelman, it really didn't have the same implications as it does today. For one, at Spelman, I wasn't married and cheating on my husband. But on that campus, it was like a sexual revolution, an awakening for me. Sleeping with more than one man for this college girl was, I don't know, empowering almost, because I was beholden to no one, you know? I didn't have to answer to any man, or be responsible for his sexual well-being or feelings. My expressed intent was to enjoy myself, to find out who I was, what I liked, how I liked it, how I could make someone else like me. And that took experimentation. With boys. And if I happened to like Rob and Joe at the same time and I wanted to have sex with one and the other in the same week, well, I wasn't about to tell Joe we couldn't do it because I was already sleeping with Rob. Both of them were going to get some because I wanted it.

That's how it is for women on college campuses, or at least the way it was with my friends. Our hearts twisted from all the abuse we'd taken from our high school boyfriends, we went to college determined to first learn, and then play. A lot. Taking special care not to get played. And the way you did that was to indulge yourself just like the boys did. See a cutie, make his acquaintance, sleep with him if you were attracted, and keep it moving. There was nothing whorish about it. It was revolution—female revolution—no different from being pro-choice or swearing off marriage and babies for a career that hadn't even formed itself yet, or smoking and drinking with abandon and sleeping through classes because you could, without someone telling you it wasn't ladylike. In college it was like, fuck ladylike. We were women. And unlike high school, under the watchful eye of our parents and our neighbors and our churchfolk and our society's notions of what a woman's place was, no one was going to tell us girls what to do, how to do it, who we should do it with, and damn for sure not how many. Anyone who questioned that behavior, was, without question, simply anti-woman.

This was my mindset at least. And I wielded it like a sword. Like in my junior year. There were these three guys, see, all equally attractive, smart, accomplished, forward-moving. There was James, the football player/criminal justice major from Georgia Tech, and Altimus, the business major/wanna-be-college administrator from Emory, and Donald, the club-hopping English major from Morehouse. And I, at some point during the year, had sex with all three of them. Not at the same time, you see. The relationships—or, as we called it, the friendships—that we had all kind of overlapped at some point, with me meeting and dating James in October at some football rally my girls had dragged me to, and Altimus at some college business fair we'd bumped into each other at in March, and Donald in some club we'd gone to to unwind from studying in early May. You know how those college relationships work; meet the guy wherever, exchange numbers, talk on the phone and lunch and club together for a few weeks, then do what animals do on the Discovery channel—have sex. There were no emotions involved for me, no yearning to turn any of them into my husband. I just wanted to have a good time with them.

But at the end of the semester, you know, you have to say good-bye to folks—let them know that they'll be missed, even if things on the relationship front didn't work out. I just happened to have to say good-bye to three guys that week before summer break rolled around. And seeing as none of them knew about the other—hey, if I was dating someone else before them, it really wasn't any of their business—they all kinda just showed up on my doorstep, damn near one after the other.

And I happily obliged them, and endulged myself, by sleeping with all three within days of each other. Felt good about it, bragged about it to my girls even. I'd gotten over on all three of them; made them feel special one minute, gave them the boot the next, with no promises of commitment, much less assurances that they'd be invited back.

I felt like a man. Or at least that I'd had their sexual power. It's funny how quickly those ideals change, how circumstances and knowledge and, I don't know, maturity and loneliness turn them on their ear. Not immediately after college is over, but close to it, after you find yourself scraping by in some cramped studio apartment, eating Ramen noodles and taking in movies alone, wondering if your girls—all of whom are off living lives of their own—are as lonely and bored as you are. You realize that the things you held so dear just a few years before really aren't all that important. Your priorities have just changed. With your career comes responsibility. With your success comes a desire to share it with someone special. Even my pro-choice views in college took a right at some point. I mean, I would have rather chewed off my left arm than tell someone they didn't have a right to have an abortion while they were at Spelman—thought it too important that women have the right to end a pregnancy if they knew it would stop their lives dead in their tracks before they'd hardly begun. But today, even though I certainly don't want any rugrats of my own, I'm a little more torn on the issue, with the larger part of me thinking it's more important for women to either close their legs or reach for a condom rather than kill a baby for their own convenience. I think that came from watching Zaria have her babies despite the fact their daddy wasn't taking care of them properly; it certainly didn't end her life, and those kids, bad as they are, are truly a blessing to my family. When I look at them, I think, okay, their mom was right, they deserved life.

And my man—whether it be Randy, Marcus or whoever—deserves

all of me. Not just every other night, but all day every day, exclusively. That stupid desire I had in college to sleep with every man with a cute face and a hard penis wasn't empowering, now that I'm grown and can look back at it. It was ridiculously whorish, for one. And stupid, considering what kinds of diseases I could have gotten sleeping around with this one, that one, and everyone in between.

And, at its base, it was unfulfilling. I wasn't getting over, I was giving it away. I certainly wasn't hurting the men I was sleeping with by demanding our relationships be strictly sexual; in fact, I was letting them off the hook—telling them that they could get free ass with no commitment. How did that help me any?

It didn't.

It was just plain, dry, boning—no different from being a dog in heat, letting the neighborhood mutts mount her. Not special.

But making love—my God, there's nothing on this earth more deliriously pleasing than sharing your body with the person you adore. The emotions that come with it turn sex into a sensual, mind-blowing experience. You look deep into each others' eyes and you whisper tender words meant only for each others' ears, passionate words that really mean something to your heart, your soul.

You become one.

I can't, however, become one with Marcus—the one I love—while I'm sleeping with Randy. It's just impossible for me to split those feelings into two. I love Randy, he's my husband. But I'm not in love with him. Which means that when we have sex, it's just that—sex. There's no passion, there are no emotions that come with it. The night of his homecoming, I wasn't feeling anything for him. At least not at first. I'd come into the house with the purpose of screwing him, so that we wouldn't have to talk. Because I knew that if we got to talking, I wouldn't be able to continue to hide from him the fact that I was being unfaithful and that our relationship, in essence, was basically through.

But he was trying so very hard to please me, to make me feel special. And I'll admit that, for the first few minutes, I suspended time and squeezed my eyes real tight and made myself believe that Randy and I were new again, that we were truly in love. In an instant, I felt like I was making love to him and he was making love to me.

But it didn't take long for me to get smacked back into reality. I don't know exactly what turned my thoughts to it, but I couldn't help but begin thinking that I was, somehow, cheating on Marcus. I was under some other man giving him my body, making him feel special, wanted, loved, and I wasn't getting the same for myself in return. Not because Randy wasn't giving his all, but because the man on top of me wasn't the man I thought I was in love with. And the moment my attention turned to that, I felt compelled to get up—just get out of there, leave the house, go to another neighborhood, or at least another room. I needed to breathe. I needed to rush to Marcus's arms. I needed to make Randy come.

So I pushed him off me and flipped myself over and lifted my ass in the air, with all its glory. Randy loved my ass, worshipped it. I knew that the moment I let him bump and grind against it, he would come almost instantly. And with every moan and yelp he let out—with every drop of his bodily fluids flowing into that condom—I recognized that I had just lifted my ass in the air for the sole purpose of helping a man get a nut.

I had treated Randy like a trick. Only thing missing was the cash.

Even more so, I felt guilty for doing it, even more so than I did for cheating on him. Because Randy deserves more—someone whose heart truly belongs to him. For that reason, I just can't sleep with Randy anymore, can't and won't.

I'm having a hard time convincing Marcus of this, though. Mainly because of the way I performed—or didn't—that following Monday, when I snuck over to his apartment to see him. Before I could get into the door good, he was all over me, pulling at my shirt, pawing at my ass, pulling my hair back and biting my neck. He was an animal.

I didn't need an animal. Or sex. I needed to talk to him, to have him put his arms around me, calm my spirit, ease my fear. Assure me that it was going to be all right.

Not happening.

"What? You don't want me now that Randy's home?" he said, grabbing at my ass.

I let him touch it, then I brushed his hand away. "Come on, Marcus," I said quietly. "This is hard enough as it is."

"Come on, baby—what's hard about it? You don't sleep with Randy and you sleep with me. I don't see the difficulty there."

"You don't see the difficulty?" I said, incredulous. "He's my husband, Marcus!"

"No shit, he's your husband. That doesn't mean you have to fuck him."

"What do you mean that doesn't mean I have to fuck him? We sleep in the same bed. How on earth would I be able to live in the same house with my husband and not sleep with him?"

"Easy," he yelled. "You don't."

I snatched my arm away from him and rushed across the room, then started pacing back and forth so furiously that I knocked some videotapes off the sofa table and onto the floor. Finally, I twirled myself onto the sofa, and buried my face in my hands.

"You're acting like I want to sleep with him."

"Well, don't you?" he said back, quickly.

"No, I don't," I shot back. "Despite what you think, I'm not comfortable sleeping with men I'm not in love with."

"But it doesn't stop you from doing it," he said. "And I'll tell you this much, I'm not the man to be fucking if you're rolling around in somebody else's bed. You can understand why I feel that way, can't you?"

With that comment, he brought tears to my eyes. "Look, I'm not going to sleep with him anymore, okay? I'll figure something out."

"How you going to do that while you're still wearing his ring?" he asked, his voice tinged with a little disgust now.

"Oh—I'm sorry," I said, equally disgusted. "You want me to stop wearing his damn ring? Well, tell you what: why don't we just call him right now and tell him all about us so that I can take his fucking ring off and we can be together." I took off my ring and threw it as hard as I could at Marcus. But I throw like a girl—and I have a wicked curve—so it landed somewhere about ten feet to the right of where he was standing. He looked at me like I was crazy, and burst out laughing.

"Damn, Mick—were you trying to hit me or the next door neighbor?"

I wasn't laughing. I was breathing hard—from anger more than physical exertion. But his eyes were bright again—almost like the argument that we'd just had didn't happen. He walked over, sat on the couch beside me, and took my hand into his.

"Baby, it's not time to tell Randy anything," he said quietly.

"Well, then, why are you stressing me over this?" I yelled. "Do you have any idea how hard it is to go into that house and look into his face and pretend I'm in love when I know damn well the man I love is somewhere else?"

"Mikki, calm down, baby. I'm sorry," he said, again quietly. "I guess that when Marti and I fell off it was easy for us not to sleep with each other, seeing how much we just coudn't stand each other. I was trying to compare the end of my marriage with yours, and that's not fair. Everyone's different, and I understand that you have to do what you have to do until we can figure out how to tell him." He paused. "But, Mikki—we can't say anything yet, okay? Not a word. Randy can't know anything about this until we decide how we're going to handle this."

"Well, when are we going to decide? Because I just don't know how much more of this I can take."

"Mikki, there are a lot of things we have to consider. When you break up with Randy, are you going to keep the brownstone or are you going to let him have it? If you let him have it, where are you going to live? What about the business? Doesn't Randy own a large portion of it? Are you ready to give that up? Do you have any plans for what you'll do if he decides he wants to pull out his financial support? Are you ready to deal with the implications of leaving your husband for his best friend? Have you thought any of this through?"

Damn. He was right. I hadn't thought any of this through. I was quiet. My breathing was easier, but my mind was working overtime. What the hell was I going to do? I loved my business. I loved my home. I loved my life before Randy went off to Paris without me. How was all of that going to change if I left him?

Marcus, recognizing that I was thinking about all that he'd said, got up and walked over to where my ring had landed. He found it, then walked back over to where I was sitting, and took my left hand into his.

"Keep this on, Mikki—just for now. We're going to work this out, I promise."

And with that, he took me into his arms.

We made love.

Or at least that's what it felt like while we were doing it. But when I got up from his bed and pulled my clothes back on, I felt dirty. Nasty. Ridiculously immature.

This wasn't going to work. Something had to give.

He

The sex was on Saturday. But now it was Friday, six days later, and we hadn't had sex again. As I sat in my new office at Trier-Stanton, looking out at my new view of midtown Manhattan, I derived no pleasure from the majesty of the clustered skyscrapers looming all around me like redwoods. I was agitated. What was wrong with my wife? I had tried everything I could think of over the past week, but she hadn't been interested in anything having to do with me, or so it seemed. She had pushed me away, literally and figuratively, always managing to avoid me until she claimed she just had to go to sleep.

The first few nights, though I was bothered, I had dismissed it. We had never been one of those couples that screwed every night anyway. But by Wednesday night, I was deeply disturbed. So disturbed that I risked a big blow-out argument by mentioning it to her. But she had even managed to deftly sidestep the question. Like she couldn't even summon the passion to argue with me.

"I've just been really tired, that's all," she said, yawning—for effect, I wondered? "You know, June is fast approaching. This is a busy time for me in the store."

As a matter of fact, I had been beating Mikki home from work all week, even with my increased responsibilities as the head of the entire creative department. I could remember the previous Octobers and Novembers of years past; she hadn't seemed overly busy then. Why the sudden rush now? Had her store grown that much more popular, or was something else going on?

I could no longer figure it out by myself; I picked up the phone and called Marcus. He sounded rushed, but agreed to meet me at seven that night. We were supposed to meet on Wednesday, but Marcus predictably had canceled on me, saying he had to work late. He *always* had to work late.

"What do *you* think I should do, man?" I asked for about the fifth time in the past hour. Marcus, seemingly intent on downing an entire six-pack of Coronas by himself, had gotten less helpful with each bottle. Now he was spending more time gaping at a honey-coated sistah perched on a nearby bar stool than listening to me. And to think I had been telling myself with great admiration how skilled a listener Marcus was. Well, at least he was skilled when he was sober.

"Randy, man, I can't tell you what the problem is," Marcus said. I could see that Miss Honey-Coated was staring back at Marcus now. Not for the first time, it occurred to me that Marcus might be hitting quite a lineup of grade-A booty now that he was back on the market again. He was handsome and gainfully employed. What else did a brother need these days to have the sistahs—and, in many cases, the white girls—lined up?

"I know you don't know what the problem is," I said. "I was just wondering if you went through any of this with Marti before things went bad."

At the mention of his wife's name, Marcus's attention was yanked back to the table. He looked me in the face, then dropped his eyes down to his beer. He almost appeared to be sober again. Damn, just her name could sober the brother up? If I had to guess, I'd say that Marcus was still in love.

"I don't even know what was going through Marti's mind in the end," Marcus said, shaking his head. "I'm sorry, but I'm all out of insights, bro."

Something had been sneaking up on me, a suspicion, and I thought I'd try it out on my friend, who had spent some time around Mikki over the past few months.

"I was kinda wondering if"—I took a swallow of spit—"maybe she was, like, having an affair or something." Once I said it, I couldn't even look Marcus in the face. It was terribly humiliating for a man to even consider such thoughts about his wife. To give voice to it, even if I was talking to my best friend, made it much worse.

"An affair? Really? Mikki? Nah," Marcus said, sitting back and dismissing the thought with a curt wave of the left hand—the one not holding the beer.

I was relieved that Marcus had dismissed it so quickly, but I still wasn't totally convinced.

"I know it sounds unlikely, but I can't think of anything else. I mean, I've cooked for the woman, I've offered to give her massages, I've tried to stay interested in what she's doing at the store. I even cleaned the house the other day."

That one caused Marcus to study me more closely. I knew it would. That was quite an admission to make.

"Wow," Marcus said, staring off into the distance. "You cleaned the house? The whole house?"

"Yep," I said sheepishly, still not sure if I should be embarrassed. "All four goddamn floors."

Marcus whistled to show his surprise.

"I don't mean to sound like a chauvinist or a Neanderthal, understand, but that's some serious love, man. Cleaning four floors. What was her reaction?" I shrugged. "Believe it or not, she didn't really have much of a reaction. She mumbled something about the house not really needing a cleaning anyway. She seemed surprised, but it wasn't like she was overly grateful or anything. I think her reaction was like, 'Hey, it's his house, too. He *should* be helping with the cleaning.' And we *are* supposed to split things up, but we rarely get around to it and we usually wind up calling the cleaning service. Or at least that's what used to happen before I left."

"Damn, I think she's leaving," Marcus said, his gaze trained on the bar. I looked over and saw the lovely lady, who had a short, natural hairstyle—her hair wasn't much longer than mine—and the cheekbones of a cover girl, give a barely perceptible glance in the direction of our table and move toward the front door, her round ass and slightly mushrooming hips visible underneath tight black pants.

"Damn, she got more ass and hips than I thought," Marcus said. "You see her look over here?"

I nodded. I wanted to finish talking about Mikki.

"You think I should try going after her?" Marcus asked me.

I shrugged. "I don't know, man. Go 'head."

Marcus instantly recognized my pique. "All right, I'm sorry, man." He leaned toward me and straightened himself up in his chair, as if to put himself in a better listening position. "You were saying that you even cleaned the house. And you still got nuthin'?"

I shook my head.

"Well, maybe if you really suspect something, you could get a private detective to follow her for a coupla weeks. That'll ease your mind."

I reared back in shock. "You mean, like *Magnum, P.I.* or something?" I laughed. "Or maybe that chick from *Murder, She Wrote*, what's her name?"

"I'm serious, man. There are some really good private detectives out there. I know of a few that we use at the firm. I could hook you up with one."

I studied Marcus's face. Apparently, he was serious. Hiring somebody to follow my wife around would be taking this to a whole other level. Was I ready for surveillance and spying and the implications of all that? True, it did make me uncomfortable, but what was there to lose—besides my wife if I didn't do something in a hurry?

"Okay, let's do it," I said firmly, locking eyes with my best friend. I had said it with conviction, but I still wasn't absolutely certain it was the right thing to do. However, I doubted that I was going to receive a message from on high, spelling out on stone tablets the actions I should take. Advice from Marcus was about as good as it was going to get.

The private detective's office was about a dozen blocks from Trier-Stanton, so I decided to walk over. It was an unseasonably warm fall day, and the beautiful female portion of the city's population was taking advantage of the lingering sun to let their nubile young limbs stretch in preparation for the winter covering. I was almost blinded by the dizzying array of hotness that strolled before me, nearly everywhere I looked—black ones, white ones, Latino ones, Asian ones, Indian ones, short, tall, very young, a little longer in the tooth, long-haired, short-haired, virtually no-haired, and all sauntering like they were the stars on a Milan runway. The women in Paris were lovely, but there wasn't the stunning variety that one finds in New York—a variety that almost brought tears to my eyes. I was pleased to see that in the midst of profound marital distress, I still had the use of enough of my senses to appreciate the gift that is a warm day in the city.

The detective—I couldn't bring myself to think of the guy as a "private dick," which Marcus sometimes called him—was named Joseph Perrot and his office was in a modest office building on Lexington Avenue, the entrance of which was squeezed in between a pizza parlor and a florist shop. As I walked through the building's revolving door, the smell of pizza and the fragrance of the flowers tangled to make me hungry and nauseous at the same time. I was impressed to see that the building had a security desk with a guard behind it, but I was less impressed when the guard, a fat, middle-aged white man, barely glanced in my direction as I walked by the desk and headed for the elevators.

I wasn't sure what to expect from this private detective. Marcus hadn't given me much information except to say that the guy was very thorough and very discreet. The word "discreet" had jarred me for a second—that's what you called it when you were about to meet somebody you weren't supposed to be meeting to do something you weren't supposed to be doing. Perrot told me over the phone in a deep, no-nonsense tone that his fee for individuals was fifty dollars an hour, plus expenses, and he expected a five-hundred-dollar retainer up front. I figured I could spare about a thousand dollars for the entire project without causing myself too much financial pain. I didn't think the detective should need much in the way of expenses—how far could Mikki possibly go?—so I figured I could afford about twenty hours or so of spying. I wanted Mr. Perrot—pronounced "pair-rot"—to concentrate on the early evening hours when Mikki claimed to be working late. I hadn't told Marcus, but one evening—it was Wednesday, in fact, the night I was supposed to be meeting Marcus—I had gone by the store after finishing up at work at about eight p.m. and the lights were off and my wife was nowhere to be found. That's when I had started to become suspicious. Mikki's movements were normally as predictable as the tides.

Mr. Perrot's floor seemed to be jam-packed with small law firms and "production companies." I couldn't imagine what kinds of "productions" were being put together behind those cheesy wooden doors. For some reason, perhaps my own attraction to sleaze, I guessed those grainy porn flicks filmed on videotape with a budget expansive enough to buy the "actresses" some fried chicken and a subway token home.

I knocked on the nondescript wooden door that said "Perrot Enterprises" and was buzzed into a small, clean outer office with a few chairs and a large rubber tree plant that appeared to be real, though I was far from an expert. In an instant, Joseph Perrot emerged, smiling politely and extending a hand. For some reason, I had assumed that Perrot was white. He clearly wasn't completely white, but I couldn't tell what else he was; he could have been mixed with black, Latin, or even Asian, judging by the dusky-colored skin and the short, straight-looking hair.

"Welcome, Mr. Murphy," he said. His voice offered no clues about his nationality, though I knew from my own experiences that the voice was no sure giveaway. How many times had I seen that startled-but-trying-not-to-let-it-show look on someone's face when meeting me for the first time after many phone conversations?

I followed Perrot into a large but spartan office. There were no diplomas or citations from the mayor or pictures of Perrot with the rich and famous up on the walls. As a matter of fact, there was nothing at all on the walls, not even a print from the Met or a tacky framed portrait of a Lamborghini. I quickly got the impression that Perrot preferred to keep a profile so low that you'd need an electron microscope to find him.

Perrot sat behind his almost-bare wooden desk and got right to the point.

"So, who is it that you want me to tail and what is it that you hope to find, or not find, Mr. Murphy?" Perrot said, sitting back and folding his hands over his abdomen, which I could tell was quite flat and tight, even under Perrot's crisp white shirt and red print tie. I wondered how old Perrot was. The man could be anywhere from thirty-two to forty-six, I guessed. But I didn't think I'd ever find out the answer.

"It's my wife," I said. I leaned forward to get closer to Perrot. I wanted to convey the secrecy of the whole matter. "I think she's having an affair."

Perrot simply nodded. His face showed no expression, no judgments. He probably practiced that expressionless reaction in the mirror, I imagined.

"Okay. I'll need to know her likely whereabouts at various times of the day and a picture."

Damn, I could have kicked myself for not figuring that I'd need a picture. I could have taken that sexy picture of Mikki from my desk. (Funny how I wanted to show off my wife in her best light even to the private detective.) I did have a wedding picture of the two of us in my briefcase, though Mikki's face was nearly in profile as she gazed at me lovingly. I snapped open the briefcase and handed it to the detective, who looked nothing like Magnum, P.I. or the old lady from *Murder, She Wrote*. I wondered how Perrot felt about being called a "dick."

Perrot glanced at the picture, nodded, and put it down on the desk.

"She owns a clothing store in Fort Greene, Brooklyn," I said. "She's been coming home quite late the past week and I know she's not staying at the store the whole time. So I think it'd be best to tail her in the evening."

Perrot smiled. "Leave the tailing up to me," he said. "I'll report back to you in a week—sooner if I find something."

After I handed him a check and shook his hand, I soon found myself back in the afternoon sun, staggering up Lexington Avenue in a daze. I had just hired somebody to spy on my wife. Based on her arriving home late a few nights and not sleeping with me. That was some pretty flimsy evidence, wasn't it? How could I know if I was doing the right thing? The night before, for the first time in a long time, I had gotten down on my knees and talked to the Lord, asking for guidance, a clue, confidence, anything that could be a help to me.

"Please, Lord, tell me I did the right thing," I muttered to myself. A young white woman with about five hoop earrings sticking out of her eyebrow stared at me with a bemused smile as she walked by. Oh, so she thought *I* was strange? *She* was the one who had mutilated her face, yet *I* was unusual for talking to God out loud?

She

"Hold up—he did what?" Zaria practically yelled, her eyes zooming all around her. We were having brunch at the Blue Tea Cup, a greasy little soul food diner in Chelsea that served grits, eggs, corned beef hash, and pancakes every day, twenty-four hours a day. People went there more for the ambience than the food—what with all the hip, young bohemians crowding the tables with their copies of the *Village Voice* and the *Times*, arguing about whatever kids with no responsibility and no allegiance to anyone but hip hop and the Internet think is important. They kept the prices low and the music cranked up, hoping, I'm sure, that it would distract the young 'uns from paying attention to what that kitchen really looked like behind those closed swinging doors.

At least I was hoping they weren't paying attention, because Zaria practically told the entire restaurant that my husband was having me tailed. I thought I'd seen this Erykah Badu knock-off swing her face in our direction after Zaria yelled, but she was really looking around for the waitress. It appeared that something that wasn't supposed to be in her plate was in her plate. That's why I was having tea and toast.

"You want to keep it down," I whispered to Zaria, leaning in for emphasis. "He could be here."

"Who could be here?"

"The private detective," I said, looking around.

"Oh, my God," she said, all dramatic. "Has your marriage sunk this low?"

"No, Marcus has sunk that low."

"What does Marcus have to do with this—well, other than wreaking all this havoc in my little sister's marriage?"

I rolled my eyes at her, let out a heavy sigh, then proceeded to tell her how my boyfriend talked my husband into hiring someone to spy on me, to find out if I'm cheating on him. Ain't that something? I was home cooking dinner for Randy and trying to think up an excuse for why I was too tired to sleep with him when Marcus called me from his cell phone to tell me what he'd done.

"How you doing, babe?" Marcus said into the phone, making me smile and reel back in terror all at once.

"Aren't you out with Randy?" I asked hurriedly. "Where is he?"

"Come on, Mikki—relax," he said coolly. "You don't actually think I'd be calling you 'babe'—or even calling you at all—if your husband was here, do you? Give me some credit."

I was put instantly at ease, but he didn't need to be nasty about it. I let that slide. "Where are you?"

"I'm still at the bar. Listen, Randy's on his way to the house, so I need to make this quick. He's going to hire a private detective to have you followed."

I was taking a pot out of the cupboard for my rice, and seeing as I have more pots down there than Macy's, I was making a whole lot of noise trying to get it out from under the wok my mom had given me for Christmas a few seasons ago, and the pasta pan I'd bought on sale at Bloomie's, and the cookie sheet I used to bake for Zaria's PTA meetings. Needless to say, I thought I heard him wrong, with all that noise. I was hoping I did.

"What did you say?"

"What you doing?"

"I'm about to make dinner. Fried chicken, rice, broccoli, salad," I said slowly. "What did you say?"

"Mikki, stop with the pots and listen to me for a minute, okay?" he said, just as slowly. "I told Randy to hire a private detective to have you followed."

"Marcus? Have you lost your goddamn mind? You told my husband to have me followed? What, you want him to find out what we're doing?"

There was silence on the other end of the phone, and since he was on the celly, I wasn't sure if he was being quiet or he'd lost his connection. "Marcus? Are you there? Can you hear me?"

"I'm here, Mikki," he said. "I'm waiting for you to calm down so that I can tell you what's up."

I put my frying pan down, placed the rice pot on the counter, then lined myself up against the refrigerator door. "Okay," I said, settled. "Tell me why you told my husband to have me followed."

"He knows something's up," Marcus said quickly. "We were here having a few beers and he asked me if I thought you were having an affair."

You could have knocked me flat on my ass with one, simple breath, I was so shocked and scared from what Marcus had just told me. I couldn't say anything, so it was my turn to be quiet. Marcus didn't say anything; I guess he was waiting for my reaction. The house made a settling noise, scared the mess out of me. I darted around the corner of the kitchen to see if it was Randy coming in the front door. But it wasn't.

"Mikki, you there?"

"Explain to me why you would tell my husband to have me followed—" I said, clearly upset.

"Because—" I didn't let him finish.

"—knowing full well that a private detective could go back and tell him everything about us." I was yelling into the phone now, albeit a restrained yell.

"Mikki, listen to me and I'll explain, okay?" His tone was gruff; I could tell he was getting annoyed, so I shut up and listened. "He told me he thinks you might be having an affair, and he kept pushing the issue, even though I told him you weren't. So I told him to have you tailed, just to throw him off."

"Did it ever once occur to you that a private detective might mess around and find out that we've been sleeping together?"

"That won't happen."

I was incredulous. "What do you mean that won't happen, Marcus? Spies do what they do to find out stuff. How is he not going to find out?"

"Because I know the guy he's going to hire."

"So?"

"So that means that I can call him and tell him what the deal is and he'll make sure he doesn't find anything. That way, Randy will be satisfied that you're not fucking around, and we'll have bought some time."

"And just how do you know you can trust this guy?" I said, still angry about the whole thing.

"I just know, okay? Can you trust me on this?"

I walked over to the picture window and sat in the window seat. I could feel the headache creeping into the base of my head like it usually snuck up on me when I was angry or upset or scared. Right now, I was scared—scared of the fact that Randy hit the target dead on the nose with his affair theory, scared of the idea that Marcus would think he could head it off with some snoop tailing me, scared that some snoop was going to be tailing me. Scared isn't even the word. I was terrified of the prospect.

"Is this guy really going to follow me?" I asked Marcus quietly.

"Well, I thought about that, and I think it would be best if he did actually follow you, so that he can have evidence on hand to prove to Randy he really did the job."

And then my questions started tumbling one over the other. "So, some strange man is going to be watching my every move? For how long? Do you realize how scary that's going to be? What does he look like? What's his name? Will he introduce himself to me, or is he just going to hide in the bushes? How do you know—"

Marcus cut me off. "Mikki, just chill with the questions, damn. You have to trust me on this. I'm not going to introduce you two because any contact between the two of you could come back on both of us if you slip and say you know him or you mention anything about him. He's going to follow you for a week, and you won't even know he's there."

"What do you mean I won't even know he's there?" I said. "Of course I'll know somebody's there. This is so fucking creepy. I don't know about this."

There was silence. And more silence. "Marcus? You there?" He didn't answer. "Marcus? Can you hear me?"

His phone went dead.

And I was going crazy.

My eyes were darting wildly around the room. My God, were there bugs in the phone? Recorders in the TV? I'd seen countless television news shows where suspicious parents stocked their VCRs and alarm clocks with secret recorders filled with tapes that would later reveal the nanny was beating the shit out of their babies. Was Randy that suspicious? Damn—he was. He was hiring someone to follow me, wasn't he?

How fucked up is that? He couldn't just ask me what was up? I mean, I know I haven't been the most pleasant person in the world and he hasn't had any ass in a week, but damn, it's only been a week. Weren't there leagues of married men on this earth who were denied poontang on a regular basis? Who were more shocked when they actually got some, rather than when they didn't? Did those men think their wives were cheating, too? Did they hire strange men to follow their women?

I spun around and backed up against the wall, sliding across it like I was in some bad *Mission: Impossible* episode. I creeped closer to the window and slowly pulled back the curtain to look out and see if anyone was standing there, looking. No one. I ran into the bedroom and did the same, peeking out at my backyard to see if some man was trampling through my tiny flower garden or planting some high-tech CIA spy devices in my bushes. Nothing.

Then I heard the front door open. Randy was home. I darted into the bathroom just off to the left of our bed, turned on the light. The sight of my reflection—I thought it was someone standing in the room—made me jump back so fast that I smashed into the half-closed door, a move that made me crash to the floor. Randy walked in just as I was collecting my body off the floor.

"Hey," he said, barely looking at me as he dropped his jacket onto the bed. Then he turned around and ran his eyes across my body, which was splayed all across the carpet. "What are you doing?"

I struggled to get up off the floor. "I, uh, I tripped walking out of the bathroom and fell. I'm all right, though. You know how clumsy I can be," I said, faking a smile.

His smile was equally fake. And I noticed pretty quickly that he was trying hard not to look me in the face. Now, I was mad at him. He had the nerve to shell out our hard-earned money to have someone follow me, his wife, everywhere I go. And now he was going to stand here and try to act like nothing's up. He couldn't even do that right.

"You know what?" I said, emotionless. "I'm going to go get some water and then I'm turning in. Had a long day at the shop and I'm just dog tired. I was going to cook, but why don't you just order a pizza or something?"

"Okay," he said. "I'm going to go watch a little TV. I'll be in in a little while."

And with that, he walked out the door—and I turned in for a sleepless night.

I was still yawning when the waitress at the Blue Tea Cup brought Zaria her super-sampler plate full of eggs, grits, hash browns, bacon, sausage, pancakes, and French toast. "Damn, that's a lot of food. You are not going to eat all that, are you?"

"You're going to help me," she said as she dumped a pile of salt onto her grits.

"No I'm not." I laughed. "I told you already—nothing but tea and toast for the kid. You ain't gonna get me to slop down any of that dirty food. Don't know what crawled across it before they brought it out here."

"Thank you, Mikki, for making my breakfast special, girl. That's a great thought to have in my head before I get to eating," Zaria said. She quickly dug in. She can be so, so, animal. "Anyway," she said, opening her mouth wide enough for me to see the grits mixing with her cheese eggs, "have you figured out who it is that's following you?"

I looked around conspiratorially, then leaned in toward Zaria. "Girl, I've been looking over my shoulder for the past forty-eight hours and I can't figure out who it might be. I've been walking around, looking suspiciously at men sitting in cars, looking out windows. I've been looking at my new customers all funny, wondering if they've been sent by someone to check out what's going on in the shop. I'm afraid to walk down the street. I would have stayed home for the next week, but then Randy might have caught on that I know what's up."

"Hmm," Zaria said. "That's deep. How's Randy acting?"

"He's trying really hard to act like nothing's up. Marcus told me I should try to be a little more affectionate, which is a trip in and of itself because that Negro goes off every time he thinks I might have so much as kissed my husband. But anyway, despite my affection, Randy acts like he can't look me in the eye and barely talks to me. Yesterday, he left for work early, came in late, and watched TV all night," I said, taking a sip of my tea. "Maybe I should assume his distance means he's having an affair and have his ass tailed."

"Aw, you know that boy ain't cheatin' on your ass," Zaria said.

"How do I know that?" I asked. "Randy is an extremely sexual person, Zaria. Don't think for one minute that he didn't get some of that French booty while he was over in Paris. He was over there for three months. He can't go three days without some ass without thinking his wife is cheating on him. You know he was wallowing around in somebody's drawers over there."

"Yeah, you got a point there."

I settled back in my chair. Somehow, for just a moment, I felt justified for sleeping with Marcus. Yes, I decided, Randy left me, his wife, alone for months, cheated on me with another woman (Lord knows how many) then came home and paid someone to follow his wife around. He was no angel.

Zaria broke into my thoughts. "So, you think it might be that cute dred over there?"

"Huh?" I said, shaking my head a little.

"The dred—you think he might be Mr. Private Dick?"

I looked into the direction that Zaria was nodding. There was an extremely cute guy sipping on a cup of coffee, peeking into the *New York Times*. He didn't look up, so if he was supposed to be keeping tabs on what I was doing, he wasn't doing a good job. But my eyes had met several times with the guy sitting one table away from him—a Maxwell reject pretending to flip through an *Essence* magazine.

"Nah, I think it's the guy next to him. You know damn well no black man reads *Essence* magazine, unless it just happens to be sitting on the bathroom counter when he's taking a dump."

"Nice, Mikki. I'm eating here."

"No, seriously—look at him, trying to act like he's really into the makeovers and makeup stories. Give me a break. He's the stalker."

"Nah, his hair is too big," Zaria said, dismissing him with a wave of her hand. "The guy who's following you has to be discreet—someone who blends in. He's not going to have eighteen feet of hair spiraling from his scalp."

We went back to scanning the room, picking the men apart, giving ourselves excuses for why this one and that one couldn't have been the spy. Zaria, surprisingly, was making me laugh all through breakfast. I didn't have anything to laugh about, but it sure felt good doing it anyway—even if it was just for a few hours.

He

The next week was utter agony. Every time my phone rang at work, I thought it was Perrot. I was trying to dive into my new position with gusto, but I feared that my co-workers could sense my distraction. I desperately wanted to call Perrot myself, but I knew that wasn't the way this thing worked.

On the home front, things were still strange between me and Mikki, though Mikki was more affectionate than she had been the week before. In fact, one night she even sat down next to me on the couch as I watched a Knicks game in our second-floor den and she rested her head on my shoulder. It was a move that touched me; for a time, I surmised that perhaps I was wasting a whole lot of money with Perrot. She even rested her hand on my chest, though she didn't start stroking it the way she used to do when she was trying to signal to me that she wanted to get busy. Still, I wondered if this was her way of initiating sex. Even before I went to France I had discovered how much of their evenings husbands spend anxiously watching their wives for any sign that some sexual activity might be on the night's agenda. It was a part of married life that I disliked immensely, for I thought that there should be enough communication between us that she could tell me when she wanted some. But I had come to learn that that wasn't the way most women operated, even around their husbands. So I watched, waited, looked for some sign, a lingering glance, a suggestive gesture. Since I had returned home, my booty watch had intensified, with very little to show for it. I was especially sensitive about not wanting to make a move on Mikki and risk rejection, yet I was growing hornier and more confused with each passing day.

"You want to go into the bedroom?" I had asked, holding my breath as I felt her body tense up just a slight bit next to me on the couch. There was silence, an interminable silence. I watched the Knicks prepare to blow another close game at the Garden. It was still early in the season. I heard sirens race by outside. My heart pounded and I wondered if she could feel it, too.

"No." Her tone wasn't mean, but it was a "No" nonetheless—just as painful a rejection as if she had slapped me. I had risked the question and now I suffered the consequences. I wanted to jerk my shoulder away and tell her to move, but I didn't. I sat there in silence, growing more incensed and befuddled. I just did not understand where Mikki was. She seemed so far away from me. And I was now doubting that it was another man; she was too listless, too lacking in energy to summon the passion for an illicit affair. Clearly, the problem was me. I couldn't blame it on someone else. But what was it? What was I doing wrong? I was trying everything I could think of, but my wife was nearly indifferent. Maybe she just didn't want me anymore. Maybe she didn't find me engaging or interesting or attractive anymore.

I had swallowed hard when that last came to me. No longer attractive? Was that possible? I ached to ask her, but I knew I'd get no truth, only fire and hostility. Is this what happened to marriages when they went bad—the passion and intensity just drains away slowly as one partner loses interest, siphoning off the love until all that remains is an empty, unsatisfying shell?

Precisely a week after the meeting in his office, Perrot called me at the office with his oral report. I was proud of myself for being able to wait for Perrot to reach out to me. It had taken every ounce of willpower I owned.

"Well, I got some news for you," Perrot said. I almost gasped audibly.

"The news is that there's nothing to report," he continued. "I spent a total of twenty hours on her trail. In the morning, in the afternoon, in the evening. Everything seemed to be in order. The only things she did were run errands or look around in clothing stores in Manhattan.

I never saw her with another man. She barely even spoke to anybody when she was out of the store. And I never once saw a man go into her store—any man. Plenty of women, but no men."

I exhaled. I was enormously relieved to hear that—though it did throw my problems right back onto my own lap. If it wasn't somebody else, then it must be me.

"All right, then," I said softly. I was drained—somehow that news had wiped me out. I realized how much tension it had caused me to have Perrot sniffing around my wife, looking for something to explain my troubles.

"I'll send you a final bill," Perrot said.

"Thank you for your time," I said. I paused, wondering if this next statement was necessary. "Uh, can you please send the bill to my office?"

"Of course," Perrot said curtly, clearly insulted but trying not to let it show.

As I hung up the phone, my mind was already weighed down with the reality that my marriage was crumbling before my eyes, and I had no idea why. Mikki having an affair would have been easy, obvious. So now what?

She

I'd closed down the shop early, but only after kicking out a customer who wanted to sit and talk about what kinds of shoes would go best with this georgeous fitted shimmery organza gown I'd made for her wedding. I'll readily admit that I'd thrown myself back into the business ever since this whole Randy mess blew into town. I was stocked to the gills with orders from anxious brides looking for my trademark afrocentric bridal designs, and all too happy to oblige them by opening the shop early in the morning and staying there until late into the evening to meet the demand—something I'd never done before. But this particular night, I had somewhere to go, which is what I explained to my customer as I pushed her out of my door. I ran down to the corner of Lafayette, looked around to make sure I didn't see anyone I knew, and hailed a gypsy cab. The dirty velour seats smelled like a combination of smoke and funk—no doubt a scent consistent with the smell of the driver—and for a minute, I'd considered getting out of the car and trying to catch another one. But I'd made it safely in without anyone seeing me, at least I thought, and I wanted to just get to where I was going without drawing attention to whoever was following me. I had Stinky drop me at Bloomingdale's on the Upper East Side, where I proceeded to walk all throughout the store to make sure no one was watching. Then I left through an exit different from the one where I'd entered, and hopped into another cab that took me to the corner of the street where Marcus lived. I ducked into the deli, looked around to see if I noticed anyone that I'd seen at Bloomie's, then ducked back out into the crisp air and walked—fast—to Marcus's. He answered the door almost immediately.

"Hey, babe," he said, reaching out to hug me.

"Marcus—maybe you should give me that hug in the apartment, where no one can see us," I said, looking over my shoulder.

"Aw, girl, come here," he said, grabbing me by the waist. "Ain't nobody looking at you."

"Uh, okay Mr. Loverman," I said, pulling his hands off me and pushing past him. "You're the one who talked my husband into having someone watch my every move."

"He's not doing it anymore."

I was headed for the sofa, but I stopped dead in my tracks and spun around. "He's not? It's over?" I yelled.

"Yup—all done. He told Randy today that he didn't find anything and that you're not cheating on him, so you're cool now. No one is going to follow you anymore."

"Praise God," I said, flopping down into the sofa. I had some nerve, huh? Thanking God for calling off the goon who could have proven to my husband that I was breaking several commandments. But I was just happy, because now we could move on, unencumbered. Marcus came and sat down next to me, and put his stockinged feet on the coffee table. He laid back and looked at me.

"Are you happy?" he asked.

"Hell, yeah," I said. "You have no idea how weird it is to know someone is following you. I did all kinds of crazy things to get away from this man, whoever he was. I still can't believe Randy actually went through with it."

"Yeah, well, guilty consciences make people do crazy things."

I was quiet for a moment—wasn't sure if I'd heard him right, or had heard him at all. Did he say "guilty conscience?" "What do you mean, 'guilty conscience?' " I said to Marcus, turning to face him.

"I don't know . . . you know, I was thinking about the conversation Randy and I had the night he decided to hire the detective and he said something that made me think he may not be as innocent in all this as he's making himself out to be."

I wasn't sure if I wanted to hear the rest of this, but I knew I needed to. Because if Marcus was about to tell me what I was thinking he was going to tell me, there were going to be some serious problems up in the Chance-Murphy household—even more than there were now.

"What," I said, "did Randy say to you? What are you talking about, 'innocent?' "

"I don't know, maybe I was reading into it, but when we were at the bar that night, he was talking about all the pretty women in France and how 'down' they were to get with African-American men."

"Down for what?" I said slowly. "What does 'down' mean? Explain 'down.' "

"He didn't really say it, but I understood it to mean those white girls over there were giving him some play and he was obliging."

"You mean Randy cheated on me with some French bitches—some stringy-haired, lanky, stank, white girls?"

God—I was floored. Yeah, I knew that Randy had been gone for months and that he was a man of considerable sexual appetites and that he was probably longing for some tail—that he'd probably even considered on a few occasions getting with some of those pretty French girls over there, with their perfect model-thin bodies and sexy accents. They certainly made it apparent that they were ready, willing, and more than able to give him some, I noticed that much when I went to visit him. Some of them were so bold that they openly flirted with him, even with his wife holding on to his arm. There were a few times where I even considered checking a few of them, but Randy convinced me that they didn't mean anything by it—that they just admired good-looking people, were a little bit more forward than Americans, and were probably shocked by the fact that a black man was holding on to a black woman, considering how high jungle fever ran over there. So I kept quiet. But it did make me wonder whether they were actually stepping to him when he didn't have a wife holding his hand.

Turns out they were. Turns out Randy was obliging them. Turns out I was mad as hell. "That muthafucka was over there screwing other women behind my back? Cheating on me? That self-righteous bitch had the nerve to come home and accuse me of being an adulterer, and he was doing more dirt than me?"

"Mikki . . . calm—" Marcus started, but I didn't let him finish.

"That mutha has more balls than an elephant," I said, the venom lining each of my words.

"Calm down, Mikki, please," Marcus said forcefully, nearly yelling. "This is a good thing."

I looked at him like he'd just stepped off a UFO. "What," I said, "are you talking about?"

"It's a good thing, Mikki—because it'll help us when we tell him about us."

Oh. He got me with that one. I snapped my head into his direction, and stared in his eyes. In an instant, I'd forgotten everything he'd told me in the last few minutes. It was almost as if the words sucked out all the memory from my brain so that I could focus on these new words and the meaning behind them—"when we tell him about us."

"Really?" I said, smiling. "You're ready?"

Just as Marcus had opened his mouth to answer my question, his phone rang. He got up off the sofa and walked over to the phone, looked at it as it rang again, then came back to the sofa and sat down. "I'm just going to let the machine get it."

One ring later, the machine did pick up, and a few seconds after that, some woman's voice—a sexy, breathy one—started talking into the speaker. Marcus leapt up and ran into his bedroom, just as she was saying something about how she was looking forward to seeing him tonight. I saw him pick up the phone and push a button on the machine, then start talking really low into the receiver. It was a short conversation—a quiet one, too—characteristics that made me slightly uncomfortable. Who was that woman on the phone, and why did she make him jump off the couch and run for the machine when he'd just said he didn't want to talk? And why was he whispering?

He came back into the living room.

"That was a client of mine—I've been waiting for her to call so that we could get together and discuss her case," Marcus said hurriedly.

"You have to go see her now?" I asked, my voice tinted with a hint of anger. "Who is she?"

"I told you, she's a client," Marcus said, equally hurried. Then he paused for a moment, looked at me, and sat back down on the couch. "Mikki, I want you to go to dinner with me tomorrow night. Find something to tell Randy—tell him you're going out with the girls, whatever. I made reservations at this beautiful restaurant in Little Italy. It's nice and cozy and intimate, the food is great, the perfect setting to talk about our plans together."

Client schmient—did boyfriend say what I thought he'd just said?

"You think you can have dinner with me tomorrow?" he continued.

I was so excited I could barely speak. We were going to go to a beautiful restaurant to talk about our future together. Finally, we were going to bring an end to all this frustrating sneaking around and ducking behind buildings and secret rendezvous and lying our way through our relationships with Randy. We were going to tell the truth and set ourselves free.

"Of course I can have dinner with you. I'd be absolutely delighted," I said, a grin spreading across my face.

"Okay, then," he said, getting up from the sofa as quickly as he'd sat down. "Let's touch base tomorrow afternoon so that I can give you all the details, okay? I have to run." He stood over me, waiting to help me up. It took a minute for that to register with me, but once I got the hint, I got my ass out of the chair. I was too happy about what was going to happen tomorrow to be bothered by his rushing out the door. I gave him a kiss when I got to my feet—a light peck—and then a long, strong hug.

"I'm so happy," I said, wrapped in his embrace. "So happy."

"Well, get your happy ass on, then," he said, pushing me back and then tapping my booty. "I have to get out of here and meet with this client. If I leave now, I might not be late."

"Okay, okay, I'm going," I said, giving him a final peck before I headed to the door.

When I got to the corner of Marcus's block, I ducked into the deli, but this time it had nothing to do with my trying to determine whether I was being followed, thank goodness. This time, it was to get a pack of gum, some water, and the paper, which I planned on reading on the subway. Even the long line and the slow-ass cashier didn't bother me, because I was free. I was going to take the subway home, something I hadn't done in a while for fear that the crowds and lengths of the subway cars would make it easier for someone to tail me. But no one was tailing me anymore. And I was one day away from not having to sneak around anymore. I walked out of that store, practically skipping, but what I saw next made me reel back just a little. It was Marcus, bounding down the front stairs of his apartment. He was dip from head to toe in a fly suit that he wasn't wearing when I'd seen him. And he was shining—skipping, almost. And in his left hand, he carried a single red rose. I watched him get into his car, check his face in his mirror, pop a mint into his mouth, and pull out of his parking spot.

What client of his was getting a rose?

He

The phone call came early for a Saturday, nine a.m., from one of my old tennis partners, Roger Bluebird, seeking a doubles team.

"We're playing against a club from Queens and I just found out we're gonna be short a doubles team," Roger said. "I thought maybe you and Marcus might be available."

I hadn't played tennis in months, since before I went to Paris. Roger remembered me from the year before, when Marcus and I never let a week go by without getting in a few hours either indoors or outdoors. I certainly was in no shape to play a competitive match, and I thought it'd be virtually impossible to get Marcus out there on such short notice anyway.

"I don't know, Rog. I haven't played in months. I'm bound to be pretty rusty. And Marcus has been working like crazy lately. He's probably at the office now."

"As a matter of fact, I just talked to Marcus. He wants to play. So I really only need one more player. How 'bout it?"

How did Roger convince Marcus to play on such short notice? And why didn't Marcus call me if he wanted to go out and hit with somebody? That didn't sound like Marcus. And why wasn't Marcus calling me now to make the appeal instead of Roger?

"All right, well, if Marcus already committed, I guess I can do it, too."

As I stood on the court three hours later sweating profusely and wondering how frequently thirty-two-year-olds suffered from heart attacks, I couldn't help but notice that my partner wasn't even breathing hard.

"Hey, Marcus! How come you ain't tired?" I called out to him as we waited for the older white man on the other side of the net to serve.

Marcus looked back at me and grinned.

"I been running, man," he said.

"Running? You mean, like, jogging?" I asked. "Damn, what brought that on?"

Marcus didn't answer because the serve was on its way. I was on the receiving end; I saw the heavy topspin and knew it would bounce high and short. I took several quick steps in and twisted my left shoulder around to prepare for the forehand. I swung—and hit another one into the net. Largely because of me, we were down four games to two in the first set. The only games we had won came when Marcus was serving.

"Damn—what the hell is wrong with me!" I yelled out loud.

"Calm down, man. You haven't played in months. It's no big deal." Marcus was trying to be calming, but it wasn't working. I hated to lose and I hated even more to play badly on the way to losing. And it was all the more painful because the two white men on the other side of the net were at least twenty years older than me and Marcus.

On the next point, when I was winding up to smash an overhead at the net, I was abruptly moved out of the way by Marcus, who brought his long right arm down and pounded the ball into the ground across the net, causing it to bounce high over our opponents' heads. Marcus's move had violated a whole list of the protocols of doubles tennis. I glared at him, but Marcus pretended not to see me.

"I *had* that," I said, trying to keep my temper in check. The last thing we needed was to get into an argument during the match.

Marcus glanced over at me and shrugged.

"Sorry. I thought I had the better angle."

For the next forty-five minutes, I found that my anger at Marcus improved my play immensely. My forehand started clicking, and I even was greeted by the return of my backhand slice, which I had been afraid to even try. During one rally, I tracked down a slicing shot that hit the line deep on my backhand side and returned it with a perfectly placed backhand straight down the line for a winner. I looked over at Marcus and grinned.

"Man, what got into you?" Marcus called out, returning the grin.

"I got mad," I said, still smiling.

With my game resuscitated, the two of us went on to reel off seven straight games and snatch the match away from the old guys, who were bent over at the end, clutching the hem of their shorts and gasping for air. I walked off the court on such a high that I didn't think anything could bring me back down. I sat with Marcus for a beer, still replaying some of my winners in my head and still wanting to talk about how I had managed to turn it around. Marcus, for the most part, was willing to oblige my ego.

"All right, enough of your bragging," Marcus said, rising and stretching out his long frame. "I gotta run to the office for a little while."

I shook my head. "Don't you give that firm enough of your time? You can't chill out and enjoy one weekend?"

"Easier said than done," Marcus responded. He slipped on a jacket and strode out of the club without even saying good-bye.

"Damn, well, good-bye to you, too," I said, muttering to myself.

I was in such a hurry to peel off my sweaty clothes that I took the steps two at a time as I made my way up to our third-floor bedroom. I heard the radio playing, so I knew Mikki was home. I entered the bedroom and was about to call out to her, but I heard her voice rise above the R&B crooner on the radio. It sounded like a laugh. Apparently she was on the telephone, probably talking to her assistant at the store. Sometimes Mikki came home during the afternoon if things were slow and she didn't have any fittings. She liked to play music and work on her designs in the small office she had created on the other side of our master bathroom. I stepped quietly into the bathroom so I could hear what she was saying. I felt a little strange snooping around, but I couldn't squelch my curiosity, especially considering our recent troubles.

"Okay. Well, I can make it there in about a half hour," she said. "Randy took the car, so I'll have to take a cab—if I can find one."

I noted the warm cheer in her voice. It didn't sound like she was talking to a customer. Especially not if she was referring to her husband by his first name. Perhaps it was her sister, or her friend Angelou?

"I'm not sure," Mikki continued. "It's four now, so we should have about four hours or so."

I heard her laugh—a low, seductive laugh. As soon as I heard it, my stomach went into a spin cycle.

"Yeah, we could do a lot in four hours," she said, laughing again. There was no mistaking the suggestiveness in her tone. This was not her sister.

"All right, babe. I can't wait either. I really really miss you."

I was frozen. I heard her hang up the phone, but she didn't immediately move. There was no way I could let her see me. I darted back into the bedroom and scooted into my closet. I left the door open just enough for me to see out into the bedroom. I tried to slow my breathing, but my soul was in such turmoil that I almost felt like I was about to pass out.

Mikki came bustling into the bedroom like a woman in a hurry. She practically ran over to her closet and dove inside. I saw several items fly out onto the bed. I angled my head so I could see Mikki tear off the white blouse and the tight jeans she was wearing. She held up a little black dress and pranced in front of the mirror, admiring herself. Clearly she was prepping herself for a steamy date. There was no other way to interpret the talk and the clothes. I felt the hotness start somewhere down around my feet. There was no doubt what it was—it was the start of a most intense and blinding anger. I had the ability to almost remove myself from my body for an instant, to observe from a distance what was about to happen. I knew that my temper was about to overwhelm me; this was the kind of anger that acquired a mind of its own. I just prayed that I'd be able to control myself. At that moment, what I needed most of all was enough cool to allow me to follow this woman to see where this path was going to lead. Who was she going to meet? My craving to find out was so strong that I had to clench my jaws shut to keep from crying out, to keep from spraying my anger in this woman's face.

In no time flat, Mikki had slid into the black dress and dabbed her face with touches of makeup. Then she dashed out of the room and down the stairs. I moved out of the closet, where I had been stepping on top of my shoes. But the state of my beloved footwear was not something I was even capable of considering at that moment. I exhaled and inhaled deeply. I got a whiff of Mikki's freshly applied Issey Miyake perfume—which I had bought her in Paris—caught in my throat and I almost coughed. I hadn't heard the front door close yet; I couldn't let her hear me. My eyes almost teared up as I struggled to keep the coughing sensation down in my throat. I stuck my head back into the closet and let the coughing run its course, my body wracking from the effort to get the bitter taste of the perfume out of my mouth.

As I took my head from the closet, I heard the front door close. That was my cue to spring into action. I raced down the stairs, barely bothering to look down at where my feet were landing. If she caught a cab, I'd be in trouble because I had had to park around the corner, so I'd need a few minutes to reach my car. I slipped from the front door as quickly but quietly as I could. I saw her striding purposefully down the street, heading for DeKalb—a major thoroughfare where she'd be most likely to find a taxi. I jumped down the front stoop and sprinted in the other direction, toward my car. As I ran, the same thought kept running through my head: "I can't believe this is happening. I can't believe this is happening."

When I reached my car, I had that familiar bitter taste in my mouth that was common for the out-of-shape after exertion. My chest and side hurt like hell, but I couldn't afford to slow down and try to catch my breath. I maneuvered the BMW out of the tight parking space and took off, headed for DeKalb, gasping for air like a drowning man. I let out a relieved gust of breath when I got to the next corner and saw Mikki still standing out in the street, looking frantic and upset. I moved my car into a space at the intersection so I'd be ready to spring when she got into the cab.

As I sat and waited, I felt the waves of humiliation start to wash over me. I had never been so ashamed in my life. Not only did it appear that my wife was fucking another man, but here I was following her around like one of those psycho stalkers who get regular featured spots on the evening news when they wipe out their whole family, children included. I never understood why those men killed the children when they were upset with the wife. But I guessed that questioning the motives of psycho stalkers was pointless folly. I was no psycho stalker, merely an aggrieved and suffering spouse. And I had tried so hard to make things right. Apparently she looked on all my efforts with indifference. She was getting her bread buttered elsewhere; her husband was superfluous, extraneous—a pain in her ass.

I saw the taxi pull to a stop and Mikki hop in. I felt buckets of additional adrenaline dump into my bloodstream, like I had just injected it through my veins. The cab pulled off and, after waiting about ten seconds, so did I. The chase was on. Mikki wasn't the most observant of women—I had no fear that she would notice me following the cab.

The taxicab took me over the Manhattan Bridge, which was moving surprisingly well, and into Chinatown. Was this her destination? Chinatown would be clever because she'd be unlikely to run into anybody that could get her into trouble. The taxi fought through traffic on Canal Street, then made an unexpected right turn just as the light changed from yellow to red. I cursed my misfortune and banged on the wheel with both hands. I was four cars back, so I couldn't even creep up and crane my neck to see down the street the taxi had turned onto. I kept my eyes trained on the light, willing it to change. Of course, it didn't move. It just stayed red, in defiance of me, no doubt. I felt the sweat start trickling down my sides. My face was already hot and wet. I reached over and turned on the air conditioner, cranking it all the way up. Still, the light didn't move. I looked around wildly to see if any other drivers felt as crazed as me at the light's stubbornness. Surely it must be broken. Just as I was about to step out of my car and yell at the front car to drive through the red, the light flipped to green. But the light fiasco had increased my anxiety tenfold. I pressed down on my horn when the cars in front of me didn't move fast enough.

Finally, I turned the corner.

I didn't see a cab anywhere. I sped up the street to the next corner, even more wild-eyed now. The entire mission would be rendered meaningless if I couldn't find her. I'd have to suffer through not knowing, not being sure. I stamped down on the accelerator and zoomed to the next intersection. I craned my neck both ways. Where did she go?

Just as I was about to fly to the next intersection, I saw her! She was hopping out of the cab and slamming the door shut. Nervous, terrified, relieved, I made the left turn and moved slowly down the street, my eyes trained on her like a bloodhound's. She pranced onto the curb and walked toward a restaurant with a red awning. It was called Ponticello's; I glanced around quickly and realized I was now in Little Italy. My car was still behind her but she was only about forty feet away. I checked the rearview mirror—there was no one behind me. I pulled the BMW to the side, double-parking so cars would be able to get by.

What happened in the next five seconds will surely go down in the archives as *the* most shocking and painful five seconds of my life. My eye was still locked on Mikki, so I hadn't looked ahead to see what she was heading toward. But now I saw, and I audibly gasped.

It was my best friend Marcus. I could see the big, satisfied grin spread across Marcus's face. I couldn't see Mikki's face, but I guessed that she was smiling, too.

Mikki did a quick glance around her, checking out the surroundings one last time before she stepped into Marcus's arms. Her quick surveillance was only about a half-hour too late, I wanted to scream out to her. They stood underneath the awning and squeezed each other. Though they were in the shadow of the restaurant, they were still virtually in public. Mikki craned her neck upward and their lips met briefly. It wasn't a long kiss, but the passion and the intent were evident. Mikki and Marcus were lovers.

I felt the nausea building, the turmoil of the past half-hour culminating in the core of my stomach. I hadn't eaten much that day, but whatever was down there was now working its way up my esophagus, eager to exit the storm-like conditions below. I saw Mikki take Marcus's hand in hers as my best friend pulled open the door of Ponticello's. I saw the giddy smile on my wife's face and I knew I couldn't hold it down any longer. I shoved open the car door and unleashed a torrent of liquid onto the street, a little of it hitting the small white car that was parked to my left. I pulled my head back into the car and lunged for the glove compartment, where I hoped to find some napkins. But it was empty. I peered around the street to see if anyone had witnessed the double humiliation of Mikki's infidelity and my vomit. The bile sat in my mouth, dancing around my taste buds in a taunting tribute to my weakness. I opened the car door again, this time spitting the rest of the yuck into the puddle I had already deposited. I wiped my mouth with the sleeve of my stinky sweatsuit. I willed myself into action again, cruising the car slowly past Ponticello's, trying to stop myself from craning my neck to see inside. Once I was a few feet past the place, an idea germinated among my jumbled thoughts. I needed to make a statement, to do something so dramatic that the infidels, who were no doubt basking in the glow of their secrecy at that moment, would be scarred by it forever. A gesture that'd be worthy of a Verdi opera. I brought the car to a halt and shoved the door open once again. I stepped onto the sidewalk and stopped long enough to stare up at the sign above the awning. Let me never forget this time and place. Let Marcus and Mikki never forget it either.

The rage that I had encountered in the closet had returned in full bloom. I was primed, so rabid that I no longer even had the capacity to think about what I was about to do. I was just doing. I reached for the front door of the restaurant and I almost felt giddy. I was floating, removed from my body, watching myself, suffused with the unconquerable spirit of moral outrage. I shoved the restaurant's front door, satisfied at the way the door obligingly flew open and made a loud banging noise, drawing many sets of eyes in my direction. I swept my gaze across the small, intimate dining area and saw Mikki and Marcus in a corner, grinning happily at each other, virtually oblivious to everyone and everything around them. Good—everyone would see me coming except them. I took a deep breath, reaching down to make sure the full complement of rage was still present. It was. I marched toward their table, ignoring the pudgy, smiling host and his alarmed "Can I help you, sir?" In the corner of my eye, I saw what I thought was fear cross the host's face. But Mikki and Marcus were still oblivious, still grinning as they pulled their chairs up closer to the table—and to each other. As I headed toward them, I got another idea. I looked around for an extra chair. I grabbed it and slid it next to their table, right in between them. At the same time they both looked up, just as I deposited myself in the chair.

I have to admit I was deeply satisfied by the gasp I heard from Mikki. Her audible noise from shock and surprise already had made this whole scene well worth it. I wasn't sure where more of my anger was concentrated—at Mikki, or at Marcus. I directed my searing stare at both of them, first Marcus, then Mikki, then back at Marcus. I was also satisfied to see that Marcus was unable to look me in the eye. In fact, Marcus seemed to be looking more at Mikki than at me.

"Well, ain't this nice and fuckin' cozy?" I finally said with a snarl. I wanted to appear under control to them, but I wasn't sure that was possible. I glanced behind Marcus and saw that my presence was still being keenly followed by the other diners. I shook my head as I looked back and forth at them again. Both of them appeared so stunned that they couldn't form words.

"This looks like a real nice place. I bet the food is great. Something tells me you two have eaten here before. Maybe even more than once."

I looked back and forth but got no acknowledgment. I wanted to create more drama, to blow up the spot and spread audible gasps from one end to another, but my sense of propriety—my home trainin'—was just too strong to allow me to be too ghetto.

"Listen, Randy . . ." Marcus began. Evidently he had decided it was his role to speak up. But he clearly didn't know what to say. His voice trailed off.

"Randy, I—I'm really sorry this had to happen like . . . like this," Mikki said. She was near tears, but they still hadn't come. She was probably still too stunned, I thought. It wasn't unlike what happened when you got a scrape so deep that it took long minutes before the blood even started seeping into the wound. Mikki would cry buckets of tears before this was over, but the torrent hadn't yet found its way to the surface.

"Yeah, I bet you are," I said with a sarcastic laugh. "Would have been much easier if y'all could keep fuckin' undetected for a while longer, I'm sure, then maybe dump my ass when y'all didn't want me around anymore. Was that the plan?"

I looked back and forth at them again, noticing the nervous and pained looks they were exchanging with each other. Obviously this scenario hadn't come up in their planning. Over my left shoulder I saw the host, peering at us nervously. I almost let go a chuckle at the worry evident on the man's face. No doubt he had constructed all kinds of zany possibilities in his mind of what I was up to. Any sudden movements on my part and I was sure the host would spring into some sort of action.

"It wasn't like we *planned* this, Randy," Mikki was saying.

"Planned what?!!" I asked, looking at her wildly. "You mean y'all just happened to meet at this cozy little hideaway by accident! Your arms just happened to wrap around his, your lips just happened to meet his? I bet you just happen to accidently fall on his dick too, right?"

Of course I knew what she meant by the lack of a plan, but I couldn't resist the opportunity to make them squirm a bit more. I didn't realize the decibels had reached warning-stage levels until I saw the host striding toward the table.

"Excuse me. Uh, is there something wrong over here?" he asked, looking at Mikki and waiting for a sign from her.

I saw a prime opportunity and leaped.

"Yeah, there is most definitely something wrong!" I said so loudly it was almost a shout. I wanted the entire restaurant to hear every syllable to increase the host's embarrassment.

"My wife is fucking my best friend! I'd say there's something wrong with that—wouldn't you?!!" I pivoted in my chair so that I could catch every nuance of the expression on the host's face. First the man turned a shade of red I didn't think it was possible for white people to reach through natural causes. The flush in his face and neck could accurately be described as scarlet.

The host seemed to choke on a response. I had rendered him frozen and speechless. It was a delicious moment for me amidst the most surreal experience of my life—up to that point. I turned my head back around so I could enjoy the reactions of Mikki and Marcus. My best friend was staring down at the table. They hadn't been in the restaurant long enough to be served even drinks. Mikki was staring at me with her mouth open wide enough for me to crawl inside. I saw the surprise in her eyes—apparently she didn't think I was capable of this. Well, we were even, because I hadn't thought *she* was capable of this either.

"Oh, you surprised, Mikki?!" I said, relishing every word out of my own mouth. I wondered for a moment if my enjoyment of their public embarrassment was greater than my rage at their actions. That was a troubling thought—so troubling that I quickly banished it.

"Well, imagine my fuckin' surprise five minutes ago when I saw you run into his arms!" At the word "his," I jerked a thumb in Marcus's direction without looking at him. I saw the moisture start to glisten in my wife's eyes. The wound finally was starting to bleed. She mouthed the words "I'm sorry," but no sound came out. I saw the pain etched across her face. Her tears had instantly taken nearly all of the fun out of the scene. I was still angry enough to chew off my own arm, but the sadism was leaving me now. Replaced by—what? It wasn't compassion. Maybe I was just quickly tiring of the drama. I abruptly pushed my chair away and stood up. The movement startled Mikki, Marcus, and even the host. I could have sworn I saw Mikki cower just a bit, as if she expected me to strike her. Where would she get that idea from, I wondered angrily? I glanced toward Marcus.

"Marcus, my friend, all I got to say to you is this one thing: Thanks a lot for all your fuckin' help!" Then I remembered the private detective and smiled. "Perrot was a stroke of genius, man. Did you have to pay him to cover for you guys?"

I shook my head and started away from the table, staggering just a little—drunk from the exhaustion of the performance. I wasn't sure if I felt better or worse than I had before I entered the restaurant. The pudgy host stepped out of my way, still carrying a terrified look. I smiled at his fright. In this guy's mind I could be on the scale of a Ted Bundy or Mark Barton, one of those psychopathic white dudes who bludgeoned their entire family 'cause their stock portfolio had taken some hits. I moved in close to the host, observing the widening of his eyes and his two steps of retreat. I pointed at Marcus and said, loud enough for the surrounding tables to hear—it was all an aspect of the performance—"Hey, if you want to stay married, don't ask him to be the best man at your wedding."

As I turned and calmly walked from Ponticello's, I pictured myself in the scene from the first *Godfather* movie when Michael Corleone assassinated the Corleone family rival, who had an appropriately cool name like The Turk, and the crooked police captain in that little Italian restaurant in the Bronx and dropped the pistol as he calmly walked into the street. God, I loved that movie. I hadn't shot anybody, but I had fired my rage around the restaurant enough to leave some frightened faces, almost like I was packing. I had no idea what to do next. If I took my cues from the Corleones, Michael had fled to Sicily for a few years and gotten married. But I had nowhere to run. So I decided to go home and await the return of my wife.

She

Completely oblivious to what had just occurred, our waiter walked over to our table with his tray full of drinks—Pinot Grigio for me, Cabernet for Marcus, water for both of us—with a grin spread across his face. "Your drinks, sir? Miss?" he said, as he began to set them on the table. Neither Marcus nor I said anything to him; I just remember thinking how odd he was, wth his hook nose and his droopy eyes and his rail-thin body. I don't know if he was just a klutz or if the host's sudden move toward the waiter caused it to happen, but when he lifted that Cabernet off the tray, it toppled—almost in slow motion—over into my lap. Equally slowly, I looked down at my dress, watching the dark red liquid ooze across my lap, down my stockinged leg, and onto my cream and black Manolo Blahnik slingbacks, mixing with the linen on the pointed toe of my shoe. The waiter grabbed Marcus's napkin and scrambled toward me, bumping into the host, who had already rushed over to me and started dabbing at my legs. With the two of them apologizing in my ear and stabbing at my legs and everyone in the restaurant staring at my table—at me—I completely lost my entire damn mind. I closed my eyes, put my hands on my head, and started screaming like a madwoman.

The waiter, still oblivious to the prelude to his fuck-up, stopped dabbing and lurched back. So did the host. And then, suddenly, I felt two really strong hands lifting me out of my chair. It was Marcus. He didn't say a word—just picked me up, screams and all, and started walking, first toward the back of the restaurant, then down a flight of stairs, then to a bench just to the left of a bank of pay phones and the bathrooms. He put me down on the bench, then went to work.

"Okay, Mikki, stop it," he said. Marcus was sitting next to me, but he wasn't looking at me; he was staring out with his hands clasped, and sort of bending over his knees. I'd stopped yelling by the time we hit, like, the third step headed downstairs, but my screams were replaced with an hysterical round of crying. My face was soaking wet and snotty. My throat was sore, but I kept on crying. Marcus had had enough. "Mikki. Stop it, already," he said, a little louder this time. He turned toward me and put his hand on my wet knee. "Just—just stop it."

I was more surprised by his tone than I was by the decibel of his voice. I was gasping for breath, but I managed to say a few words. "Why—why are you yelling at me?" I said between sobs.

"I'm not yelling," Marcus yelled. "Just stop crying, already. Show's over."

He might as well have slapped me, rather than say that. "Show's over?" Did he think I was crying for someone else's benefit? That I'd purposely drawn my husband to the restaurant so that the three of us could act out our own ridiculous ghetto drama, replete with cursing and crying, in front of a crowd of white folks in a chi-chi restaurant? Marcus should have just slapped me; it would have felt better.

"What the hell did you just say? 'Show's over'?"

"Yeah, Mikki—the show is over," he said, lowering his voice. Then he turned to me. "You can stop all that fussing now."

"Were you there?" I said, turning to him. "Were you even in the room? Did you even see what just happened? Randy caught us, Marcus! Randy marched into this restaurant and caught us in a dark corner, staring into each others' eyes—"

"You don't have to re-live the moment for me," he snapped. "What I want to know is this: How in the world did he know we were here?"

I opened my mouth, but nothing came out. I was stunned into silence. How did Randy find out we were there? He wasn't home when I'd left, so he couldn't have heard me talking to Marcus on the phone. Was he still having me tailed? Did he figure out Marcus's boy was a ruse and hire someone else? Did Marcus's boy—what did he call him? Perrot, was it?—come clean to Randy and tell him about us? Did he tap the phone or put one of those taping devices in the VCR? Did Angelou call and tell him what was going on to get back at me? Did Marcus slip and tell him something?

That last one hit me in the head like a bolt of lightening. I can't describe it; it was almost as if I blacked out for a moment, it hit me so quick—so fierce. Marcus told him—had set the whole thing up. How else would Randy have known to come to this restaurant on this night at this specific time to that specific table?

"What did you tell him?"

"What do you mean, 'what did I tell him?' What did I tell who?" Marcus said, looking at me, annoyance mixing with his words.

"Well, I know I didn't tell him," I said coolly. "And only three people in this restaurant knew we were coming here tonight. One of them is the maître d', who I certainly don't think met my husband before the last half hour. One of them is me, and I know damn well I didn't tell him. I'm just figuring the only possible way Randy could have known we were here was if you told him."

"Why," Marcus said slowly, "would I possibly tell my best friend that I was betraying him like this, Mikki? What could I possibly get out of telling him that I'm fucking his wife?"

"I don't know, maybe it's some kind of weird male bonding thing— you two swap stories and get all giddy about sharing a bed with the same person. It's been known to happen."

"Oh, you know what, Mikki? You need to grow up," he said, spewing his words so hard I could feel the warm moisture of his spit throttle my face. "We're not in college anymore and this isn't some game or an episode of *Soul Food*. This here is real life, Mikki, and we commited the ultimate sin against your husband and my best friend. We cheated on him, and he found out. That's all that matters now—that's all that counts. He found out. Who knows who told him, who knows how he found out we were here? The point is that he did. And no amount of blaming it on someone else is going to change that, Mikki. Stop thinking about yourself for just a minute—just one lousy minute—and think about how Randy feels right now. And how I feel right now. And how you should be feeling right now. Because we all have to go home and live with this shit. Figure that out, Mikki. Figure out how we're going to live with this—not who told."

And with that, Marcus ran his hands across his thighs and, with his hands on his knees, lifted himself off the bench. He took one quick glance at me, then headed slowly up the stairs, leaving me sitting right there on the bench. Alone.

He was right. What was wrong with me? My husband, who had loved me unconditionally for almost seven years—despite my whining, my cursing, my silliness, my madness—was off somewhere with his heart broken. And I was the one who took the sledgehammer to it. Justifiably so, but I—the woman who promised to love him until the end of time—committed the ultimate betrayal against him. He had fire in his eyes when he walked over to our table. I'd never seen him that way before, outraged, outrageous, uncontrollably angry. I'd given my body and my heart to someone else and, in effect, given our marriage "do not resuscitate" orders, without checking to see if it's what Randy wanted. I should have given him that benefit—of knowing that I was in love with someone else, and the chance to fight for our married lives. And now, Randy was probably somewhere tearing things up, undone. And there I was, focusing on stupid stuff—like who told him we were in some restaurant.

The tears started flowing again, but I didn't linger in that basement—didn't want to. One of the ladies who had been staring at us as the drama unfolded upstairs had just come out of the ladies' room with her girlfriend and the two of them were staring at me and whispering to one another. I felt naked. Lonely. Insecure. Like I wanted to stab myself in the heart.

I needed to get out of there.

Fast.

When I got to the top of the staircase, Marcus was walking out of the door. He didn't even wait for me—didn't even say good-bye. But I was too embarrassed to stop and stare at him like I wanted to, or to call out to him like I should have. I could feel the heat of the patrons' glares on my neck and my cheeks and my back. I surveyed the restaurant, then made my way over to our table to retrieve my pocketbook and shawl. Before I'd even made two steps in that direction, the host jumped out at me with my belongings, startling me. "Here you are, ma'am," he said, shoving my purse and wrap into my arms. "Your, um, gentleman friend settled the bill." And then he extended his arm toward the door.

"Why don't you just say 'Get the hell out,' " I said, bass in my voice, neck rolling. If he was going to treat me like I was ghetto, I was going to give him a taste of ghetto. "What if I told you I wanted some spaghetti? Some penne? Risotto? You have risotto? With seafood in it?"

He put his arm down and closed his gaping mouth and stared at me for just a moment. He opened his mouth, and then quickly closed it again. Clearly perplexed, he extended his arm and said, "This way, ma'am. I can show you back to your table. Indeed, one of our specials tonight is scampi served over mushroom risotto. If you'll follow me . . ."

He walked to the right.

I exited left.

I was praying all the way back to Brooklyn in that taxi cab that Randy had gone back home and that he'd parked the BMW somewhere on South Oxford, out of his view but where I could find it. I wasn't going into that house—no way, no how. There was such rage in Randy's eyes that I half-expected him to lean back and hit me in that restaurant. In fact, I thought the only reason he didn't swing on my ass was because Marcus was sitting there. Randy isn't stupid. But he is angry. He's never so much as lifted a finger toward me, but then again, I'd never cheated on him. I wasn't trying to roll up into our house expecting that he wouldn't give me a shot. So I'd decided practically before the taxi got out of Little Italy that I would simply get into the BMW and drive to South Orange—stay there with my mother for a few days.

Sure enough, when we pulled onto Lafayette Avenue, I saw the car sandwiched between some raggedy old station wagon and one of those mammoth Land Cruisers. I hated when he did that. He was really good at parallel parking, but he'd squeeze into the tiniest spaces, each time adding some kind of nick or scrape to the bumper of the Beemer, and making it near impossible for anyone but him to get that bad boy out from between the squeeze of the other cars. I particularly hated this, because I couldn't parallel park to save my natural born life—had failed my driving test twice because of it. I'm the first to drive a half dozen blocks out of the way to find a space I can just drive into, and the first to tell Randy that if he wants me to drive, he has to pull the car out.

But this time, I was on my own, and I had to work fast. I put the key in the ignition and started the car. Abbey Lincoln was blasting in the speakers—a signal that Randy was depressed. He loved her singing, had every single one of her albums. But the only time he played her was when he was upset about something and needed her melancholy voice to help him drown in his sorrows. She was hitting those bottom notes in "Laugh Clown Laugh" when I hit the station wagon, then pulled forward, narrowly missing the bumper of the Land Cruiser. For sure, I'd jacked up the rim on the back right tire, but it was something that I would have to deal with later. I pulled out of the space and, zoning, made a left onto South Oxford, which I didn't want to do because I didn't want to drive past the house and have Randy see that I'd taken the ride. When I realized what I'd done, I stepped on it—hard. Had a little child, a small animal, or a really slow old man stepped so much as a toe onto the street, I'd have run them over. I'm almost sure I left tire tracks rushing through the yellow light to make a left onto DeKalb, and I narrowly missed a double-parked car just around the corner. I pushed on the pedal, getting a rush from the power of the metal surrounding me, carrying me down Flatbush and Tillary Streets, over the breathtaking Brooklyn Bridge, past City Hall, through the evening-serene downtown Manhattan and the Holland Tunnel, onto Route 280. When I hit the open roadway, I rolled down both the windows, letting the rush of wind slap my face as the cities of northeast New Jersey whirred by—Harrison, Newark, Orange, East Orange. And before I knew it, I'd come to the exit for South Orange.

I hadn't heard it when it started playing, but as I turned on to the roadway leading to my parents' house, I heard Donny Hathaway struggling through the speakers. I looked down at the stereo, then back at the road, then reached down and turned him up loud, letting his words stroke and caress and move me to tears. He was such a beautiful singer—had one of those sexy, butter silky voices, rivaled by few. I remember his songs well; they were practically a soundtrack to my parents' marriage, and my childhood. Daddy played him constantly—pranced around the house singing (well, yelling, really) the words to Donny's "Song for You," and "The Ghetto," and "To Be Young Gifted and Black." He'd jab his finger at the speakers and into the air and turn to me and Zaria and say, "Y'all don't know nothing 'bout this here. This here is good music. Real music. Soul music. Them boys y'all listen to can't hold Donny's applejack." I would giggle; Zaria would make a half-hearted attempt to argue the merits of listening to Run-DMC and Public Enemy and De La Soul versus "that old-people music." I never looked at it as old-people music, though—just hoped the two of them would shut up long enough for me to hear Donny's "Someday We'll All Be Free" minus their silly pecking and bickering. It was a stunning song, with its lush strings and Donny's stirring lyrics, about the perils of life and self-esteem and the shackles black folks' wear from day to day, and our need to believe that it wasn't always going to be like this for us. You didn't have to be old to appreciate any of this—Zaria knew it, too. Always, by the time the song came on, we'd all be standing somewhere, shouting the words and swaying and throwing our hands in the air like a bunch of church ladies moved by the spirit. My mother would just look at the three of us and shake her head and laugh.

I'd rediscovered Donny when Randy and I were planning our wedding. Well, actually, we were arguing over it. Randy, who was in love with the jazz singer Dianne Reeves, wanted us to dance our first husband/wife dance to her smoky-bluesy version of "For All We Know," a wonderful jazz standard that any singer worth her mettle had to record at some point or another to be taken seriously by enthusiasts. It's about unrequited love—a demand from one lover to another to love hard and strong with abandon, because God promises tomorrow only to the sun. I thought the song was an excellent choice, but I wanted Donny's more soulful, gospel version because, you know, Dianne can sing, but Donny's the man. Well, we fought over that for days—even went without speaking to each other, too. Then, on the third day of our bickering, I walked into our study to fetch a book and found Randy listening to Donny's version on our mini-stereo. He just looked up at me—didn't say anything, just stared. Donny wailed, asking his lover to love him tonight because tomorrow may never come. I walked over to my intended and kneeled at his feet. He slipped out of the chair, down to his knees, and we fell into a long passionate embrace. With Donny's words falling uneasily from his lips, Randy slowly unbuttoned my blouse and unbuckled my belt and slipped my skirt down past my waist and then undressed himself too and made love to me like that day was the last day on Earth we'd have together. We decided afterward to play both versions at the wedding, and Randy put the two of them on an hour-long cassette back-to-back so that when we made love for the very first time as man and wife, our song was playing.

Now, I could barely listen to it—it dredged up so many memories. The day I'd first laid eyes on Randy. Our first date. The first time we'd slept together. Our first vacation. The day he proposed. The look on my parents' face when he asked my father for my hand in marriage. All of it came back in a rush as I drove slowly toward my childhood home, past the big houses and the lake, the middle school, the train station, and the Pathmark. By the time I'd made it to Ridgewood Road, I'd already replayed the song three times, and was in the process of listening to it again when I decided to just drive past my parents' house. What, after all, was I expecting my mother to be—sympathetic? Hadn't she already kicked her husband out of the house for doing the same exact thing I'd done to mine? Wasn't she still salty about the Joe incident, with me acting all mean to her—ugh—boyfriend? Wasn't she just crazy about her son-in-law, and likely to tell me I deserved whatever I had coming?

I wasn't going over there.

Angelou's wasn't an option.

Marcus was probably still mad.

I definitely wasn't in the mood to hear Zaria's "I told you so's."

So I just kept driving—me and Donny, on the highway, with nowhere to go, no one to see. Nothing to look forward to. I don't know how long I pushed the tin around the roadways of Essex County. I do know that the sun had long set and I was hungry, yawning, and in serious need of a toilet. And at some point, I took my behind on home.

He

It was well past midnight when I finally heard the clank of the dead-bolt announcing Mikki's return home. Was it even proper to call it her home anymore? I wasn't sure. At the moment, there wasn't much I was sure of. I was actually a bit surprised that Mikki had come home. After a few hours, which I spent sitting on the couch in our rec room staring at the moving images on the television screen but not really seeing them, I had given up the expectation that I would get to confront my wife once again. I figured she would stay away as long as she could to postpone another scene. But here she was, trudging up the stairs, slowly, probably excruciatingly, walking into the breach.

As was usually the case when I expected a huge conflagration with my wife, my stomach roiled and tossed like the hurricane-buffeted surf. My anger had accumulated strength again during the wait. In fact, I used it like a lighthouse beacon to keep my focus against the distractions of my nerves. Yeah, sure I was angry, but I was also frightened. This might prove to be one of the most devastatingly transformative days of my life up to now. I couldn't bear to think beyond this coming confrontation, to imagine what my life might be like if I lost my wife and my best friend on the same day. Who would I run to with my pain if both of my dependable shoulders were snatched away from me? Who could I talk to?

Like two wary heavyweights, the two of us began without much action—silence, as a matter of fact. I tried to pretend that I didn't see Mikki as she glanced into the rec room and quickly kept moving toward the bedroom on the next floor. I was anxious to see what kind of approach Mikki would take toward me. In the past when I had flung some rage in her direction, she would respond with a bit of rage of her own, almost as a defense mechanism, even if she was clearly in the wrong. She had never been more wrong than she was tonight. I couldn't imagine her trying that one again. But I knew I'd never get very far trying to predict what Mikki was going to do.

Once she passed me by, she effectively tossed the ball back in my court. Now I had to decide how long I was going to wait before moving into the bedroom. I couldn't race in there too quickly unless I planned on kicking off the argument. But I couldn't wait too long or she would crawl into the bed and pretend to be asleep, ending any possibility of me exercising my broiling anger tonight. It was confusing stuff, this marital combat. I didn't want to make the wrong move and lose my current tactical advantage, which was huge. I had anger and moral outrage on my side. Mikki had squat.

I decided to wait fifteen minutes before moving to the bedroom for the big confrontation. I knew there wasn't a woman alive who could get ready for bed in less than fifteen minutes. With my heart in my throat and a simmering outrage dancing on my tongue, I stepped into our bedroom. I saw that Mikki was still in the bathroom, going through her face regimen. I would have to wait a little longer. I sat down on the edge of the bed, stealing a few glances into the bathroom to see how close she was. In an instant, she breezed into the bedroom and walked right by me as if I weren't there. Oh, she was going to try to ignore me? That was her tactic? Oh, hell no.

"I still can't believe that shit," I said, starting off in a voice I hoped sounded calm yet outraged. "I think I'm still in shock."

I looked straight ahead, not at her, almost pretending that I was talking to myself. Still, she said nothing. More of the silent treatment. I forged ahead.

"How could you do that to me?" I said venomously, spitting the words in her direction. Finally, Mikki stopped and gave me a taste of her mindset.

"You know, Randy, you can cut the fuckin' drama queen act, okay?" she said angrily. "I'm not in the mood for it. I've had quite enough of it for one day. Sorry I don't have an Academy Award to give you."

Oh, damn, she was making fun now? She had jokes now? After committing her mortal sin, she was trying to make *me* look silly? The nerve of her.

"*You've* had quite enough? You think I care about how much *you've* had? If I wanna be a drama queen, then I'll be a goddamn drama queen! I didn't create the drama—that credit can go right to you and my so-called best friend. Y'all created all the drama when you started sneaking around like little roaches and fuckin' behind my back. You're the ones who belong on a damn soap opera!"

I wanted to let go of the drama analogy, since it wasn't mine anyway, but first I needed to grind it into her face as hard as I could. As I looked at the angry set of her eyebrows and the scornful snarl she wore, I wanted to inflict as much damage as I possibly could, to pay her back with some hurt of her own.

"How do you know we were fuckin'?" she snarled. "You can jump to all the conclusions you want, but you really don't know a damn thing except what you saw. And all you saw was a kiss between two friends. As far as I know, that's not a felony. So you can just let go of the outrage."

Despite the snarl, she said this rather coolly—much more coolly than I. She was trying to say they weren't having sex? I had been so sure of that one—come on, I saw the way she melted into Marcus's arms!—that I hadn't even questioned it for a moment. Now she was trying to slow me down with denials. And it was working just a tiny bit. I couldn't be one-hundred-percent certain they had been screwing, right? But I knew what a clandestine meeting between lovers looked like. The furtiveness, the passion. Why would they be eating in Little Italy if they weren't having an affair?

"So you're going to stand there and try to tell me that you never had sex with him?!" I snarled.

Mikki hesitated a short beat, as if she were trying to decide on the appropriate lie. That was enough for me; I knew she was not to be believed. I had a flash of inspiration.

"Before you make something up, you should know that I just talked to Marcus," I said, flashing her a dastardly smile. I could see her stumbling, unsure of whether to believe me.

"You talked to Marcus?" she repeated, the doubt evident in her voice.

"Yep," I said, still smiling. "So, let me hear it. Tell me about how you never had sex with him."

I saw the confusion, the uncertainty, on her troubled face. I soaked it in; I was almost enjoying myself.

"What—what did Marcus say to you?" she said, trying to sound belligerent. But I could see right through the fake belligerence to her fear. It sat there on her face like a neon sign. Sure, mine was a nasty, boldfaced lie, but it was a means to an end—and it was a mere atom, a tiny particle of matter, compared to her elephantine deceit.

"Why don't you ask *him* what he said?" I said. "Go call your boyfriend and ask him what he said to me."

I had a smile on my face, a wicked, taunting smile that I could tell didn't sit well with her. She glared at me for a long moment without speaking.

"Fuck off, Randy!" she spat at me, turning on her bare heels to leave the room.

"Oh, that's clever!" I shouted, following behind her. "That's just lovely! You fuck my best friend behind my back and you tell *me* to fuck off? I don't think so. I think—"

"You think I care for a second what you think?!" Mikki said, pivoting and sticking her index finger in my face. "You forfeited any right to an opinion a long time ago when it comes to me and my life, okay? You deserted me, Randy. You left me here, and I just had to find a way to, to"—the tears were starting to inch down her cheeks as she tried to find the right words—"to stay sane. Marcus gave me a way."

"Oh, I *deserted* you now?!" I couldn't believe my ears. She was trying to transform my time in Paris into a desertion? How jacked up was that? "Three stupid months in Paris and your little spoiled behind couldn't survive? What the hell did you do before we were married, Mikki? You just pullin' some craziness out your behind now."

I could see her anger through the tears. I saw her nostrils flare. I knew her rejoinder was going to be ugly. I almost flinched when she turned her lips up into another snarl.

"You know, maybe you could ask your best friend to teach you a little something about how to treat this 'little spoiled behind,' " Mikki said, clearly going for the hurt. Now she gave me a wicked, taunting smile. "Matter of fact, there's a lot he could teach you."

The implication was clear and it reached down and sliced me in places I didn't think Mikki still had the power to touch. In two sentences, she had demonstrated how far we had fallen by eagerly going to that place women normally would walk over hot coils to avoid: the minefields of sexual slur. I had been raised in a household where a major cardinal rule, a childhood commandment, was that boys never hit girls, men never hit women. Over the years, that rule hardened into a philosophy that affected the way I talked to women, the way I thought about women, the way I treated women. They were precious, to be adored, to be treasured. Not abused. So how hard was it going to be for me to resist every muscle, every tendon, every blood vessel in my right arm that itched, burned, and begged to reach out and smash my palm into my wife's face? Could I possibly extricate myself from this encounter without the use of physical force?

I closed my eyes and grimaced as if I had just been slapped. When I opened them up again, I thought I saw terror in Mikki's face—maybe she could sense how close she was to a smackdown. What I needed most of all was to get this woman out of my face before I spent the night in a jail cell. If that happened, I couldn't even call my lawyer to come rescue me.

"Get out."

At first I said it softly, almost as if I were talking to myself. Mikki surely heard me, but she said "What?" anyway. For some reason, at that moment I remembered a scene from an old movie I had watched as a boy, *Philadelphia Story*, starring Cary Grant and Katharine Hepburn. Grant smashed his palm into Hepburn's face in the movie's first minute and shoved her back through the front doorway and to the floor. The scene was clearly intended to amuse, but I didn't think Mikki or any other woman I knew would find it amusing if a man's palm connected with their face to shove them to the floor.

"I said, 'Get out,' " I repeated, more loudly this time. Mikki blinked rapidly in surprise. I could see she didn't expect this one. She probably didn't think I had the balls to throw her out.

"This is my hou—"

"Get the fuck out, Mikki, before I do something I might regret!" I said, interrupting her protestation. I pointed toward the front window, a la Ralph Kramden in *The Honeymooners*.

"You don't throw me out of my house! You must be crazy! I paid— hey, get your hands off me!" I firmly pushed Mikki toward the stairs, somehow finding a way to turn a deaf ear to her screams. She grabbed onto the banister at the top step.

"Randy! Stop it!"

Oblivious now to any hurt feelings she might have, I reached down and pried her fingers loose. Before I could push her again, Mikki started walking down the steps—and cursing me loudly every step of the way.

"Muthafucka, you'll regret the day you put your hands on me! My hands decorated every room in this house! I will not be thrown out of my own house!"

As I reached out to push again, Mikki kept walking to stay just beyond my touch. When the front door grew near, Mikki realized all she was wearing was a T-shirt and panties. Hardly appropriate dress for standing out in the street.

"Randy! Listen to me!"

But I stepped forward more quickly this time and gave her an extra hard shove. She tried to shove me back, but I outweighed her by almost a hundred pounds and she couldn't get any leverage as she found herself moving toward the door. I was acting like a machine, as intent as an unthinking robot. For an instant, I thought of myself as Schwarzenegger in *The Terminator*, reacting and doing without even the capacity to worry about anybody's feelings.

With Mikki screeching my name at the top of her lungs, I opened the heavy front parlor door and shoved her out. Mikki grabbed onto the side of the door, but I once again pried her fingers loose. This was a well-cast ghetto drama. A few passersby paused their strolling to watch the juicy action. I gave her one last push and slammed the door in her face. Her screeching stopped in an instant. I heard just one word seep through the door, delivered in a voice mixed with desperation, shock, and all-consuming anger.

"Bitch."

As I made my way back up to the bedroom, my body was overtaken by a paralyzing numbness. I had to sit down on the steps because I wasn't sure if I could walk any farther. For the next hour, I sat on the stairway in my well-appointed four-story brownstone and I stared at the front door. If a doctor had been around to see me, he might have guessed that I had gone into shock. But my condition wasn't nearly as treatable as shock. The medical establishment hadn't yet come up with an emergency room protocol for heartbreak.

She

"What are you staring at?!"

I swear to you, every person ever to cross my path in Fort Greene, Brooklyn, had their eyes trained on my stoop, watching the Angry-Buppies-'N-the-Hood theater Randy and I had just played out, live and in color. Frank Parks, our neighbor who owned the brownstone across the street and to the right of our house, was hanging outside his window, a look of disgust on his face. So were Andrea and Monique, the twenty-something sisters who lived a few stoops to our left. On the stoop to the right of their building was Lana and her crackhead ho ass, shaking her head at me—like she'd never found herself in a compromising position on South Oxford Avenue with any of the numerous drug-dealing thugs who terrorized the block on the regular just so that bitch could get her fixes. Sitting with her were two of said thugs, pointing and yelling "oh shit" into the palms of their hands as they released loud, harsh, rumbling laughs in my direction. "Yo, you need some help, ma?" one of them yelled out. "I got a place for you to go and I won't ever kick yo fine ass out if you walkin' 'round my crib lookin' like dat dere."

I looked down and, Lord have mercy, realized once again that I was practically half-naked on that stoop—with nothing on but a half-shirt and a black pair of cotton drawers not quite covering my behind. And my neighbors—particularly the men, with their pointing fingers and their gaping jaws—were raping me with their eyes. They knew where I lived, where I worked, who I was, and now they knew me intimately, the way my bra-less breasts hung, the true shape of my thighs, the way my ass rested on them. That my husband was so angry with me that he probably wouldn't care right now at this moment whether any of them decided to sample the goods I had to offer. Randy had pushed me on that stoop and left me ass out—literally and figuratively.

Instinctively, I threw my arms across my body—one arm hugged my breasts, the other draped my hips. I started down the stairs, my feet rushing over the dirt and cold rocks peppered across my stoop. As I ran toward the home of our neighbor, Ms. Elly, one of the thug boys started making his way off Lana's porch. Now, I was scared.

"Ms. Elly! Ms. Elly!" I yelled, my eyes on thug boy, who was standing on the curb, waiting for several cars to pass. "Ms. Elly! It's Mikki. Can you open up? Please, Ms. Elly!"

I heard the deadbolt smack against its metal casing and then the twist of two locks and finally the creaking of the wooden door as my elderly neighbor cracked it open and peeked out the small, chain-draped crack. She crinkled her brow, a look of sheer puzzlement crossed her face. "What's the matter, child?"

"Ms. Elly," I said hurriedly, turning to look over my shoulder at thug boy crossing the street. "Please, Ms. Elly. Let me in."

"Hey, shortie—let me holla at cha," thug boy said.

"Who's that?" Ms. Elly asked.

"Ms. Elly, I don't know that man and I'm begging you to open this door and let me in before he gets across that street."

When she slammed the door in my face, I swear my life began to flash before my eyes—my mother wrapping a scarf around my three-year-old neck, my father teaching me how to ride a bike at age seven, Zaria and me desperately trying to beat each other's behinds for the remote, my grandmother's funeral, my college graduation, my first meeting with Randy. In an instant, I saw it all. Weird, huh? But I snapped out of it, though, when I heard her undoing the chain, and, almost as quickly, I saw the door fling back open again. "Get on in here," Ms. Elly said quickly, pulling my arm. With me safely behind her, she gave one last quick look at the thug, who was standing at the foot of her stoop, then closed the door forcefully. When she turned around, her eyes landed on my breasts and slowly made their way down to my panties, then naked legs and bare feet. "Mikki—you want to tell me what's going on?"

I was shivering and sniffling and talking all loud between tears and gasping breaths. "Ms. Elly, I, I—"

"Calm down, honey. Here, come up the stairs and let me get you Jeremiah's robe to put on you," she said, pushing me toward the stairs. "Jeremiah! Jeremiah!" she yelled up the stairs to her husband. "Throw your robe on down the stairs for me, hear?"

"Whatcha say, Elly?" he yelled back.

"I say throw your robe down the stairs for me," she yelled back.

"Well, what you need my robe for? Ain't you got one on?"

"Jeremiah!" Ms. Elly yelled so loud I jumped a good three feet into the air, or at least that's what it felt like. She looked at me and put her hand back on my arm. "Don't ask me no damn questions, just throw me the damn robe!"

Almost instantly, a big ball of blue-and-gray-plaid flew down the stairs, right into Ms. Elly's face. It landed in a heap at her feet. Now, Ms. Elly's got to be, like, 102—or at least that's what you would think with all her "ailments." Her back is bad, and her legs, and her veins are blue and thick, and she's got arthritis and can barely move her wrist and she's constantly in need of some help from somebody for something or the other. That's how we met, actually—with her putting Randy to work the day we moved into our home. Randy was outside giving orders to the movers who were on the verge of busting up my sleigh bed when Ms. Elly called over to him and asked if he would help her bring her groceries into the house. Randy obliged—how could he deny a grandmotherly old woman?—and, in carrying the paper bags up her stairs, instantaneously sealed a friendship and workhorse relationship with Ms. Elly and Mr. Jeremiah. They always had us doing something around their house, and in return, Ms. Elly would shower us with sweet potato pies and lemon pound cakes and yeast rolls she made from scratch. We'd come to love the old couple, and Randy and I, in turn, became the children they never had.

"What are you doing outside in the freezing cold standing around in your underclothes, Mikki?" Ms. Elly said sternly, draping Jeremiah's robe over my shoulders.

I was trying to get the words out, but I couldn't for all the crying. I wasn't so sure I wanted to tell her anyway. I just wanted to use the phone—call Marcus and ask him to come get me.

"Where is Randy?" Ms. Elly demanded. "Lord, when he finds out you were standing out on the stoop in your underclothes he is going to be fit to be tied. What happened, you locked yourself out?"

"Randy—" I said between gulps. "Randy—"

"Have mercy, is Randy okay?" Ms. Elly said, covering her mouth with her hand, aghast.

"Randy did this," I managed to blurt out.

"Randy did what?"

"He put me out—"

"Put you out?" she said, incredulous. "Put you out in the street with no clothes on? Randy?"

"I, I—" I stammered.

"Lord have mercy on my soul. I'd have never imagined in a million years Randy would raise his hand to you. You need me to call the police for you, baby? Lord, I thought he was such a nice young man, and here he is abusing his beautiful wife. Shame on him. Shame on him! Ain't no kinda man put his hand on no woman. I swear before God, Jeremiah ain't never done nothing like that, and if he did, I'da gave him a faceful of grits—that's right. There'll be none of that in this here house, hard as I work around here, many years as I done gave that man . . ."

Well, Ms. Elly, indeed, was fit to be tied, and she had the phone in her hand, ready to call the police and have Randy locked up for life. Thing is, she didn't have her glasses, and she couldn't quite find the 9 on the dial-pad, so she was so distracted by her quest that she didn't hear me tell her not to call the police. I didn't want Randy to go to jail for kicking me out of the house. I was mad as hell at him, but not so mad that I'd want them knocking on our door with the butt of their nightsticks, with their itchy fingers on their gun holsters, waiting for some deranged black man to give them a reason to shoot. No, this wasn't that kind of battle.

So I carefully lifted the phone out of Ms. Elly's hand and placed it in its cradle.

"I don't want to call the police," I told her quietly. "I'd like to borrow a shirt and a pair of pants and then I want to call a friend of mine and ask him to come pick me up."

Ms. Elly just looked at me, puzzled. And then, a smile spread across her face. I amused her. "You want to call a friend and tell him to pick you up, you said?"

"Yes, Ms. Elly. That's all I want—some clothes and a phone call, and I'll be out of your hair."

She just stood there, staring at me for the longest time. "All right then," she finally said, resigned. "You young 'uns just kill me with all these here shenanigans and carrying on. But if that's what you want, that's what you'll get." She walked slowly toward the stairs, then stopped and looked back. "But I'll tell you one thing, ain't no good ever come from a woman stayin' with no man who beats on his wife. Jeremiah and I been at each other's behinds for years, and some days I wish the good Lord would just put us both out of our misery, but so help me God he ain't never so much as laid a hand on me or put my body into harm's way. No sir. Been together fifty-two years, and he been there watching and protecting me every step of the way, even when he didn't want to. That's what husbands do, baby. Now you go on over to where you got to go and do what you got to do, but don't you forget what happened this here night, hear? Can't no good come from it."

And she walked on up the stairs.

I waited for her to hobble into her room on the second floor before I picked up the phone and dialed Marcus's number. I was expecting him to pick up on at least the second ring, seeing as it was one a.m. and he should have been home. But it just rang and rang, until the answering machine picked up. I listened to the message, then talked hurriedly into the receiver.

"Marcus, please pick up the phone. I know you're there—pick up. It's me, Mikki. I really need to talk to you and I need you to come get me. I'm in trouble. Please, Marcus, pick up." I stopped talking, and waited to hear his voice. Still no answer. I talked some more, confident that he was there, but too mad at me, still, to answer. "Marcus, please. I need your help. Randy kicked me out of the house and I don't have any clothes, any keys, not even shoes on my feet. You have to help me."

I heard the receiver pick up, but it wasn't Marcus's voice that I heard on the other end of the phone. It was a woman's. "Who is this?" she asked, a hint of annoyance in her voice.

"Who is this?" I asked back, unsure whether I should be stunned or outraged that a woman was answering his phone.

"This is Marcus's girlfriend," she said, more indignant this time. "He's busy right now. So how can I help you?"

The pit of my stomach was roiling, like the soft rumbling that fills the night air just before a roaring crash of thunder pierces through it. All at once, I was dizzy, unstable. I needed to hold on to something, so I grabbed the back of the chair Ms. Elly had resting next to the phone table. Then I sat in it. Girlfriend? Girlfriend?! Marcus had a woman? Someone he was so close to that he let her answer his phone and do his bidding? I had betrayed my husband, alienated myself from my best friend, embarrassed my family and myself, groveled in front of the entire neighborhood and now, Marcus had a girlfriend?

I honestly didn't know how much more of this I could take. I was standing on the edge of sanity, about a half-second from swan-diving into the abyss. In one day, I had lost my husband and my boyfriend—both the loves of my life.

Now what was I going to do? Where was I going to go? How was I going to survive? Who was going to love me? Who was I going to love? Was I even capable of it? Did I even want to ever again in life?

I heard her speaking into the receiver, but I didn't really *hear* her. Didn't want to, really. I think I thanked her for her time, and told her I didn't want to leave a message and hung up the phone or something. I don't know—it's a blur now. I kind of remember Ms. Elly walking back into her foyer and helping me into some old flowery dress, and me thinking it smelled like the foot rub Randy put on his feet when he'd had a rough day on the tennis court, and her asking me what my sister's phone number was and me telling her and her dialing it and asking Zaria what her address was because she was putting me in a cab and sending me to Teaneck.

I woke up the next afternoon, head heavy and throbbing, to my nephew's fingers poking me in the eye.

"Hi, Auntie Mikki!" he yelled into my ear. "I went to church today. Are you still sleepy? Mommy wants to know if you want bananas in your pancakes. Wanna watch *101 Dalmatians* with me? Huh? Wanna?"

I opened my one, good, non-poked eye and stared at my nephew.

At first, I didn't know where I was or who he was either. And then, the night's events came rushing back into my head. Instantly, I wanted to cry out, but instead, I reminded myself that James was a child and probably didn't know the words I wanted to say, much less deserve to hear them. So I kept it simple.

"Tell your mother Auntie said leave her alone forever."

He

When I woke up on Sunday morning, I stared in disbelief at the bed-side clock advertising the time as eleven-thirty. How had I managed to sleep the entire morning away? But as I considered rising from the bed, I couldn't even summon the motivation to convert the thought into action. What would I do? Where would I go? Not only was an empty, pointless Sunday staring me in the face, but I couldn't bear the thought of going to work the next day and the day after that and coming back to Brooklyn every evening to a desolate house that seemed to mock my heartbreak in every room. Mikki had lovingly decorated every inch of this house, and she had decorated it to within an inch of her life. My woman—God, could I even think of her as that anymore?—had a flair with interior spaces that would always leave me in awestruck wonderment. She could convert a dank cellar into a Taj Mahal showpiece. She revered Martha Stewart's over-the-top class and resourcefulness, but I believed she made Martha look like a dull WASPy pretender. All this was to say that my wife stared back at me from every wall, every picture frame, every sofa set, every mirror, and every throw rug in my entire house. Even lying there alone in the bed, I felt her presence suffocating me, screaming at me for what I had done to her the night before.

Had I really forced my wife onto the street wearing nothing but a T-shirt and panties? It was so ridiculous that I almost started laughing. I had never thought of myself as a dramatic gesture kinda guy; I wasn't particularly interested in letting the world in on my good moods and bad ones. But that act the night before had been the Oscars of dramatic gestures and attention-grabbing spectacles. I allowed myself to wonder what Mikki was thinking when it was happening. Did she ever imagine I could do something so horrible to her? I was sure that she had been as stunned by the turn of events as I was. And why hadn't she tried to beg me to let her back into the house? If I had been standing on a Fort Greene street practically butt-ass naked, shivering and embarrassed, I would have been pounding on that front door to get back in—even if the pounding attracted all kinds of attention to my plight. I knew Mikki was a proud woman, but how had she managed to restrain herself from asking to get back inside? She had probably knocked on the door of the older black couple who lived next door and used their phone to call Marcus. What was my former best buddy thinking right now? Was he even allowing his mind to wander to me, to envision the pain that his actions had caused his best friend? I thought back on my afternoon tennis match with Marcus, how Marcus had raced from the courts after our satisfying victory. He had been in such a rush because he was excited about getting to Mikki, that much was now clear. The stress that must have been coursing through Marcus's veins out on that court. But in retrospect he had done a good job of hiding it, I thought. If the situation were reversed and I had been boning Marcus's woman, I didn't think I'd be able to look my boy in the face. And how about the boldfaced treachery that led my so-called best friend to set up that duplicitous private detective farce? Did Marcus have to pay Perrot to participate in the ruse, or did the detective go along willingly as some favor to Marcus? In effect, Perrot had taken my money without delivering an iota of service—he had reneged on our agreement. The more I thought about it, the angrier I got over the detective's actions. I had been treated like a stupid little child as Marcus and Mikki and Perrot carried on their game at my expense—literally. I knew there were consumer protection agencies I could call to drop a dime on Perrot, but they were slow, cumbersome bureaucracies that would probably take years to act. I needed some action, some satisfaction, right this moment. I needed to let Perrot know that I was wise to him and I needed some sort of revenge.

As I sat up in my den later that afternoon and watched the Knicks turn in another lackluster performance on national television, I could barely concentrate on the game. I was concocting a plan that would make Perrot regret the day he gave his assent to Marcus's nasty deception. A professional wasn't supposed to lower himself to act as a dupe in the craven world of marital infidelity. *Professional* was one of the first words that I would have used to describe Perrot. So just how had Perrot come to be involved in Marcus's plan? Marcus must have worked with Perrot for quite a while—or maybe Perrot owed the lawyer some big-time favors. At any rate, Perrot would be getting another visit from Randolph Murphy. Until I could find a way to inflict damage on Marcus and Mikki, I would have to content myself with getting back at Perrot.

I jerked my head toward the clock and again shook my head in disbelief. It was ten-thirty? I had nearly slept through the morning for a second day in a row? The Trier-Stanton Monday morning engine had already been chugging away for two hours. It would take me at least another hour and fifteen minutes to get dressed and to the office. There was no point in waltzing in at 11:45 a.m., I'd never catch up. No, it was best to stay away from the office now, to call my secretary and tell her I had the early winter flu and would need to stay in bed. In fact, the flu would buy me at least three days of recovery time—time to develop a place to deposit, or at least hide, the pain and hostility that would certainly block any productivity in the workplace. I was overseeing a massive push by Trier-Stanton to make a run at the Reebok sneaker contract. It was the first major project since my promotion to head of the creative department. Reebok was entertaining pitches on the sly, without the knowledge of its longtime agency, Olds & Harper. It was back-stabbing and cold-blooded—but hey, that was the ad business. The same thing had happened to Trier-Stanton a few years back with a major airline contract. Somebody had slipped in beneath us—wasn't it Olds & Harper, in fact?—right under our radar that was constantly sweeping for poachers. If I could successfully engineer the Reebok coup, I would earn a spot in the legendary line-up of mythical corporate tales that get passed on through generations of awestruck drones. Reebok was as high-profile as they come, with an unparalleled opportunity for out-of-the-box edginess and artistry in the ad campaign. On Friday I had wanted Reebok so badly that I had ripped off numerous heads in the department in an effort to push my people further than they'd ever go on their own. But now Friday seemed about as far off to me as the glee-filled early days of my marriage. Right now Reebok could kiss my ass. Besides, we had at least two weeks before we were scheduled to meet with the Reebok people and make our pitch.

I needed to make the mental effort to force Reebok away from me. That was really somebody else's business, even if the Reebok campaign would do magical things for my career. I couldn't allow myself to be trapped by the glory of career advancement into neglecting the things that really were my business. I had already tripped over that boulder on too many occasions to count. Right now I had to bore in on what was mine. This Monday morning, that thing was revenge, marital infidelity, a shattered friendship, and enough heat and fury to propel me as if my ass were bolted to a missile.

As I passed through the revolving doors to enter Perrot's Lexington Avenue building, I was actually a little frightened. I thought my anger would be enough to get me past the trepidation I was feeling about confronting the detective, but now that the scene was upon me I wanted more than anything to flee. I hadn't been sure whether I should call Perrot first to see if he was there; I didn't get the impression that the man spent a lot of time at his office. Once I decided that I should call and then hang up if Perrot answered, I smartly realized that it wouldn't be wise to call from home. A private detective would surely employ caller ID or at least Star 69 if he suspected there might be danger looming. I didn't want Perrot to know that I was coming after him. Virtually the only thing I had working in my favor was the element of surprise.

As the elevator began its ascent, I tried to wade through my apprehension enough to come up with a plan of action for this encounter. I was fairly certain that Perrot had been a participant in Marcus's ruse, but what if the man denied it? Did I have any proof? Would my anger have any effect on Perrot besides inciting some anger of his own? What if things escalated to a physical confrontation? I didn't relish the idea of having to fight Perrot—the man had the look of someone confident in his response to violence, like he had been there before. I hadn't been in a fight since college, when I tangled with a drunk white boy who had slurred some racial nastiness in my direction outside of a frat party that

I just happened to be walking by. In fact, Marcus was with me at the time. We both thought we heard the boy mutter the word "nigger." That was all it took. Yale wasn't the kind of place where racial epithets were likely to fill the air, so we both had been taken aback. I had walked up in the white boy's face and asked him to repeat his comment. Apparently the white boy thought his frat brothers had his back, but he was wrong. The frat boys stood silently by as I shoved the drunk in the chest and told him he was a stupid, racist idiot. Maybe his frat brothers agreed with my assessment. The drunk had cocked back his right arm so slowly that I would have been tempted to laugh if I wasn't the intended target of the coming roundhouse. The punch sailed lazily through the air in my general direction; it wouldn't have landed even if I hadn't stepped deftly aside. In response, I lashed out a quick right hook that caught the boy in the left side of his face, approximately in the cheek. I felt a pain shoot up through my fingers as the fist connected; I was lucky I didn't strike jaw or I probably would have sustained more damage than my racist classmate. The single punch dropped the drunk like an overstuffed laundry bag. All along, Marcus had been glaring at the other frat boys, his sizzling stare keeping them all from forming the idea that they should defend their buddy's honor by inviting more violence. I looked down at the hapless white boy, whose face was a shade of crimson even deeper than we had seen earlier that day on the football uniforms of the Harvard players. I shook my head, gave Marcus a satisfied smirk, and we were back on our way. The fight grew in stature and legend each year as we told the story so many times that listeners were eventually led to believe me and Marcus had beaten down an entire fraternity by ourselves, standing back to back and cutting down one after another drunken frat boy like heroes in a martial arts flick.

I inhaled deeply before I knocked on Perrot's door. I heard footsteps approach. I saw that there was a peephole at about the level of my nose; no doubt Perrot was looking out at me and wondering what I could want. The door opened up. Perrot was standing there with a slightly quizzical look.

"We didn't have an appointment, I don't believe," Perrot said.

I shook my head.

"No, we didn't. But I just wanted to speak with you a minute." I tried to make my voice sound warm and non-threatening, but I hoped Perrot couldn't detect any of the fear and nervousness I was feeling.

His face still an open question mark, Perrot nodded and stepped back to let me in. I let Perrot lead the way as we went into his still-spartan inner office. For just a second I thought about running out and forgetting this whole confrontation thing. After all, Perrot was very much besides the point—my real anger should have been concentrated on Marcus and Mikki. Perrot was just a bit player, an extra hired to assist in their secret, illicit cause. I had very little to gain by unleashing my venom on Perrot. But it was too late now to turn back, wasn't it?

Perrot sat down in his familiar pose behind his sparsely decorated desk in his barely decorated office. He leaned back in his chair and looked up at me quizzically. The moment of truth.

"So, how can I help you, Mr. Murphy?"

I paused an instant. How do I do this? I tried to locate some of that outrage.

"Well, I had a very upsetting weekend, Mr. Perrot," I began.

"Sorry to hear that," he said.

I watched him closely to see if his comment contained any sarcasm. I didn't see any.

"Yeah, I bet you are. I made a startling discovery. I discovered that my wife is having a very open and public affair with my best friend. A man named Marcus Peate. I believe you know him."

Perrot's face was contorted into a frown. He didn't look embarrassed or ashamed that I had thrown the covers off his ruse. He just looked a little confused. This was not going as I had expected.

"I'm sorry to hear that, Mr. Murphy. I had hoped that it wasn't true, and you know I saw no evidence of it. But who the hell is Marcus Peate?"

Damn. Perrot was going to play stupid? I knew it was going to prove uncomfortable that I had no evidence of his complicity.

"He's my former best friend and he's the person who referred me to you. I think I told you that. He works at Hatch, Doyle and Roberts, the Wall Street law firm that I believe you've done a lot of work for."

Perrot nodded. "Yes, I'm certainly familiar with the firm. They are a client of mine. But they have several hundred lawyers at the firm and I've probably worked with at least a quarter of them over the years. You can't expect me to remember all their names."

Perrot was so calm and unfazed that virtually every ounce of my outrage had dissipated. It did me no good to get into a debate with

Perrot over which lawyers he remembered and didn't remember. Talk about your pointless tangents.

Perrot leaned in toward me. "What exactly did you expect to accomplish by showing up here?" he asked me. "I could only report to you what I saw. Certainly you understand that. Hiring me is no guarantee of anything. If your wife and this lawyer had no contact during the week I followed her, how was I to report that to you? Most people hire my services for a longer time period, for just this very reason. Their lover could go out of town—hell, the woman could be on her period that week. You never know."

"You didn't say anything about a week being too short when I hired you," I said. I feared that my voice had too much whine in it. I didn't feel like pursuing this anymore. It was clear I wouldn't get the kind of satisfaction I was looking for—that look of shock on Perrot's face when he realized he had been busted with his hand in the cash register, the deer in the headlights sort of image. I didn't think Perrot was capable of appearing shocked, not even if you plugged a lamp up his ass.

"Well, I'm sorry if you feel I didn't give you the proper guidance. I got the impression that your funds were limited."

My eyes snapped to his face to see if he meant it to be as insulting as it sounded. In effect, he was calling me cheap. What an asshole.

"No, the funds weren't the problem, Mr. Perrot. My problems were . . . you know, I have a hard time believing that it was just a coincidence that Marcus Peate sent me to you and he was the one having an affair with my wife. That one just kills me. But I guess you're not prepared to be straightforward about it. So I guess my deed here is done."

I got up from my chair in a sudden rush. I was starting to feel embarrassed that I had even come to his office. He was the one who was supposed to feel embarrassment upon my departure.

"Again, I really have no idea what you're talking about," Perrot said as he followed me to the door.

I pivoted. "I hope you're telling me the truth, Mr. Perrot," I said. "If you're not, I *will* find out." I tried to introduce some menace to my voice at the last minute—with limited success.

Perrot just shrugged. He certainly didn't appear to be frightened by the veiled threat. Maybe he didn't even pick up on the threat. I turned back around and scurried out of his office. At least it felt like I was scurrying.

As I've said before, I hate to feel like a big walking cliché, but after my encounter with Perrot I felt such a searing shame that I needed to reach an altered state. I needed to get drunk or high or something that would enable me to escape the pain that seemed to reach down to my toenails. It had been years since I had smoked a joint. In fact, even though I lived in Brooklyn, probably within blocks of dozens of drug dealers, I had no idea where to find marijuana. So that left me with alcohol.

I looked up in time to see a Lexington Avenue spot with the inappropriate name of The Goodtime Grill. I could see a nearly empty bar just inside the door and figured, if I was going to pursue an altered state, this was as good a place as any. In Brooklyn the places that catered to serious drinking tended to be dives, and I didn't want to get toasted in Fort Greene anyway. I might run into somebody I knew. There wasn't much chance of that on Lexington Avenue and—what was it?—Twenty-ninth Street.

It was almost an hour before the five p.m. rush, so there was only one other person, an older Latino-looking man, at the bar besides the bartender. I ordered the hardest thing I could think of, a shot of Jack Daniel's, and grimaced as I threw it back and ordered another. The bartender gave me a subtle raising of his eyebrows as he poured the second shot. But he didn't say anything. Surely this was not the first time someone had sat at his bar with the intent of getting pissy drunk.

The problem with doing heavy drinking when you're out of practice is that you lose all self-monitoring abilities. You can no longer gauge how far you've gone and when you need to stop, nor can you control your actions once you've passed the point of no return. By the time The Goodtime Grill filled up with the after-work happy hour crew, I was already feeling more than happy with the state of the world. "Feeling no pain" is the common expression. I briefly considered pressing my case with a few of the lovely women who had filed into the bar in large, unapproachable after-work groups, but none of them even glanced in my direction, and I was not anxious to have my ebullience dampened by some angry single women. In my experience, single women in New York got angrier rather than happier when they drank together in groups, as if the alcohol was laced with bitter arsenic. To have any chance at even the barest interaction, you had to separate one from the group, like a lion hunting antelope, then move in quickly before her sisters returned to hurl their collective bile in your direction and bring their girl back to her senses. I know it's common practice for lonely, pathetic men like me to deride the big-city single woman, but it's too hard not to.

I even considered snagging the bartender's ear, but he looked too busy and distracted to risk it. Besides, that was probably just some well-rehearsed myth anyway, that bartenders could provide a sympathetic ear to the drunk and dejected. At least that kind of counsel was not part of the bartender's job description at trendy places like The Goodtime Grill. I sensed I'd have to wander into one of those old-man bars to find one of those types of bartends—the pretty people who poured drinks in midtown were too busy with the mirror to give more than a thought to anyone else's problems.

A group of African-American women came into the bar and sat at a table not far away from me. These were the kind of groups in which I knew the talk invariably turned to trifling brothers; any brother who happened to be in the group's vicinity would get tarred and ostracized by association. I could have sworn a few of them kept glancing in my direction, but I wasn't sure what to do about it. Even if a sister in a group wanted to talk, the logistics were quite daunting for her in the presence of her friends. I knew I'd look silly wandering over to the table and trying to engage the group in conversation—even drunk I knew that. So I had no option but to sit there and wonder what they were saying about me.

After a few more minutes, I thought I saw one of the women—naturally, the heavyset one—gesturing at me. Were they actually calling me over to their table? I looked behind and on the sides of me, pretending that they couldn't possibly be calling out to me. The oldest sight gag in the goofy guy manual. The women—there were five of them—understood my corny little joke and laughed on cue. Were these women going to make me eat the thoughts I had been having about their probable unpleasant attitudes? I picked up my drink—I had moved on to Hennessy and coke—and walked toward the table, pleased that I was still sure and steady on my feet. I clutched the alcohol like a security blanket. In fact, it *was* security of sorts. I felt only a tiny bit of the trepidation I'd normally feel in a situation like this.

"Hello, ladies," I said, trying to hide the nerves. I hesitated for a moment, not sure if I should sit down. The heavyset woman, who was sitting one woman from the end, nudged her friend with a meaty thigh, indicating that they all should scoot over to give me room. They were not unanimous in their willingness to move. Grateful, nevertheless, and perhaps a little frightened at what lay ahead, I sat down in the space that had been created for me.

"We saw you drinking alone, and it looked like you were doing some serious drinking too." That line got some chuckles from the group. "We thought you might like some company. My name is Arlene."

Arlene, she of the meaty thighs, was either the group's spokesperson as the most aggressive, or she was merely the most desperate. She shoved her right hand in my direction. I took it, wondering if she were the only one who had wanted me at the table. The other women seemed to have amused—or maybe bemused—looks on their faces, like this was a little comedy show produced for their entertainment. So I was called over here to be a minstrel show?

"Hello, Arlene. I'm Randy." I looked questioningly at the rest of the group, waiting for some more names.

"I'm Charlotte," said a small, light-skinned woman with eyebrows plucked so thin that she couldn't help but look surprised.

"Hi, Randy. My name is Kendra," said a lovely, caramel-colored woman who was easily the best-looking of the group. She extended her hand with a practiced ease, obviously accustomed to the fawning interest of my gender. I didn't want to give her the predictable overexaggerated attention, so I declined from producing the big broad smile I wanted to throw at Kendra. I knew Rule Number One in a group such as this was not to give too much attention to the prettiest woman. To violate it was to incur the considerable wrath of the rest of the hornets' nest. From what I knew already about the heavyset one—now named Arlene—she'd call me out on that blunder. The other two introduced themselves, one of them—Carla—with what appeared to be much reluctance.

"So, tell me, Mr. Randy, what are you trying to run away from that you need to consume so much alcohol so fast?" Arlene said.

"Arlene, you don't know him," Charlotte said, laughing. "He might come here every night and drink like that."

The other women chuckled and nodded their agreement. But Arlene wouldn't go along. She shook her head.

"Come on, ladies," Arlene said. "You can look at him and tell he's not a hard drinker."

I smiled at Arlene. "Thank you, Arlene, for your well-placed confidence in me. As a matter of fact, I've never been in this bar before. I work farther uptown." I considered giving them the title and job description, but I decided to wait until they asked.

"What do you do?" asked Carla, the reluctant member.

"I'm a vice president at Trier-Stanton, the advertising agency. I'm in charge of creative—you know, creating the ad campaigns and such."

I could have sworn I saw the lovely Kendra perk up a bit at the job description. That was entirely too predictable. Suddenly, I flashed on the unpleasant memories I had stored away of phony conversations with legions of smooth-faced mercenaries all over the city. I remembered the relief I felt after I got married—the relief coming, of course, after the well-documented panic over eternal monogamy— and could appreciate the joy of regular female company without the aggravation of lame bar chatter. Kendra quickly became a lot less lovely to me.

"That sounds like a great job," said the perpetually surprised Charlotte. "You get to do all those clever television commercials and stuff like that?"

I laughed. "I hope they're clever, at least. Sometimes we succeed at cleverness a little better than at other times. Did you ladies see any of the commercials for the Women's Professional Basketball League? Like the one with the sassy little girls talking to the female basketball star, telling her what was wrong with her game?" There were five bobbing heads around the table. "That was me."

"You mean you wrote that commercial, or directed it or something?" Arlene asked.

I nodded. "Yeah, I pretty much wrote it." Just as I was about to feel good about myself and my job, I thought about the first time I met Mikki, on a commercial shoot for Domino's. She was so sweet and shy. Of course, these thoughts led me straight to the hopelessness of my current state—the reason for the bar shots in the first place.

"So why are you drinking by yourself up in The Goodtime Grill?" asked Carla. She said it like she had been reading my mind. I didn't know the woman, but I got the immediate impression that she was skilled at dampening a good mood. I considered spinning a compelling yarn, but actually no yarn was more compelling than the truth, at least in my case.

"Well, I'll tell you why," I said, sweeping my gaze around the table. "I just found out that my wife has been cheating on me." I heard the audible gasps around the table. But I wasn't done yet. "With my best friend."

There was a collective moan as the women all felt my pain simultaneously. Then, again at the same time, they all looked at Carla, who visibly squirmed. I swung my attention to her, too. There were several seconds of uncomfortable silence at the table.

Carla stared at me. "Well, what did *you* do to her to push her into someone else's arms?" She was throwing the focus back in my direction.

I was taken aback. This lady didn't know me like that.

"Excuse you," I said. "I didn't do anything that warranted that kind of betrayal."

I saw Arlene shaking her head.

"You still trying to push that one, Carla?" Arlene said. "Your husband practically pushed you onto Kevin's dick, right?"

The table all laughed at Carla's expense. I winced because I knew her well enough already to know her response would be ugly.

"Y'all can kiss my ass, okay? Y'all don't live up in my apartment. You don't know anything about my situation."

"How much do we need to know about your situation to know that what you're doing is wrong?" Charlotte piped in, sounding angry. I clearly heard her use of the present tense. Apparently, whatever it was that Carla was doing behind her husband's back, it was still going on.

"I told you, just because I don't have any hard evidence of him cheating doesn't mean it's not happening." She snapped her eyes to me. "Right, Randy?"

I'm sure I looked startled. Suddenly my preoccupation with my own situation had disappeared. I wanted to know Carla's details.

"Well, I don't know about that," I said. "I caught them kissing and eating dinner all snuggled up in this out-of-the-way restaurant in Little Italy, obviously somewhere they thought they wouldn't get caught."

"I'd say that's pretty solid evidence," Arlene said, nodding confidently as she looked around the table for agreement. She got a few nods, but nothing from Carla.

"All I'm saying is, there are usually some reasons—maybe psychological or maybe more obvious—why a woman decides to cheat on her husband," Carla said angrily. She had one of those perpetually angry-looking foreheads that creased and buckled from temple to temple without much provocation. The result was that you strove to avoid disagreement with her. "It's not as simple as y'all are making it sound."

Charlotte was shaking her head. "I'm not trying to get all up in your business, Carla, but you been kinda lusting after Kevin for a long time. Since before you even got married."

There were nods of agreement around the table.

"So, what are you trying to say?" Carla said, knowing damn well what she was trying to say.

I was starting to grow suspicious of the timing of this conversation, almost like these women had been thrown into my realm by my wife to pass along a message. But what it really told me was that every person had a story to tell that could easily be more compelling and troubling than my own. Marriages, children, siblings, parents—they were all guilty of introducing troubles into our lives at any given moment, weighing us down, killing our joy. Ask anyone a question about how they're doing and you could very well be prying open a bulging Pandora's box of personal angst. Sometimes you didn't even have to ask a question. Just wander into an anonymous bar and order a drink.

"What she's saying is that sometimes a woman just wants to fuck!" Kendra said, sending the table into a fit of boisterous laughter.

I chuckled too, despite my fear of Carla's reaction. Under different circumstances at a different time, I could have some fun with these ladies. They had jokes.

Carla's face was one gigantic, angry frown.

"Kendra, you know it wasn't that damn simple," she said. "You know I wouldn't have touched Kevin if my husband hadn't fucked up first. I was telling you all this as it was happening, for heaven's sake. Anyway, of all people, you shouldn't be talking about no men and sex, with your ho-ish, gold-diggin' ass."

I looked to Kendra, expecting more anger and vitriol. But she was laughing. Her sparkling white teeth and the dimples imbedded deep in her caramel skin seemed to light up the entire bar. Apparently, she and Carla had been down this road before.

Charlotte, she of the sheared eyebrows, let out a deep sigh with drama intended to draw all attention to her. We all obliged at the table. I think she even sucked in a few people from surrounding tables.

"See, that's what I'm talking about," she said, sweeping her eyes around the table but spending extra time on me, Carla, and Kendra. "Every single married person I know is always going through all kinds of shit, all kind of crazy drama. What's the damn point? Sometimes when I'm alone in my apartment at night, I have a hard time fighting the loneliness. It eats away at me, makes me scared, makes me horny, makes me mad. Sometimes I almost want to run down to the nearest club and just jump on the first guy that I see. But then I think about the alternative, about actually being with somebody for more than one night. I think about every person I know who has a ring on their finger, and then I don't feel so bad—because all of y'all seem so incredibly miserable. Why should anyone even bother anymore? It really doesn't seem like it has a point. I'm talking about any long-term relationship. I'm starting to think they're just designed to spread misery. Like my mother used to tell me, 'Charlotte, you can do bad by yourself.' "

She

This time, Zaria didn't bother to send her kid to do her bidding—she came herself. She was demanding I get out of bed "right this minute," her voice ringing in my ears like a triangle in the hands of a five-year-old, just loud and uneven and totally, unsympathetically annoying. I managed to ignore her for the few minutes she stood over me, screaming like a damn banshee in my ear. But when she snatched the covers off me and pulled the pillow from up under my head, I was thoroughly prepared to beat her ass, no matter that her kids were in the next room.

"Zaria! Damn—stop playing," I said, squinting through one eye at her tall, menacing figure lording over my bed. "Put the covers back over me and give me my pillow."

"I don't think so, buddy. It's time for you to get your butt outta bed," she said, a little less stern, but just as loud.

"Zaria," I said slowly and quietly. "Give me my cover and my pillow and leave me alone. I am not in the mood for you right now. I'm tired and I want to sleep. Be gone."

"Mikki? Do you know what time it is? What day it is, even? You've been sleep for damn near two days. You haven't eaten, you haven't gone to the bathroom as far as I know of, and, to be honest with you, sis, your funky ass is starting to make my guest room smell. You need to get out of bed now."

I looked over at the clock. It was four-thirty p.m., but I didn't know what day it was. Did she say I was in bed for two days? What would that put us at—Monday? Good grief, had I really been buried under that down comforter for that long? I did remember getting up a few times to go to the bathroom, and a couple times I swatted James and Jazzy out of the room. But two days?

And then, in a rush, I remembered why I was there in the first place. Because I had no husband. No boyfriend. And no dignity where I'd made my home. Hell, I didn't even have a home. What was the point of waking up?

I looked up at Zaria, then back at the clock, then back at Zaria again. "You know what?" I said. "You need to get the hell out of my face. I am not in the mood for you right now."

Zaria's mouth dropped open. She started a sentence, then stopped herself from talking, then started and stopped again. After a few moments of silence, she spit her words at me. "Look, little girl," she said. "You are in my house, in my room, in my bed, okay? Don't get it twisted. I know you got some problems right now, but that's no reason to get all ignorant up in the middle of my house. Shit, keep it up and I'll do you like your wack ass husband did you."

"Oh—this is amusing to you?" I shouted back. "My fight with my wack ass husband is just one big ol' revelation for you, huh? Just some more fodder for your 'I hate men' campaign, huh? Some material for your 'Niggas ain't shit' speeches? Okay," I said, sitting up in the bed and dramatically positioning myself in the middle of the mattress, "let me just settle in and pay careful attention, because I don't want to miss a word. Which lecture am I going to get today? The one where you proudly proclaim that women who depend on men are weak, silly bitches? Or will it be the one about how men can't do shit for you but write a check and stand aside? I particularly enjoy the lecture where you say marriage is for desperate dummies too stupid to recognize divorce is the inevitable ending. Can I hear that one today? Go 'head, Zaria—I'm listening."

Zaria looked me dead in my eyes with such disgust that, for a minute there, I thought she was going to haul off and smack the mess out of me. And I can't say that I would have blamed her; we'd come to blows in the past over sillier matters—like the time when she was fourteen and I told her boyfriend that she had chin hairs that had to be shaved off every three days or they'd grow into a full-fledged beard, and the time Zaria hid her birth control pills in my room, then refused to 'fess up when Mommy found them. Our house was ground zero for an ass-whuppin', because even though I'd managed somehow to convince my mother that the pills weren't mine, I still had to sit there for the most embarrassing three-hour lecture ever on sex and boys—despite the fact that, at the time, I was a sixteen-year-old, shy, boyfriendless virgin. When Zaria got back in the house that evening, I swung on her before she'd barely gotten in the door. My father had to pull us apart, which was a good thing, because Zaria was kicking my behind.

But Daddy wasn't anywhere around for this one, so if Zaria decided to pounce, I was going to get it. After all these years, I still had lots of bark, but absolutely no bite whatsoever. Couldn't fight a lick. But to her credit, Zaria didn't raise her hand to me; instead, she walked out of the room, quietly closing the door behind her. I was still sitting Indian-style, staring at the back of that door, when she walked back in moments later. She had one hand on the knob, the other on her hip—and tears in her eyes.

"You know what, Mikki? You can sit there and be the drama queen if you want to. That's fine by me," Zaria said quietly. "And I'll even let you do it in my house, because I'm your sister and I wouldn't dream of putting you out, no matter how ugly you're being, because I know that at the root of your anger is hurt and loneliness. But I'm not going to stand here in my own house and let you put me down one more minute for choosing a path different from yours."

"Zaria, I—" I said weakly, but she threw her hand up, signaling me to let her finish. I closed my mouth.

"You and I are so very different, Mikki. We were raised by the same hands in the same house with pretty much the same rules, and somehow, we grew up into women with polar opposite personalities and goals and ambitions. Yes, you finished college and yes, you built yourself a career, and yes, you got married and waited to have kids the way that Mommy and Daddy and all of society said you're supposed to. But I didn't. And that doesn't make me any better or worse than you, just different. You go out of your way to make it seem like I hate men and the institution of marriage, but let me tell you this much, little girl: I chose not to finish school, Mikki, so that I could take care of my babies. I chose not to get married to their daddy—not because I hate men, but because I didn't want to be in a dead-end marriage with a dead-end man. It's that simple. I love everything there is to love about men, the ones who are strong and independent and unafraid of women who are strong and independent, too. And if the man who stands before me can't measure up, then he's got to go. That doesn't make me anti-marriage—that makes me pro-Zaria, and pro-James and pro-Jasmine, because me and my kids deserve the very best. I haven't settled for less up to now, and I'm not going to start just for the sake of being able to say that I'm married. And if that means that I have to be alone and my kids have to go without a father in this house, then so be it.

"But I think it's time you stopped acting as if your life and your way and your decisions are somehow better than mine. I think the fact that you're here instead of in Brooklyn with your husband is proof positive that not even your perfect, by-the-rules ass is guaranteed a happy ending. The sooner you realize that, the sooner you'll understand that Mikki has to do things for Mikki, and not for anyone else—not Daddy, not Mommy, not Randy, not me. Just for Mikki.

"Now, you can lay in here and wallow in misery and act like the world has come to an end if you want to. I'm not going to stop you if that's the way you need to deal with this. But I will not allow you to insult me just because my decisions don't line up exactly with yours. We both want the same thing, Mikki—to be happy. I know what's making me happy. Do you?"

Zaria stood in that door and stared at me a while longer. I didn't know what to say—had nothing to say. So I watched her wipe the tears off her cheeks, and then I did the same for myself. She walked out without saying another word, closing the door behind her. This time, she didn't come back.

The next time, I woke up on my own. Well, kinda. It was actually the smell of Zaria's dinner that got me stirring. It smelled like my mom's soul food dinner, the kind she'd make just before waking us up for Sunday School when we were little. It was a wonderful aroma: the smell of made-from-scratch onion gravy mingling with the smell of roast beef and parboiled rice and turnip greens and corn bread. That smell always found its way into my dreams—the ones I'd have in my REM sleep, when reality stole scenes in my inner-mind's fantasies just before I woke up. In my dream, I'd see my mother lifting the cornbread out of the oven, smelling it, then carefully placing it on her pot holder on the marble countertop, then closing the oven door before making her way to my bed to shake me awake, kiss my forehead, and tell me what I needed to put on for church. And then I'd wake up for real and my mother would be bent over my bed, kissing me out of my slumber, the smell of her very real Sunday dinner wafting through the house.

Zaria's house smelled like that regularly. Both of us had turned out to be pretty good cooks, but while my meals were more soul food nouveau, Zaria was a down-home southern cook through and through. She could make roast beef better than my mother, and greens, too. Everyone raved about her fried chicken, which always turned out to be perfectly seasoned, perfectly crispy, and perfectly juicy on the inside. And that's the smell that woke me up. I slowly opened my eyes and squinted at the clock; if my eyes were serving me correctly, it was eight p.m. I'd managed to cry myself back to sleep after all that drama, and sleep a few more hours. I sat up in the bed, waiting for the blood to finish rushing to my head and for my eyes to lose their blurry edge and truly focus. My stomach was growling and I had to use the bathroom really bad. I swung my feet over the edge of the bed and pushed myself up, then slipped into the shorts Zaria had left for me on the bureau. I felt dizzy—surely from sleeping too long—but I pushed myself over to the door and walked through it. James and Jazzy, both of whom were in the playroom next to the guest room where I'd been sleeping, saw me first.

"Auntie Mikki!!!" they both screamed, rushing over to me. Jazzy grabbed my leg, James wrapped his little arms around my stomach. The two of them nearly toppled me. "Auntie Mikki," Jazzy said through her stuffed nose, "can you help me make a wedding dress for my dolly? Huh, huh? Can you, Auntie?"

"Sure, honey," I smiled. "But Auntie has to go to the bathroom and if you don't let her leg go, she's going to have to borrow one of your old diapers."

They both giggled and raised up, then tumbled back into the playroom. Zaria came into the hallway just as I hit the bathroom. "Glad to see you rejoin the land of the living," she said, her arms folded across her chest. "There's some fried chicken and rice and string beans on the stove if you're hungry. I made some cornbread, too."

"I'd like that," I said. "Just let me hop into the shower right quick."

"Oh, you don't need my permission, honey—you need the soap," she said, a smile crossing her face. I could hear the kids giggling in the other room. I smiled back, closed the door, and plopped down onto the toilet. I looked up at the shelf just opposite the commode and noticed a collection of candles, and decided practically at the same time that I spotted them to forgo the shower for a long, hot, steamy bath. Zaria had all the essentials—bath salts, bubble bath and a bath pillow—perfect for the mini-escape/rejuvenation I was going to take. I didn't linger in the tub long; I hated when the water got cold, and especially when the bubbles disappeared, only to be replaced by soap-scummy water. About twenty minutes is all I gave it, but it was the perfect pick-me-up. When I rose out of the water, I no longer felt weak or dizzy, just refreshed. I wrapped the towel around my body and headed for Zaria's room. She was already there, a fresh T-shirt and pair of shorts in hand.

"I don't have any new underwear and I know how you are about wearing other people's drawers so you're going to have to let it hang under these," she said, handing me the clothing. "Not that I have the cooties or anything."

I chuckled and took the clothes, and stared at her without saying a word. She simply stared back. I can't explain it; it's like she could hear me trying to find the words in my head to tell her that I was sorry—for what I'd said earlier, for what I'd long criticized about her.

"Don't say anything," she said quietly. "Just come over here and give me a hug."

I happily followed her order, and collapsed into her arms. She absorbed each and every sob I cried into her shoulder, just stood there and rocked me back and forth and patted my back and said "It's going to be okay Mikki, it's going to be okay," over and over again. It felt like we'd been standing there forever, but Zaria didn't let me go until I was ready for her to let me go. When I pulled myself back, she gently placed her hands on my face and told me it was going to be all right again.

"You'll live," she said. "Nobody dies from a broken heart."

"I know," I said. "But it's not really me I'm worried about. What I did to Randy was just lowdown, Zaria. You had to see the hate in his eyes."

"He doesn't hate you," Zaria said.

"No, Zaria—you had to see his face, his eyes. I'd never seen him that way before. It was like he was an animal, like one of those lions on *National Geographic,* crouched in the bush, waiting to take out the hyena. He had blood in his eyes. If his mama didn't give him good home-training, he'd have beat my ass."

"You sure are right about that," she said, nodding in agreement. "But you're missing the point here, babe," she said, taking my hand and leading me to the bed. "Right now, the only one you should be worried about is you. Randy is really inconsequential right now, Mikki—can't you see that? When are you going to start thinking about you?"

"I am thinking about me—about us," I said. "When I took those marriage vows, I swore before God that Randy and I would not only become one, but be one."

"I was there at your wedding, Mikki, and I don't remember that being in the vows," Zaria said.

"Well, regardless of if you heard the exact words, it certainly was implicit in the meaning behind the ones that were said. We vowed to be one, and I betrayed him, thinking about myself."

"But that's what I'm talking about, Mikki. For once, you did think about yourself, and now you're beating yourself up over it because it didn't turn out exactly the way you planned it. It may not have gone perfectly, but Mikki did what made Mikki happy, even if it was for a brief few months.

"Look, I'm not going to tell you what to do," she continued. "But I will say this: Right now, you need to take your mind off how Randy's feeling and deal with your own emotions, because if you don't, they're going to get the best of you. Figure out what will make Mikki happy."

Zaria got up off the bed and walked toward the door. Then she turned back toward me. "You know, Mommy and I joined a book club a few months ago, over at the Mahogany Space Gallery. We're meeting next week at the gallery for tea and to talk about that book *Their Eyes Were Watching God.*"

"By Zora Neale Hurston?"

"Yeah. It was a great book. A little confusing, but it was good."

"Gosh—I haven't read that since freshman year in college. I barely remember what happened."

"Doesn't matter. Just come with us. Get up out of this house and get some fresh air. We can go over to your house to get some clothes while Randy's at work, and then we can go shopping before the book club meeting."

I just looked at her, didn't answer her right away. Zaria sensed my hesitation. "Mikki," she said. "You can't sit in the guest room forever. Besides, because you funked it up, I have to air it out. And I'm running out of T-shirts to lend yo ass, and you need to put on some drawers—preferably your own."

We were both still giggling when she walked out the door and closed it behind her.

I can't quite explain why, but when I woke up that next morning, I had a ridiculously strong desire to call Angelou. I needed to see her, to hear her voice, to tell her that I was sorry for the drama. Truth is, I missed the girl. We'd been through so much together—had loved each other so very long—that it felt almost as if I was in the middle of a battle with my own sister. Except worse, because I was closer to Angelou than my own sister. Funny how that happens, huh? You treat your best friend better than your sister, because blood? Well, you know you can pretty much get away with murder with them, and somehow they'll get over it because they're, like, blood. They have no other choice but to accept you—warts, faults, and all—because you're family, and you can't cut off family. So you treat them like dirt, talk to them any old kinda way, take advantage of them, piss them off. They'll be mad for a minute, but they won't cut you off. Because you're family. I think it's, like, written in a book somewhere that you just have to accept the bull and move on back to loving them because, you know, they're your people.

But friends—that's a whole different dynamic entirely. You don't pull half the crap you do to family on your friends, because you want to keep them and you know if you totally fuck up, they're history. They don't have any blood ties to you, so they have express authorization to drop your ass over the stupidest of things. Like, if you borrow money from your sister and you don't pay it back, she'll get over it. She'll give you hell for it, and she'll harrass you about it, but she'll get over it, even if years pass by and you don't ever hand over her dough. You'll still get invited to Thanksgiving dinner, you'll still see her children, you'll still be your mother's daughters. Pull that mess with your girl and she's outta there. Why stick around and continue to be friends with a lout that can't return favors, and especially money? Who will take advantage of you? I believe we all know this going into a friendship, and so we give our best friends all the love usually reserved for family, without most of the complications, just so they'll stick around, if we really like them, that is.

Of course, this theory gets shot to hell when I think about the friendship Marcus and Randy shared. I mean, I know I didn't help in the situation, but what kind of friend sleeps with his boy's wife, anyway? What the hell was going through his mind when he decided that night at that concert to rub up against me in such an inappropriate way? How did he know I would respond the way I did? It could have just as easily gone in the other direction, with me smacking his face and calling Randy to tell him Marcus touched me. What made him take his chances? With his best friend's wife? Had he planned this all along? Could it have been that Marcus was lusting after me well before Randy went to Paris? Did he see something in our relationship that allowed him to believe I'd be down?

I started doing all kinds of mental gymnastics with that one, recalling times when we all were together before any of us had walked down the aisle, during our simultaneous courtships, after we all got hitched, during our marriages. Nothing. I couldn't think of one instance where Marcus remotely flirted with me, or said something suggestive or gave any hint that he wanted to get into my pants. From where on Earth did his attraction stem? And why did he pursue it, knowing the dangers—the danger of losing his best friend?

I couldn't figure it out. Anyway, I didn't want to think about it anymore. I wanted to talk to my best friend. I needed her. Missed her. Wanted to commiserate with her. I hadn't talked to Angelou in weeks—hadn't so much as thought about dialing her phone number. But my fingers flew over the phone keypad, dialing her number just as easily as if I'd dialed it just five minutes before. The phone rang twice before she picked up.

"Hello?"

I wasn't sure what tone I should take. Should I be all girlfriendy, like nothing ever happened? Apologetic? Business-like? I went for apologetic.

"Angelou? It's me, Mikki. Girl, I miss you so very much and I want to say that I'm truly sorry for all the mess that I put you through, and specifically for dragging you into the middle of it. I hope that you can forgive me, because I don't know what I'd do without my best friend."

The words tumbled out of my mouth, one after the other, after another. I didn't want to stop talking, because I was afraid that if I did, she would say something that I didn't want to hear. Finally, I took a breath and waited for her response. She paused—a long pregnant silence. Then finally, she spoke.

"Damn, I was going to tell you a joke, but I forgot the punchline," she said. "Shit was funny, too. Oh well, what you up to?"

Just like that, it was on again.

"You can't remember it?"

"Nope."

"Not even some of it?"

"What's the point of telling part of a joke if you don't remember the best part?"

"Yeah, I guess you're right," I said, laughing. "When you remember it, then you can tell it to me over lunch. What you doing?"

"Waiting for you to take me to lunch."

"Well, damn—why I gotta take you to lunch? How 'bout you take me to lunch for once."

"Well, I figured since a sister was being all apologetic and shit, I might as well take advantage."

We both laughed, big hearty, booming laughs. It sure felt good to hear her voice, and to know that she was listening to every word I said—without judgment—as I recounted the events of the past three weeks. She didn't say a thing, just let me get it all off my chest, almost in a long run-on sentence. Until, that is, I got to the part about Marcus's girlfriend.

"He let that tow-headed weave-ado answer his phone?" she asked, incredulous.

"What you talking about, Angelou? You know her?" I quizzed.

"I don't know her, but when I go over to the West Side to visit my boyfriend, I see her bouncing all around the neighborhood like she owns that bitch, sipping wine in the afternoon like she don't have nothing else to do with her time."

"I don't understand," I said, even though I did. If I understood her correctly, Angelou knew who it was that answered the phone at Marcus's house, which meant that she knew he had a girlfriend, which meant that she knew Marcus was cheating on me, when we were cheating on Randy. "Marcus has a girlfriend and you know her?"

"I didn't say I knew the girl. But Marcus and my man do live in the same neighborhood and we do run into each other from time to time, and I've seen him around with this tall light-skinned chick with a weave down her back—going to dinner, to his apartment. I don't know if that's his girlfriend, but she is around quite a bit."

"And how long has she been around?"

"Now, I don't know all those details, but I do remember seeing her around for about a month and a half."

I was quiet. Over a month? That means that he was with her while he was sleeping with me, doesn't it? That he was two-timing me. I honestly didn't know what to say. Angelou sensed that, so she took over.

"I wanted to tell you, but you were so head-over-heels for this guy and I needed you to find out for yourself, because I knew that if I told you, you would hate me and not him."

"Angelou, I could never hate you—not over some man," I said weakly. But I already had. Over the past few weeks, I hadn't called her because I didn't want to listen to her voice of reason.

"Yeah, well, it's over. Now you know. Marcus is a dog. A fucking Rottweiler. That guy goes through women like you do white thread at the bridal shop. I wasn't worried about your breaking up with Randy as much as I was about you getting your heart broken with Marcus."

"Great. Nice to know my marriage was ruined over some bullshit Negro with a million women on the side," I said, nearly whispering the words. "I can't believe I let myself be suckered like that. Basically, I was just a piece of ass to him. Amazing."

"Mikki, you can't beat yourself up like this, you hear me?" Angelou said, her voice strong. "You and Randy had problems well before Marcus came into the picture. But instead of helping you two work things out, Marcus took advantage of you and his best friend. He's the one who did dirt, not you. Will you remember that? For me?"

I didn't answer her. I couldn't make that promise. Whatever ill intentions Marcus had—or maybe it was just that he wanted to get his dick wet and it didn't matter who he slept with—I was still complicit in the breakup of my marriage. I couldn't blame it on anyone else but Mekhi Chance-Murphy, that much I was sure of.

"So," I said, trying desperately to change the subject, "where are we going to lunch?"

"Well, I have a jazz class around the corner from my apartment at three o'clock, so could we grab a bite here in Bed-Stuy? Maybe you could come to the class with me."

"Sounds good," I said. "Zaria and I were going to take the train into Brooklyn anyway, to find the car and try to gather up some clothes from the house while Randy's at work."

"You got keys? I thought he threw you out with nothing but a T-shirt and underwear," she said, then started giggling. "Lord, I would have paid good money to see that shit."

"Yeah, ha, ha. I'm glad you're amused," I said, dismissing her. "Zaria has a copy of all of my keys. I'm going to use those."

"Okay—so I'll see you around, what? Say, one o'clock?"

"Make it one-thirty. Be standing on the stoop, Angelou—I don't want to have to wait for your ass."

"Oh," Angelou said, as if she suddenly remembered something. "I have to introduce you to someone."

"Damn, what happened to ol' boy? You kicked him to the curb already?"

"No, no," she laughed. "He's still around, hanging in there. It's another friend of mine."

"Who, Angelou? You know what? I don't care who he is—I don't want to meet him. I don't need any more trouble."

"No, you have to—he's really nice and sweet. His name is Mr. Tone." And with that, she slammed the phone down.

I looked at the phone receiver and laughed. Lord, that girl is a fool.

He

I had never understood the thrill that the urban male apparently got from stealing cars. In all those urban thug-boy gang dramas that Hollywood churned out like *Menace II Society* and *New Jersey Drive,* miles of celluloid was wasted on the evident thrill of screeching away in an auto that didn't belong to you. But as I crept around the streets of Manhattan's Upper West Side looking for the BMW that Mikki and I jointly shared, worried about being spotted, juiced by the vision of their faces when they realized the car was gone, I felt the adrenaline rush and suddenly comprehended the car-theft movies. My only fear was that they had given up on trying to find a space in this notoriously space-starved neighborhood and had opted for the high-priced parking garage that Marcus used for his Mercedes that he seldom drove.

I wondered if Mikki had felt any of the rush I was feeling when she took the car from Fort Greene. Mikki would now have a commute to get from Marcus's condo apartment to her Fort Greene store—the nasty, unpleasant subways that she hated so much, or perhaps a pricey cab ride. I didn't think she'd want to drive the car from Fort Greene to the Upper West Side every night, trying to park up here was way too much hassle. Knowing Mikki, she wouldn't at all appreciate the convenience of an Upper West Side parking garage when it came with a ridiculous price tag. That's why I was sure that the car was somewhere on the street.

It wasn't like I didn't need the car, anyway. I had decided I would drive out to Jersey to visit my mother during the week, when she'd be shocked to see me. It was a Wednesday, and she'd probably gone to Bible studies at the church. No doubt she'd be so happy by my presence that she would bless me with one of her fabulous dinners.

As I scurried up and down the blocks, my mind wandered back for perhaps the two-hundredth time to the damning, depressing statement that the eyebrow-deprived Charlotte had made about marriage the week before. I had to admit that there didn't seem to be overwhelming evidence around me of the prosperity of the matrimonial state. Of the few friends—I still unconsciously included Marcus in this category—I had who had actually managed to stay together long enough to get married, I could only think of one couple who really seemed to be thriving. It was my friend Charlie, a white guy I had met on the tennis courts, and his wife, Michelle, who was black. Could the interracial angle have something to do with that, like the taboo giving them an extra bond or incentive to make it work? I had no idea. But anyway, I probably wasn't close enough to their marriage to see any fraying at the seams. It was a valid question to ask: was the state of marriage truly endangered at the close of the twentieth century? Perhaps American society had transformed so radically that two individuals rarely had the emotional strength and psychological fortitude to sustain a monogamous relationship anymore. Marriage was very difficult work, a fact that hadn't been shared with many members of my generation. The common response to the discovery of the labor involved was to throw up the hands and surrender, to conclude that survival was a skill most of us hadn't located. We were all drowning in the muck of conflict and dissension, wondering why we had ever thought a life could be shared with another person. We weren't used to the everyday pain, the incessant struggle, the regular ingestion of pride. When the storms came, we had no choice but to flee—for we had learned no alternative. I had thought somehow we were different, that my bond with Mikki had been cemented by the joys and struggles we had shared to the point where it could never be severed by something as lame as separation. But apparently that's exactly what happened.

Actually, in acknowledging that it was the separation that had really severed our bond, for the first time since I had caught Mikki and Marcus at Ponticello's I was accepting a large part of the blame for what had happened. I had no doubt that Mikki would have remained faithful to me if I hadn't flown off for months, leaving her to fend for herself in Brooklyn. I knew, as she had told me many times, that a man could never fully appreciate the security concerns that women carried with them, particularly in a city as notoriously scary as New York— and the notoriety had a lot to do with it because much of their mental state had to do with perceived fight. It stayed in the backs of their heads at all times, the notion that they were never really safe when they were alone. And I had galloped off halfway around the globe and left her by herself in Brooklyn, of all places. I guess maybe that was a bad idea. Maybe I had in effect shoved her into Marcus's arms.

And what about my best friend? What could have been going through his head? Or maybe it was his loins I should be wondering about. It raised a troubling question in my mind—if I couldn't trust Marcus, of all people, to be alone with my wife without taking advantage, did my gender really have *any* control over the impulses that raced through us? How many of us had the stuff inside of us to walk away? I would have bet large sums that Marcus had the stuff, but I had found out how painfully wrong I was.

For more than an hour I paced the streets of the Upper West Side, looking desperately for my ride. I gave up when the side streets off Broadway were blanketed in darkness. Where could my wife be stashing the car? I was furious that she was clearly hiding it from me. I vowed that when I finally did track it down, I'd put it somewhere that Mikki would never think to look. I didn't know where that was just yet, but I'd think of something.

The next day, I sprinted out of the office in the early afternoon, inspired by my new plan. I figured that the car was in Bed-Stuy, somewhere near Angelou's apartment. Mikki wouldn't want to drive it to work because she knew I'd find it, but she also wouldn't want to put it in a garage. Angelou's street was fairly safe, as far as Bed-Stuy streets go. I was able to snag a cab and, as the taxi crossed the Brooklyn Bridge and headed across Atlantic Avenue toward the historic Brooklyn neighborhood where Angelou showed off her carefully tended brownstone, I became more convinced that I was right.

It took only about five minutes to spot the car, which was around the block from Angelou's. It was sparkling in the sunlight, wedged tightly between an SUV and a Mercedes. The car made me smile. Yes, I was a red-blooded American male—my car made me happy. I pressed the magical button and heard the lock disengage with the peppy two-tone laugh that announced to the world that a driver was returning. In fact, the sound made me glance around warily. I couldn't help but feel a little bit like a car thief, even if it was my own car that I was stealing. I wondered if Mikki or Angelou would actually try to confront me if they were to stumble upon me at that moment. Probably not. I certainly wouldn't if I were them. Mikki had done all she could to avoid me in the days since I had thrown her out of our brownstone. I knew she had come back to pick up some clothing; I could smell her perfume and see the evidence of missing toiletries. We would have to talk at some point, wouldn't we? Tossing her onto the sidewalk in a T-shirt and panties was hardly closure.

It was shortly before six in the evening when I arrived in West Orange and bounded up my mother's porch. As I waited for her to answer the door, I hoped none of the neighbors on this comfortable and closely knit street would see me and ask after my wife. I wasn't in a lying mood. I looked out at my mother's lawn and saw that it was well tended, as were her flowers that surrounded the front porch and the edges of the lawn. I knew she paid a little Italian landscaper to take care of the greenery, as he did for most of the neighbors and had done since I was a teenager. I had always thought this suburban town to be boring, but the older I got the more I could understand its attractions for a family with young children. It was a very pleasant place to grow up. When I had gone to Yale and found myself naturally attracted to the more urban types like Marcus, I had been slightly embarrassed that I hadn't grown up amid the concrete jungle of a city, with its attendant laundry list of delinquencies to entertain the growing juvenile. I even lied a little about West Orange's dangers—going so far as to create a neighborhood gang, in which I was, of course, a major figure—and the fibs held up until Marcus visited me in West Orange during my sophomore year. Marcus, a child of the rough-and-rumbling Bronx, had laughed as he recalled some of my scary West Orange declarations. But he also hadn't been too ashamed to say that he would have liked to have grown up in a nice neighborhood with a lawn and a backyard. It made me start looking a little differently, and less abashedly, at my upbringing.

"You got here just in time to take me grocery shopping," my mother said as she swung open the door. She was wearing slacks and a sweater. Grocery-shopping clothes.

"Oh, look at you. You look so sad," she said as she craned her neck upward to kiss me. "It's going to be all right, baby."

I didn't realize my sadness had been etched on my face that clearly. Hearing it was a little disconcerting. After all, I was a man—the last thing I wanted was to walk around attracting the sympathy of everyone who glimpsed me, particularly if they were giving me their sympathy on the sly without my knowledge. I wanted to hold my pain inside, not let everybody know about it. That would be weakness, right?

"Ma, I'm all right," I said, returning her kiss.

She looked at me sternly. "Oh, stop it. You know everything's not all right. You've lost your wife *and* your best friend at the same time? You don't have to hide the hurt from me, Randy. I *know* it has to hurt. And I can see it on your face. You can't hide from your mama."

It was an interesting concept, in fact, whether my mother actually did have the ability to see and feel the things I was feeling, like we still had some long-lasting umbilical connection. I had heard about mothers whose intuition would tell them, like a thunderbolt, when something awful had happened to their children. Could my mother empathize with me that completely?

"Yeah, it's been pretty tough, Ma. You're right." I walked into the living room and sat down on the couch. The room looked exactly as it had for the past ten years—like it was barely lived in. My mother was such a neat freak; she probably still cleaned the room every day, even if it went weeks without being occupied.

"I just have a hard time accepting that I did something wrong in going to Paris. I mean, how could I have turned it down?"

As my mother gathered her coat and pocketbook, we headed out to my car while we continued the conversation. All the way to the grocery store, I recounted for my mother exactly what had happened when I returned from Europe, how I had followed Mikki to the restaurant, even how I had thrown her out of the house in her underwear.

"The girl was only wearing a T-shirt?" she said, as she squeezed nectarines in the produce section. "In the middle of the night, you kicked her out of the house?" My mother shook her head as she reached for the oranges. "Y'all sound like you belong on the stories or something, all that drama. That's a shame—I know you really love that woman."

The peculiar thing about spending considerable time as an adult with your parents is that you start recognizing gestures, expressions, and mannerisms that you assumed were yours alone until you see them reflected back at you. You realize how much of you is really just an amalgamation of them, melded together with a few things you pick up over the years. Mikki was always annoyed by my obsession with expiration dates when we went to the grocery store. I'd check the dates on everything, from the milk carton, which was customary, to the dish detergent, which was not. I watched my mother prowl the aisles, flipping over everything in sight looking for dates. I got the excited thrill of discovery that would usually compel me to seek out Mikki and share it with her, but just as quickly I realized there was no one in my life now who would understand my excitement. I was all alone with this one.

As we approached the checkout counter, I saw a large woman who looked vaguely familiar pushing a cart in front of us. Something about her movements and the shape of her head told me I knew her. My mother leaned over toward me.

"There's one of your old girlfriends, Randy. I see her here all the time. She just recently went through a nasty divorce. As you see, she got big."

As if she could hear my mother talking about her, the woman swiveled her head around. A big grin spread across her face when she spotted us, particularly when her eyes settled on me. I hoped my face didn't give away my shock. Renee had gained at least seventy or eighty pounds since we dated. I hadn't seen her in about fifteen years and, frankly, probably hadn't thought about her in just as many years. The face had the same features, but it looked like it had been inflated to twice its size.

"OhmyGod, Randy!" she cried out as she moved toward me. I put on a big smile to match her own, but for some inexplicable reason what I thought about was the stunned look on her face the first time I slid my head down below and performed—or tried to perform—oral sex on her a few weeks before we graduated from West Orange High School. I had read my parents' copy of *The Joy of Sex* so thoroughly that I could recite passages by heart, and I was anxious to give the cunnilingus chapter a shot. My hope was that Renee would be inspired to return the favor. Renee had been a little reluctant, more out of fear than any moral opposition, I guessed. But after a few weeks of heavy conversation, we finally tried it in my room one day when we left school a few hours early. As I went south, I saw her eyes widen like headlights. Staring at the curious arrangements of folds and flaps, which looked *nothing* like the vagina diagram in *The Joy of Sex*, I wondered what in the world *she* had to be afraid of. I was the courageous explorer.

"Renee! How have you been! How long has it been?" I gave her a big hug, wrapping my arms around her considerable girth. I added ten pounds to my estimate—she was packing another hundred easy. She pushed me away and peered closely into my face.

"You look great, Randy," she said, smiling happily. I froze for an instant, probably too long. It was one of those "Dear Abby" moments. Dear Abby, what do you do after an old friend tells you that you look great, but they in fact look quite terrible? Do you lie and return the compliment, knowing that they know you're lying? Or do you try to change the subject as quickly as possible?

I don't know what old Abby would advise, but I chose the latter option: evasion.

"Hey, I heard you have some kiddies!" I cried out, guessing that the thought of her children could immediately change a woman's focus.

"How'd you hear that?" she asked, smiling.

"Hey, a little birdy told me," I said, looking at my mother.

"Would that birdy's name happen to be Mrs. Murphy?" Renee asked, laughing. "I hear you're married now. Finally," she continued. "How's your wife doing, anyway? When am I going to get a chance to meet the lucky woman?"

I could feel my mother's eyes burning a hole through my head. I didn't want to get into any details of my marital situation. In fact, I didn't really feel like talking to Renee anymore. How could I get out of this as painlessly as possible?

"Well, we'll have to set something up, Renee . . ." I knew I was trailing off, but I didn't know what to say. Fortunately, Renee had been blessed with keen social intuition. She could sense my unease and she immediately jumped to another subject.

"Have you run into anybody from high school lately?" she asked. "I saw Keenan Stuart a few months ago. You remember him?"

I got an image of a tall, smooth, good-looking brother who used to keep all the girls busy. Like about half the male population of West Orange High School—or at least the black male population—I harbored a rabid jealousy of Keenan Stuart. But to his face we were the best of friends. It *was* high school, after all.

"Yeah, of course I remember him. We were boys. What's he up to?" Renee shook her head sadly. "He's not doing very well, unfortunately." I thought I saw glee on her face, but perhaps I was projecting my own feelings. "He has about four kids but he's never been married, and he keeps getting locked up because he owes like a billion dollars in child support to the babies' mommas, but he don't ever hardly pay them nothing. I think he drives a bus out at Newark Airport, like for long-term parking or something."

We both shook our heads, sharing a pitying moment at our former classmate's expense. It was the kind of scene that gets repeated with regularity anytime an adult goes back to the place he used to call home. I wasn't really sure what Renee was doing occupation-wise, but I felt pretty good about my showing if the conversation moved to my job situation. But Renee had no need to take it there—she certainly had done all the research on me that she needed for her purposes, whatever they may be.

Renee and I drifted away from each other after exchanging good-byes.

As my mother was putting away her groceries, she continued her lecture. Her goal for the day seemed to be to convince me that marriage was indeed worth the apparent pain. Just what you'd expect your mother to do. But, as usual, my mother took an unexpected route to get there.

"What I'm seeing now is that when you live by yourself for too long, you become an extremely strange person. You can start getting into some really sick stuff. I know from experience."

She saw my eyebrows raise up almost into my hairline. What kind of experience could my mother have with this sort of sickness—and did I really want to hear about it?

"I don't know if I want to hear the rest of this, Ma," I said, laughing. She laughed too, but she wasn't about to stop. She was on a roll now.

"Some of these gentlemen that I've met have been allowed to develop some pretty strange interests. That's all I'll say." I could see her glancing over at me. Oh God, what the hell could she be talking about?

"I think when you have a spouse, all that freaky stuff gets stopped before it ever gets a chance to start. Now I'm not saying that everybody has to be all pure and everything, but if you heard the stuff I'm talking about, you would understand. Let me just say that men especially need to have somebody else in the house with them. Then they can't be getting into no trouble with video cameras and all that kind of stuff. They all need wives, and they need to stay with them."

I had heard very little about my mother's romantic pursuits. Maybe she had revealed more to my little sister, Diana, but I doubted that. They had been furiously feuding in recent years because of my mother's unhappiness with my sister's career decisions. She had gone out to Los Angeles, supposedly to break into films and television, but my mother suspected that she was making money working in strip clubs. Diana had once let it slip that she was tending bar at an "exotic club" on weekends to make money, but Mom thought she was really dancing—don't ask me why she concluded that. She called it mother's intuition. Anyway, they had kind of stopped speaking, and frankly I didn't speak to my sister much either. I didn't even know if she had had any steady relationships in recent years. She had gone out to the West Coast and virtually fell off the side of the planet.

"I know it's almost a cliché to say this these days, but I don't know if young people really have any idea what they are getting into when they walk down that aisle," my mother continued. "It seems like all of y'all are so unhappy. Like you wake up one day and realize that marriages are hard, and y'all don't want to be bothered."

"Well, I can certainly agree with you about how hard marriage is," I said, nodding. "It requires nonstop work. I've never worked so hard at something in my life, and it still didn't work."

My mother watched me closely. "How hard were you working at it when you were halfway around the world?"

My head snapped around. What was she saying? It felt like a slap. "Are you saying I shouldn't have gone to Paris? I thought you agreed with me that it was the right thing for me to do!"

My mother held up her hand, halting me like a traffic cop. "Hold it right there. First of all, I'm not telling you that going to Paris was the wrong thing. I'm not saying that at all. But you sat there and told me how hard you worked at your marriage. I'm not doubting you, but I *am* wondering if perhaps you kinda put things on hold when you went away, maybe saw it as a vacation."

I was about to protest loudly, but I stopped myself. I could remember the burden that I felt was lifted when I got on that plane at JFK, as if I *did* have a three-month break from my marriage in store. And that feeling did carry over to the weeks that followed because sometimes I would get annoyed when Mikki made demands on me from across the Atlantic. It was like I no longer felt obligated to deal with her while I was away. Maybe I *had* wrongly assumed that Paris was a vacation from the marriage work. Was that enough to snuff a marriage?

"But that still shouldn't have been enough to end it, Ma. Okay, I didn't call her as much as I should have. But it was still clear to her that I loved her. Just because I wasn't around, that was enough to send her into the arms of my best friend?"

She shook her head. "I'm not justifying what she did. Not at all. But maybe both of y'all need to take a little bit more responsibility for what happened in your marriage. From what I'm remembering, y'all were having problems before you went to Paris, right?"

I shrugged. "I don't know if they were anything more than any other married couple has."

"Is that what you thought, that it was normal-type problems? And what are you basing that assessment on? What do you really know about what kind of marriages most people have? All you're really doing is guessing, just like everybody else. But you know what the difference is between now and when I was your age?"

She looked at me and paused, as if she were waiting for my answer. I shook my head.

"We didn't know anything more about marriage than you did, but I think we figured that this was about as good as it was going to get, no matter how bad it actually was. We really had no illusions about marriage at all, so we weren't sitting around waiting for the fairy tale. But you all seem to assume that happiness is always waiting for you around the corner, and all you need to do is just break free from whatever you're in now and go look for it."

When the terrifying phone call came, I had been staring out the window of my midtown office, wondering if I had managed to destroy my career in just a few short weeks. I often spent Friday afternoons in meetings with my boss, Peter Webber, sifting through the success or failures of Trier-Stanton's recent campaigns, planning for future campaigns or corporate directions. They were meetings I had looked forward to since my elevation to vice president because it was a time to solidify my role as the company's brilliant and courageous creative force. I had always heard that Webber used the meetings as stroking sessions, to feed his praises to his needy and grateful upper-level executives, and I had eagerly awaited my turn. So the parting words I had received from Webber this afternoon had shaken me down to my sweaty feet.

"Randy," he had said, staring through me with his ice-blue eyes. I returned the stare and saw no warmth or bonhomie—only something that looked disturbingly like anger. "I am somewhat alarmed about the quality of your recent work. Whatever it is that's troubling you, I suggest you get it fixed." He had reached into his marble-encased desktop humidor, and now he leaned toward me as he softly caressed his Cuban. "Soon."

I had walked back to my office on legs whose numbness gave me a floating sensation. It was the most damning threat I had ever received in my career, and it left me frightened. I knew the Reebok account had slipped through the firm's grasp largely because of my inattentiveness, but I thought I had covered my ass with enough evasion and buckpassing that Webber wouldn't even know the blame should be assumed by me. But as the head of the company's creative endeavors, I had virtually no one around me who I could pass the buck to.

No more than ten minutes after settling down in my office chair, an unexpected call came through on my private line. Aside from Mikki, Marcus, and my mom, I didn't know of anyone else who had the number.

"Hello," I said quickly, feeling the thump-thumping of my quickening heartbeat through my suit jacket, which I still hadn't removed.

"Ran-dee! Is that you, dahling?" It was the unmistakeable Paris-accented tones of my old friend Paula, the sexual gymnast. And she sounded disturbingly close.

"Paula?! Is that you? My God, you sound like you're right around the corner."

"But I am, Ran-dee! I am around the corner!" she said gleefully.

The thump-thumping tripled in speed. "Wh—what do you mean, Paula?"

"Oh, Ran-dee, I'm in New York! Didn't I tell you I would visit. I am in the office, I think one floor below."

I panicked. Paula was here, in New York, in Trier-Stanton's offices? And she was calling me internally, and had somehow gotten my private line. It was probably too late to attempt a getaway. What could I do?

"I will come upstairs right now to see you, Ran-dee! I miss you very much."

And with that, the phone went dead. She hadn't even given me a chance to protest. She was on her way to my office! I was trapped.

"Mr. Murphy, there's a woman out here to see you," my secretary told me through the intercom. "She says she's an old friend."

I had no time to think, to protest, to hide. "Okay," I mumbled weakly toward the phone.

"Does she come in?" Alice asked, sounding slightly annoyed. Maybe she disapproved of Paula, or maybe my extreme paranoia had already set in—and the woman hadn't even yet stepped a foot inside my office.

"Yeah," I mumbled again.

"Excuse me?" Alice said, sounding even more annoyed.

"Yes," I said a little more forcefully. I noticed that my throat was terribly parched.

Before there was an answer, the door swung open and Paula stood before me, smiling broadly and sporting a short, clingy dress that advertised every well-constructed curve. Her hair was longer than when I had left Paris, and she somehow looked prettier than I recalled. Must have been the invigorating New York air. Paula raced toward me and practically jumped into my arms. Curiously, at that moment I caught myself thinking about Mikki. I knew she'd virulently disapprove of this sight—me clutching a white woman in my arms. Somehow it had seemed safer, less transgressive, in Paris. I could tell myself that I was merely consorting with the locals. But on native soil, amidst the hothouse sexual wars that raged between black men and women, I felt enormous guilt even wrapping my arms around her.

Which is why I would have had a hard time explaining to a jury of my peers how, six hours later, I wound up rolling around butt naked on her hotel bed with my tongue down her throat. But first let me recount how we got to the hotel bed.

So not only was Paula now standing in my office, but to my horror she had been doing research. Paula possessed two pieces of information that would prove very disturbing to me: she had found out that Mikki and I were separated, and with that knowledge she had gone on a hunt for a restaurant in which to celebrate our first day together in the big city. But these were to become later concerns. My first preoccupation was how to avoid having anyone at my company see me with this woman. There were several very nosy and very talkative black women in the office, and a few of them had made Mikki's acquaintance over the years. The thought of one of them passing along to Mikki the news of my parading around the office with this white Parisian chick was too much for me to bear.

As Paula held me tightly in her clutches, I had no choice but to hug her back, and I must say that she felt wonderful. Even better than I remembered her feeling. I looked over my shoulder at the doorknob and prayed that it wouldn't turn. I had read many tales—usually in dubious publications like *Penthouse Forum*—about people doing their thang thang on a desk in an office in the middle of the daytime. That would never be me. First of all, I was much too fearful of intrusions. I think it was still baggage from the time that my mother walked in on me "making out" with a college girlfriend in the basement while home for a holiday break. Anyway, my secretary was much too nosy for me to risk sex in the office.

Paula threw me off-balance again when she moved her head to my ear and whispered: "Ran-dee, I'm not wearing any underwear." Then she proceeded to grab my right hand and to pass it slowly, caressingly, over her behind, which was only too accessible through the fabric of the clingy dress. My mind raced with thoughts, concerns, fears: How was I going to get out of this? What would Mikki think? Where could we go? How could I get her out of my office without being spotted? What would Mikki think? It even occurred to me that it was quite peculiar that I was even concerned about what Mikki would think, considering that we were apparently now "separated."

"Ran-dee, I've been waiting for this moment for months," Paula said as she pulled back and beamed into my face. "I missed you so much. It's been very lonely in Paris without you. I think from the day you left I've been planning this trip and counting down the days when I'd be able to hold you again."

These words sounded too much like the declarations of a love-sick woman, much to my alarm. I knew it was trouble if she had anything close to a love jones for me. This was what I was trying to avoid when we were in Paris together. And now here she was in my lap, on my doorstep, in my backyard—in other words, every cliché in the thesaurus for "all in my stuff." Just as I was forced to do in Paris, I knew I had to play along at least a little bit with Paula. I did not want this woman to leave here feeling rejected and dejected—that would only lead to trouble. In addition to these new worries, my knees were still weak from Webber's parting threat.

"How come you didn't tell me you were coming, Paula?" I asked. "I could have planned something special for us to do."

"Oh that's okay, Ran-dee," she said. "I've already made plans." And she leaned a little closer and she said more softly, "I heard that you and your wife were separated. I hope it's not too presumptuous of me to be happy about that, but I can't help but be honest with you. When I heard that, I got so excited"—and lowering her voice a little more—"and so horny. God, I can't wait to be with you."

These words were sending my stomach into a round of somersaults. I was truly scared.

"I've already gone through the trouble of making plans for us," Paula was saying. "There's a restaurant I've been reading a lot about that you just have to take me to tonight, Ran-dee. I even made reservations for us."

Immediately when she said reservations, my first thought was "Under whose name?" Did she mix my name up in there somewhere?

"Oh yeah, Paula? That's . . . great," I said, halting before choosing the adjective. "What's the name of this restaurant?"

Paula beamed at me again. "It's called May-lory's, or Mallory's, or something. I hear it's one of the hottest restaurants in New York right now."

I hoped that the horror was not evident on my face. This woman wanted me to take her to perhaps the most public spot that a black man in New York could go to display a white woman. This was a restaurant that had been started by one of those young, megalomaniacal, hugely successful rap stars and producers. Every African-American celebrity of note under the age of thirty had to stop through there whenever they came to town, if only to make the gossip columns. Now Paula was asking me to bring her there on a Friday night, and she had even made reservations. What in the world could I do to get out of this?

If I had handled the reservations, of course, we would be tucked away in a quiet little corner of one of those hidden Manhattan gems, where no one I knew or cared about would ever see me. Now, I would be advertising my new partner at a spot that was akin to mid-court at Madison Square Garden. There was no way in hell I was going to go to Mallory's with Paula. It was not happening. Thinking quickly, I came up with something.

"Oh, Paula. Mallory's is a hot spot, but they've been getting some very bad press lately. I think the health department is on the verge of closing that place down. It's very unclean and people have even gotten sick eating there. I don't know what they're doing in that kitchen, but I wouldn't trust anything that was cooked in Mallory's."

Her face fell. "Oh no, that's horrible," she said. "And I was so proud of myself because I had done all the research and found a place that I thought you'd want to go to."

It was clear to me what was happening: Paula thought that since she was now trying to slide her way into the life of a black New Yorker, what she needed to do was to think like a black New Yorker, to come to New York and become a black New Yorker. In her mind, one of the easiest ways to begin the process was to eat at Mallory's. I wondered what was next. A trip to the Apollo Theater? Or perhaps a tour of the Studio Museum of Harlem? Whatever else some Paris tour book had told this woman was what black New Yorkers did, that's what would be on the agenda. You had to respect the effort.

"I have just the place for us, Paula," I said. "It's really romantic and very special. I think you'd really like it."

She was still beaming. Something told me she didn't care at all what restaurant we went to, as long as we ended the night together. Another scary thought occurred to me.

"Paula? How long are you going to be here in New York?" I asked.

"Oh Ran-dee, I'm not sure. I'm going to be working here now, in the research department, at least for a few months. I was able to—how do you say?—pull some strings. A friend of mine in Paris had an apartment that I could sublet. It is somewhere in, I believe they call it The Village? I haven't even been there yet. I just arrived in the city a few hours ago."

That was not welcomed news. Paula was not leaving. She could very well attach herself to me and make things quite difficult. This was exactly what I didn't need, particularly after what I had been told by Webber. My boss had given me all weekend to wonder if I would still have a job the following week. But then again, perhaps a weekend with Paula wouldn't be the worst thing to take my mind off my troubles, I thought, as I recalled our wild sessions together in the Saint-Germain. Maybe fate had sent Paula to me at this moment. Nah, forget fate—it was a more elemental force at work here: the loins of a lonely French woman.

After I made the decision to not fight the night, things went much easier. Paula and I spent a few hours drinking wine and leaving fingerprints all over each other's bodies while seated in the corner of a little Italian restaurant in the Village only blocks from Paula's new apartment. As opposed to that final night I spent in Paris, this time I let Paula's fingers do all the walking they wanted, and I even went on a few finger walks of my own, taking particular advantage of Paula's absence of underwear. We got so carried away at one point that Paula's moans became audible to the couple sitting about ten feet away from us at the next table.

I didn't believe it was possible, but Paula even looked a little embarrassed when she saw that the couple kept glancing over at her as she squirmed and tried to move her pelvis ever so slightly back and forth, working against my right middle finger. She leaned toward me.

"Ran-dee, I can't wait to get out of this place. I can't wait until other things are replacing your finger. You turn me on so much."

And so there we were, hours later, rolling around on a strange bed in a strange, crazily decorated apartment in a not-so-attractive corner of the East Village. Though the place could accurately be described as the East Village, it had many more of the characteristics of Alphabet City, which was only two blocks away—a notoriously run-down and underserved Manhattan neighborhood. But as my hands roamed over Paula's body and I felt her magical fingers doing the same on mine, I could have been stretched out on concrete in an alley somewhere and I still wouldn't have wanted to stop.

The night with Paula was just as remarkable as I remembered in Paris. At one point as I looked down at her, with one of her legs draped over my right shoulder and the other one wrapped around my waist and fervently pulling me closer—thus pushing me deeper inside—I again had the thought that I could not make this a habit or otherwise I might get seriously hooked. Though as I got older I learned that good sex wasn't enough to keep a relationship afloat, it occurred to me that I had never actually tested the buoyancy of fantastic sex. I wondered if Paula would become just as distracted and disinterested in frequent amorous adventures as virtually every other woman that I had become involved with became over time. I wondered if it was something that women did consciously: portray themselves as ravenous sexual dynamos at the start, only to have the hunger wane into merely a desire for occasional nibbles over time. In speaking with my friends, I knew that mine had not been the only relationships in which this sexual dissipation occurred—which is why it wouldn't have been implausible for me to think that the whole lot of females had gotten together at one of those massive Circle of Sisters expos and decided that the best marketing strategy was to promote "all pussy, all the time" in the early months to keep the brother's nose so wide open that a tractor trailer could drive through it. And once he was reeled in like a flopping, floundering grouper, then they would quickly let things return to their normal state. In other words, the nymphomaniac would be summarily booted from the car and left to expire at the side of the road.

As I stared down at Paula and saw the unadulterated glee on her face, I knew she had a sexual appetite that was unlike any woman I had ever encountered, and I couldn't imagine it disappearing. On this night Paula turned in a virtuoso performance. She even sucked my toes at one point, making me wonder, not for the first time, if this was something she had added to the repertoire specifically for my benefit—to complete her bold grab for a piece of my heart—or did she do this with all her partners. In all honesty, I didn't dwell too much on the thought 'cause the toe-sucking felt too damn good to question it. But I hoped that she didn't expect me to return the favor. Toes didn't exactly rise to the level of foodstuffs in my mind. Most people's toes spent most of their days in some pretty unsightly places. The poontang was good, but Paula hadn't yet been elevated to my toe-sucking file, which actually contained one name: Mekhi.

It was a good thing I enjoyed myself during the marathon lovemaking session with Paula because the next morning, as my eyes pried themselves open and took in the orange-painted ceilings, the purple walls, and the hanging purplish velvet that spanned the room like a spider web, I wanted to scream out and ask myself, "What the hell had I done?!"

I craned my neck to peer over at the other side of the bed. Paula was awake and grinning broadly at me with that same satisfied smile I remembered when she first strolled into the bathroom at the Saint-Germain and allowed me to take in her naked form. Again I was disturbed by the thought that this woman could very well be falling in love with me. Oh, how impossible a situation that would be. I could not let these encounters continue, I told myself as I felt Paula's hand sliding down my chest. I was starting to feel like a pathetic heroine addict who keeps telling himself that he must quit as he slides the needle into his veins. Was I pathetic, I wondered? As I lay there and allowed this woman to stroke me to erection, I felt a queasiness in my stomach. I wanted to think of myself as stronger, as somehow more capable of whatever it took to make a relationship work. I had never wanted to become a cliché, a loosely scrawled caricature of a black man, driven by money and ass, with no firm commitment to anything more meaningful than a fifteen-minute fuck and the pleasure of a dollar well spent.

But there comes a time when we must recognize that our wishes for ourselves and our inflated images of ourselves are often separated from reality by miles of lies and deception. I had abandoned my wife, rushed to another corner of the world for my job, raced into the arms of the first pretty woman who smiled my way (well, not exactly the first, but you get the picture), virtually thrown my wife into the waiting grasp of my best friend, and now here I was, continuing to make the same mistakes.

I looked down and watched Paula's mouth take me in and I wondered where I would find the power to stop it. Did I love Mikki? Had I ever loved Mikki? I knew that I did and had. I knew that I had opened my heart to her and allowed her to take up every inch of space that existed there, to fill me up and lighten my head so completely that I literally floated around New York during the climactic days of our courtship and early marriage. It had been some heady and wonderful stuff and I thought that it would never end. But I guess that was naive because the work and commitment to keep it going had to remain as high and strong as they were in the first days. I had let my commitment wane; I could admit that now. And I had to take a large part of the responsibility for what had happened.

It literally pained me to do so, but I reached my hands down and pulled Paula's mouth away from my straining and ignorantly woeful member.

"Paula, that feels wonderful, but I can't let you go on," I said.

I saw the hurt on her face. I think I even saw her flinch; she probably knew what was coming.

"You think this was a mistake, don't you?" she said with such pain and longing that it reached down and touched me in deep places I didn't even think Paula could reach. I turned toward her and I felt my eyes start to moisten. But I was not crying for Paula, not really. It was actually myself for whom I was beginning to become misty-eyed. It was for the depths that I had allowed myself to sink that I mourned. My life was in disarray; my heart had been rended to pieces. I wasn't sure if the damage wasn't irreparable, but I knew that this woman with whom I was now sharing a bed was not the answer.

"Yes, Paula, I can't do this anymore. I have to go. I can't let myself do this to you. I fear that if I keep this up, I won't even be able to look myself in the mirror anymore."

Her face was already wet from the tears.

"Oh, Ran-dee, I prayed that I would never hear you say this, but a part of me knew that it would happen. I just wanted as much of you as I could get my hands on. But I knew it was temporary because you belonged to someone else."

She moved across the bed and our lips met. I felt the saltiness of her tears. I wasn't sure if they were mixed with some salt of my own. I think that they were.

She

I half expected my mother to give me the silent treatment when Zaria and I walked into her house. I had, after all, disgraced her and the family with all my shenanigans, and here she was, trying to get over the ultimate betrayal—a cheating husband—only to find out that her daughter had followed her daddy's footsteps and messed around, too. With all that Daddy and his other kid had put her through, how could she not transfer that anger to me for breaking that very same commandment? Mommy took that "Thou shalt not commit adultery" really seriously, and it had seemed quite clear that she was willing to break the "Thou shalt not kill" one to get back at my father. I had the feeling that I would be picking up the sloppy seconds in that line. I did know this much: I deserved whatever I had coming.

Zaria had assured me that Mommy wasn't going to trip if I went with the two of them to the book club meeting at the gallery. In fact, Zaria had said, Mommy had asked about me on several occasions—wanted to know how I was holding up and all after the drama. "If she really wanted to know, she could have called and asked me herself," I'd told Zaria on one occasion, as we made our way to Brooklyn. I had been staying at Angelou's house, because it was simply easier to get to the shop from Bed-Stuy than it was from Teaneck—particularly since I didn't have access to a car. Randy had taken the Beemer from the streets around Angelou's place and hidden it somewhere I couldn't find, even after an exhaustive four-hour search. So I was perched in the guest room at her brownstone, commuting by cab to the store. Even if my mother didn't have Angelou's number—and she did, mind you—she could have called me at the shop. "She knows how to reach me, right?"

"Sure, she does," Zaria said, a bit of hesitancy crowding her voice. "She just doesn't know what to say to you."

"All these years, Mommy's never been at a loss for words. You must mean she has nothing to say to me," I said back, trying to appear nonchalant.

"Yeah well, think what you want," Zaria said quickly. "But she knows you're going to the book club meeting, and I'm not going to miss the discussion on Zora Neale Hurston because you're afraid to be around Mom. Get over it and let's go," Zaria said, just as the man from the car service honked his horn.

When we got to our parents' house, I was quite surprised to see my father's car in the driveway. I hadn't anticipated that he would be there; he'd been staying with my uncle over in Westchester and, as far as Zaria and I knew, hadn't been back over to the house since he'd packed up his clothes and sadly walked out the door over three months ago. He'd tried desperately to get back with my mother—called her, sent her flowers and little letters professing his love for his wife. My mother had ignored his advances, turning away his flowers, writing "return to sender" on his cards, giving him only short, curt responses when she actually bothered to answer his phone calls at all. My father and I had gone to lunch about a week or so ago, and he'd told me that the last time he'd spoken with Mommy, he tried to tell her what a wonderful young man his son turned out to be. He was on the verge of becoming a heart doctor, a cardiologist, at a hospital in New York, about to complete his residency. He had recently married—Daddy sat front and center at his wedding—and his wife was about to have their first child. "A grandchild," Daddy said he'd told Mommy. "We're going to be grandparents."

"That ain't none of my grandchild," Mommy snapped. "I don't have any illegitimate children—just two daughters, and two grandbabies."

And then she hung up on him.

He'd told me just a few days ago that he hadn't tried to contact her again, which is why I was so surprised to see him at the house. I looked at Zaria, and she looked back at me, but it was clear she was just as in the dark about all of this as I was. We didn't say a word to each other; just walked into the house to see what was going on. Mommy greeted us at the door.

"Mikki, Zaria—hello, my darling daughters," she said, extending her arms to both of us for a group hug. As I embraced my mother, I saw my father standing at the top of the stairs. His face was ashen, and there was no light in his eyes. It was clear that while my mother was putting on the appearance of being happy, my father was making it painfully clear that all was not well in Denmark.

"Come on upstairs, girls—let me get you guys something to drink," Mom said, dragging our arms behind her. "Sit down in the living room. We need to have a talk."

A talk? We needed to have a talk? Oh, God. I hated this. What did we need to have a talk about?

Minutes later, after we'd taken off our coats and exchanged pleasantries and gotten our cool drinks in our hands, my mother sat in the reclining chair positioned just opposite the couch onto which Zaria, Daddy, and I had squeezed. "Well," she said, "I don't want to drag this out any longer than it needs to be. We have the book club meeting anyway, so we might as well get this over with. Your father and I are getting a divorce."

The word *divorce* punched my stomach like a Mike Tyson blow, and I instantly felt moisture on my cheeks. My mouth opened, but I couldn't say a word. In fact, nobody said anything after that—not my sister, not Daddy, not even Mommy. The silence just filled the air, the word hanging thick like smog in Harlem on an extra nasty, hot summer night. I was staring at Mommy with my mouth wide open when I heard the heaving sobs to my right. I thought it was Daddy, but when I looked over, I saw him holding on to Zaria, who had lurched into hysterics.

"After thirty-eight years together, you're just going to let it end like this?" she screamed. "You're going to let thirty-eight years just disappear into thin air, and break up this family over something that happened so long ago it's not worth even talking about?"

"Shhhh," Daddy said, rocking Zaria in his arms. "Shhh. Calm down—it's going to be okay."

"No, it's not," Zaria said, jumping off the sofa, waving her hands in the air. My God, I thought, she's stealing my part. I was supposed to be the dramatic one. Where the hell was this coming from? "What's wrong with you people? You guys love each other. You guys loved each other for over thirty-eight years. You can't just turn that off. Honest to God, I can't get over you and Daddy and Mikki and Randy. People like me would kill for the relationships you guys have. I dream about it every night, pray for it over my babies when I put them to sleep—that God will give me the same happiness that he's given my parents and my sister. And what happens? Nothing but destruction. Can't you guys see how stupid all of this is? Doesn't love count anymore? Can't you all just be happy?"

My father was up off the couch now, and my mother was out of the chair. Both of them were trying to comfort Zaria, who, after her soliloquy, had collapsed into a heap. I reached for my glass and took a sip of my orange juice, a long, inviting gulp. I started to shake the ice around in the glass, watching, through my tear-filled eyes, the pulp cling to the ice, then bounce back into the liquid. I rocked back and forth, hoping that the motion would stop the headache that was working its way up my neck and into the back of my skull.

"Zaria, baby, calm down," Daddy said, as Mommy raced into the kitchen to get a wet paper towel for my sister's forehead. "It's going to be all right."

"No," she said weakly. "No. No, it's not going to be all right. It's not going to be all right. It's not."

After pressing the towel to Zaria's head, my mother picked her daughter up off the floor and helped her into her old bedroom. Mommy turned around after she stepped over the threshold, and gave me a final glance. She blew me a kiss, and closed the door.

My father, after some struggling to get up off his knees, hobbled over to the recliner, sat down, and looked over in my direction. I could feel his eyes on me, even though I was still staring down at my nasty, pulp-filled juice.

"This was my idea," he said to no one in particular. "If your mother can't trust after all these years that I would never intentionally do anything to hurt her, and accept that what's done is done and that we have to move on, then I don't need her in my life. I love her so, Mikki. But I can't be married to her anymore—not if all we have to look forward to is mistrust and anger. Your mama and I, we've done the majority of our living already. We need to be happy during the time we have left here."

"And you think you'll be happier without her than with her?" I asked, finally looking at him.

"I don't know about that, honey. I've been with her for thirty-eight years—been with her longer than I have without her. So I don't right remember what it means to be happy without her. But I do know I can't be happy staying with your mama, and that I can't make her happy by forcing her to stay with me. So we agreed that we would just go our separate ways."

God. My parents were getting a divorce, and there wasn't anything I could possibly do about it. For as long as I can remember being able to remember, they'd been together—there to tuck us in at night, to kiss our hurt away, to cheer us on, encourage us to do better, even when we'd thought we'd put in our best. Who was going to carve the turkey on Thanksgiving? Who was going to say the blessing at Christmas? Who was going to sit next to my mother at church? Or drive her around when she needed to go shopping? Or comfort my father when he had a cold—make him hot toddies to sip and wash his laundry and fold his T-shirts into three-quarters and stack them neatly into his bureau?

Who was going to love my mother and father like they loved each other? And if they couldn't make it after thirty-eight years together, how in the hell did I ever expect that Randy and I would last? We hadn't been through nearly ten percent of the mess that my parents had lived through during their marriage—the Civil Rights movement, women's liberation, free love, Reaganomics, disco—and we couldn't even get three years' worth of loving right. What was the use in trying?

Just then, my mother came out of Zaria's room and shut the door behind her. She was looking at her watch when she came down the hall. "Okay, well, then," she started, looking up at me and my father. "Can you look after Zaria? Mikki and I are going to go to the book club meeting at the gallery, and if we don't leave now, we're going to miss the beginning of the discussion."

I gave my mother a quizzical look, then my father. He looked back at me, then my mother, and said, "Sure, I'll look after Zaria. You two go on ahead to the gallery."

My mother turned on her heels and headed for the coat closet. She snatched out one of her sweaters—a light blue one with what appeared to be clouds at the bottom—put it over her shoulders, put a coat over that, and looked over at me. "Well," she said. "Are you coming?"

I got to my feet, walked over and hugged my father, then followed my mother on out the door, into the bright, crisp fall evening. When we got to the end of the walkway, my mother stopped and looked over at me. "Mikki," she said. I braced myself for some big speech, the one where she would tell me that I messed up and my father messed up and that we were always just alike and, worse of all, that she was disappointed in me. But she said no such things.

"It's so beautiful out this evening," she said, taking in a huge breath of the chilly air. She looked up at the sky. The stars were twinkling in her eyes. "Can we walk to the gallery? I want at least one good thing to come out of this day."

"Sure, Mom, we can walk," I said.

After that, we didn't say another word to each other. We simply soaked in the silence.

I was surprised to see so many women in the tiny gallery, nestled between a computer store and a chi-chi Italian restaurant on the main road in the center of town. Years ago, it was more of a shop that specialized in African artifacts—masks, walking sticks, small furniture—and books, art, and other gift collectibles created by African-American authors and artists. But about two years ago, the owner, a fabulous artist in his own right, gutted the place, redesigned it from top to bottom, and turned the shop into a gallery featuring his own work. Smartly, though, he realized that he couldn't possibly make a living depending on the good people of South Orange to buy his pro-black pieces, so he designed a sort of café on the gallery's second floor and opened it to poets, authors, and other creative types willing to rent the space to put on their programs. My mother's book club—the Mocha Girl Reading Group—was one of the many groups that regularly met in the gallery parlor.

By the time my mother and I finally made it up the stairs and got ourselves settled into our seats, the book club was well on its way. There were about a dozen or so women there, deep into discussion about whether or not Janie, the main character in *Their Eyes Were Watching God*, was wrong for rebelling against the stability her second husband gave her and loving, as one woman put it, "that broke-down Tea Cake and his crazy self."

"All I'm saying is, if a man gives you prestige and security, he's good on the eyes, and he dies, why not go find another one just like him? Why fall for a man who doesn't have anything to offer besides good sex and fast talk?" the woman asked. Judging by the rock on her well-manicured finger and the navy blue pants suit tailored to her thin frame, one could kind of assume why she didn't get Janie's preoccupation with ol' "broke-down Tea Cake."

"Maybe she just wanted to be happy, Lynn. There are women out there who actually marry men for reasons other than what they have in their wallets," another woman chimed in. By the way she said it, with attitude and a twist of her mouth, and the way she looked—a big, strapping, dark-skinned woman with the beginnings of what appeared to be locks and mudcloth from head to toe—it was obvious this sistah-girl was rebelling against more than Ms. Chic's argument; she was rebelling against Ms. Chic's "kind."

"Of course there are, Sarah," Lynn snapped back. "But, as you could see in Janie's case, love won't put food in your stomach or a roof over your head. And after the love is gone—or, in Tea Cake's case, your man dies like a rabid dog in the street—what do you have left for you?"

"Confidence in the fact that I knew what it felt to love someone and have him love me back," Sarah said, dramatically crossing her legs and rocking to and fro in her chair for emphasis. Lynn didn't respond; just rolled her eyes and fingered her rock.

"Well, I think both of you have strong arguments," a voice of reason called out from my left. "But aren't we all looking for a combination of the two? I think Janie's Nanny represents that part of society that sends out the message that he's not right for us unless he can afford us. But there's a larger part of society that says he's not right unless the mere sight of him makes our stomach fill with butterflies—that we love him and he loves us. Now if he had both he'd be a perfect man. But we all know men are not perfect."

Uh, that was my mother talking. Now, I suppose I shouldn't have been shocked, seeing as she'd joined the book club in the first place. I mean, what you do at book clubs is discuss books. I guess I just didn't expect my mother to speak up and actually have an opinion on something like this—on literature and an author's motivations and a character's sensibilities. Mommy is outspoken, yes—smart, even. But matters of academia—outside of struggling through mine and Zaria's algebra and checking our English papers for grammatical errors when we were in high school—weren't her bag. My mother, who'd hardly ever displayed an interest in critical academic thinking, was, well, breaking it down.

"So," Mommy continued, "if we can't find both in a man, can't we simply accept in him what makes us most happy? I think that's what Janie was doing, or at least that's what I got from the book."

She was doing great, and I probably would have continued to be shocked and amazed and proud of my mother if she didn't drag my personal damn business up into the conversation.

"You know, I've been trying to tell my daughter Mekhi, here, something of the same thing. Her marriage is on the rocks and she's conflicted over what to do about it. I think what's most interesting is that no matter how evolved we think we've become since Zora's day, we're still dealing with the same issues that the author was talking about in her work, which was written, when, in the thirties?"

How we got here, I do not know. I do know that I was using my eyes to shoot daggers into my mother, who was flipping through her worn copy of *Their Eyes* to find the copyright date in the first few pages of the book. If she weren't my mother, I would have smacked her dead in her mouth for sitting up in the middle of that gallery and telling all those women I'd never met before that my marriage was in trouble and I didn't know what I was doing.

"Well, that's an interesting point you make," the bookclub moderator called out to my mother from behind the podium. "The issues Zora was writing about with regard to relationships had to do with society's influence on the way we think, and whether or not those teachings can ever help us become proud, independent women, right? It's the question of the ages: can you ever be happy with a man who's not perfect, and keep yourself from, I guess, compromising your independence in the process? I'm interested in what your daughter has to say about it."

I swung my head over toward podium girl and rolled my eyes. At that moment, I was debating whether I was going to simply get up and leave that place, or talk some shit, embarrass the hell out of my mother, and then leave. I chose the latter, but it just got me deeper into trouble—and everyone throwing in their two cents about Mekhi Chance-Murphy's dealings with her man.

"You know, my mother here was my society—and she's the one I've always looked to as a role model for how to conduct my relationships," I said. "As far as I'm concerned, her marriage serves as the perfect model for what inevitably happens to marriages, and it's very simple: you fall in love with someone, you marry them, you stick it out through all kinds of weather, then you break up."

Everybody in the room turned their bodies around to look at my mother, whose face was now beet red. She shot me a look and started to say something, but was cut off by a younger-looking woman sitting two seats down from us.

"How long were you married, Mrs. Chance?"

"I'm still married," she said abruptly.

"For now," I said, twisting my lips up on the side of my face.

"I'm still married," she said, forcing her words. "It's been thirty-eight years."

"And how long have you been married—I'm sorry, what's your name?" the young woman said to me.

I hesitated, then said, "Three years."

"Hmm," young buck said. "So with the problems that you're having with your husband, how do they compare with the problems your parents had in their relationship?"

Sarah just couldn't resist. She had to have in on the action.

"Surely, you two young 'uns aren't going to try to compare a thirty-eight-year relationship that survived racism, sexism, and decades of black economic depression to a simple three-year relationship between two children too spoiled to know they have it made."

"Excuse you," I said, turning to Sarah, my voice rising an octave. "You don't know me like that."

"I know this much," she said. "You kids today don't know how good you have it, and you rush into relationships only to run away from them at the slightest hint of trouble. I can't be too far off if you and your husband are breaking up after only three years."

"For your information," I said, seething, "the reason for our breakup wasn't 'slight.' It was much more complicated."

My mother, still reeling from my dis just a few moments earlier, couldn't resist digging back. "She broke up with her husband because he went away to work in another country so that he could come back with a better position, making more money."

Everyone in the room was quiet. All their eyes were on me. And then, the conversation took on a life of its own—and neither my mother nor I nor podium girl had any control over it.

"Wait a minute," Lynn said, her disgust evident. "You left your husband because he was working too hard? Well, did you ever stop to think that perhaps he was working hard to get nice things for his wife?"

"But a husband is supposed to be there for his family, and you can't do that from another country," Young 'un reasoned. "A wife needs her husband."

"Ugh," Lynn sighed. "You young girls are so incredibly naive. I'm just constantly amazed by your belief that a man can't be anything more than an emotional crutch for women. Surely it's no crime to expect that they should be able to provide some financial stability, too."

"But chasing the dollars surely can't come at the expense of being there for your loved ones," Sarah said, peering at Lynn. "Women these days can get the riches on their own. Shoot, some of these girls don't even need men for much else but some tender loving care, what with all the money they're pulling in from high-paying careers."

"I don't know about all that," Young 'un said. "I have a whole lot of friends who don't have the career or the love, and they'd do anything to get one or the other, specifically the man. But I don't know— I don't know anybody who would go throw away a good man she loves because he's actually trying to *make* money, at least not legitimately."

Sarah said, "Well, I'm with you there, so long as he makes your boat float, there's no need to punish him for bringing in the cash."

A chorus of "I know that's right" rose throughout the room. Pockets of quiet conversation broke out all over the gallery, with women looking at me and my mother and shaking their heads and wagging their fingers and twisting their necks and probably making all kinds of assessments of me and my relationship and my financial situation and assuming they knew enough about me to come to one specific conclusion: I was dumb to leave Randy over that Paris job.

Well, I don't really know if that's what they were thinking. I do know this, though: it certainly was what was running through my mind. Those women had conducted a virtual relationship war council on my ass after hearing just the bare essence of what initiated the breakup of my marriage. They were divested of emotions and opinions in the issue, and were making their determination based on the bare-bone facts: Randy went to another country and our relationship went south, and I was wrong to let it go.

And then I began thinking, "What if they're right?" I'd accused Randy of deserting me when he went to Paris, but maybe it was I who'd deserted him. Sure, he'd gone there of his own volition, with dollar signs in his eyes. But did he really have a choice in turning it down? Randy is an extremely ambitious man, a man who takes pride in his work and won't stop until he's perfected it. And, I guess, that doesn't make him any different from any other man in that regard.

But he's also a black man working in a cutthroat medium full of people standing at the ready to cut him down, not just because he's the competition, but because he's the black competition. Randy often came home stressed-out over the perceived slights he'd received from coworkers waiting to take his place the moment he fucked up. He'd tried to tell me that he didn't have a choice—that he had to go to Paris because if he didn't, his boss would have considered him weak, not willing to put in the work necessary to hold a top position at Trier-Stanton. I wasn't listening to his words, though, I was looking at the gleam in his eye. He seemed too excited about the prospect of leaving me—more excited about climbing the corporate ladder than he was sad about having to leave me to do it.

But maybe I read him wrong. Maybe I should have told him how I felt. Maybe I should have gone with him if I was so concerned.

For the first time since Randy climbed onto that plane headed for Paris, I was thinking that maybe I was the one who messed it all up.

Podium lady was clearing her throat and pounding lightly on the podium, trying her best to get everyone's attention back.

"Well, now that we've gotten all into the Chances' private affairs, maybe we should turn our attention back to Zora Neale Hurston," she said, all business. She directed her attention to a piece of loose-leaf paper with a bunch of scribbles on it. "*Their Eyes Were Watching God* has been hailed as much for its language as it has for its feminist ideas. What did you all think of the southern dialect she weaved throughout the book and how essential do you think it was to Zora's storytelling?"

I tried not to make too much noise as I stood up from my chair and made my way out of the gallery, but my mother, chasing after me,

knocked over her chair. I heard her calling my name, and another chorus of murmurs rising throughout the room. But I just kept running
down the stairs.

I burst through the heavy wooden doors into the night that had
spread like a blanket over South Orange Avenue. The cold air stung
my ears and made my nose throb. But it couldn't freeze my tears.

My mother ran out onto the street seconds after I did.

"Mikki, wait, baby," she called to me. But I kept on walking.
"Mikki, please wait for me. Slow down, baby, I can't keep up with you
at this pace."

"Why?" I shouted back, still marching down the road like a ma-
niac. "So you can tell some complete strangers on the street all my
business, too? How about we go into the restaurant and tell all the diners? Oh, I know—we can go over to the train station and announce it
over the loudspeakers: 'Mekhi Chance-Murphy is an idiot because she
let the best thing that ever happened to her go over some dumb shit.' "

"Is that how you feel—like this was your fault?" my mother called
to me, clearly out of breath.

"Never mind, Ma. I don't want to talk about it," I said, stopping
and turning around to tell her to her face. She walked up to me and
stopped, squaring off her shoulders so that we could stand face-to-
face.

"I want to talk about it, Mikki, because I'm your mother and I can
tell when my daughter is hurting. I want to help."

"I think you've helped me enough today," I said hurriedly. "The
whole town witnessed that."

"Mikki, I know you're angry—" she started.

"You don't know anything about me," I said, interrupting her.
"You don't have a clue."

"Mikki, I'm your mother and I may not know all the details, but
I can tell when my daughter is upset," she said quietly. She hesitated, probably waiting for me to say something nasty. But I was
tired, and I'd run out of things to say. So she took over. "Oh, Mikki.
I wish you would just let people love you, instead of always telling
them how to do it. Love is unconditional, my darling, and you have
to just accept it as it is and learn to iron out the wrinkles. You can't
keep running."

Again, I was silent.

"You know, what happened between you and Randy wasn't your fault solely, or his," she continued. "Both of you need to take the blame."

"Mommy," I said, breaking down. "He left me. He went away and left me sitting right there in Brooklyn."

"So?"

"So? He left me," I said, incredulous. "Doesn't that count for anything?"

"Does it count for anything in your ideal relationship?"

"Yes, it does. It counts for a lot," I said.

"Well, then, you were right to leave him."

"But it wasn't right, can't you see? It was my fault. If only I had supported him more, or stopped being so selfish . . ."

"Mikki, I'm sorry, but I'm confused. Are you mad at him for leaving, or are you mad at yourself for not supporting his decision to leave?"

"I don't know," I whined. "But I know that I made mistakes and Randy didn't deserve what I did to him. And now the issues are all clouded up by what I did with Marcus. If only I would have—"

Mommy cut me off. "You have to stop with the 'if only' and think about the here and now. You can't change what happened—you can't call it back and analyze it and tear yourself to pieces over it. You have to figure out what it is that you want right here, right now."

"Oh, God," I yelled. "Stop it, will you? I'm so tired of everyone preaching to me and telling me what I should think and do and how a 'real' woman would react and what society says I'm supposed to do. It's like I'm in the front row of a never-ending church service, and the pastor just won't shut up, already. I wish everyone would let me figure this out for myself."

Just as I said that, a woman walked past, pushing a stroller in front of her with one hand and holding the leash of a terrier in the other. The baby—he looked to be about a year and a half—smiled up at me, pointed, and looked back at his mother. "Yes," she said to her son. "That's a lady. Nice lady."

"Nice na-dee," he said back to his mom, before turning his attention back toward me. And then, just as easily, he was off to pointing at something else. I turned my attention back to my mother and looked her in her eyes. She was so beautiful.

"What if I don't know what I want?" I said, my words forming into a near whisper.

"Well that's okay, too," Mommy said. "But don't let the past taint your decision. The past is a confusing, jumbled mess. Take some time to clear your mind and reflect on what you do have and decide what it is that you do want. But take your time, baby. Take your time."

He

Sunday was spent staring into a bottle of Hennessy. It was the only way I could pull my mind away from my troubles—the state of my marriage and the beheading I feared I was due on Monday. Perhaps the worst part was that I knew the beheading was not undeserved. My work had suffered terribly in the month or so since Mikki and I parted. Missed deadlines, missed meetings, late arrivals—the list of my misdeeds was embarrassingly long. I had always been the type of person who prided himself on putting in a full and hard day's work. I truly believed that hard work was one of the qualities that made Americans special. There weren't many personality traits that Americans could boast about, but that old Protestant work ethic had propelled the country to unparalleled heights and taken along many individuals within it. I had always counted myself among those, but now I was one of the slackers—those no-count and unmotivated creatures who peopled every office and confounded their superiors with their stubborn and unabiding desire to avoid work at all costs. Sure, I had my excuses. My personal problems were monumental and haunted me seemingly on an hourly basis during the course of my days. But we all had personal problems. I knew I wasn't the only one in the office with a troubled marriage and wouldn't be the last to have to find some way of fighting through marital discord as I completed my daily rounds. If a company allowed its workers to become slackers when things went sour at home, it would soon find itself out of business. I knew that and it troubled me that there was really nothing I could say in my defense. Therefore, my solution was to seek answers in the comforting presence of a nice fat bottle of top-shelf cognac.

By three p.m., I was so drunk and experiencing so many hallucinations that several times I thought that Mikki had entered the room and was sitting on the couch with me having a conversation. Once I even found myself talking back to her and telling her how much I loved her and missed her and how sorry I was. It was the roar of the Giants Stadium crowd on the television set when the Jets scored a touchdown that shook me out of my stupor. I even considered calling Mikki, or going by Marcus's apartment and begging her to see me and talk to me. I assumed that she was still staying with Marcus, but I had heard very little news from or about Mikki in the past month, so I didn't really know where she was. I knew she had taken most of her essential items out of the brownstone and whenever I had gone by the store in an effort to catch a glimpse of her, she had not been there. I wondered if her business affairs were suffering as severely as mine were. If they weren't, I would have been truly impressed by her mental resiliency. I believed that, though men were better compartmentalizers in terms of keeping our emotions out of sexual entanglements, when things went bad with women we loved, we suffered mightily. Perhaps more so than our women did. But I knew there was not a man out there who would be willing to admit that to their women or to themselves.

Curiously, during this time I didn't really give many thoughts to Marcus's state of mind. My anger at him had dissipated over the weeks and had now been replaced by a sadness, almost a longing. He was the person that I was closest to, and not having him around was causing me great hurt. This was also something that I probably would not have been willing to admit to anyone else. There were many times I considered picking up the phone and calling Marcus, trying to have a conversation with him about what he had done. Sometimes I wanted to ask him if I was in some way responsible.

I don't remember much of my Sunday evening after about five p.m., but I do know that I woke up at five-thirty a.m. to the blaring of an infomercial featuring a big fat former heavyweight boxing champion trying to sell me some electrical gadget to make better hamburgers. I stood up and tried to assess my physical state. How hungover was I, where did I ache, would I be able to perform at work? Would I look as bad as I'd felt as I sat across from Webber?

The meeting with Webber was ugly, though in retrospect I guess it was no worse than I'd expected. He had been keeping a file of sorts of my screw-ups, and he was able to list them, one after another, a stunning and disgraceful listing of the lowest moments of my professional life. This was not supposed to happen to me. Yalies were supposed to be special creatures. I had always been told that I was more talented, more deserving than the others, ever since I could remember. It had always been second nature to me to impress my superiors, whether they be teachers, professors, or employers. And I began long ago to take it for granted, to know that as soon as I walked into the joint, the respect would be instant and the admiration total. But yet here I was, sitting before this man who had trusted me with a great deal of his company's financial responsibilities, and I had let him down. I had cost him money, even. So I guess it could have been worse. I guess I should have felt lucky that I emerged from the meeting still in possession of a job at Trier-Stanton.

But the job would be out of my hands for a month. Webber had told me that he was "strongly requesting" that I take a one-month leave of absence to get my "ducks in order."

"I'm not really sure what you're going through, Randy, but I do know that whatever it is, it must be consuming a great deal of your attention, because I have never known you to be anything less than incredibly competent. Until now." Webber was looking at me, but I couldn't bring myself to return the look. My embarrassment felt like it was seeping down to my bones.

"I know that you are one of the most talented people I have here," he continued, "so I've never even given a thought to letting you go." The statement made it clear that he had been thinking about doing exactly that. "But whatever your problems are, they must be taken care of. Our personal lives can seem at times like they are distracting us from our work. But in actuality, our work should only be a distraction or a respite from our personal lives because they should have the top priority. It may sound hypocritical for me to be saying this, but I have learned this lesson through time and experience. And I know that if my wife and my children are getting anything less than my best, then something is wrong."

I had never given Webber's personal life more than a cursory thought over the five years I had known him. He didn't provide his co-workers with many openings to consider his world outside of the office. The fact that he was giving me just this glimpse into his family philosophy was, I suppose, intended to be meaningful. But what I still felt more than anything was stultifying embarrassment.

Webber leaned closer to me. "I suggest that you think carefully about what is most important to you and make decisions that are based on the best interests of the people you love," he said. "I want you to call me in two weeks to let me know how things are going, and just so that I can hear your voice. Don't worry about your salary and benefits—everything will remain intact while you are gone. What's most important is that you figure out what's wrong and what you need to do about it."

I wanted to fold myself up into a molecule and drift out of the room. That I needed the boss to lecture me on the importance of my personal life said everything about the sad state of my affairs. As I walked out of Webber's office, I wondered, "What do I do now?"

For the first three days of my banishment, I rooted around my house and wallowed in self-pity. On Thursday, my mood was thoroughly shaken when I returned to the brownstone in the middle of the afternoon after a walk in Fort Greene Park—these walks had become increasingly necessary to avoid the temptations of the bottle—when I ran into the unmistakeable scent of Mikki's presence, which I had apparently just missed. I raced through the floors of the house, trying to breathe in as much of her fragrance as I could, trying to consume it, to eat it, to imbibe it, to take in every atom that I could locate in the corners and crevices of the four stories.

Mikki had been here! She had just been in this space. My heart pounded and my stomach flip-flopped at the thought of seeing her. God, I had just missed her. What would have happened if I had been here when she arrived? She didn't expect me to be home in the middle of the afternoon. What was she doing here? Was Marcus with her—was she by herself? Would she have been happy to see me? Would she have been upset? Does she still love me? I stopped. That was not one I had asked myself before. But it was a question that had been walking with me like a shadow. Did she still love me? How could she not? Just because she had run away with my best friend didn't mean that everything that we had built, that we had shared, that we had enjoyed, was gone, did it? It couldn't have been that easy, for, during my gymnastic sessions with Paula, as enjoyable as they were, they in no way diminshed my passion for my wife. She was still my wife, right? It was okay to call her that, right? Why was I no longer mad at her? Perhaps I still was mad—but why was I so excited about the idea of seeing her? What did this mean?

I considered running from the building and racing down the street to the store. I had avoided the store, even though every part of me was desperate to run in there and drag her back home with me. But why did I want her back? Hadn't she betrayed me? But in fact the betrayal seemed so long ago; it was the least of my concerns, the most distant of my thoughts. The scene in Ponticello's, my Godfather-like performance, was not even something that brought me pride or joy. It was a kiddie tantrum in the middle of the supermarket and I was almost embarrassed by what I had done, even though it had caused me a great deal of satisfaction at the time.

When Mikki came to the house, did she miss me, too? Did she wonder where I was, what I had been doing? Had she been as excited by the proximity of my presence as I was by her perfume? Could she smell me as I smelled her? Did she feel a longing race through her loins, as I felt now? Did she run her hands longingly over the clothes in my closet, or the bed I just slept in? Was any of this heart-rending pain reciprocal, or was it just me? Was I alone now in my hurt and craving? Please, Lord, tell me that some of this was shared by her. It would be too devastating to know I occupied this space by myself.

By the second week I had become a stalker. I was hiding behind bushes that were near Mikki's store, waiting for her comings or her goings. I had spent seven hours there on Wednesday and had not seen her once. When I stumbled back to the brownstone, frozen and humbled and more than a little frightened by my uncontrollable obsession, I wondered where this all was leading, and what I would have done if I had seen her.

I got my answer on Saturday: nothing. She walked into the store at eleven a.m., strolling up, somewhat carefree in her walk, much to my annoyance. She opened the door with not a glance around her and went inside. I was paralyzed. I truly had not planned a course of action. There she was now, inside the store, and here I stood outside the store. What an idiot. What did I expect would happen when she arrived? Did I think she would somehow smell me, or sense my presence, and come racing across the street to embrace me—or perhaps slap me? And from where I was standing, I couldn't even see inside the store. So there really was no point in my remaining. Again I stumbled back home, depressed and hurt and even more frightened this time.

By the end of the third week, I was so devastated, distressed, and dumbed, that I actually got hit by a car. It wasn't serious, but it was bad enough to attract a large crowd of curious Fort Greene onlookers as I lay in the middle of the street, dazed and staring up at about two dozen widened eyeballs.

I tried to struggle to my feet and a pair of hands reached out and pushed me back down.

"Don't get up!" the older female voice said. "We called an ambulance. Stay there until they arrive."

I looked to my right and saw a middle-aged black woman who appeared to be very shaken. She must have been the driver. I couldn't even recount what had happened. All I knew was I was crossing the street on my trip back to the house from Mekhi's, and the next thing I knew I had been knocked onto the ground. Apparently what happened was that this woman had stopped at the light, and hadn't realized that she had eased up on the brake. Her car lurched forward just a foot or so, but enough to make contact with the side of my knee and push me onto the ground.

I was not hurt and I certainly was not eager to wait around for an ambulance. I did feel a dull ache in my leg, but it was no worse than what I felt sometimes when I banged it on the side of my bed.

"It's okay, it's okay," I said to the woman and to the crowd, whose curiosity was now somewhat annoying to me. "I'm okay; I did not get hurt. I don't need an ambulance."

The woman was peering into my face. Surely she did not want me to be hurt, and I could see it was with some relief that she asked again whether I was sure.

"Yes, I'm sure. Let me just get on back home," I said, wanting to escape the stares of the crowd as quickly as possible. What really concerned me was that Mikki, drawn by the commotion only a half block from her store, would come outside to see what was going on. But it was now mid-December and the day was quite cold. In fact, the full-length cloth coat that I was wearing had done much to lessen the impact of the woman's bumper. And I knew Mikki was not likely to come outside in the cold to look into some of what she would probably call "Brooklyn foolishness." We would often sit up at eleven and watch the news, shaking our heads at the long litany of "Brooklyn foolishness" that passed before us on the screen.

When I got back home I tore off my clothes and settled into a steaming hot bath. By the time I got out of the water, I couldn't even tell the spot on my leg where I had been hit. No, the only thing that had been bruised that day was my already fragile pride.

She

I'd been looking at apartments all over Kings County for weeks. I love Angelou, don't get me wrong, and I'm grateful that she let me live with her while I got my act together, but damn if we were meant to be roomies. I needed out. I had to have my own space to think and create and spread out, and I was finding that the only time I was able to do that was at the shop. And while business was thriving, there was only so much time I wanted to spend there. Too many memories. So I started my exhaustive search for that ever-unattainable, perfect New York apartment.

A few weeks before Christmas, I thought I'd finally found one in Boerum Hill, just on the other side of downtown Brooklyn. It was cute—a nice-sized one-bedroom with an efficiency kitchen and beautiful, sparkling hardwood floors. The pièce de résistance was the spiral staircase leading up to the roof, an exclusive feature of that $1,150-per-month rental, which was at the top of a three-story walk-up. Transportation would have been easy; it was just a short walk away from all the major subway stops, and I could easily hop a gypsy cab to the shop or over to Angelou's.

Basically, it was perfect.

And all I had to do to get it was run very quickly over to my old brownstone and pick up some paperwork that would prove I could afford it. I'd picked up a lot of my clothes and other personal belongings over the past month, going over to the old place when I knew Randy would be at work. Angelou and I would scour the neighborhood for the Beemer, to make sure he hadn't called in sick or anything, then head on in, collect some things, and hail a cab to help us transfer it back to her place. I couldn't figure out for the life of me why Randy hadn't changed the locks. I'd assumed that since we never talked after the night he kicked me out of the brownstone that his anger was still pure, hot, and that he would do anything within his power to simply screw me over, like changing the locks, or parking the car somewhere where I couldn't find it, or getting the lights and the phone turned off at the shop or something like that.

I wouldn't have blamed him if he did do all those mean things. He's human, and I'm sure his stomach is still turning from the vile, nasty sequence of events that lead to our relationship's demise. How, after all, does a man get over the fact that his woman was sleeping with another man? We women are so much more forgiving when it comes to cheating hearts, you know? He screws around with the neighbor, we give him shit for a few weeks, he cries, we let him back in. He screws the secretary, we give him shit for a few weeks, he cries, we tell him to fire the bitch, and we let him back in. He screws one of our friends, we give him shit for a few weeks, we curse her out and cut her off, and we let him back in. Why? Desperation, maybe. We've deluded ourselves into thinking that there just aren't that many available men out there, and so we do our best to train the one we've got—you know, smack him on the nose with the *Times* when he pees on the carpet and then give him a doggy treat when he wags his tail and rubs up against our legs. All is (mostly) forgiven.

But men, they don't operate that way. At least not in my experience, they don't. Even when you two have no real commitment except to screw each weekend and every other Wednesday and he's sexing this one over here and that one other there, boyfriend still expects that his bed partner is going to be sleeping with him exclusively. Any woman who tries to change those boundaries is immediately labeled a ho and curbed with a quickness. The man who helps her violate the rules? Pity him. I don't care what anyone says; a man doesn't carry his manhood in his penis—it's in his woman's vagina. I fully expected that my violation of Randy's manhood would reserve me a nice, toasty spot in hell—and it would be Randy who would send me there.

So I'd braced myself for his wrath. But it never came. I was able to walk in and out of the brownstone as I pleased, and the shop was running without any trip-ups, thriving, even. And I was genuinely confounded by it—a little pleased, even. Because maybe that meant that he wasn't as angry as I'd thought. And if he wasn't as angry as I thought, then maybe he'd be willing to talk to me. And if he was willing to talk to me, then maybe we could start down the road to recovery.

This, after all, was what I'd concluded that I wanted. And while I'm sure that none of you think I have the right to make any demands on my husband, I'll tell you this much: I still love him. And I know that I was wrong. And the least he deserves is an apology. And closure. I don't know that talking to him will lead to a reconciliation. Randy and I had a host of problems before he went away to Paris and I ever even considered sleeping with Marcus. All of those problems, as far as I'm concerned, are just as important to work out as the issue of abandonment and infidelity. But he is my husband, and I don't want my marriage to end like this, if at all. And it would be nice if we could open the door to the possibility of reconciliation, or at least move on to being friends.

Maybe his not changing the locks and not giving me a hard time was his way of telling me that he was willing, at least, to have a conversation—to hear me out. Then again, if he truly did want that, he could have easily called me at the shop, or stopped by. I answered the phone with bated breath every time it rang, hoping that it would be him—held my breath and felt my heart leap every time the bell on the shop door rang, hoping it was him. But it never was. He didn't call, he didn't come by, he didn't try to reach out to my sister or my mother or Angelou, even though I'm sure he must have known that he could easily find me through one of them. He had, for all intents and purposes, dropped off the face of the Earth.

Indeed, the only time I remotely had any contact with my husband was when I was sneaking back into our home. I'd hit the block at about ten a.m., and head on over to Ms. Elly's house—sip tea with her for a minute while I watched the neighborhood awaken. And then I'd ask her if I could use her phone to call over to the house, and she'd always oblige. I'd dial the number, wait for it to ring four times, then listen to my husband's voice on the answering machine. "Hello. We're not here to take your call . . ." his voice would chime. It was cheery. He was saying "we're." Signs of happier times. I'd hang up without leaving a message; if Randy were home, he'd answer the phone on the second ring. He's anal like that. That he didn't answer was a signal that I could go on over and do whatever it was that I had to do.

I always tried not to linger while I was there, but I would look around—take in my home, my husband, what he was doing. The refrigerator was always empty save for some juice and take-out containers from the Mexican and the Jamaican restaurants over on Fulton Street. Randy didn't even much like taking the food out of their take-out containers, much less cooking, so it was clear he probably wasn't eating very much or very well. In the bathroom, the laundry would alway be piled up, no doubt because Randy was avoiding the laundromat. He hated it—the way it smelled, the kind of people who frequented it, the idea that his underwear was being washed in the same tub as the underwear of half of Fort Greene. It was no surprise, then, that the hamper was overflowing.

When I'd go into the bedroom, I'd have to resist touching the bed, wondering whether he still slept on his same side or if he'd taken to spreading across the entire queen-sized mattress after I'd left. I wondered, too, if anyone else had been invited to our marital bed—if he had a girlfriend or an acquaintance or something. Another woman ready to take my place. I checked the garbage cans for strings of womens' hair, the floors for bobby pins, the dresser drawers for teddies and thongs and stockings or evidence of the same. There never was any. Just signs of Randy, living without me.

Something was different though, the day I'd gone over to collect my paperwork. I could smell Randy—his cologne was hanging thick in the air. It was Cool Water, the scent I most loved to smell on my husband. I'd mentioned to him once that I'd smelled it at one of those counters at Macy's and really liked its cool, fresh fragrance. A week later, Randy went out and bought himself a bottle and sprayed it over our comforter and in the pillows, lit candles all around our bedroom and put on soft music—all of which greeted me when I walked in from work. He was lying there on the bed, waiting for me. I remember I was dog tired, and just not in the mood, even with his entreaties beckoning me into his web. He could tell I wasn't down, and you know what he did? He laid me down, massaged my back and feet, then proceeded to talk to me for the next two hours. No sexual advances. No begging. No pleading. Just talking. Until we both fell asleep.

She

God, that was a beautiful evening.

When I walked into our brownstone and smelled my husband's special scent, I got nostalgic. I wanted to see him, desperately. I wanted to talk to him, to apologize, to tell him that I still loved him and that we should at least try to work it out—to be friends if we couldn't stay married. I walked over to the phone and picked it up out of its bed. I dialed the number at his job, then hung up. Then I dialed it again, and heard his secretary pick up the phone. I hung up again. I didn't know what to say. I didn't know how he would respond. I didn't trust, even though my husband had so far avoided getting ugly, that he wouldn't be ugly now. If it was going to be that way, I didn't want it to happen while he was at work. I needed to do this face-to-face. I decided then and there to call my husband, and make the first move toward healing.

I ran downstairs and grabbed my paperwork out of the filing cabinet and then headed quickly out the door. But somewhere between the stoop and the gypsy cab that I caught at the corner of South Oxford and Lafayette, I decided not to keep my appointment to sign the lease on my perfect walk-up in my perfect brownstone in my perfect neighborhood. Instead, I went shopping for the perfect dress—the one that I planned to wear when I next saw my husband.

He

As we got closer to the holiday season, I began to consider just picking up the phone and calling my wife. Though her state of mind was now my obsession and I definitely wanted to talk to her, there was something holding me back. Perhaps it was my interest in justice being served. After all, she was the one who had committed adultery—or at least she believed she was the only one—therefore I didn't think that I should be the one to make the initial entreaty.

But then again, I couldn't even be sure that she wasn't somewhere in Marcus's arms, not even remembering what her husband's name was, soaking in the giddiness of a new love. That thought sickened me, that perhaps I had already lost her, that maybe it was totally over.

And so it was only two days before the end of my banishment when the phone rang on a Saturday afternoon and I picked it up to hear my wife's voice. God, how it rocked me. The chill that flashed down my spine told me everything that I needed to know about the feelings I still had for her. But I had no idea where she was, what she was thinking, so I tried to play it cool, distant.

"Hi, Mikki," I said. "How have you been?"

There was a pause as she searched for the right words.

"I've been meaning to call you, to talk to you. There's a lot that we need to talk about," she said.

"Yes, there is. I've been thinking about you a lot," I said.

"Oh, really?" she said. "I guess I've been thinking about you, too. I need to say something to you, Randy."

My heart leaped. This sounded like the beginnings of an apology. Could that be possible?

"Randy, I want to apologize. I . . . what happened to us should never have happened. I-I cannot believe I allowed myself to get carried away with this other foolishness and put you through what must have been some really painful times. Marcus and I just got carried away with the moment. I know there's no excuse for it, no way to erase what happened. But if it will make you feel any better, I'll tell you my so-called fling with Marcus was over before it even started. He turned out to be exactly what I didn't need. And I've realized I made a big mistake. I just pray, I ask the Lord every day, that you find a way to forgive me. I don't know what kind of future we may have, but can we at least, um, get together and talk about this?"

The clearly heartfelt emotion that poured through the phone lines and reached me at a time when I was wide open for it made me want to do somersaults in my living room. This was precisely what I was hoping for. I wanted to burst from the house and sprint to wherever Mikki was and wrap her so deeply and snugly into a giant hug that she'd never want me to let go. I wanted to scream into the phone that I loved her more than I thought was possible and that she made my life one big carnival and I sometimes felt like I couldn't go on without her. I wanted to tell her that everything was already forgotten and that it was largely through my own neglect that she felt compelled to screw around with my best friend.

But did I tell her any of that? Of course not. Because that would have put me in a position of weakness. So all I said was, "Yeah, I think we should get together and meet. Let's do that. I'm glad you called."

There was a long pause. She was waiting for me, obviously. I was not yet ready to give her more. If we were going to work our way back, it was going to take some smaller steps than perhaps she was hoping for. Hey, she had screwed my best friend.

She

"Are you sure these earrings are okay?" I asked Angelou for the fourth time as I twirled my ass toward the mirror.

"You look great," Angelou said, her voice monotone. "If you ask me one more time if the earrings are right, if the dress fits right, if your Jimmy Choos match, if your hair is cute enough, I'm going to draw a smiley face on your forehead with this lip gloss."

She's so stupid. I couldn't help myself, though. Randy agreed to meet me at the Kings Square Café, a trendy French bistro in Soho, and I was about as excited as a senior on her way to the prom. He wanted to see me! Randy, my husband, wanted to have lunch with me, and to talk to me—to take that first step.

I don't know if I was more happy or grateful. I do know that for the first time in a very long time, I was happy—skipping and shit at the shop, at the grocery store, at the laundromat. And this time, when I went to the hair salon to get my new 'do and to Nicole Miller to get my new outfit, I was doing it not to hide my feelings from my husband, but to express some to him. I threatened to stab my stylist if he remotely considered cutting so much as a strand of my hair. Randy likes it long and dark—and while it was still much shorter than it was when I first cut it all off, it had certainly gotten some length to it, and damn if I wasn't going to keep it that way. And when I picked out that tight Nicole Miller number? The one with the pink satin trim, the flirty short skirt, and just enough material to stretch over my glorious ass?

Oh, I knew that when he saw me, his mouth would drop open with wonder, instead of surprise.

Yes, I did look good. I didn't need Angelou to tell me that.

I only hoped that Randy would think so, too.

He

As I sat in the café, I was as nervous as a high school freshman on his first date. The sweat poured down my sides, trickling from my forearms and telling me I was losing control. What I wanted more than anything was to appear in control at this meeting. Well, that's not true—what I wanted more than anything was to leave the meeting knowing that my, our, ordeal was over. That we would be able to find our way back to that loving place, the path that had been obscured for us.

A key piece of information for me was what Mikki would wear. What message would she send? Would she go casual and conservative? Casual and sexy? More formal and sexy? It was a Sunday afternoon; the dress code was wide open. If she showed cleavage, her tight form, and some leg, then I knew we were back in business. If her form was concealed, than I was supposed to believe her intent was to let me know that it was no longer available to me. At least not yet. The clothes would tell me everything I needed to know and would inform me which tack I needed to take, how my mindset should be positioned.

The café door opened slowly. I hadn't seen her coming; I was hoping I'd see her walking up the street toward the place, but I must have been lost in thought. So here she was. She turned and spotted me. Already, underneath the short leather jacket—and it was a somewhat chilly day, meaning a short leather jacket wasn't the ideal outerwear—I saw leg, I saw thigh under a clingy skirt, I saw makeup, I saw teeth, I saw a smile. I felt bliss.

Oh, yeah, we were back in business.

If you enjoyed *Love Don't Live Here Anymore,* read on for a special preview of Denene Millner and Nick Chiles's sensational new novel . . .

In Love and War

A Dutton hardcover on sale now

Okay, now that I think about it, maybe I did go a little too far.

I had pledged to be more honest with the mothers and look what it got me—the harshest attack that I had ever suffered from a parent. Zaria Chance had strolled into my classroom and torched the place. She actually suggested that I couldn't control my class, that maybe I didn't know what I was doing. I was so stunned that I was almost speechless—which is a rarity, believe me.

As with so much in life, it was all about the timing. In fact, that's a lesson I often push with both my seventh graders and with my basketball team. Timing. Knowing when to make a move.

Zaria Chance walked into my classroom at the wrong time. I had been getting angry, thinking to myself that right there on the sheet of paper in front of me was the problem with the public education system. According to my class register, thus far I had seen parents for sixteen students. All were the parents of my better students. The difficult kids, the knuckleheads? Their parents were missing in action. So in effect most of my evening at the parent-teacher conference was spent preaching to the choir, so to speak. The ones I really needed to convert, the mothers and fathers who were failing to do their jobs, couldn't find the time to come down to the school and talk to their child's teacher. As if whatever they were doing this evening was more important than that.

Yes, I could get self-righteous about it when pushed. I considered what I did to be on the level of missionary work in its importance. After twelve years in the classroom, I had seen plenty of evidence that a teacher could pull off miracles. Okay, maybe *miracle* was too strong.

Work magic. But I needed help from the parents. At least backup, the appearance that the parents cared and would smack the kid upside the head—they didn't literally have to hit the kid, of course, but at least put the fear of God in him, as my grandmother used to say—for messing up in my classroom.

Back to Zaria Chance. As I said, her first mistake was walking into my classroom just after I was getting pissed that I wasn't seeing any of the parents I wanted to see. I'm not saying Zaria's son, James, is a knucklehead, but he definitely had his knucklehead moments. I could tell the kid was smart—he had "potential," a term we teachers definitely overuse (don't they all have potential?)—but there was something missing in the discipline department. My guess was that there was no man in the house. I had become quite skilled at picking up on that one over the years. Especially with the boys. That's why Principal Bell tried putting as many of the male students in my class as she could get away with without attracting too much attention.

When Miss Chance walked into my class, I was a bit surprised by how pretty she was. It's not that I never saw any pretty moms, but by seventh grade most of the suburban mothers in Teaneck had been overtaken by resignation. They had given up on pretty—they seemed to be settling for awake. But Zaria Chance looked different, fresher, carrying a hint of sensuality that I had assumed didn't even exist in these comfortable split levels and colonials. Her skin was a rich caramel, her face so smooth and flawless that you instantly knew she was a woman who took care of herself.

Right away, as I watched her settle into the small chair, I braced myself. I didn't want to let her attractiveness distract me. It had happened before and I was still embarrassed. I was doing a stint in fifth grade three years earlier and the sexy, kittenish mother of a top-shelf knucklehead had talked me out of a suspension with her clearly calculated sexual codes. I had kept looking down at the glimpse of chocolaty thigh gleaming at me and I totally forgot the point of her visit. Never again.

"So how's my James doing?" she said, presenting a polite smile. She had dimples. Nice.

Her James was getting on my nerves. That's really what I wanted to say. But that was much too frank. You had to ease into it with the mothers. I had gotten the sense over the seven weeks that he had been in my class that James didn't have much interaction with adult males.

It was something about his needy, attention-grabbing swagger—he was calling out for me to give him extra time. These were the kinds of observations that Principal Bell counted on me to make. I hadn't thought about how I would get to it, but I suddenly got a flash of inspiration. Why not just come out with a simple question?

"Does James have a father figure in the house?" I asked, smiling warmly, kindly. Or so I thought.

Right away I knew the question had been wrong. The bulging of Zaria's eyeballs told me this, as did her snort of disgust.

"Excuuuse me!" she said. "What kind of question is that? Aren't we here to talk about his academic performance?"

Her eyebrows arched so drastically that I thought they were going to merge with her hairline. She was wearing a conservatively cut business suit, light brown, and I noticed that her nails were not decorated with any brightly colored polish. Like she didn't have time for all that adornment. Right now her hands were clenched tightly, angrily. And of course there was no wedding ring, which I noted early on. No rings of any type.

"Well, there's a good reason I asked you that," I said, trying not to let her reaction rattle me. "James has acted up quite a bit in my class. He spends too much time in homeroom out of his seat, and he often seems distracted. Sometimes he seems to be, uh, kind of searching for attention. In my experience, males frequently do that with male teachers if there's a lack of a, uh, male figure in the house."

She stared at me coldly, not responding right away. I tried to return her stare, but not very successfully. Her glare made me look away, at a spot above her head and to the left. I wanted my statement to sound strong, convincing, but I knew I had been a bit too hesitant, unsure of what I was saying. With parents, particularly mothers, uncertainty was lethal. They picked up on the scent of it like a bloodhound.

"He has plenty of male figures, thank you," she said crossly. "He's never had any problems in other classes with his, um, discipline."

I waited for more. I got the never-had-this-problem-before defense all the time. Frankly, it was not at all convincing. Most of the time, the student in fact *did* have the same problem in other classes but the other teachers just never bothered to complain. But I believed I was doing the parents a favor by giving them as much info as possible, even if it was negative.

"Uh, well, that doesn't really concern me," I said. "I'm much more interested in what's going on with him right now."

Right away I knew it sounded too cold, a little heartless. I wanted to take it back, but it was out there, like a finger in her eye.

"That doesn't *concern* you?" she said. "Is that your way of saying you don't care what he was like in his previous classes? That would seem to be totally relevant, if you ask me. 'Cause what it would be telling me is that the problem with James might not be with James at all."

She sat back and crossed her arms in a huff. I waited for more, but she was waiting for *me* to respond. She was telling me that the trouble with her son was his teacher. I took a deep breath, told myself not to overreact. This, in fact, was the other problem with the public education system: parents unwilling to take responsibility for their children's behavior. It was always someone else's fault—usually the teacher. Sometimes when they were called to school because of their youngster's wild antics, they'd actually wind up confronting the teacher right there in front of the child. Obviously, I had one of those single mothers in front of me who thought her child could do no wrong. Boy, I was sick and tired of the Zaria Chances of the public school world. I wanted to gather them all together, scream until my voice was gone, then teach Parenting 101. No, my daughter, Lane, had never lived with me, but I still knew a thing about parenting—enough to teach all these blameless single moms, that's for sure.

"You know," I began, "it would be a lot more helpful to your child if you could listen to what I'm saying. James doesn't need you trying to put the blame on somebody else for his actions. He's in seventh grade, starting to become a young man. Frankly, he needs somebody to crack down on him *more,* not to give him excuses. He won't—"

"No!" she interrupted loudly. Her exclamation made me draw back, away from her, as if she had swung.

"*No,* sir. I will *not* sit here and listen to you lecture me on how to raise *my* son! That's what's wrong with the public schools—teachers always wanting to blame the parents for their own shortcomings. If you can't figure out how to reach my son, then maybe you're not a very good teacher. Maybe he needs to be in a different social studies class. If you could control your class, I *know* you wouldn't be having any problems with my James. He doesn't have any discipline problems."

I think I gasped audibly. I noticed a nasty glint in her eye; she had enjoyed her little speech. She had actually accused me of not knowing how to teach. I was so stunned that I almost wanted to laugh. This was by far the worst confrontation I had ever had with a parent because never before had any of the angry ones made it so personal, so quickly accused me of not knowing what I was doing. That was astounding. She wasn't nearly as pretty to me anymore. I glared at her, trying to gather my thoughts, trying to craft the perfect response to her unprovoked attack. Here I was, dragging myself up to Teaneck every morning, pouring my heart and soul into the classroom, trying to keep these knuckleheads still long enough to stuff something into their heads that might prove useful one of these days. It was the most thankless job in our thankless society because we were always getting ganged up on, used as a handy scapegoat by every politician from the White House down to the town council. Test the teachers, monitor the teachers, mentor the teachers, punish the teachers, blame the teachers. So they pay us peanuts, kick us in the teeth at every opportunity, then place their children in our care for the majority of their days. It made absolutely no sense to me. I mean, would your average mother hire a nanny to watch her baby after the mother had spent the previous year smacking the nanny upside the head every five minutes? I don't think so. But we come in every morning and do our job like professionals, knowing that each child who's not paying attention, who is too depressed or distracted or excited or aggressive or uncaring, is still our responsibility, even if it's clear that he has no intention of learning anything.

These are the messages I wanted to shout at this woman who had the nerve to blast my teaching abilities. I wanted to invite her to follow me around for a day, to watch me in action as the students grinned and laughed and squealed and applauded and listened—that one was key—on my cue as I did my thing every day in this classroom. I couldn't control my class? Sheeeit.

"You know, Miss Chance, I sit here all night hoping that the parents I really need to talk to find just a little bit of time in their busy schedules to come out and hear the things their kids need to work on. But usually the parents I talk to are the ones I don't really need to see. I'm still not sure why that is, but I've come to accept it. But every once in a while I'll get a parent—and I'm going to be honest here, usually a single mother—who seems unable to hear what I'm saying. For whatever reason, she doesn't want to believe me, as if it's impossible that her little boy could be anything but perfect. And that's a problem. James doesn't need you to blame me or anybody else for his difficulties. That's not going to do him any good. If more parents took responsibility, we would all be a—"

"Oh, *hell* no!" she said, bolting up from the chair and grabbing for her pocketbook. "I'm not going to sit here and listen to this." She started toward the door. Then she turned on her heels and pointed a long finger at me.

"You need to take a good look at yourself, Mr. Roman! You seem to think that you are God's gift to teaching, that you can do no wrong, but you need to think again!" And then she was gone. Just like that.

The rest of the conversations with parents over the next half hour zipped by in a blur. Right after she left the classroom, I was literally shaking. I had to run to the bathroom so that a parent wouldn't see me flustered. I stared in the bathroom mirror, looking myself in the eyes. What had just happened? I turned over the entire conversation with Zaria Chance, pinpointing the places where I had erred. Surely, the opening was all wrong. I should have suspected that she would be sensitive about a grown man asking her if she had a man. In this age of single mothers multiplying, that was a question loaded with tons of baggage. Some single mothers were frank and unashamed about their single status and the lack of positive role models for their sons; they were often engaged in campaigns to find role models wherever they could—but those were usually the parents whose sons weren't knuckleheads. Again, Zaria's son wasn't a knucklehead, but he did have some knucklehead tendencies.

Once the conversation between me and Zaria started off wrong, I didn't know how to make it right again. So I made it worse, it seemed. Telling her I didn't care what he acted like in his other classes had been a mistake—even if it was true. What was wrong with me? I needed to go somewhere and have a tact transplant, I thought, as I splashed cold water on my face. Now the question was, did I reach out to her and apologize—or just let it go? Surely I was a big enough man to construct an affecting apology—right? Maybe I could send a letter home with James. I nodded to myself. That was what I'd do: sit down over the next few days and write a strong apology letter—warm but not too apologetic—perhaps even invite her out for a cup of coffee. But she might misconstrue a coffee invitation, thinking it was an attempt at a pickup. I certainly didn't want that evil woman thinking I had any interest in her other than professionally. I preferred my women to be a bit funkier and a whole lot sweeter. Not that sweet is enough to make a relationship work, as I discovered about six months earlier with a woman from Queens named Cynthia. Long story, but it's enough to say that surface sweetness doesn't necessarily mean a woman won't eventually try to cut out your heart and feed it to her dog. Actually, Cynthia had a cat, but he was a mean little bastard who might as well have been a dog.

Being an unmarried, reasonably attractive male teacher in an elementary or middle school was like tossing a hunk of chum in the middle of a pool of sharks—they all tried to devour you whole, and they didn't care who got nipped in the process. The ones who were married themselves were trying to fix me up with their single friends—inside and outside the school—and the single ones were trying to send me as many loud and clear signals as possible without appearing to desperate. A challenge at which they usually failed. I tried to mess around with a few teachers in my earlier years—had even had a couple of brief but deliciously scandalous sexual relationships with two different married teachers (one of whom transferred out of the district after we mutually decided to end it because she felt she was on the verge of getting caught)—but it typically ended badly and messily. Nothing worse than breaking up with a fellow teacher—not only did every female in the building know all your business by the first lunch period, but you instantly became archenemy number one of the entire staff (though that only lasted long enough for another single teacher to decide that she now felt kindly enough toward you to invite you over to her place for dinner). I'm not even trying to brag here—two other male teachers in the school who I had grown fairly close to over the years got just as much attention as I did, and one of them was rocking the sunnyside up, balding-pate-with-a-circular-fringe-of-hair look. Well, he didn't get quite as much attention, but he did all right. In fact, he was dating a sixth grade English teacher.

When my classroom clock hit nine p.m., I quickly gathered my things and practically sprinted for my car. . . .